roping trouble

SWEET PEA RIDGE BOOK TWO

AMORA BLAKE

Cover Design by Lorissa Padilla Designs

Editing & Interior Formatting by Sarah Fraps Editorial Services

ISBN 979-8-218-66222-6 (paperback)

To the lonely. It's worth the wait.

kate

The cool metal ridges of the horse trailer dig into my shoulder blades, but my focus is on the cowboy inching closer to me. Ronnie rests his forearm above my head, and his fingers skim the line of my jaw as I take a shallow breath. When his lecherous stare returns to my mouth, I know it's finally about to happen. I moisten my lips under his hungry gaze and lift my chin in silent invitation. Bowing his head closer, my eyes flutter shut in anticipation.

Should I be cozying up to a stranger like this? Probably not. This isn't who I am, but I'm tired of playing it safe and always doing the right thing. Plus, as his body heat chases away the Montana spring chill, he appears to be off to a good start giving me the crash course on living in the here and now.

Instead of the warm lips I'm expecting, though, a biting sting clips the end of my nose, startling me. My eyes fly open as the rope that swiped me tightens around my cowboy's shoulders, tugging him away from me. I search for the asshole who is clearly more worried about cockblocking than cowboying right now. When I spot him, a frustrated huff escapes through my gritted teeth, and I roll my eyes. The butterflies that have been fluttering around in my belly take flight, and I deflate against the side of the trailer.

"We're a little busy here," Ronnie says, angrily grabbing at the rope to free himself.

Another tug sends him stumbling back a few more steps, and I grab hold of his shirt to steady him.

"Yeah, I don't think so." The newcomer's voice is gruff and he's clearly irritated. He drops his end of the rope and takes slow, deliberate steps toward my new friend.

"What the hell, man?" Ronnie finally frees himself then takes a good look at his captor.

His brows shoot up, and his Adam's apple bobs with his hard swallow. I spin away, fisting my hair at the roots, and let out a groan. It's clear how this is going to end—another one bites the dust.

"You know who I am, don't you?"

Ronnie nods. "You're . . . Austin Farley."

"Good. But the bigger question is do you know who that is?" Austin motions to me, maintaining eye contact with Ronnie.

I pivot to watch the remainder of Austin's shakedown, my arms crossed tightly over my chest. It shouldn't surprise me that Austin caught us, but it pisses me off just the same. Austin's like a damn watchdog, and I'm the bone he has to guard.

"I didn't kn-know, man . . . I swear . . ."

Ronnie stumbles, trips over a trailer hitch, and lands flat on his back.

"Really?" Austin looms over him now. "Are you always this big of a stammering fool, or are you lying to me now, too?"

"Austin, stop." I step between them, planting a hand against Austin's chest and glowering up at him. "Let him be. I'm the one that came on to him, not the other way around."

"He made his choices."

Austin gently pushes me aside before grabbing Ronnie by the front of his Western-style button-up shirt and lifting him back to his feet with one hand. Austin's eyes are slits as he glares at my blubbering cowboy before shoving him away. Ronnie scrambles backward, and when he's several feet away, he takes off running through the maze of trucks toward the rodeo arena. Austin stoops, grabs his rope off the ground, and coils it.

"I'm not a personal possession you get to control," I say, my fists planted firmly on my hips.

My brother is a big guy. He's tall and strong and doesn't give a shit about anyone except the few people in his circle, which basically consists of me, my mom, his best friend Caleb, and possibly a couple of the guys at the ranch.

"I'm not trying to control you."

When Austin barely looks my way, I grab hold of his rope and yank it, demanding his attention. He huffs, his scowl firmly in place.

"Then how exactly would you describe what just happened?" I motion in the direction that Ronnie took off running.

"You're better than some no-name hookup, Kate. And in the parking lot of a rodeo? Come on, now."

"His name was Ronnie, and again, that's not up to you." I poke at his chest.

Austin snorts and tucks the rope under one arm.

"You're right. It's not up to me. But you're better than this, Kate. The last thing I want is to stand by and watch some dick hurt you, especially when he never deserved you to begin with."

"And I appreciate that. Really, I do," I say in a sarcastically buoyant tone, "but after watching you scare away nearly every guy that's ever been interested in me, I'm thinking the real problem is you."

Austin straightens and scrunches his face as though I said something completely absurd.

"As self-revealing as this conversation is, we'll have to finish it later. I've got to prep for my event." Austin pulls me in for a hug, but it's a quick one. His fingers go to his mouth, and he whistles, trying to get someone's attention. He focuses on me again. "Do me a favor? No more cowboys tonight. If you're around after my event is over, let's hang out. We can stay for the concert after."

Austin reaches over my shoulder to fist bump the buddy he whistled at. Pissed off, I walk away, not caring who he's talking to, but I've only made it a few steps when Austin's hushed voice catches up with me.

"Keep an eye on her, would you? Keep the cowboys from her."

Typical Austin behavior. He still treats me like I'm fourteen. Putting as much distance between me and my babysitter as possible, I keep walking and kick a dried-out clump of horse dung as I go. It skitters across the dry dirt lot, sending up dust in its wake. Heavy footsteps quickly gain on me from behind.

"What's happening, Trouble?" the deep, familiar voice of my brother's best friend, Caleb, calls out.

Before I can respond, a giant palm comes down on the top of my head and ruffles my hair. Damn him. I try to shove the massive man aside and walk away, but he's unfazed. Wrapping his muscle-bound arm over my shoulders, he walks along with me. Despite my above average height, Caleb towers over me. His Viking-like build gives me a glimpse of what it feels like to be dainty and delicate—two things that are typically foreign to me with my pioneer-stock genes. Perhaps that's why he has such an overwhelming effect on me, sending my senses into overdrive when he's nearby.

I ache to run my fingers up his chiseled jaw and through the longish swirls of his blond hair that blend into the short-cut sides. The man is magnificent. But men like him don't notice girls like me. And even if he did notice me, I wouldn't have any hope of holding his attention for long. It would be foolish of me to think I could persuade him to stick around.

"I've told you to stop calling me that." I roll my eyes at him.

"What's got your panties in a twist?" As usual, Caleb's

undeterred by my bad attitude as we weave through the empty trailers.

"Austin does . . . And stop talking about my panties."

I shiver under his arm, hating the way he treats me like I'm his little sister, too. The last thing I want is to be Caleb's sister. Talk about the therapy I would need. They would probably commit me.

"Why?"

"Because you don't have the right to talk about my panties. Anyway, I'm not wearing any, so they can't be in a twist." I jut out my chin at him.

It's Caleb's turn to cringe. He groans and his giant hand slides over his face. If I'm not mistaken, a faint blush spreads across his skin.

"Ugh . . . Kate, I didn't want to know that! I was asking why you're mad at Austin."

"It's nothing."

He stops us in our tracks, and his hands grasp my shoulders, turning me to him. He studies me as I shift under his heavy scrutiny—suddenly not feeling so brazen as he inspects me with those steel-blue eyes that seem to bore straight into my mind, leaving my thoughts on clear display for him to pick through. I bite my cheek and divert my gaze from his, trying to focus on the comforting smell of hay and livestock rather than the musings currently plaguing my mind.

"What's wrong, Trouble?" His voice wraps around me like warm velvet.

Austin is always ready to fight my battles, but Caleb is the one who listens. He's the safe place I can pour my worries into. Most of them, anyway. Some things are best left unsaid.

"It's not important." I shake my head but still can't look at him. How am I supposed to put this swirl of emotions into words without exposing myself to him? Slowly, the words tumble out. "As soon as a guy hears I'm Austin Farley's little sister, he tucks his tail and runs for the hills." I carefully study the ground, afraid Caleb will see what I'm holding back. "It's so frustrating," I add in barely a mutter.

Caleb throws his arm over my shoulders again, giving me a squeeze as we walk through the mess of parked trailers toward the arena.

"Any guy worth your time won't be afraid to fight for you. If he runs, it means he's a pussy, and Austin saved you from having to learn it the hard way."

"Nice, Caleb. That's real helpful." I shake my head at his eloquent spin on my discouraging situation. "I'm twenty-five years old, and I've never had a serious boyfriend."

"Don't stress it. You'll meet someone eventually. In the meantime, have some fun."

Between his heady scent and the short circuit his touch causes in my brain, I'm lightheaded. I dip out from under his arm, needing space. The truth is, I already know the someone I want. The problem is, he doesn't want me.

For eleven years, I've been waiting for Caleb to notice me. Whenever I decide I need to move on from him and stop waiting, there's nobody for me to move on to because my brother has successfully scared away the entire male population within a 50-mile radius of me. It's a no-win situation, and without a way to distract myself from my hopeless feelings for this man next to me, I'm likely to end up a complete grouch like my burley big brother.

"Yeah, just have some fun . . . Easy for *you* to say. My brother doesn't cockblock you."

At the arena, we choose a spot along the fence rather than fight the boisterous crowd in the stands. Towering snow-capped mountains backdrop the familiar sea of cowboy hats floating around the perimeter of the metal panels and livestock bucking and tearing through the center of the dirt-packed enclosure. Dust floats in the air, stirred up by the bucking horse currently in the arena, and drifts in our direction. The saddle bronc riding is almost finished, and my brother's event will start next.

"He's not got anybody to cockblock me from," Caleb says with a wink, his grin spreading easily across his face. I swear this man is always happy-go-lucky.

"Uh, *me?*" I say without thinking.

As soon as the words slip from my lips, I freeze, tingles dancing over my skin. Caleb tenses at my side, but his expression is unreadable.

Shit. Shit. Shit. Did I really just say that? Of all the things to come out of my mouth, *that?*

My stomach churns with regret. A mixture of fear and shame bulldozes through me on the spot, and I flounder over my thoughts briefly before trying to cover my slip. Already uncomfortable with the taste of my foot in my mouth, I can't look at him. "He thinks he has to protect me from everyone is all I mean."

"His intentions are good." Caleb's reply comes too quick. He remains focused on the arena, his brow pinched, and me, I'm an utter fool.

"What is your type of girl, Caleb?" I ask, trying to point the spotlight on him instead. He shuffles on his feet, and I keep talking. "Lacey was pretty, and you were quick to lay your claim on her when she moved into town. Is she your type? Petite and sweet, with long, wavy brown hair cascading perfectly down her back?"

The complete opposite of me.

I spent the majority of my time with Austin as a kid and became way too comfortable in his hand-me-down button ups and T-shirts, playing poker with the boys and participating in far too much tomfoolery in general, including the occasional scuffle. It's no wonder Caleb hasn't ever noticed me. At best, I'm the opposite of his type of girl, and at worst, I'm just one of the guys.

"I don't have a type." Caleb smirks. "I like all women equally."

"Gag me. You sound like Austin, and I know better than that." I nudge him with my shoulder.

We stand quietly side by side watching the saddle bronc riders wrap up. Soon the team roping starts. Austin and his roping partner, Josh, take the arena. When the steer is released, Josh and Austin fly after it, silently playing their parts like a well-oiled machine. Josh's rope flies over the steer and wraps around the horns, followed by Austin's rope taking the heels. They pull the rope taut, finalizing their time for the run—one they can be proud of, starting their season off strong. By the end of their event, the uneasy tension between me and Caleb has faded, and we fall back into our roles as Austin Farley's little sister and best friend.

caleb

"Did you see that?" Monty screams despite me standing only three feet away.

I give him a high five. We've been working on making it across the monkey bars at his favorite playground all month, and he finally did it.

Monty and I have been buddies for two years now under the Buddy Up program I volunteer with for children in need of support. It's something I fell into while searching for my own salvation and in the meantime fell head over heels for this seven-year-old boy. Monty doesn't have the best home life. It's only him and his mom, and she's been busy fighting her own demons. I try to hang out with him at least once a week and make sure things are going okay at home.

"Heck yeah, Monty. You bet I did. Way to go, little man!"

He smiles up at me with his snaggletooth grin. My feet sink into the soft wood chips that make up the ground covering of the squared-off playground, the faint oak scent surrounding me.

"Watch me do it again!"

Monty returns to the monkey bars, jumps up, and grabs the first bar, wearing a look of sheer concentration. His little tongue sticks determinedly out of the corner of his mouth, and his scrawny form swings back and forth. With each forward swing, he reaches a brave hand ahead to grasp the next bar. One by one, he gradually makes his way to the opposite end of the monkey bars. Monty jumps up and down in celebration, his joyful "Woo-hoo!" resounding over the chatter and laughter of the other kids running about the playground.

"I think you've officially graduated from the school of monkeying around. You probably even earned an ice cream cone for that one. What do you think?"

"Yeah!" Monty jumps, stretching his little hand up in the air to give me another high five.

"Real food first, though. You ready to go get some lunch? Your mom is going to be expecting you home soon."

"Can we get cheeseburgers?" Monty asks, his big brown eyes wide with excitement.

"Sure. Let's go get in the truck." I ruffle his shaggy brown hair and motion in the direction of the parking lot.

"It doesn't matter if we take a while. My mom probably won't notice. She already met with the CPS lady this morning, so she's probably sleeping anyway. You should let me hang out with you all day." Monty takes my hand and skips along with me toward the pickup.

"How about I check in with her and see if she's fine with it? Has she been sleeping a lot lately?" I've had my suspicions that she may have fallen off the wagon again recently.

"Yeah. She sleeps a lot during the day. Sometimes she doesn't even wake up to get me off the bus. But the neighbor walks me home when she forgets." I lift Monty into the back seat and wait while he gets buckled.

"Hopefully, she'll be caught up on her sleep by the time school starts again. What are you doing during the day now that you're on summer break?"

"I hang out with you"—Monty lists out on his fingers—"I watch TV, play on my phone, and sometimes, I walk to my friend's house."

"Where does your friend live? Is he a neighbor?" My brow furrows.

I'm not liking the sound of this. There aren't many kids that live on Monty's street, and I'm pretty sure he's not refer-ring to any of the ones who do. Most of the kids on his street are older.

"No. You know the stop sign at the end of my road?"

"Yeah."

"You go there, then you go by the little blue house, then you count two more streets. He lives on that road in the big red house with the tree in the front yard."

"You probably shouldn't be walking over there by yourself anymore, bud. Okay? It's not safe. If you want to go see your friend, call me."

"Okay, Caleb. Hey, can we buy some more snacks for home, too? Mom forgot to go to the grocery store again, and I'd give someone my left shoe for some bananas."

"Absolutely. But I'm putting you on a budget this time," I say, watching him through the rearview mirror.

"You don't want my left shoe?"

I scrunch up my nose. "Are you kidding me? That sucker is rank. No way I want it."

"Good. I really didn't want to be walking lopsided anyway."

This kid. One thing I will never understand is how I got lucky enough to have a spot in this boy's life. Looking out for Monty may not serve as restitution for the role I played in my little cousin losing her life, but it's about more than that now. Monty needs me. And I'm beginning to see that I need him, too.

By the time we finish our lunch, Monty's mom has given me approval to extend our outing. Monty is excited, but not surprised, and for that, I feel bad. Even after I destroyed my parents' dream of having more kids, they still made it clear how important I was to them. Still am. Which drives the shard of guilt even deeper into my chest.

"What should we do for the rest of the day?" I ask.

"Let's go to the ranch. I haven't cowboyed since last week."

I chuckle. This kid wants so badly to be a cowboy. He worships all the ranch hands, and they enjoy having him around, too.

When we get there, everyone is gathered around the corral. Monty and I join Austin, and it doesn't take long to figure out what is going on. I probably shouldn't let Monty hang around the guys when they are doing stupid shit like this, but everyone is good about watching out for him so he stays safe.

How does the saying go? It's all fun and games till somebody winds up hurt? If I got a penny for every time Austin and I had that phrase thrown at us growing up, I'd be a rich man. Evidently, it was wasted words on us because we still haven't learned the wisdom behind the phrase.

It just so happens that we took in a new bronc yesterday, and our dumb asses are feeling frisky. The agitated bronc trots around the corral. To one side is the large weathered barn while open fields lead to more pasture on the other. Austin and I stand along the perimeter, our arms folded over the top of the corral, with Monty between us. He mimics our stances by standing on one of the lower rungs of the panel.

After college, Austin took the job of ranch foreman on our buddy George's ranch and convinced me to move back and accept a position as a ranch hand. In a lot of ways, it's like we never grew up.

Now we're watching as the new guy, Trevor, tries to saddle the beast. He gets the saddle pad over the horse's back, and when he grabs the saddle, a grin fills his face as though he's accomplished an unmatchable feat.

"What's your bet?" I ask Austin. "Does he get the saddle on?"

"Not a chance." Austin chortles, shaking his head.

Monty studies him closely then observes me, waiting for my response.

"Alright. I'll vote for the underdog. Twenty bucks says he pulls it off."

"Yeah," Monty chimes in. "He's definitely going to pull it off."

"You're just saying that because you're copying Caleb," Austin says.

"Nuh-uh. Anyway, Caleb is smarter than you, so I trust what he says."

Austin and I erupt in laughter. Witnessing Monty's personality shine through might be one of my favorite things. He's sharp as a tack and has enough spirit to spare. He's going to be a force to reckon with one day.

We turn back to the corral as the kid slowly approaches the bronc again, saddle in hand and sheer determination marking his face. The horse whinnies and stops, backing away. Eventually, after several attempts, Trevor makes it to the horse's side. Slowly, he lifts the saddle, but as he's about to drop it on the horse's back, the bronc jerks and trots away, causing Trevor to face-plant over the top of the saddle in the middle of the corral.

Boisterous laughter erupts from all around, everyone enjoying the show. Austin holds out a hand to me, a wide smirk spread across his face.

"Twenty bucks, man."

"Yeah, yeah, yeah." I pull the bill from my wallet and slap it into Austin's palm.

"You sided with the wrong cowboy this time, little man," Austin says.

Monty replies by sticking his tongue out at Austin and hopping off the panel to go play.

Ducky takes mercy on Trevor, and by the time he's back on his feet, dusting off, Ducky is picking up the saddle and showing him what he did wrong. Within minutes, he has the horse saddled, and we're ready to get started.

It's been a long month of calving on the ranch, and all the ranch hands are ready to let loose and have a little fun. During calving season, we have to keep 24/7 surveillance on the cows in case one goes into labor and needs assistance. It's cold and exhausting work, even with several ranch hands around.

Some of the guys from the ranch rode in the rodeo last weekend, and it was a good start to help us unwind, but we haven't got it out of our systems yet. This bronc has a major attitude problem and a stubborn streak a mile wide. He belongs in the rodeo, but we'll have our fun with him for now. One by one, we take turns trying to stay on the wild beast and outride each other. Is it a smart idea? No. Is it safe? Depends on your definition of safety. Is it what we need today to boost morale? Absolutely.

I take my turn, already knowing the odds are not in my favor. He's bucking and twisting, and for a couple of seconds, I think I might surprise myself. When the flash of Kate and her friend Emily walking up to the corral catches my attention, the moments of lost focus result in me getting bucked off. Even if I had the skill to stay on, my massive build wasn't made for sticking to bucking animals. I don't have the low center of gravity that's needed. Between my lack of skill, my unhelpful size, and my disrupted concentration, I don't stand a chance, and I know it. Win or lose, though, I'm always up for a good time.

"That sure is one rank son of a gun!" Grinning, I rise off the ground and dust myself off.

Grimacing at the grainy taste of earth on my tongue, I spit off to the side in hopes of clearing out the bland stickiness. Nothing like a quick display of failure in front of a pretty girl to keep you humble. I climb over the gate as Josh, Austin's roping partner, readies himself for his turn on the horse. Claiming a spot next to Kate, I throw an arm over her shoulders, giving her a squeeze. I spot the hint of cleavage that peeks out from the neckline of her sweater and silently scold myself for noticing.

"I see you boys are working as hard as ever." Kate gives me a gentle nudge.

"Oh, you know, we work a little, play a little, and maybe play a little more when the boss is out." I smile at her. "What are you girls up to today?"

"Both working later. *Somebody* was begging to swing by and see what you boys are up to."

With Kate's smile appears the dimple that claims her left cheek. My urge to press a kiss against it has me clearing my throat, and I take a casual sidestep away, letting my eyes drift around the corral. It's an impulse I've been fighting for the last year. I rub my thumb across the scar on my left palm, massaging the muscles.

"Your hand still giving you trouble?"

"Not much. This little spot here tingles now and again. Massaging it helps."

"If I'd known you were going to try to chop your hand off, I would have called someone else for help that day," Kate says, referring to the day last spring she'd asked me to help her repair a damaged fence on her family's homestead.

"If you hadn't distracted me I wouldn't have cut myself."

"Multitasking never was your thing, but I honestly thought you could handle a little conversation while you worked. Lesson learned."

But it wasn't the conversation that distracted me that day— it was the captivating woman that my best friend's little sister had turned into while I was away at college.

"Maybe if I'd had a better doctor, it wouldn't be bothering me a year later."

It was while I watched Kate doctoring me up that it hit me. Somehow, we'd evolved from the parts we'd played as kids with tightly defined boundaries to a whole new set of roles with bigger consequences. And I, late to the realization of what we'd become, was already in over my head before I even saw it coming.

"Excuse me?" Kate twists away, feigning offense. "This from the man who was going to put duct tape on it and call it a day."

"Duct tape fixes everything."

"Then why don't you stick a piece of duct tape on your tingles and make them go away?"

"That's a good idea. Maybe I will," I say, winking at her.

"Let me know how that works out for you."

Kate props her chin on her arms, along the top of the panel, and I ignore the impulse to wrap my arms around her and hold her close. Trying to push those thoughts from my mind, I scan the group of cowboys gathered around the corral. Sure enough, Emily has already found her spot next to Austin, flirting shamelessly. Kate catches sight of them, too, rolls her eyes, and lets out an exasperated sigh.

"I'm not sure if she's going to get anywhere with that one," I say, referring to the fact that Austin isn't exactly known for having committed relationships.

"You're probably right. I tried telling her, but I think she took it as a challenge."

Somehow the space between us has already disappeared again. We stand side by side, watching the guys try to get a hold of the horse. The coconut scent of Kate's shampoo permeates the air. My heart beats faster, and my entire body stands at attention, ready to respond to her touch. What has gotten into me? I'm not supposed to have feelings like this for Kate, and yet, my thoughts keep betraying me. She's like the match to a bundle of fireworks, sending my senses into an explosive array.

Out of nowhere, Monty plows into Kate's side, wrapping his scrawny arms around her waist and knocking her into my side. My arms instinctively wrap around her, and once she's steady, I have to force myself to let go.

"Hey, Kate." Monty grins at her, still clinging to her waist.

"Hey, Monty. I didn't know you were here today."

"Yeah. I'm hanging out with Caleb."

"I see that."

Kate's fingers comb through Monty's hair affectionately

then rest on his shoulder, holding him close. She's going to be a good mom one day.

"I want you to come hang out with me and Caleb again. Hey, can you come to the cattle auction with us next time?"

"I don't know, but I'm here right now."

"Right now doesn't count. You need to come to the cattle auction."

"We'll see."

Monty takes off again, returning to the haybale he was pretending to ride like a bronc. Hopefully he'll stick to haybales for several more years before graduating to the real ones.

The horse in the corral neighs in protest and stomps his hoof on the ground before bolting again. The other ranch hands are causing a ruckus, kicking up dirt that assaults our eyes and lungs.

"Does it bother you?" I ask. Kate looks up at me, confused. "Emily flirting with Austin."

"Oh." Kate shrugs. "I don't know. I don't love it, but I doubt Austin will ever act on it."

We return our attention to the corral and the captured horse. Josh is up next. His involvement in a lot of the bunkhouse shenanigans is coming to an end soon, so he has a smidge more pressure than the rest of us to come out on top. It won't be long before Josh and Austin take off on the rodeo circuit, and a few months after they get back, Josh and his fiancée plan to tie the knot.

Ducky holds the horse steady while Josh climbs on. The bronc is calm for about half a second after Josh mounts him but then takes off spinning and bucking around the corral. Dust slings off the bronc's hooves, leaving a cloudy trail behind them. For several seconds, Josh maintains his grip, his motions in tune with the horse. With a quick twist, he shifts in the saddle, leaning too far to one side. With another jolt, he gets slung off on the outside as the bronc edges the corral, crushing him against the steel panel. In quick, fluid motions, several of the guys and I hop over the panels and rush across the corral to Josh. He's still flat on his back by the time we reach him, but his limp arm is cradled across his torso, his face scrunched up in pain.

"Kate, run and grab my truck," Austin yells, taking charge of the situation and tossing his keys to her. Kate catches them with ease and runs off.

Josh's injuries seem to be limited to his arm and shoulder, and we slowly get him sitting upright. Once Kate has returned with Austin's pickup, gravel popping under the tires of the dually, Austin and I carefully lift Josh to his feet. Despite our hesitant pace, his painful groans continue as we walk him toward the gate and gently load him inside the pickup.

"Come get in the truck, Monty." I wave my hand, motioning for him to get in, too.

"Don't worry about Monty," Kate says, grabbing his shoulders. "I'll take him home."

"Thanks, Kate. I appreciate it."

I hop in the truck, and the tires spit gravel behind us as we rush to the hospital.

HOSPITALS ALWAYS PUT me a bit on edge. I usually avoid the place as much as possible and have been successful in that venture for over eight years now. Ever since the accident. I slouch into a vacant chair in the waiting room and suck in a deep breath, hoping to clear the knots in my stomach.

"I didn't think about it in the rush to get over here, but if you want to leave, I can see if Kate or someone can pick you up. Or you can take the truck and come back for us when Josh is done," Austin says.

"I'm fine. It's not reasonable to think I'll make it the rest of my life without having to step foot in a hospital again. Might as well learn to deal with it."

Several more minutes tick by. I lean forward, resting my elbows on my knees as I try to ignore the familiar smell of antiseptics permeating the clinical space around me. A few discarded paper cups sit scattered about. The rumble of the automatic doors fluttering open startles me in the quiet as another patient walks in, heading straight for the front desk to check in.

"Volunteering with the Buddy Up program seems to have done you good, man," Austin says, breaking the silence again.

"Yeah, I think it has. Monty is such an awesome kid." I lean back in my chair, my nerves eased by shifting my focus to Monty.

"You should bring him to the cattle auction Sunday. He had a blast last time."

I chuckle, remembering his amazement over the auctioneer. The rest of the day, Monty did his best to mimic the auctioneer's chant and tried to convince everyone else to give it a try, too.

"Yeah, he did. I'll check with his mom. I'm sure she'll be fine with it. Monty was just telling Kate she needed to come with us next time."

"He seems pretty smitten with her."

"He is."

"I'm glad things ended up working out like they did," Austin says, patting my shoulder. "You had me worried there for a while, but you snapped out of it, and life seems to be going pretty decent for you these days."

"Yeah, thanks, man. Even if I didn't deserve to feel better after what happened. Couldn't have done it without you. It still haunts me, if I'm being honest, but working with Monty has helped."

When the accident with my cousin happened, I took it hard. As I should have. Her death was my fault, after all. One of several lives I played a part in destroying. It wrecked my world, and I couldn't find my way back from the pain and guilt. They consumed me. Austin gave me time to grieve and work through it, but when I gave up and couldn't do it anymore, he was there for me. I fought his every attempt to free me from my past, but nothing I did could make him turn his back on me. If he hadn't been there for me like he was . . . Well, I try not to dwell on what could have been.

"Everyone has told you several times, Caleb: The accident wasn't your fault."

"Maybe. And maybe I see it differently. One day, I'll figure out how to repay you."

"No need, man. Knowing my best friend is the one man in this state I don't have to worry about trying to get with my little sister is payback enough. It's good to know I have a friend I can trust."

The shudder of the automatic doors to the hall of treatment rooms interrupts our conversation. Josh walks into the waiting room, his arm in a cast and sling, his head hung low. We hop up from our seats, closing the space between us and Josh.

"I'm sorry, Austin," Josh says, dipping his head. With his uninjured arm, he runs a hand through his hair. "It's broke pretty bad. Doc says I'm going to need surgery. He says my rodeo year is over."

Austin blows a disappointed exhale from his lips and pats Josh on the back. "It's alright, man. We'll give them hell next year."

CHAPTER THREE

Emily sets the ketchup bottles she's gathered from the white and red booths and tables around the diner on the counter in the center of the room. We've been best friends since we started working at the diner together our junior year of high school. She's had a crush on Austin for most of that time, too, but he's never been too interested in relationships, much less my friend.

"Are you sure it's not awkward for you if I date your brother?" Emily asks, nudging me.

"I'm sure. As long as you promise that if things turn sour between you two, you won't take it out on our friendship. You know I don't think it's a good idea, and I don't want to lose my best friend over my brother making an ass of himself."

Being such a tomboy growing up, I didn't have a lot of girlfriends. Typically, the only girls that were interested in a friendship with me were the ones who had a crush on Austin. As soon as he turned them down, they were done with me. In fact, Emily is the only one who has stuck around for any length of time.

"I know. You've told me all about Austin's track record, but I think I can be the exception. Honestly, I don't understand why you think Austin would be guilty of any assholery that Caleb wouldn't. Like seriously. You're always trying to warn me off him, but meanwhile, you've been pining over Caleb for years. They're best friends." Emily slumps onto one of the cushioned stools at the counter.

"Um, because my brother is an asshole and Caleb isn't." I cock an eyebrow and scoot the ketchup bottles over to her as a reminder there's work to be done.

"How do you figure? They're best friends."

Emily rolls her eyes at me, the gum in her mouth popping as she chews. I dump ice cream into the blender, starting on the milkshake my table ordered.

"Listen, Austin is a good guy. I'm not denying that. But he's not a romantic. He doesn't believe in love and relationships and stuff. Caleb, though . . . " I smile, remembering the night Caleb first swept me off my feet. "Remember Shawn Jennings from high school? I was supposed to go to homecoming with him our freshman year. Thirty minutes before he was supposed to pick me up, he texted me saying that he wasn't taking me anymore, but he was still going—with a girl who didn't wear her brother's hand-me-downs or get in fistfights. Austin found me in a ball of tears on the front steps. He offered to take me, but I didn't want to crash his date. Plus, how lame would that be to show up to homecoming as my brother's third wheel? No thanks.

"Twenty minutes later, Caleb showed up. Without a word, he pulled me up off the front steps and slipped a corsage on my wrist. He didn't drop me as soon as we got to the dance, either. He didn't even humor the offers from other girls. He spent the whole evening dancing with me and showing me off like I was a prize. Caleb, a senior, was proud to go to homecoming with a tomboy freshman like me."

How could I not end the evening totally smitten? Caleb single-handedly gifted me the best night of my life up to that point. He dropped me off at home after the festivities, starry-eyed and gushing with feelings I had never experienced the likes of before.

"Oh, that's the night that Austin messed Shawn up. I remember hearing about that. Didn't he run him over with a car?" Emily asks, her chin propped up on her hand.

"That was a rumor. Austin escorted him out to the parking lot for a little chat. He may have bloodied him up a bit to get his point across, but Shawn walked away. He had nothing to do with Shawn getting hit by a car."

"Can I give you some advice, girl?" Emily asks as she marries two partial bottles of ketchup and pulls me back to the present.

"Do I have a choice?" I pour the milkshake into two cups.

"You need to forget about Caleb. It's never going to happen. If he liked you, he'd have already made a move. At this point, I think it's in your best interest to move on."

My muscles stiffen at the sting of her comment, and the room grows suffocatingly warm. I blow out a heavy breath, trying to vacate her comment from my mind as I top each milkshake with a swirl of whipped cream. Plopping a cherry on both peaks, I carry them to their table and slide the milkshakes in front of the two cute kids out to eat with their dad. I hand them each a straw then move a couple booths down to collect my tip and clear the recently abandoned table.

The ache in my feet doesn't allow me to forget what a long day it's been, working a busy double shift. I allow the dull discomfort to occupy me in my continued endeavor to avoid facing the disappointment brought on by Emily's comment. I'm not sure what room she has to talk, anyway. She's been chasing Austin for nearly as long as we've been friends, and it's only recently that Austin has had anything to do with her. Caleb and I, however, talk at least a couple times a week. My friendship with Caleb is something I have had for years and have come to depend on.

The eight teenagers previously huddled around the table left it a sloppy mess. A glob of melted ice cream sits on top of my three-dollar tip—fabulous—and I wipe it off before doing the same to the melted mess all over the table. Unfortunately, tables like this are common. Most tables full of teenagers work out similarly: chaotic orders, messy tables, and lacking tips. Somehow, they were all seated in my section tonight, letting Emily off scot-free from the headache.

I check the time on my watch—barely over an hour till I'm free. It will be too late to do anything once I'm off work, but after the day I've had, I'm ready to be home. With the bulk of the spill wiped up, I carry the sticky piled-up dishes to the kitchen to be washed and grab the spray and a fresh rag to wipe down and reset tables. Emily joins me, making quick work of the task. My heart sinks when the bell over the door chimes, signaling another customer. If they aren't quick, I'll be here longer. And the late ones are rarely quick. I turn to the rowdy chatter that commandeers the near-empty dining room, only to be faced with a pleasant surprise: Caleb.

He sends me a wink, accompanied by his ever-present, contagious grin, which dissipates my exhaustion in an instant. He follows Austin, Josh, and a few other guys from the ranch over to a vacant table. Emily is already headed their way. Straightening my apron, I take a steadying breath and approach the table, too. Emily is shameless, and I wish I could be free like that. She connects her body to Austin's with every opportunity and laughs a little harder at his jokes. All the guys tease her, and she eats up the attention, especially from Austin. If it's a game, she's in first place.

My welcome at the table is noticeably different from Emily's. When I approach, the guys chorus my name and fist bump me like I'm just one of the boys. Fan—fucking—tastic. No flirty banter for me. I station myself next to Caleb, flush against his side, resting a hand on his firm shoulder, trying to follow Emily's lead. Caleb doesn't even seem to notice. I don't know if I should take it as a compliment for how comfortable he is with me or a sign that there will never be anything more than air between us.

"Get me one of those Angry Rancher burgers and fries, would you, Kate?" one of the guys asks.

"I want the cheesesteak and fries," Josh says, repositioning the strap of the sling stabilizing his broken arm.

"What was that burger I got last time, Kate?" Caleb dips his head back to peer up at me, and I want to deep dive into those steel-blue eyes of his. As if I wasn't already knocked off-balance by his presence, a warm tingle runs through me, and the ruckus at the table dwindles as I lose myself in him. I could swim the depths of his irises and never come up for air. "Do you remember?" he asks after I take too long to resurface into reality. Of course, I remember.

"It's not on the menu." My voice comes out unintentionally hushed. I clear my throat and try again. "It's just something I concocted for you, but I can make it happen again if that's what you want."

"Wait, Kate created a special burger for you, Caleb?" Ducky asks. "I want to try Caleb's special burger."

"What did you have to do to get a special burger made for you?" one of the ranch hands asks, wiggling his eyebrows.

My cheeks light on fire. Subconsciously, I lean further into Caleb's side in search of refuge from the insinuations bouncing around the table now.

Austin's fist comes down on the table. "Knock it off."

Emily jumps as the table rattles along with everyone's nerves.

"Oh my gosh, Austin, you scared me. Warn a girl next time, would you?"

The conversation among the ranch hands picks back up around the table.

"I want the chicken sandwich and sweet potato fries," a guy I haven't met yet says. The conversation goes cold, and all the men stare at him with disgust. Selfishly, I'm grateful the attention has been placed elsewhere.

"Chicken and sweet potatoes?" Austin asks incredulously.

"Dude, what's wrong with you?" Josh adds, playing off Austin's comment, feigned disgust covering his face.

"I like chicken . . . ?"

"Grow some balls," Austin says. "Men eat beef." Uncomfortable silence hangs over the table, but then laughter rings out from the group. "We're just fucking with you, man. Eat whatever you want."

A rush of breath drains from the new guy's chest, and he grins as Ducky gives him a friendly slap on the back. His smile returns, and he lets out a halfhearted laugh, reading the room.

It takes me a couple trips, but I get everyone's food out while Emily forgets she has a job to do. After everyone is settled, I steal a fry off Caleb's plate, swiping it through his ketchup and popping it into my mouth. The mixture of the warm, crispy spud and the sweet tang of the tomato satisfies my craving for the moment.

"Pull a chair over and hang out," Caleb says, flashing his gorgeous smile at me. He scoots his plate toward me, a signal for me to help myself.

"Maybe if I get everything else done." I peek over at Emily who has somehow positioned herself on Austin's lap and is feeding him a french fry. "I don't want to be stuck here any longer than necessary tonight."

Emily has a one-track mind when Austin is around. Unless I want to wait for him to leave before starting the list of closing chores, I know I won't be getting any help from her.

Slowly, as closing time approaches, the guys start to leave. It isn't long before Caleb and Austin are all that's left, Emily still anchoring Austin down. I return to the table to grab the last of the dishes.

"Let me help you."

Caleb's chair screeches across the floor as he jumps to his feet and takes the dishes from me.

"That's really not necessary."

"Please. You'd be doing me a favor."

Caleb motions behind him where Emily has her tongue down my brother's throat. That's new. I pretend to gag and motion for Caleb to follow me. I know his offer wouldn't have changed regardless of Emily and Austin's behavior. He's always ready to help.

"That progressed quickly," I say once we're behind the swinging door of the kitchen.

It's only us now since I sent the cook home half an hour ago, after we were done seating people for the night. Being alone in the kitchen with Caleb while my brother and best friend make out on the other side of the door has left my nerves feeling raw and exposed.

"She's been working hard for it." Caleb props himself against the counter and watches me work. Even with my back to him, his trailing gaze heats me, keeping his presence on the forefront of my mind. Self-consciously, I work my way through my mental list of closing procedures.

"She's had a crush on Austin for years."

"With as little attention as he's given her before now, you'd think she'd have given up," Caleb says, making my heart plummet.

Is he dropping a hint? Does he know that I've been pining over him, and this is his way of politely telling me he'll never be interested? Surely, he isn't. Regardless, I focus on scrubbing the sink, where maybe the steam from the water will get the blame for my burning cheeks and I can avoid Caleb's gaze. I'm not ready to give up on the possibility of us yet.

"I think I'm done," I say, changing the subject as I dry my hands on my apron and try to untie the strings. Whether it's my fingers numbed by the nerves dancing through me or these damn stubborn strings, I can't seem to free the knot.

"Let me." Caleb pushes off the counter and gingerly brushes my fingers aside, taking his turn at the knot holding me hostage.

I stand silently, hoping the aroma of burgers and grease clinging to my clothes goes unnoted. Caleb's warm breath skims over the back of my neck, inducing a shudder, and I squeeze my eyes shut, concentrating on not letting the blood rush to my cheeks again.

"There."

The strings fall loose off my hips, but he doesn't move and neither do I.

My senses are overloaded, and all I seem capable of doing is breathing in and out in long, ragged breaths. I must be imagining the weight of his hands on my hips. Aren't I? My heart is beating out of control, and I wonder if he can hear the heavy thuds reverberating from inside my chest. His fingers abandon my sides, but rather than vacating my body, they slide faintly up the edges of my arms, making my skin tingle, and rest on my shoulders ever so lightly. The urge to lean into him wins, and without analyzing the possible outcomes first, I relax against him, sneaking a peek over my shoulder at him. His gaze dips from mine, pausing on my lips.

Just as quickly, the spell is broken by Emily's squeal on the other side of the door. Clearing his throat, Caleb pats my shoulders and navigates around me, studying the floor and leaving me to follow him into the dining room. His absence allows me to shake my thoughts clear again. He had to feel it, too. Right? I lift a shaky hand to my chest and take a deep breath, hoping to steady my erratic pulse, then push my way through the swinging door.

"We can have fun, but I don't do relationships," Austin is saying to Emily in a hushed tone.

"I can do casual." Emily presses into him.

"Kate, can you give Caleb a ride to your house? I'm going to be a bit," Austin says, watching Emily. She gives him a sultry smile, twirling her black hair around her finger.

"Yeah, not a problem." I look over at Caleb.

"My truck is at your place," Caleb says, reading the question in my mind. "We were fixing the loose rail on the porch earlier."

Of course they were.

The four of us make our way out of the diner. Austin leads Emily over to his pickup as I lock the door, Caleb waiting at my side. Inside my truck, Caleb turns on the radio, playing some Nitty Gritty Dirt Band, and settles back with his arm draped across the top of the bench seat. I try to ignore his hand resting above my shoulder, sending invisible sparks shooting straight into me the whole ride home.

Finally, I pull into the driveway next to Caleb's truck, lifted high enough to make running boards a necessity. A light chill hangs in the air, though the clouds covering the stars keep the temperature from dropping lower. Caleb offers me his arm, a habit that started off as a joke when we were kids, and I accept it, linking my arm in his, my hand resting on his forearm. He walks me to the door like the gentleman he is, our joined arms dropping gradually until my hand finds its way into his. I'm honestly not sure if I put it there or he did. Regardless, I savor the warmth of his calloused hand that completely engulfs mine. Neither of us speak or rush the walk to the door. We don't need to fill space with our voices. Instead, we stroll and quietly soak in the sweet comfort that always finds us in moments like these.

When we make it to the door, Caleb rather conspicuously observes our intertwined fingers, lifting our joined hands between us. His lips press together, almost into a grimace, making my heart shrink. Shit. Maybe it was me who grabbed his hand.

"Sorry." I yank my hand back, heat spreading across my cheeks.

"Come here." Caleb wraps me up in a hug, his strong arms pulling me close and his woodsy scent enveloping me. "Good night, Trouble." Caleb retreats without delay, taking the steps two at a time.

"Good night," I say after clearing the lump in my throat and turning away.

Inside, Mom is on her hands and knees on our kitchen floor, soup soaking into the knees of her pants and her hands shakily trying to pick up the shards of ceramic from her broken bowl. I drop my apron and keys on the counter and rush to her side, pulling her up from the floor.

"I'm sorry, bug. My hands have been so bad today. You know how they get when my nerves are on edge. The bowl just slipped right from my fingers." Mom shakes her head with pursed lips.

"It's okay, Mom. I've got this. Can you get yourself cleaned up, or do you need help?" I take over picking up the pieces of her broken bowl.

"I can manage."

"Why are your nerves on edge? Did something happen today?" My mother's health has steadily deteriorated the last couple years. The doctors haven't been able to offer any real explanation, only labeling it as fibromyalgia and giving her pills to treat the symptoms.

"I was fired today." She leans against the counter for support. "They say I've been too far under quota for too many months." Mom shrugs her shoulders and shrinks into herself, completely defeated.

"Oh, Mom, that's horrible. Can they even do that? You're only behind because of missing work for your doctor appointments." I pause cleaning up the mess to study her expression. She stops picking at her disheveled clothes and smiles a touch too brightly at me.

"It's okay. Really. They're right. I've been struggling to keep up at work, and I think the stress of it has been making my symptoms worse. I think the change will be good for me. I only worry about our house. We still owe on it, and we're already behind on the payments. It'll break my heart if the bank makes us sell."

"What do you mean we're past due, Mom? How bad is it?" I lean back on my heels to study her, my skin heating with frustration. If we were going to lose the homestead, we could have sold it years ago and saved ourselves most of the sacrifices we've made. The thought of losing it now feels like a slap in the face.

"It's been a few months since I've been able to make a full payment." She dabs at her soaked knees with a dish towel. "A man from the mortgage company is coming tomorrow to discuss options. I'm hoping to refinance or something."

"They aren't going to let you refinance now that you don't have a job, and I don't make enough to put it in my name. You need to call Austin."

"Oh, I don't want to worry Austin with my problems. You kids already do so much." She waves off my suggestion.

"Mom—"

"That's the end of it, bug. I'll talk to the mortgage man tomorrow and see what I can work out." She turns and leaves the room so I can't argue.

I finish mopping up the mess and pull out my phone. She will be mad when she finds out I told Austin, but if there is anything we can do to keep the house that Austin and I grew up in, I have to try. Austin and I have been helping Mom with the bills since we were old enough to hold a job. It was hard for her to make ends meet after Dad left.

With no health insurance, Mom's bills have become astronomical as the doctors run tests to find her a diagnosis, but I had no idea we weren't contributing enough to keep her up to date on her bills. She handles the finances, and we each contribute a certain amount, then she lets us know when she needs more. Or so we thought.

I send Austin a text with only a little guilt for ruining his evening with Emily. Knowing her, she'll make herself available to him whenever he wants, and we have to figure this out.

CHAPTER FOUR

caleb

I hang my hat on the hook by my bed in the bunkroom and sling my towel over my shoulder, whistling some George Strait on my way to the shower. Despite the cool spring temperatures, I worked up a sweat and smell like a fresh manure pile. It was a long day of work, but I thrive on days like these. They occupy my mind, leaving no time for stray thoughts that feed the feelings I'm not supposed to be having.

The bunkhouse bathroom houses shower stalls on one side and sinks and mirrors on the other. I reach into one of the stalls, flip the knob to hot, and wait for the water to warm up.

After making a few calls today, I may have found a temporary job a couple hours away. Far enough to shake things up and get some space from Kate and the bombardment of feelings I've been having for her lately, but close enough—and in the right direction—to put me right under an hour away from Monty. The possibility gives me the boost of encouragement I need. It won't be easy leaving all of this. Some days I wonder if I even know how to function without Kate and Austin. We've been inseparable for so long that I guess, in some ways, it was unavoidable for me I would end up falling for Kate.

I don't want to leave, but maybe getting some space for a few months is what I need to finally squash my desire for Kate and put her neatly back in the box labeled "danger." I've tried ignoring my feelings and finding someone else, but nothing I do seems to help. Every part of me wants Kate, but acting on those feelings will destroy the bonds we both rely on.

The warm stream of water pours over me now from the showerhead, and I break into Billy Currington's first verse of "Must Be Doin' Somethin' Right" while soaping up my hair and body.

"Hey, Caleb, don't quit your day job," a voice yells over the chatter from the other room. There's a door to the bathroom, but since it's shared by the whole bunkhouse in a locker room–type fashion, it never gets closed. Steam billows out of the shower as I stick my head out of my stall to shout back at him.

"You're just pissy because you can't find a lady to sing it to." I belt out the tune even louder now. The guys are used to listening to me sing in the shower, but we also don't like to pass up perfectly good opportunities to give each other hell.

"You don't, either," he says, accusingly.

No, no I don't. But that doesn't mean I don't have someone I'd like to be singing to. As I wash the grime off my skin, my mind takes me back to last night at the diner. Kate's touch, nearly as intoxicating as her rosy lips, sent shivers through my body.

My resolve almost slipped last night when I helped Kate with her apron strings—being that close, feeling her, but not being able to touch her the way I so desperately want to . . . I shouldn't allow these thoughts to hang around. It will only make denying my feelings for her harder in the long run, but fighting it continually is wearing me down, too.

With Kate filling my head, I don't even see it coming: a bucket of slushy, ice-cold water dumped straight over my head and down my bare skin. In sudden shock, my eyeballs roll back in my head for all the wrong reasons, and my balls jump so high up inside me they pummel my stomach and I think I'm going to puke.

"Fuck!" I finally scream once my throat muscles relax enough to let sound out. The heckling hyenas retreat, undoubtedly knowing retribution will be paid.

The slush, too thick to go down the drain, sits in the bottom of the shower, covering my feet. Rather than wait for the water to melt it away, I shut the shower off and grab my towel, hopping out into the cold before it's even secured around me. With goose bump–ridden skin, I dry off as quickly as possible and throw some warm clothes on.

The guys are snickering, a couple of them giving each other high fives, as I head to the fridge for a beer.

"Yeah, laugh it up now, you assholes. I know where you sleep." I shake my head but can't hold back a chuckle as I make a mental note of my next victims.

After taking a swig of the lager, I pick at the stew sitting in a pot on the stove. Steam swirls from inside, and I shovel a scoop into a bowl for my dinner. The chunk of potato in the glob I cram into my mouth scalds my tongue. I grimace, playing a literal game of hot potato back and forth in my mouth until I can swallow it down, as I head across the room and claim an empty seat at the table where some of the other guys are playing a round of cards.

"Don't say I didn't warn you," Josh says, his voice projecting over the laughter and chatter. "I told you it's not so easy when you play with the big boys." He tosses his hand down for everyone to see but holds eye contact with the new kid, Trevor. "Straight flush."

Trevor groans through clamped teeth and slumps in his seat, showing defeat, before he places his cards on the table one at a time. With his hand displayed, his eyebrows lift, and he straightens in his chair.

"I guess I'm lucky I got a royal flush." A grin the size of

Texas spreads across his face, and he sweeps up the pile of bills from the center of the table.

"Bullshit." Josh stands abruptly, sending his chair flying behind him. He slaps his good hand on the table. "Bull. Shit. Who's feeding you cards? Someone has got to be feeding you cards."

The guys around the table all hold their hands up claiming innocence, despite rolling with laughter. Josh inspects each of them anyway and peers under the table, determined Trevor has an accomplice.

"Come on now," Trevor says, patting Josh on the back. "Call it luck, call it whatever you want. I personally call it playing cards with the big boys."

Josh turns on Trevor like he's ready to swing at him, and Trevor jumps over his chair on reflex, putting space between them again.

"Okay, okay," Ducky butts in. "Let's simmer down."

Austin storms into the bunkhouse, slamming the door behind him. His presence quiets the room, and the entire bunkhouse watches him pace back and forth across the floor. He pauses and scans over us till he zeros in and points directly at me.

"Caleb, we need to talk," Austin says and motions to the door. I'm pretty sure the color drains from my face, and I momentarily forget to breathe.

Maybe it's his authoritative tone, but guilt sweeps over me like I've been caught doing something I shouldn't. He might be my best friend, but he's also my boss. I haven't done anything that would upset Austin, though. Of course, he wouldn't be too happy if he found out that I've fantasized about his sister, but unless I've started talking in my sleep, there's no way he would know about that. A couple of the guys slap me on the back in solidarity as I hop up from my seat and follow him out the door. Evidently, they agree that I'm about to get an ass-chewing for something.

"You told me the other day you need a change, right?" he asks once the door is closed behind us.

The floodlight hums above us, casting a glow over the front of the bunkhouse. Fighting the chill of the brisk night air, I bury my free hand deep in my pocket.

"Yeah." Remembering I'm holding my beer, I raise it to my mouth and take another drink, keeping my arms stiff against my body.

"Come on the circuit with me. With Josh injured, I don't have a reliable header. I've got to make some money, and you need some excitement in your life. It's the perfect solution."

Rather than the anger I thought was driving him, desperation hangs in the air, leaking from my friend as he stands in front of me.

"I don't know, Austin. I haven't competed in years, and I might be taking a job out of town for the summer, in which case, I probably won't have time to rodeo." I rake my fingers through my hair and try to decipher where all of this is coming from.

"Taking another job? The hell you are, man. Get that nonsense out of your head. This is your home. We're your family. Please tell me you're joking, man." Austin's shoulders slump like he's had the wind knocked out of him.

"I haven't committed to anything yet. And it's temporary if I do take it. I'd be back by the end of the summer. End of the year at most. Regardless, I don't think I'm your man for this. You've got plenty of good choices from the cowboys here."

"Come on, I don't want one of the other guys. I want you, Caleb. I can't trust any of them like I can trust you. I know you'll take it seriously. You rope every day here on the ranch, and you know how the competitions work. We can do some practice runs before we sign up for the next rodeo. It'll be fine."

I finish off my beer and set the bottle next to the door, buying myself a few seconds to formulate a response. This is a big commitment and would give me so much more to figure out.

"It's not going to hurt anything if you take the year off and wait for Josh to heal. And seriously, things are up in the air for me right now." I shake my head, slowly building up to telling him no.

"I can't wait on Josh. I need the money now." Austin runs his hands through his hair, pacing again. I shuffle my feet, his anxiety now settling on me, too.

"If you need some extra cash, I can help you out."

"It's not the kind of money you have lying around."

Austin is typically in a bad mood. He's been that way most of his life. The added frustration tonight is something new though.

"Why do you need money all of a sudden?"

"Mom's house. She's behind on the payments. I met with her and the mortgage guy today. We were able to set up a special payment plan to buy us a little time, but if I don't come up with the money, she's going to lose the house, the land, everything, Caleb. Honestly, I don't know how the bank hasn't already taken it all. She told Kate she was a few months behind, but it's been more like eight months since she's made a full payment. They kept letting her do these partial payment extensions that put her in a mess."

I audibly exhale. That was unexpected. Buying myself a little extra time, I chug down the rest of my beer. I could tell Austin no, walk away and take that new job, and choose to live with the guilt of letting him down, or I could return a favor to a friend in need. When I was desperate for help and giving up on everything, Austin was there for me. Even when I didn't want him to be. He saw that I was past knowing what I needed, and he took the abuse I dealt him without complaint. He just kept showing up. I owe him.

I know the home they've built is important to Austin and his mom, but I also know how important it is to Kate. She gave up her own opportunities after high school to take care of her mom and keep up the homestead. Kate would be devastated if they lost the place.

"Okay. I'm in."

Austin grins and slaps me on the back. "Thanks, man. This means everything to me."

CHAPTER FIVE

caleb

Lounging against a tree, I toss a rock into the creek, not bothering to move from my spot on the bank. I've been debating how to handle my growing attraction to Kate all week, contemplating the choices that are weighing me down. There's no way I can take the temp job and rodeo with Austin this summer. Leaving isn't an option. If I'm being honest with myself, it never really was—more like hopeful thinking that I could simply escape it all.

Just the same, I can't entertain the idea of being with Kate. We can never be more than friends. Relationships are fickle, and as much as I'd like to think Kate and I would last forever, there are no guarantees. It would be so much easier to give in and enjoy whatever moment we'd have, but deep down, I know it's not worth the risk. Too much is at stake. Hopefully, a summer out of town with Austin will give me enough separation to get my head on straight. Kate is an infatuation. That's all. At least, that's what I'll keep telling myself until I'm over her.

Standing, I brush the specks of earth from my pants and head over to where BoJack, my palomino horse, is waiting on me. He steps toward me and nudges my shoulder as I pull on

39

my boots, prompting me to run my hand down his nose before I claim my spot in the saddle.

BoJack and I go on a solo ride every Saturday. It's a routine we started years ago as I tried to heal and find closure from the nightmare of the day I lost my cousin. I found a solace on those peaceful morning rides that was missing in everything else I tried.

BoJack and I emerge from the trees, into the open field. We have a decent ride ahead of us before we'll make it back to the barn, and I urge BoJack into a gallop. His powerful muscles work beneath me, and the wind whips against my body as we race across the expansive landscape, my blood pumping. My lungs fill with the fresh mountain air, and it's as though BoJack and I are the only ones left on earth. It's a measly moment where I have control, chasing a fleeting freedom from the worries on my mind.

We slow again and take the remaining ride at a leisurely pace. Along the way, I make peace with my decision to remain friends with Kate and nothing more. After all, I'm a grown man with self-control. I can be levelheaded and squish my unsolicited attraction for her I've been secretly harboring.

It's late afternoon by the time we're back and I have BoJack settled after our ride. My stomach grumbles on the walk from the barn to the bunkhouse. With any luck, there will be something edible in the fridge, and I won't have to run to town for food. I'm ready for an evening playing poker with the guys. But instead of the boisterous bullshit I'm expecting to walk in on, the guys are rushing around, freshly showered and wearing their Sunday best. There's only two reasons guys like us get gussied up: a funeral or a wedding.

"Who died?" I ask.

"Jacob," a voice yells back.

"The vet?"

"Yeah." Josh approaches, an envelope in his hand. "They're only joking about it being a funeral though."

He hands the envelope to me with a knowing look and pats me on the back before silently walking out the door. The others trickle out behind him, and as I remove the contents of the envelope, I'm alone again. I stare at the glossy invitation and find that the serenity I brought home is nowhere to be found.

Sinking into one of the wooden kitchen chairs, I rest my arms on the table with a heavy exhale. I study the picture of Jacob and my ex-girlfriend Lacey on the invitation to their wedding this evening. I knew the wedding was coming up, but I guess I lost track of the days. I run a hand through my hair and flop the invite onto the table. Here's the thing, though. It's not even about my ex or the wedding. It's about the way they're looking at each other in the photo. It's about seeing the same emotions on their faces that I've been fighting against feeling for Kate. And to beat it all, I didn't even notice I was falling until it was too late. It's about the promise I made to Lacey the night we broke up that I wouldn't settle for anything less than a breathtaking love and an unquenchable desire.

Jacob and Lacey represent what I can never let myself have with Kate.

I can't do this. I can't ignore the way I feel about Kate. The realization hits harder than a ton of bricks directly landing on my chest, causing the air to rush from my lungs.

So much for finding answers this afternoon on my ride. The chair screeches against the floor of the empty bunkhouse as I slide it back from the table and rise to my feet. I head to the fridge, needing a drink. Of course the fridge is dry. I slam the door shut harder than I intended. It slaps against the fridge and bounces open again, earning a kick from me.

"Fuck!"

A throat clears, followed by the front door clicking closed. With fists clenched at my sides, I swing around to the slow but steady thud making its way across the floor. Austin picks up the invite on the table then studies me with false understanding. I release a frustrated groan and link my fingers behind my head while he silently watches me.

"What do you need?" Austin asks.

"A drink."

Austin motions to the door, and I follow him to his truck, climbing into the passenger seat. We drive in silence to the bar. There's only one in town, and although it's a Saturday night, it isn't very busy. Most people are probably at the wedding, truth be told. Our town is small enough that an event like a wedding makes a dent in foot traffic around town.

We head straight to the bar, claiming two stools. Austin orders us a couple bourbons and tells Randy, the bartender, to keep the tab open. We're going to be here a while. I throw the first one back and Austin scoots his over to me without hesitation before waving for the bartender to bring us both another. He doesn't try to talk until I have a few in me.

"You good?" Austin asks, searching my face for a hint of the truth.

"Not yet." I finish off another. The loud pop of the glass meeting the wood bar top grabs Randy's attention again, and he heads our way.

"Another bourbon?" Randy asks. I nod. "You want me to put in a food order for you while I'm at it?"

"That would be counterproductive, don't you think?"

Randy and Austin share a silent exchange as he slides a couple more drinks in front of us. Austin gives a slight nod, and Randy turns and tends to the other patrons at the bar, an old country tune crooning from the speakers.

"You said you were over her." Austin sits sideways on his stool, watching me.

"Don't know what makes you think I'm not." I drag my thumb down the glass in my hand, creating a dry runway through the condensation.

"Guess I'm imagining things."

"Guess so." I take a swig, nursing it now.

The evening creeps by while I pour bourbon down my throat till I can't walk straight. After a while, Randy brings out some sliders and fries. I never noticed Austin order them, but he must have. I give in and eat a good bit of it, starving and too drunk by this point to remember why I refused food in the first place. Eventually, Austin cuts me off and we decide to leave.

"Where are you going?" I ask, my words slurring, when Austin walks right past his pickup. One of us must be drunk.

"Mom's."

"The hell?" I'm stuck in my own personal tragicomedy. Of everywhere in town, that's the one house I'm determined to avoid.

"I might not be as sloppy as you, but I'm not sober enough to drive. Mom's is half a mile down the road from here. We can walk there tonight and come back for the truck in the morning."

When we finally make it to his mom's house, all the lights are off. The floodlight on the corner flickers to life, catching the motion of us stumbling up the driveway. Austin waits for me as I follow him up to the porch.

"Hold this for me." Austin hands me his cell phone with the flashlight on so he can use two hands to sort through his keys.

Finally, he finds the right one and slips it into the lock. He takes his phone back from me and holds the door open, motioning for me to lead the way. I blunder through the entryway and down the hall, tripping over the trash can in the kitchen, sending it skittering across the floor.

"Shhhh!" Austin scolds, grabbing the can and putting it back in its spot.

"So, are you the big spoon or the little spoon tonight?" I ask.

"Neither. Your ass is sleeping on the couch." Austin hands me a bottle of water, the top already screwed off, and a couple of painkillers. I toss the pills into my mouth and suck down the entire bottle of water. "Come on."

In the living room, I plop onto the couch and kick my boots off before stretching out. Austin tosses a blanket at me, gives me a nod, and heads to his old bedroom. I fluff out the blanket and shuffle around on the couch until I'm comfortable and ready to sleep. Only I'm not tired. And I really need to piss. Grumbling, I wrestle my way off the couch and lurch toward the bathroom. Shockingly, I make it to the half bath off the kitchen without breaking anything. My bladder isn't the only thing that's empty now though. My stomach growls.

Searching the fridge for leftovers, I come up short. There's no way I'm making anything to eat. I don't feel up to it, and I don't want to wake the whole house. Instead, I perch myself on the counter with another bottle of water. The buzz is wearing off, but enough lingers to keep me at ease.

A door down the hall squeaks open, followed by the pitter-patter of bare feet. My gaze drifts to the hallway, waiting to see who will appear. The dark figure is hard to make out, but it's the same outline that has been haunting my conscience all week.

"Kate? Is that you?"

kate

I have the advantage. The dim light over the stove is the only light on, illuminating Caleb but leaving me mostly hidden by the darkness. Hopefully it disguises my flushed skin and racing pulse. What is he doing here anyway?

"Where's Austin?" I ask, slowly stepping into the pale-yellow aura of the stove light, appropriately radiating around Caleb. Taking a bottle of water from the fridge, I remove the lid and take several large gulps.

"Bed . . . Where you should be, too, Trouble," Caleb says matter-of-factly in his lazy speech.

Has he been drinking?

"And what about you?" I'm standing close enough now to touch him, and longing whirls in his charming blue eyes, calling me closer to him.

"We walked from the bar. Guess I'm stuck here for the night." Caleb's admiring gaze slides down my body, and self-consciousness dribbles over me as he takes in my yoga shorts and oversized T-shirt. "Damn, your legs keep going." His body sways as his eyes trail down my legs. Roaming back up my body, they hesitate at my chest momentarily before meeting my gaze again.

Without speaking, he takes hold of the front of my baggy shirt and pulls me into him till my hips are against the counter and his warm hands rest on my waist. His fingers send shockwaves through me as they trail up my sides, his massive hands claiming either side of my face. I can smell the bourbon on his warm breath as I stand motionless, observing him, waiting for what's about to come. His attention is locked on me, anticipation steadily building as I wait for him to dictate what happens next—the same need I feel emanating from him, too. Instead of our lips colliding, though, he rests his forehead against mine.

"Mmm . . . the things I want to do to you right now," Caleb mumbles. "I've wanted you for so long, and I don't know how much longer I can fight it."

"Then don't." The words are freed before I can give them a second thought.

"I wish." His thumb strokes my cheek. "If it was up to me, I'd claim you and never let you go."

"Who is it up to then? Me? Because I think you already know how I feel about it." My fingers curl on his thighs.

"You're Austin's sister. His little sister. Austin trusts me not to take advantage of that. Anyway, you don't want me. You're just stuck on the idea of me. I'm no knight in shining armor."

"I don't need a knight, and I don't need anyone to tell me how I feel." My words come out breathy. "Forget everything else and be selfish for once in you damn life, Caleb. If you want me, show me."

"It'll have to wait till you're sober. I don't take advantage of drunk chicks."

Disappointment takes over. He's right though. Now is not the time. Not like this.

"I'm pretty sure you're the one who's drunk."

"That's what all the drunk ones say."

"Okay. Let's get you back to bed." I pat his shoulder and step aside, giving him space.

Caleb slides off the counter, one of his strong hands

pressing into my shoulder. I lead him over to the couch where I help him settle for the night before returning to bed. My heart flutters as I slide back under my covers. Sleep is hard to find, as my mind spins with a war of emotions. His drunken confession was the last thing I expected tonight. I've waited for years for him to notice me, but maybe he has all along.

Eventually, I drift off to sleep. I only manage a couple more hours of restless sleep before the morning sun seeps through the curtains of my bedroom window. Yawning, I toss my feet over the side of the bed and stagger toward the bathroom.

Nervous anticipation fuels me, making up for the lack of rest I got last night. Blue toothpaste splatters in the white sink, and the pipes groan to life when I twist the squeaky knob, allowing water to flow from the faucet. I make quick work of rinsing, washing away the toothpaste and dabbing my mouth on the towel hanging on the wall. Stepping back from the mirror, I scan over my reflection and let out an uneasy breath. Why did I never learn how to dress myself up?

On my way to the kitchen, the faint rumble of news playing drifts down the hall from my mother's room. If she is watching in her room, Caleb must be in the living room. After a quick peek to verify, I grab bacon and eggs from the fridge and get to work.

With bacon, eggs, and a giant stack of pancakes on the table, I wait for the boys to emerge. Before long, a heavy thud followed by a groan floats from the living room. Caleb trudges into the kitchen, stopping in the doorway to lean against the wall. I pour a glass of orange juice and dump a couple painkillers into my hand, offering them to him. With a grimace, he washes them down. I watch his every move, searching for any indication of recognition.

"You hungry? I fixed pancakes." I motion toward the table.

"Thanks." Caleb pushes off the wall and plods over to the table. He dumps himself into one of the chairs, and I claim a spot across from him.

While we load food on our plates, I sneak glimpses of him, anxious to see how the morning will play out. He takes his time drizzling syrup over his pancakes, and his silverware scratches against the plate as he cuts off a bite. The rustling coming from Austin's old room now warns me it won't be long before he joins us. If this conversation is going to happen, it probably needs to happen now.

"So . . ." I say, breaking the silence.

Caleb shifts in his chair, waiting expectantly.

"You and Austin must have had a good night."

"Hmmm." Caleb chews the bacon in his mouth. "Must have."

"I didn't expect to see you last night. You scared me a bit when I walked into the kitchen."

Caleb pauses so briefly I wonder if I imagined it. Giving me a brief glance he asks, "I'm sorry?"

"When you were sitting on the counter last night and I walked in. We talked. You do remember, don't you?"

Caleb's expression goes blank. He sets his fork down on his plate and clears his throat. Leaning back in his chair, his palms slowly run over his thighs, and his eyes stay locked on mine. He's clearly buying time, searching for an answer to give me. He doesn't remember, does he? Or maybe he does, and he's looking for the right words to reject me. His lips finally part, about to respond to my question.

"You fixed us breakfast, Kate?" Austin's voice booms between us. I didn't even see him walk in. "This is perfect. Thanks."

"Yeah, no problem."

Austin plops food on his plate and digs in. I regard Caleb who is already demolishing his breakfast again. Slumping back in my seat, a huff slips free from my pursed lips. This is not how my morning was supposed to go. What do I do now? Does he not remember his confession last night? The pit in my stomach grows with each minute that ticks by, and suddenly, my own appetite is completely gone. By the time the boys are finished with breakfast, my disappointment is tasting more like fury.

"Thanks for breakfast, Trouble," Caleb says, clearing his dishes to the sink. "Oh, Kate, Monty was hoping you'd come to the cattle auction with us this afternoon."

"Yeah, I think I can."

"I'll text you about it."

"Ready to go?" Austin asks Caleb, shoveling the last of his pancakes into his mouth.

"Yep. Let's get out of here. We've got work to do."

Of course he's ready. What does he have to stick around for? I bite at my lip, trying to keep my expression neutral despite the sickening pit growing in my stomach. He went out and had his fun last night and sopped it all up with the breakfast I slaved away making him. I was so hopeful. Maybe I should have known better, but I've been waiting so long for him to feel something for me—anything. I was foolish to think things had changed.

The door bangs closed behind them, leaving me alone in the quiet house, the only voices coming from the news playing on the TV in my mother's bedroom. A hot, frustrated tear escapes, trailing down my cheek before splattering on my shirt. How could I be so stupid?

I fix another plate of food and carry it to Mom's bedroom. She's resting in her chair, her head bowed and tilted toward the light. Moving closer, the familiar pages of our old picture album come into view, the one that typically stays tucked away, forgotten. The one with pictures of Dad. I pause, watching her. She lifts the album closer, tilting it for more light from the lamp that sits on her nightstand. She's studying the picture of my dad, one where he'd brought home a new horse. Her thumb brushes over his lifeless form, almost as though she might miss him.

But ice rushes through my veins at the memory of him. Yes, there were some good times, but those have all been masked by the freshest memories, the ones that leave a sour taste in my mouth. The ones that remind me I wasn't enough to convince him to stay. I clear my throat, and she slaps the album closed, clearly startled by my presence. She shifts in her chair, draping her blanket over it.

"What have we here?" Mom asks, taking the plate from my hands.

"I fixed you breakfast," I say, studying her carefully.

"Thank you, bug."

Mom reaches for me and squeezes my hand. The last year has not been kind to her. The slightest trace of the blonde that I inherited from her can scarcely be made out on her head. Instead, coarse gray strands are taking over, hanging over her shoulders. Her skin is pale aside from the dark circles that seem ever-present. She's only forty-eight, but her health issues have tacked at least an extra ten years on her appearance.

"I've got to get ready," I say, turning from the room and making my escape.

"How does he talk so fast?" Monty tucks his hand into mine, his round eyes bouncing between me and Caleb in wonder as we walk out of the auction house.

"Lots and lots of practice. You'll get there one day." Caleb's answer seems to satisfy him for now.

We pass through the wide alleyway of pens holding livestock. I don't know what I was expecting coming to the cattle auction with Caleb and Monty. There are so many ways I could have spent my Sunday afternoon instead, and we obviously can't discuss the night before with Monty hanging around. It leaves an unusual wariness hanging over us—or me, rather. Caleb seems unfazed, and I'm not sure if it's because he's oblivious to it or adamantly ignoring it.

Austin waves us over from the open area of gravel that makes up the unloading lot.

"Did you bring your rope?" Monty asks Caleb, hopping up and down in anticipation as we continue toward Austin. "I want you to show me some more of your cool tricks."

"I didn't. But I bet Austin has one in his truck he'd let us use." Caleb ruffles Monty's hair.

"You think he does, Kate?"

"Go ask him," I say, nodding toward Austin.

Monty releases my hand and barrels the rest of the way to Austin, as fast as his little legs will carry him. Upon his arrival, Austin scoops him up and flips him upside down, holding him against his side as he helps close the gap between us. Monty squeals and giggles the whole way, until finally Austin flips him back onto his feet.

"Can we?" Monty asks Austin. He must have already asked once about the rope before Caleb and I reached them.

Austin nods in the direction of his truck parked about ten yards from us. "Go ahead and grab it. It's in the passenger floorboard. Bring the bag of chips, too."

Monty darts off without hesitating. The amount of energy that kid has is astounding. Before long, he's back at my side with the rope and bag of potato chips. He hands the chips to Austin and the rope to Caleb and points out the first target he wants him to rope—a fence post.

Caleb adjusts his loop like I've watched him do countless times before and lifts his arm, swinging the rope overhead. After a couple rotations, he lets it fly free. It lands perfectly, slapping against the wood post and then pulling tight. After a few more successful ropings of inanimate objects, Monty points at me.

"Rope Kate now."

Caleb smirks. "What do you think, Trouble?"

"Don't you dare." I reach in Austin's bag of chips and grab a handful.

Caleb may not be fazed by the other night—hell, he probably doesn't even remember it—but I'm not in the mood to goof around with him.

"Why do you call her Trouble?" Monty asks.

"Because girls are trouble. Every single one of them." Caleb winks at me.

"I guess that checks out." Monty shrugs and takes the rope from Caleb, running off to a hay bale several feet away where he tries to mimic Caleb's movements.

"He seems to be having a blast," Austin says, crunching on a chip.

"Kate, come here. I want you to watch me." Monty waves me over, and I happily oblige.

"Let's see what you can do."

Monty slings the rope a few times. Becoming frustrated, he plops on the hay bale. Scratching his head, he looks up at me, his face scrunched.

"Can I ask you a question?" Monty asks.

"Sure."

"Are you Caleb's girlfriend?"

"No." Thanks for pouring salt on the wound, kid.

"Do you want to be his girlfriend?"

"Come on, let's go see if the boys are ready to go home yet."

CHAPTER SEVEN

Clarabelle is waiting for me when I enter the barn. Breathing in the familiar scent of earth, straw, and livestock, I rub the cow's head and open the gate to her pen. She follows the clanking of grain bouncing in the metal bucket I offer, willfully going to her milking stall. While Clarabelle munches on the bucket of grain, I pull over my stool and get to work milking the old girl. This is my favorite part of my morning routine. It's my moment of peace to escape whatever problems reality decides to throw my way. Like being a caregiver to my mother before even graduating from high school. Or giving up barrel racing despite my first-place standing in the Montana High School Rodeo Association because my mother needed me close. Plus, there's the whole unrequited love thing. Yeah, sometimes reality is a bitch.

I'll miss chores tonight because of work. Thankfully, our neighbor comes over to help when I'm working. Mom hasn't been able to handle the chores consistently for a couple of years now, and I'm not sure what we would do without his help. Austin comes over and helps when he can, but he has his own work that keeps him busy and allows him to provide more financially than I can.

Back inside, I tidy up and get ready to take Mom to her doctor's appointment.

WE SIT on the thinly cushioned vinyl chairs of the treatment room that reeks of antiseptic while Mom and her doctor discuss her fluctuation of symptoms, the loss of her job, and the likely impact from that. My fingers skim over the rough ridges in the vinyl as I listen to my mother fill in the doctor on how the most recent changes in medications and diet have been working out for her. They don't ask my opinion, and it's just as well—they wouldn't like what I have to say.

"I think we're almost done here," Dr. Miller says, reading over Mom's chart through the glasses sitting halfway down his large nose. His gray hair is perfectly slicked over the thinning top of his head.

He's kidding, right? There's been no discussion of next steps or possible solutions. I can't sit here and allow this doctor to use my mother like a meal ticket.

"Why don't we have a definite diagnosis yet? She's been coming to you for years, and her health keeps getting worse. Clearly what we've been doing isn't sufficient," I say, finally deciding to speak up. "If it was, we should see more measurable improvements in her symptoms."

"I disagree," Dr. Miller says, not batting an eye. "I think we've made some good progress. We could consider adding in some more therapies if your mother would like, but ultimately, this is something she's going to have to learn to live with for now." His stool squeaks under his slight form as he turns back to his folder and jots down more notes, his pen scratching against the paper.

"Learn to live with? What kind of doctor are you? She's coming to you for help, not to be told she needs to suck it up and move on."

"Bug, it's okay. The doctors are doing the best they can," my mom says, patting my knee.

Why won't she advocate for herself? Does she even want to get better? I love my mom, and I would do anything for her. If I need to stay with her indefinitely to care for her, I will, without a second thought. But when she doesn't press the doctor for help, it makes me wonder if she cares at all that I put my life on hold for her. It's times like this I feel taken for granted.

"I think we've reached the point where we can start working on filing for long-term disability," the doctor says, ignoring me and regarding my mother again. "The front desk can give you some recommendations for attorneys in the area who specialize in that sort of thing. You don't have to use any of the ones on the list. We like to provide it for your convenience."

"Thank you, Doctor." Mom stands and pulls her purse strap over her shoulder.

Minutes later, I'm helping her out to the pickup, and we head home. The care she's receiving is infuriating, and I seem to be the only one bothered by it. If I didn't know better, I'd think they weren't concerned about finding the cause of her issues because they're afraid they'll actually be able to cure it. Healthy patients don't make you any money.

"I wish you wouldn't cause such a stir," Mom says. She stares out the window, avoiding me.

"I want you to get better. I feel like the doctors are playing games with your health."

"They're doing the best they know how. Not everything has an easy solution."

"Then maybe we need to find new doctors." The statement comes out more forcefully than I intended, but I'm not sorry. She needs to hear it.

Mom doesn't respond. Instead, she watches the empty fields roll by as I drive us further down the road. Her fingers fidget with the necklace she's wearing, toying with the charms that dangle from the gold chain. One for me and one for Austin.

She's quiet the rest of the drive, presumably upset with me. That's fine. I'm upset with her, too. Her choices are affecting all of us, and she's choosing to bury her head in the sand.

Austin says he has a plan to save the house, but he hasn't shared the details with me yet. He told me he has to work a couple things out before he knows for sure if his plan will work. If it doesn't, we'll have to start making some hard decisions. Do we sell off as much land as we can and save the house? Do we let the whole thing go? Sometimes life isn't fair, and unfortunately, *sometimes* seems to be *most of the time* for my family.

I'm still getting the silent treatment when we arrive home, so I invite Emily over to hang out. There's way too much going on, and I need a distraction before the stress boils over.

Right before lunch, Emily shows up at my house telling me all about how in love she is with my brother. While I don't mind if my brother decides to date my best friend, I'm quickly becoming aware of the disadvantages of such an arrangement. There are some things a girl should never know about her brother, and unfortunately, Emily has never been bashful about oversharing.

"Has Austin said anything about me? Things are going so good with him," Emily says after I cut off her ramblings about their night together. "I'm confident that it's not going to be much longer before I can officially call him my boyfriend."

"You think so?" Personally, I think she's overly optimistic, but who am I to say what's going on between the two of them?

"Oh, yes. He's so incredible. And I'm sure we are on the same page. He doesn't want to rush into anything, you know? I think that's so sweet of him."

Emily plops down on my bed, and the headboard knocks against the wall waking the cat. She stretches before plopping onto the floor and lazily strutting out of the room.

"Is that what he told you?" I finish painting the nails on my right foot and switch to my left, the pungent chemical scent of the polish starting to get to my head.

"Not in so many words, exactly, but yeah. He said he wants to keep getting to know each other, but he's not ready to define us as anything more than friends. I think it's sweet that he wants to focus on building a strong foundation of friendship before we label ourselves as boyfriend and girlfriend. It makes complete sense if you think about it."

Or he's the same old Austin who doesn't want a committed relationship, and she's delusional enough to interpret his explanation as something other than what it is. His flings hold onto him as long as they can before they figure out he's broken beyond repair and the declaration of their relationship is never actually coming. He's so determined that happily-ever-afters don't exist that he's afraid of either one of us giving love a chance.

"Did you meet the new guy?" Emily asks.

"Not officially. Why?"

"His name is Trevor. Does he look familiar to you?"

"Should he?"

"He's Brock's little brother. Do you really not recognize him?"

"Brock, as in the douchebag that you dated a couple years ago?"

"The one and only. I haven't heard from him in ages." Emily sighs dramatically and props her chin in her hand. "He's the one that got away."

"Didn't he break up with you to date Laurie Gibbs?"

"Yes. They got married last year. She's such a bitch. I bumped into them right before they got married. They came into the diner one day while I was working, and they were total jerks. They thought it was so hilarious that I had the same job I worked in high school and that I was still unsurprisingly single."

"What? You didn't tell me about this. I would have remembered." I twist around to face her.

"It wasn't a moment I wanted to relive by sharing the story. Anyway, I'm sure Trevor will feed information back to them about how pathetic my life is."

"Your life is not pathetic."

"How great would it be if Trevor tells them I'm dating his boss? One more reason I can't wait to make things official with him. Your brother makes my body come alive and feel things I've never felt before," Emily says. I don't bother trying to hide my cringe. "If only you could have that with someone."

"I will eventually." Turning to focus on spreading the vibrant red paint across my nails again, I hide my eye roll from her.

"Of course! I'm not sure if it's going to be Caleb though, babe. If Caleb was going to notice you, he would have already. I mean, I know he said he wanted you, but let's face the facts: He was drunk. He didn't know what he was saying. And to top it off, it wasn't even significant enough for him to remember the next day."

"Or maybe he does notice me, but he doesn't think I have feelings like that for him." I aggressively twist the top back on the nail polish bottle, my lips pressed tightly together.

I suddenly regret confiding in her about Caleb's drunken confession. Sometimes Emily really gets under my skin with the Caleb comments. I think she means well, but she could at least put a little more effort into the delivery. And although she's not totally wrong about the incident, the way she delivers the recap only twists the knife already embedded in my heart.

"Oh!" Emily sits up on my bed, her eyes wide. "You know what you need? You need a makeover." Emily claps excitedly. "Let me do it. Let me show you how to do your makeup and hair. We can pick out a sexy outfit and go to the ranch to see our boys. It will be perfect. Caleb will have to notice you."

"I don't know, Em. I'm not sure a makeover will change anything."

Part of me wishes I was one of those girls with the perfect hair and makeup, but that shouldn't make any difference.

"Please? Oh, please let me do your makeup."

Against my better judgment, I finally agree. What could it hurt? Emily pulls her ever-present makeup bag out of her purse and gets straight to work on me. The weight of the makeup on my face gets heavier with each stroke. Once she's all done and I study myself in the mirror, I'm surprised—I do look good.

"Let's find you something to wear now." Emily opens my closet. She scoots shirt after shirt across the rod in my closet, her nose wrinkled. Emily shakes her head and mutters to herself as she flips through the options. Finally, she gives up and turns back to me, her eyebrows scrunched together. "Why do you have Austin's old clothes in your closet?"

"Because I wear those." I cross my arms over my chest, unsure why her question showers me with shame. It's no secret how I dress.

"What about your mom's clothes? She used to dress cute. Would she care if you borrowed something?"

"No, she wouldn't care." I lead Emily to my mother's room.

Emily flips through Mom's clothing, not impressed by the options but much more satisfied. Dread overtakes me. What was I thinking agreeing to this? She pulls a few of my mother's frilly blouses out of the closet and sets them aside. Finally satisfied that she hasn't missed any viable options, we carry a handful of blouses to my room.

"I think the emerald one is perfect for you," Emily says, eyeing me up and down. "It looks great with those jeans, too." The blouse buttons in the front up to the low dip of the V-neck. This one doesn't have a bunch of ruffles like the other options Emily set out—which I'm grateful for—but the small clusters of white flowers add a delicate touch.

"Now we need to figure out what to do about that hair." Emily's studies me as though my hair is a tangled rat's nest.

"We've got to work this afternoon. I'm not going to spend

the whole night sweeping my hair out of my face or risking getting a hair in someone's food. I'm putting it up in a ponytail."

"Fine. But at least let me do it. I'll dress it up a bit."

Once I'm as good as I'm going to get by Emily's standards, I observe myself in the mirror. Somehow, she has turned my basic ponytail into something much fancier. I look like I'm ready to head out the door on a hot date, not go visit my brother and his friends on a ranch. Emily spritzes me with her body spray without warning, sending me into a coughing fit. The spray leaves a bitter taste in my mouth and makes my lungs burn. She could have at least given me a heads-up.

I have nothing to do now but wait for Emily to deem herself ready to be seen by my brother. As I wait, nervous anticipation builds steadily, making me dread what would otherwise be a typical visit. This isn't a petty game I'm playing to convince him he wants me, but I'm more than his buddy's little sister, and if he can't see that, I'm not sure I'm ready for the outcome of this experiment.

caleb

Monty sits across from me at the picnic table. We're under the shade of a large oak tree eating the lunch Monty helped me pick up. Joyful screams drift toward us from the nearby playground. Monty's sad little face is propped up on his fist while he picks at his french fries. He isn't taking the news of me leaving to rodeo very well.

"I'm still going to see you, bud. I'm just letting you know that it won't be on our usual schedule over the summer." The aroma of greasy burgers wafts around us.

"I know. But what if I need something?" Monty finally peeks up at me again with tears brimming and clinging to his lashes.

"You'll call me, and I'll be here."

"You promise?" Monty's quivering lip is almost too much for me to take.

"I promise. Nothing can change that."

Monty slides out of his seat, sniffling, and wraps his little arms around me. "I'm going to miss you," he whimpers into my shirt.

"I'm going to miss you, too." I kiss the top of his head.

I didn't expect our conversation to be this hard. A heavy,

invisible weight sits on my chest, making me antsy to do whatever it takes to brush it away, but I know that's not possible. I fully believe Monty will make it through the summer fine, but I can't shake the feeling that I'm letting him down.

At his request, I take him back to the ranch with me. Austin wants to get some practice in, and Ducky's agreed to keep an eye on Monty while we do so. Even if I didn't already like the guys I work with, I'd have extra respect for them based off their welcoming of Monty to the ranch. They all look out for him and make him feel like he's one of the crew.

As soon as I turn the truck off, Monty leaps out and races to the barn to find Ducky, who gives him a high five and leads him away to help with a chore. Monty's excited chatter slowly fades as they walk further away, and Austin and I get our horses ready.

Austin may have convinced me to be his roping partner, but we need to figure out if we stand a chance against other seasoned teams. Our long-term friendship and ranching career definitely work in our favor. Thankfully, we have plenty of steers to practice on and extra cowboys willing to work the chute and offer unsolicited coaching.

We've been at it for about an hour, practicing roping together. A couple car doors slamming shut snags my attention, and soon our audience has grown both in numbers and in looks. Kate steps up on the bottom rung of the panel, crossing her arms over the top. She immediately finds me with her eyes, and I can't help the smile on my face from stretching wider. Kate sends me a little wave, and I nod in return. Damn, she's gorgeous. If I thought the craving to kiss her was bad before, that moment with her the other night in the kitchen only made it worse. It has me questioning my resolve and if I'm overplaying the obstacles in my head.

Emily is at Kate's side, no doubt hoping for another chance to get close to Austin. She's been working him like a debt collector. Poor girl can't seem to figure out he's the shark. I don't agree with the way my best friend handles his relationships, probably better labeled as situationships, but I do understand how he got there. His parent's marriage did a number on him.

I shoot Kate a wink and turn to ready myself in the box for the next run, stealing another peek at her as I do. It takes me a minute to pinpoint what's different about her. She's wearing a blouse I've never seen her in before, and for a moment, I wonder if she wore it for me. The thought is quickly pushed aside. Of course, she didn't. She doesn't go out of her way to impress me. She doesn't need to.

Kate's a showstopper with the makeup and the overall look she has going on today, but I think she's just as gorgeous in her usual garb of jeans and an oversized T-shirt. While I'm not opposed to admiring today's view, if it's not for me, I wonder who it *is* for. The possibility of her dressing up for someone else makes me sick to my stomach. It's wrong, but I want to be the only man that holds her interest.

The new guy, Trevor, saunters over to Kate and Emily and introduces himself. The kid better watch himself or he's going to find out the hard way why he's the only one getting friendly with the girls. I can't hear what he's saying, but whatever it is, he pulls Kate's attention away from me and onto himself. If only looks could kill, this joker would have keeled over by now from the way my gaze is boring into him. Kate steps off the panel and turns to talk to him. She doesn't seem bothered by his attention. Actually, she seems flattered. She laughs at whatever it is he says and dips her head bashfully, pink spreading across her perfect cheeks.

The steer breaks free from the chute, and my horse takes off, but I fumble with the rope, unprepared. My focus is stuck on Kate.

"Shit, man, what happened?" Austin shouts and turns his horse back to the start.

"I wasn't ready." It's a lame excuse, but it's the best I've got when my brain can't function over the red I'm seeing.

"Well, get ready. We don't have time for fooling around."

I get into position and peer over at Kate and Trevor again. She's smiling at him, and he's standing way too close. Does the nitwit not know what personal space is? I silently will Kate to "accidentally" knee him in the nuts, but she's too wrapped up in their conversation to pay me any mind. Fuck.

This whole situation turned south way too fast. Suddenly, up here roping is the last place I want to be. I try to pull myself together and prepare for the next run, but I can't keep my eyes from wandering over to Kate.

We run through a few more steers and I blow it each time. I can't focus on roping while that dumbass flirts with her. Kate is way out of his league, and he'd better watch himself or he'll have Austin up his ass real quick.

"Okay, let's take a break," Austin finally says, probably deciding to let Emily ease the frustration I've caused before I piss him off any more with my sudden lack of performance. There's no way we'll make our goal if I rope like this the whole time.

Not having to be told twice, I'm off my horse in a matter of minutes and hopping over a panel of the corral to get to Kate. She's laughing at something Trevor said, and he's completely oblivious to my approach.

"We need to talk." I delicately grab her arm and pull her with me across the gravel lot and around the side of the barn, out of sight of everyone.

It surprises her, but she follows along without putting up a fight. That's my girl.

"Is everything okay?" Kate relaxes against the barn once I've released my hold on her.

She stands rooted to the spot while I pace back and forth, trying to escape the unquenchable fire I feel burning for her.

"No, it's not okay," I hiss, pulling off my hat and running my hand through my hair. My mind and my heart are at war with each other, one needing to declare itself to her and the other screaming out warnings to keep my distance. I can't continue to play my charade as the indifferent friend. Her effect on me is too intense, and I'm all out of strength. Pausing in front of her, I take a deep breath to steady my nerves.

Her stunned silence pulls me to her, and I lean into her, resting my forearm above her head. My free hand finds Kate's waist. Falling victim to her gravitational pull, I press into her body. The ache I feel for her is eating away at me, slowly disintegrating my willpower.

"Caleb . . ." she says, shaking her head.

Her round, questioning brown eyes are locked on mine now, and her hands hesitate between us as though they're unsure of where to land. Panic is slowly rising, threatening to overtake me as I pray those delicate fingers find rest on my body. I thought she felt the same to some degree at least. Did I misread her? Am I making a fool of myself?

Slowly, her hands finally land on my chest and slide up to my shoulders, but as she grabs my shirt, I can see Kate contemplating whether to pull me down to her or push me away. I want her to push me away, but I'm praying to God she pulls me closer.

Kate's fingers tighten their grip on my shirt.

With my nose brushing Kate's, my mouth hangs desperately over hers, wanting to give in. Just this once. Tingles dance through my body under her touch, and as if she's read my mind, she lifts on her toes and presses her mouth to mine. Just like that, I'm lost in her, tasting her, and trying to commit this kiss to memory. Her arms wrap around my neck, and my body presses harder into hers, springing to life with the desire radiating from her. My hands drop to her thighs, and I lift her, wrapping her legs around my waist, never breaking the connection of our mouths. She moans, and it feeds my craving for her.

Kate fits so perfectly to me, like our bodies are meant to be intertwined. I squeeze her ass and slide a hand up her back, past the nape of her neck, and pull the hair tie from her hair. Her locks fall to her shoulders. The coconut scent of her shampoo fills my nose, and I tug her head back tenderly by her hair, exposing the soft skin of her neck for my mouth to explore. A moan escapes her, and I'm ready to take her right here against the side of the barn.

"Kate?" Austin's voice calls out for her from the direction of the corrals, breaking the trance I've found myself in. Reality crashes down over me, stealing away this moment that I know I'll never get back. The moment I shouldn't have allowed myself in the first place.

I pull my mouth from her neck, and we stare at each other, our chests heaving with ragged breaths. I loosen my grip on her ass, allowing her legs to slide down, and Kate's feet catch her when they hit the ground. Taking a step back, I focus on my hands straightening my clothes instead of risking a look at her swollen lips that I'd rather be pressed against.

I locate the abandoned hair tie on the ground behind her and pick it up, wiping the dust away before placing it in her palm. When my eyes meet hers, she takes a step toward me again, but I stop her.

"No, Kate. We can't. Austin—we just can't." I shake my head.

"Clearly, we can. We just did." Kate watches me expectantly.

"We shouldn't have. Austin wouldn't take it well, and—"

"Wasn't it you who told me that any guy who wasn't willing to fight for me was a pussy?" Her hands go to her hips, and she faces me squarely like she has no intention of backing down.

"I want to be respectful to your brother and that makes me a pussy?" I cock an eyebrow at her and take a step toward her, too, ready for the challenge.

"If the tampon fits . . . "

We're inches away now, Kate staring up at me through her lashes. I watch the rise and fall of her chest with each breath she takes through those full, parted lips.

"Kate, don't be like this—"

"No, it's fine. You've just proved to me what I didn't want to admit. You're not man enough for me, and now that I can see it, I don't want you anymore."

"Kate, where'd you go?" Austin yells again.

I shake my head. Her words sting, but it's best this way. There can't be anything between us. Not without destroying both of our relationships with Austin. And as much as Austin's friendship means to me, I can't be the one to do that to him and Kate.

"I've got to get Monty home." I take off down the side of the barn, away from the corrals. It's not safe being close enough to touch her. I need to get out of town.

I slow the gator to a stop on the bumpy, uneven terrain of the pasture. Austin and I climb out to work on the fence made with sections of barbed wire stretched between weathered wooden posts. The tall grass dances in the light breeze, and the low bellows of the cattle reverberate through the field as we make quick work of stretching and reviving the wire. We're driving the fence line today and repairing any damages. It's not a very stimulating task, but it gives us time to plan out our last-minute roping season.

"Have you got our schedule figured out?" I ask Austin, knowing he's anxious to get on the road and start winning money.

"Oh yeah. We're going to start off this weekend in northern Montana, in Augusta. After that we'll move on to Bigfork. The first month we'll probably stay on the road. We'll have some breaks, so we can swing through town if we need to, but we may decide it's not worth the extra travel time and gas."

"Okay." I nod and stretch the wire tight and secure it. "We leave Thursday?"

"That's the plan. We'll leave bright and early. I've already got it all worked out with the boss."

I pull off my gloves and stuff them in my back pocket, my fingers sliding over the worn, velvety leather. We climb back on the gator and drive further down the fence line, keeping watch for spots that appear weak.

"What's the deal with you and Emily? Are you simply having fun, or did you finally find someone to tie you down?" I'm pretty sure I know the answer, but I'm trying to move the conversation along to the topic I actually want to discuss.

Austin scoffs at me. "It's all in the name of fun. She knows it's nothing more than a good time. I've made that clear to her several times now. She's free to take it or leave it."

"You sure about that?" I smirk as we stop at another weak section of fence.

"Hell yeah, I'm sure. Why? Did she or Kate say something?"

Austin stops working to watch me, his brows furrowed. Austin has been the "love 'em and leave 'em" type since high school. Somehow Emily has stuck around longer than most of the others.

"No, man. I was just checking. Seeing where your head's at is all." I chuckle and we move on down the fence. "Think you'll ever settle down?"

"I don't know. What's the point? You move in together just for one of you to have to move out when things are over. Or if you're dumb enough to get married, you get to pay thousands of dollars and split up everything you own for the same result. No, I'm not interested in all that bullshit. I'll have my fun and have my own place to go home to."

"You might find someone that changes your opinion of that one day."

Austin huffs and waves me off. "I don't see you handing out any rings," he mutters.

He's right. I've never even been close to proposing to a

woman before. I want it, but I want it with Kate. And that's not going to happen.

"Give me time. It'll happen one day. And you'll be my best man. We'll get you up at that altar in a fancy suit one way or another," I say, choosing to be optimistic.

"Don't count on it."

kate

The dish drainer rattles as I slam the mixing bowl into it, and several of the freshly washed dishes tip over. I grab at the dirty pot now, anger fueling my stamina to scrub the pan clean. Even if I could find reprieve from the hurricane of emotions raging through me, I probably wouldn't understand what has happened between me and Caleb this week. Not even remotely. One minute, I'm talking to one of the ranch hands, and the next, Caleb has me pressed up against the barn desperate to jump him. So, I do. *And he clearly liked it.* In true fashion, though, Austin had to ruin the moment. It's like he has a sixth sense for these things. And for what? To ask about my work schedule, of all things. Honestly, Emily could have told him when I'm working. We are almost always on the same shifts.

Caleb took the opportunity to turn and run the other way. He left me standing there dressed up for him, aching for his touch, and mad as a fucking hornet. And let's not forget his confession in the kitchen and his inability to step up and be a man. The more I roll these events around in my mind, the less I understand.

With the dishes washed, I stomp to my bedroom to get

ready for tonight. Austin wants to have a bonfire. That's why he wanted to know my work schedule. Caleb will undoubtedly be there. They've always been an inseparable pair. A part of me doesn't want to see him. Then again, I'm tired of letting other people dictate the decisions I make. Now I'm stuck with a dilemma. Do I try to dress myself up again like Emily did, or do I stick to my typical low-maintenance look? And how am I supposed to dress cute and still be warm tonight? I pull my phone out of my pocket to check the weather app for tonight's temperature: forty-five degrees.

There are two ways I can play this. I can dress in all the necessary layers to be perfectly warm, or I can dress light and trust that between the fire and someone else's body heat—a detail yet to be determined—I will be plenty warm enough to make it through the night. I bite my thumbnail while considering the options. Maybe I can come up with something in between.

I grab the bag of unused makeup I have stashed away and take a seat on my bedroom floor in front of my full-length mirror. Digging into the bag, I pull out items similar to what Emily used on me yesterday, determined to figure this out. Looking everything over, I suddenly feel overwhelmed. I can't do this on my own. What was I thinking? I'm about to toss everything back in the bag when my phone vibrates on the floor next to me. I swipe my finger across the cool, slick screen to answer the FaceTime call from Emily.

"You could sense that I was in dire need, couldn't you?" I ask her.

"Always, babe. What's wrong?" Emily asks. I switch to the front camera and scan it across my mess on the floor.

"Help me? I don't know what to do with any of this shit."

"Oh, I can definitely help you out with that." Emily takes me step-by-step, explaining the process with each product. The outcome isn't as good as when Emily did it, but for being inexperienced, I didn't do half bad.

"What do you think?" I let Emily see my finished face.

"Hot as hell, babe. The boys will be drooling over you tonight. Do me a favor though? Ignore Caleb. You've got to give the boys a chance to get to you, and as long as you're glued to him, it's not going to happen."

She doesn't know what happened with Caleb yesterday. I didn't want to tell her after the things she said about our encounter in the kitchen. Maybe I'm not ready to accept the meaning of his actions.

"We'll see." I'm still debating with myself over how to handle the Caleb mess. "But what were you actually calling me about?"

"Austin is going to ask if it'd be okay to send someone over to pick you up instead of him coming by. I wanted to ask you to kindly agree. I have big plans for tonight, and I don't want a third wheel. Sorry, babe."

"I can drive. I don't have to be chauffeured." I pack the makeup into the bag.

"You know how Austin is. He's worried about you driving out there by yourself. Please accept the ride when he calls, would you? Don't get him all riled up or you'll ruin both our nights."

"Okay, Em. I've got your back. I'll be docile and obedient when he calls." I shoot her a wink.

Sure enough, when I hang up our FaceTime call, I see a text from Austin. He wants to send someone else to pick me up just like Emily said. Which, now that I think about it, may be the perfect idea. Yes, I'm capable of driving myself, but honestly, I hate driving out there at night. It's creepy in the dark, and once you get in the desert, there's no cell service.

I scroll through my contacts, searching for the cowboy I know will be perfect for the job, and send him a text. Almost instantly I have his response. Time to fill in Austin, I guess.

Me: No worries. I got my own ride.

Austin: Who?

Me: One of your many minions.

Austin: Kate . . .

Me: What are we going to do about the homestead? Any ideas?

Austin: I have something in the works.

Me: Care to expound on that?

Austin: We'll talk later. Who are you riding with?

Me: We'll talk later. See you tonight.

Tossing my phone aside, I raid my closet. My cell buzzes again from my bed, but I ignore it. Shoved behind the rest of my wardrobe is a turquoise scoop neck top I'd forgotten about. My mother bought it for me a few years ago when she tried to feminize me. The feminization attempt didn't work. However, the fabric of the shirt clings to my body and does wonderful things accentuating my figure. Next, I find an old zipper hoodie. It's thick, and the sleeves hang a tad long, giving it a comfy feel. Zipping it up to my chest, the hoodie complements my natural fullness.

The ringing of the doorbell signals that my ride is here, and I yell to Mom, letting her know I'm on my way out. Swinging the front door open, I find Trevor standing on the front porch, his hands shoved deep in the pockets of his jeans. He's no Caleb, but that doesn't bother me. His build is much slimmer and he's only about an inch taller than me. His slicked-back brown hair almost dusts the tops of his shoulders. His face lights up with a crooked, boyish grin, and he ogles me, seeming to appreciate the view.

"Are you ready?" he asks, his eyes finally finding his way back to my face.

"Yep. Thanks again for the ride. I hope it didn't put you out coming all this way to get me."

"Darlin', you can call me for a ride any time you'd like. Shall we?"

Trevor offers me his arm, and I take it. The old wooden porch steps creak under our weight as we head down to the driveway to the passenger side of his truck. Before I can grab the door handle, Trevor is there opening it for me. Hoisting my foot up to the running board, I pull myself up into his pickup truck. Trevor's hand grazes the small of my back while he spots my ascent. I don't know him well enough yet to know if there is any future for us, but he's cute, he seems fun, and he cares enough to pursue me. That's more than I can say for Caleb at the moment.

"So that's the family homestead I've heard Austin talk about?" Trevor asks as we pull onto the road.

"Yeah. It's mostly me handling it these days, but Austin comes and helps when he can get away from the ranch."

"You know, you don't have to sit so far away. You can scoot over this way if you want." Trevor winks at me.

I can't hold back the giggle that bubbles up in my chest. I can already tell Trevor was a good choice. I'm desperate for a fun evening, and I think that is exactly what's in store for me.

A couple other vehicles are already there when we arrive at the rocky beach of the small lake. Austin is getting the fire burning steadily, and Emily is stuck to his side. A couple other ranch hands stand and watch, beers in their hands, but so far, there's no sign of Caleb.

Austin rises from his crouched position at the fire as Trevor and I approach. His eyes brush over us but snag back on Trevor as realization hits him. Austin's expression turns to the cold stone glare I'm so used to seeing him direct at men who look my way.

"What the hell is this?" Austin asks.

"Seriously, Austin? Chill. Trevor gave me a ride."

Austin looks Trevor up and down then steps into his space, glowering at him.

"Exactly how long have you been 'giving my sister rides?'" Austin asks in air quotes, his nostrils flaring.

"Austin!" I shove at him, but his shoulder barely gives.

"Today is the first time," Trevor says, his brows furrowed in confusion.

"See that it's the last time, or every nasty, miserable, shit task on the ranch will magically fall on you."

"You're such an asshole." I tug at Trevor's arm. "Come on, Trevor. Ignore him."

Austin's glare follows us as I put space between the two boys. I guess that went better than it has in the past. Probably because Austin knows Trevor will have to face him every day at work.

"I'm sorry about him. My brother's a jerk."

Trevor shrugs. "I mean, I get it. He's not serious, though, is he?"

"He's just a big bully. It's fine. Let's get a drink."

More trucks full of people pull in behind us, and the crowd quickly grows. The smoke from the fire assaults my lungs with each shift it makes in my direction. Despite telling myself not to care, I search the crowd for Caleb, but there's no trace of him.

As the sun disappears behind the mountains and the stars peek out, littered around the full moon, the party is finally reaching full swing. Music drifts in the background from someone's pickup truck. Trevor snakes an arm around my waist, hugging me close, his chin dipping down to my shoulder. He pulls me with him, swaying back and forth to the music, until suddenly he stills. I peek over my shoulder at him and follow his gaze across the fire to Austin who's shooting daggers at him. Emily hangs on Austin's arm, trying to keep his attention.

I twist around, forcing Trevor's stare back to mine. "Come on, let's dance."

Within seconds, his motions thaw, and he's twirling me to the music, making me laugh again. Before the song ends, we're interrupted.

"May I cut in?" Caleb's deep voice rumbles.

He stands about four inches taller than Trevor, his expression as he studies Trevor's face nearly as friendly as Austin's has been tonight.

"We're kind of in the middle of something—" Trevor starts.

"Absolutely not," I break in, wanting my opinion made clear. "Now if you'll excuse us, we were having a good time before you so rudely interrupted." I brush away the hair blown into my face by the light breeze and turn from Caleb, leading Trevor away by his hand.

If the fire in my veins is any indication, Caleb's eyes bore into my back, and a mixture of satisfaction and unease blooms inside me. Grabbing a couple drinks from the cooler, I offer Trevor one before opening my own. He takes it, but the smile has yet to return to his face. Instead, he wears a serious expression as though he's trying to work through a difficult problem. I take a big swig, letting the wheaty hops wash away the jitters that are creeping in and readying myself for the conversation currently brewing in Trevor's countenance.

"You know, some of the guys at the ranch tried telling me you were off-limits," Trevor finally says.

"Off-limits?" I stiffen, anger seeping inside me and spreading through my veins.

"They said you've got two bodyguards. I said they were nuts." He shrugs and picks at the label on his beer.

"That's obvious." My eyes roam the crowd, finding Caleb watching us, looking pissed. Good for him.

"Are they though? We've been here for what? Two hours? And I've had verbal threats thrown at me and every time I turn around someone is staring at me like they're ready to pummel my ass."

"They aren't going to do anything." I squeeze Trevor's arm, trying to reassure him.

"One of the guys said Austin ran someone over with his truck for taking you on a date. I thought he was kidding. Now I'm starting to wonder."

I roll my eyes. "That was a rumor. I promise."

"Maybe so. But he's also my boss and I need my job, Kate."

"What are you saying?" I pull my hand back.

"Listen, you're gorgeous. And you might be worth all the trouble, but I'm not interested in complicated right now. I'm looking for something light and fun." Trevor shakes his head. "I can give you a ride back home, but I think it's best if things end there between us."

An angry laugh rolls out of me, and I fight back tears of frustration. That didn't take long, but honestly, what did I expect? Of course, another tally goes under Austin's name on the imaginary scoreboard of my love life.

"Don't worry about it. I don't need a ride home." I start to turn away, but Trevor stops me.

"I really don't mind."

"No, thanks. Wouldn't want you to risk getting your tires slashed or something," I spit out sarcastically.

I'm ready to go home and go to bed. That's not a possibility right now though. Drifting away from the fire, I find myself a spot in the dark, several yards away from the music and laughter, to sit and lick my wounds.

I tune out the ruckus behind me and hug my legs to me, resting my cheek on my knees. Tears fight to be freed, but I'm not crying over silly boys who aren't worth my time—whether fueled by frustration or not. A chill racks my body, the sweatshirt I wore insufficient without the warmth of a fire. The cold earth only urges my shivers on, so I lift myself from the ground and onto my feet again.

This isn't the night I was hoping for. Not at all. I want to go home.

caleb

Kate made it clear she didn't want to talk to me. I should have expected as much. My lack of self-control is unjust. It's a good thing she came with someone. I'm clearly incapable of resisting her, and that's not fair to her if I can't deliver. Watching her smile and laugh with Trevor is about as pleasant as having my nose hairs slowly plucked one by one with a warped pair of tweezers. And the worst part is I could walk away and spare myself the pain, but instead, I choose misery and allow myself to wallow over every bit of her she gives to someone other than me.

Unable to stay away any longer, I make my way through the crowd and off into the shadows where I watched her run off to earlier. She's standing alone, freezing—I can tell by the way her body shivers—and she's too stubborn to come back to the fire. Coming up behind her, I slide out of my coat and drape it over her shoulders. Kate twists around to face me, stumbling in the process. I reach for her, trying to save her from hitting the ground.

"I don't need your help," Kate says.

She tosses my coat to the ground and folds her arms across her chest. Stubborn woman. I end the staring contest we find ourselves in and stoop, picking up my coat. I hold it open to her again.

"Please, Kate. You're cold. I want to help."

"I don't give a damn what you want."

I let the coat hang at my side. "What are you doing out here by yourself?"

"I want to be alone, Caleb."

"What happened with Trevor? Why aren't you with him?"

Kate laughs, turning away briefly before looking back at me. "Like you even have to ask. You know good and well what happened with Trevor. Austin happened, and you trying to interfere definitely didn't help matters."

"So, he brings you all the way out here and drops you? How are you getting home?" I clench my jaw, biting back the things I want to say. Now it's my turn to be angry. Is that fucker serious right now?

"I don't know. I guess I'll ride with Austin. Emily will be pissed, but walking clearly isn't an option." Kate waves toward the blackened desert.

"Let me give you a ride. We'll leave whenever you're ready. If you want to go now, we'll go. If you want to stay till the fire's out, we'll stay. But let me drive you home." The fact that Kate doesn't immediately turn me down tells me she wants to accept the offer. "I owe you an apology, Kate. I'm sorry about the other day. I don't want my mistake to ruin our friendship."

Kate sucks in a breath and squeezes her eyes shut.

"You're important to me, Kate. Please don't let this destroy us."

Kate nods, defeat taking over the anger that was holding her hostage. "I want to go home, Caleb."

I offer her my coat again, and this time she slips it on, overlapping it in the front to wrap it tightly around her torso.

"Come on, Trouble." I drape an arm over her shoulders and lead her in the direction of my pickup.

Kate's cold fingers wrap around mine when I offer her hand

up into my truck. I maneuver the truck out of my self-proclaimed spot, and Kate leans her head against the window as we rock back and forth, slowly making our way through the desert and toward the road.

I shouldn't have kissed her at the barn. Okay, I shouldn't have said the things I did that night I was drunk, either. I have feelings for this woman, and suddenly, I have the self-restraint of a two-year-old. This can't be a good sign. Or maybe that's exactly what it is—a sign that I've got it all wrong. Maybe giving into her is the choice I'm supposed to make. We know each other inside and out. Our feelings have morphed from a friendly respect to undeniable desire, not despite our years growing up together but most likely because of them. Kate feels like home to me.

She sniffles from the other end of the cab and wipes away a stray tear off her cheek. Her tears are daggers to my heart, and there is nothing I can do about them. I shouldn't let myself get involved.

"Did you mean what you said back there?" Kate asks, her tone timid.

"What part?"

"That I'm important to you?" She studies her hands in her lap, picking at her nails.

"I hate that I've given you any reason to doubt it." When her hushed whimpering continues, I can't stop myself. "Come here."

She hesitates, but after a moment, she slumps over in the seat cushion, lying flat on her back with her head resting on my thigh and her legs folded, resting against the seat. She's still wearing my coat, holding it wrapped tightly around her. My right hand instinctively drops from the steering wheel and rests on her head, my fingers threading themselves through her loose hair, massaging her scalp. I know, it's not safe, physically or emotionally, but this moment with her is worth the risk. And being as we are the only truck off-roading in this field right now, there aren't many ways left for us to crash. I'll make her buckle up when we get to the road.

"Do you ever feel like you're stuck?" Kate mumbles from my lap.

"What do you mean?"

"Like you screwed up at life and you're not where you were supposed to be by now."

"I guess, sometimes. I think that's normal." My fingers continue massaging her scalp.

"I don't like normal then. I don't like being stuck, and I'm not going to do it much longer."

When I dare to look down, Kate's eyes are shining up at me in the dark cab. Instead of holding her gaze, I focus on the open field in front of me before I become too accustomed to the view.

"How are you going to change it?"

"Bucket list. You have a bucket list, Caleb? I do."

"What's on your bucket list, Trouble?"

"Date a guy that's not scared of Austin, for one." Kate sighs and counts out the items on her fingers. "Move out of Mom's house. Find a way to tell my dad what I really think of him. Get a tattoo. You have tattoos."

"A couple, but I want more." The pickup jostles us as I steer it onto the road.

"You've been to a concert, right? I want to go to a concert. A real concert. Not one of the little shows after the rodeos."

"I've been to a couple with Austin. You need to sit up and get buckled."

"He's a bitch. He wouldn't let me come with you guys." Kate ignores my instructions to buckle up. "I want a piercing."

My eyebrows shoot up.

"Where?" I'm honestly afraid of the answer at this point.

"Undecided. But somewhere sexy."

"What else is on your bucket list?" I ask, wanting to move the conversation along.

"Noodling."

"What?" I chuckle and glance down at her again.

"You know, catching catfish with your bare hands."

"I think that's illegal in Montana."

"I still want to do it."

I shake my head at her.

"Maybe after I catch a big fat one, I'll bathe in a waterfall. That would be fun. And I want to ride a motorcycle. I've tried to get Austin to let me ride with him, but he won't let me. Don't know why it's too dangerous for me and not for him."

"It's Austin. Everything is too dangerous for you." I wink down at her. Kate yawns again and rubs her face. "Such as riding down the road without wearing a seatbelt. Hop up and get buckled really quick." I give her a gentle nudge.

"I want to go on a road trip. And . . . and be a fucking lady." Kate yawns.

I chuckle. "What do you mean, be a lady?"

"You know, do all the girly stuff . . . like makeup and wear . . . dresses and all that," Kate says, her eyes at half-mast now.

"Why? That's not really you."

"Because"—Kate yawns again and her eyes flutter closed, her speech becoming softer and more muddled—"maybe he would've stayed . . . " Her speech trails off into something unintelligible.

"Come again?" I ask. "Kate?"

"Doesn't matter . . . Nobody stays in the end." She nuzzles her face against my stomach.

"I'll stay. I'll always stay."

"Promise?"

"I promise."

Kate smiles up at me, her dimple claiming its spot on her cheek. She sits up, claiming the middle seat, and buckles her seatbelt. Snuggled into my side, her breathing goes slow and steady. Instead of trying to wake her, I focus on the road. She's never mentioned having a bucket list before. I'm curious if that's her whole list or if she left anything off. My thoughts wander, engulfed in the dark stillness of the night. It's only me and Kate on this lonely road, the soft roar of the truck engine humming inside the cab. The only thing visible is the small stretch of road ahead, illuminated by my headlights and the cluster of stars glimmering in the expansive sky.

Kate sleeps soundly through the rest of the trip to her house. Once I'm lifting her out of the truck, trying to move her inside, she finally stirs. She's groggy and combative at first, fighting me until I set her down on her feet. Waking enough to recognize what's going on, she leans into me again, letting me do what I do best—look after my girl.

CHAPTER ELEVEN

A new day of responsibilities comes too quickly, and I find myself rehashing the events of the bonfire the night before as I work through my morning chores. Last night didn't turn out the way I expected. I found myself in bed, dreaming of the possibility of me actually having a chance at a relationship with Caleb. Maybe I could be enough, and maybe Caleb could be the one who stays.

Placing Mom's clean breakfast dishes in the drainer, I fill her water bottle and dump her meds into my palm. The day has started out rough on her, the stress of possibly losing the house exacerbating her symptoms. Finding her sitting in her chair in the living room, I hold her pills out to her and offer her the water bottle.

"Your lunch is fixed and in the fridge. It's on a paper plate so you don't have to worry about dishes," I say. "I've got to head into work. Do you need anything else before I go?"

"No, I'll be fine. I don't plan on leaving my chair any time soon, so don't you worry about me."

Mom's fingers toy at the charms on her necklace, giving me pause. Something is off. She smiles at me, only holding eye contact for a brief moment before turning back to the television.

"You're sure you're good?"

"Yes, bug." Her fingers pause on the necklace. "You worry too much. I'll be fine till you get home."

I drape a blanket on the arm of her chair in case she gets chilly while I'm gone and grab my apron on my way out the door. Pausing momentarily in my car, I look back at the house. Maybe I should run back inside and check with her one more time before I leave. Shaking my head, I turn onto the road and head for the diner. She said everything is fine.

I make my way inside the diner, through the clinking of dishes and chatter of patrons, and head straight to the kitchen to get clocked in and ready for my shift. With any luck, it will be a busy day, and I won't have time to obsess over where things stand between me and Caleb.

"Hey, girl," Emily says with an exaggerated sigh, coming up behind me. "My head is killing me. I had too much to drink last night. Do you think Trevor noticed that I was there with Austin?"

"I think he's starting to put it together." I sign off the time clock and tie my apron around my waist.

"Good. Hopefully he mentions it to his brother. I can't believe Austin is heading out of town tomorrow. Just when things were starting to get good with him. I really thought I was going to get him to commit last night. How did it go with Trevor? Is he as douchey as his brother?"

"Wait, what do you mean Austin's leaving?" I spin around to face Emily, taken aback by her revelation.

"Yeah, for the rodeo." Emily shrugs, like this is common knowledge.

"But Josh said he was out for the season—"

"Caleb is going with him. How do you not know this? Did he seriously not tell you? They're leaving tomorrow." Emily scrunches her nose.

Stunned, I sink onto the stool at the kitchen computer while disappointment washes over me. The sizzling on the grill and savory scents of the freshly prepared meals vanish, overtaken by the knot in my stomach and a sudden heaviness of my limbs.

"I had no idea."

"Oh. Well, that's what Austin said yesterday, anyway. That's why he and Caleb were practicing roping at the ranch. It's also why they wanted to have the bonfire. It was a goodbye party, of sorts." Emily shrugs, grabs her table's order off the warming rack, and pushes through the swinging door to the dining room.

The disappointment gradually fades away as I tend to customers, and rage fills its place. How could they make plans to go on the rodeo circuit without telling me? What happened to Austin helping us come up with a solution to save the house? He asked Caleb to fill Josh's spot, and now the mortgage is one more situation for me to work out on my own? How did I completely miss the fact that they are leaving town? Were they intentionally keeping the news from me? I punch an order into the computer with overly aggressive zeal, the monitor shaking with each poke of my finger.

Slowly, the afternoon floats by. Most of the lunch crowd has come and gone, and I focus my frustrations on scrubbing the tables until they're shiny and spotless. With the last guest out the door, I don't even try to disguise my anger, resetting the tables with a heavy hand. The bells over the door chime, and I spin around to face the familiar voice calling my name. It's Austin and Caleb. Perfect. They smile at me, evidently oblivious to the fire burning down my soul. Without hesitating, I march toward them. It's not until I'm only a few feet away that their smiles fade and worry lines their brows.

"Is everything okay, Kate?" Austin asks, his eyebrows drawn together.

"Is everything okay?" I repeat, shoving Austin's chest and

making him totter backward into Caleb. "No, everything isn't fucking okay!" I close the space between us and shove him again, but it doesn't ease the fury raging in my chest. If anything, it magnifies it, making me jittery. Ready for a fight, I lay into him some more. "Were you ever going to tell me you're leaving town? You're going to leave me to figure out how to save the house? Are you that big of a pussy, Austin? Or just that selfish?" My fists are now pounding into Austin's chest and tears threaten to escape. Suddenly, it's as though I'm eleven years old all over again. "Were you going to disappear and leave me wondering where you went like Dad did?"

"Kate, you're being a bit dramatic, don't you think?" Austin asks, stepping away and blocking my attack with his forearms.

My open palm lands with a pop on the side of his face before strong arms wrap around me from behind and pull me into a solid chest. Caleb. He pulls me away from Austin, trying to calm me with the soothing tone of his voice. Tears break free. I twist around in his arms and shove away from him.

"And you're no better," I cry out to Caleb this time. "I thought you cared, but you don't. Your actions mean nothing, and your words mean even less. Maybe if you cared about our friendship you would have been honest with me. You're just like him. I don't know why I ever thought you'd stay." The words come out between sobs.

"Kate, I'm sorry . . . " Caleb reaches for my hand, pain written across his face. I pull away, embarrassed, and make my escape to the kitchen, shoving by Emily who's standing at the door, shell-shocked. I can't look at him. I can't look at either of them. They are the ones who are supposed to stay. They promised me they'd stay. And I trusted them.

Plopping onto the stool in the kitchen, I drop my head into my hands, trying unsuccessfully to hide from the memory I've been avoiding since I received the news. It's been fourteen years since my father left us, and it appears to be Austin's turn. I blow out a shaky breath and run my trembling hands down my legs, trying to steady them.

Emily stoops in front of me, her hands on my knees. "Hey, are you okay?"

"I didn't know. They didn't tell me they were leaving." I squeeze my eyes shut, trying to force the memories away.

Emily's voice is soft, trying to reassure me. "They aren't leaving you like your dad did, Kate. They're coming back."

"I know. I know that. They just caught me by surprise. I don't understand why they didn't tell me before now."

Emily takes my shaky hands in hers and squeezes. "What do you need? Want me to cover the rest of your shift?"

I shake my head, feeling foolish now for getting so worked up. "No, I'm fine. Really. I just need a minute."

Austin's right. I was being dramatic. I sit up straight and wipe the tears from my cheeks. Shame on them for not telling me their plans. Shame on me for thinking their promises meant anything.

CHAPTER TWELVE

When I walk out of the diner at the end of my shift, Austin and Caleb are waiting. I dip my head and hurry to my pickup, trying to get there before they spot me. The sweet, musty smell of the wet parking lot from the rain earlier today fills my nose, and I almost make it to my pickup when they catch up with me.

"Kate, wait up," Austin calls from around the truck. I fumble with my keys, trying to unlock the door as he makes his way around the hood, the disadvantage of driving a vehicle too old for power locks.

"Go eat shit, Austin," I yell back at him, finally getting my door open and climbing inside my truck. Droplets of water that haven't evaporated yet trail down the windshield.

"Please talk to me. We were going to tell you," Austin calls through my window. "That's what we came here for."

"Go do your rodeo circuit, Austin. I don't care anymore." The engine roars to life, and I shift the pickup into reverse, glancing in my rearview mirror. Caleb stands behind my truck, his arms propped up on the tailgate. Sliding the back window open, I yell a warning to him. "I will run you over, Caleb. Don't think I won't."

"Kate, please. We need to talk," Caleb says, his voice pleading.

He's trying to play it cool, but I can see the panic written all over his face. I'm too pissed off to care right now. When he doesn't budge, I make the truck bounce back a foot to let him know I'm serious. Caleb stumbles backward. After a brief pause, he moves out of the way and lets me go. Good idea.

The whole ride home, my mind is spinning with the things I suddenly want to say to them. Except then I'd have to talk to them, and I'm not ready to hear their excuses.

I push through the front door and force my mind to change gears. I have good news to share with Mom, and I don't want to let Austin and Caleb ruin that for me, too. I find her in her chair in the living room where I left her this morning, just stirring from a nap. The floorboards creak beneath me as I step through the doorway.

"Hey, Mom. How was your day?"

"You're already home?"

"Yeah, I told you I was just working lunch today. What happened to the lamp?" I ask, noticing broken glass scattered across the floor behind the end table.

Mom shifts in her recliner, tucking the blanket under her chin. "Oh, I knocked it on accident."

"I'll grab the broom." I head over to the closet and get the broom and dustpan. I don't mind cleaning it up, but all the ways she could have hurt herself by not bothering with it nags at me. "What do you want for dinner?"

"I'll just have the plate you fixed me for lunch." Her voice is sleepy, and her eyes are drifting closed again.

"You didn't eat your lunch?"

"No, Katie bug, I'm fine. Don't you worry about me."

All I do is worry. It's like the more I do for her, the less she tries. Pushing my jumble of emotions aside, I try again.

"After I finish cleaning up the lamp we should go on a walk. You always feel better when you do your walking."

"Not today. I need to rest."

Frustration bubbles under my skin, and with shaky hands, I dump a dustpan full of broken glass into the trash can. "I have good news. You remember me telling you about that specialist I found?"

"The one that was full?"

"Yeah. They had a cancellation, and I was able to get you the spot. You go see him next week." I pause next to her chair, waiting for her reaction. Surely this will perk her up.

This doctor could be a game changer for her. His patients have seen a lot of success, and he has a completely different approach from the doctor she's been seeing. She doesn't share in my enthusiasm, however. She doesn't even appear interested.

"I don't need the appointment. I told you I'm ready to file for my disability and be done."

"You're joking, right? Please tell me you aren't serious." A new flash of anger rings through me. I crouch next to her chair, steadying my hands on the armrest. "You can't give up like this, Mom. You have to try."

"Kate, I'm old and I'm tired. I just want to go back to sleep. Cancel that appointment for next week, would you? I don't need it."

"Is sleeping all you've done today? You do understand that's why you have so much trouble sleeping at night, don't you? I know it hurts, Mom, but you've got to get up and do your therapy. You can't give up on yourself." My raised voice toes the line of yelling. My world is slowly crumbling around my feet today, and I may never be able to piece it back together. I know I need to check myself, but between the news of Austin and Caleb leaving and now this, my nerves are frayed. I fold my arms across my torso, my jaw clenched.

"Kate, this isn't your life. You don't get to make these decisions for me. You don't have to agree with me, but you don't get to boss me, either."

"What about my life? Because you can deny it all you want,

but what you do or don't do affects me, too. I gave up my title and opportunity for a barrel racing career because you got sick. If I didn't do it, who would care for you, drive you to appointments, and make sure you get your meds? Austin can't work the job he does to support you and be here taking care of you, so it's fallen on me. I've been stuck here at home and working at that damn diner this whole time to help pay your bills and take care of you. You are not the only one who was inconvenienced by your health." I squeeze my arms around myself, hoping to hold the pieces together. I'm sweating and my head is ready to explode.

"You did that because you wanted to. Not because you had to. I was your excuse to stay in your comfort zone. I can manage just fine on my own."

The shock of her comment is like a dousing of cold water down my spine. I take a step back, tears stinging my eyes, and suck in a deep, shaky breath to quiet my nerves. It's not true. I didn't stay for me—I stayed for her. I chose her. Every damn day I chose her.

"Somebody had to fight for you, Mom, because you sure as hell haven't been. Why do you think I've pushed so hard for you to see another doctor? Obviously, I want you to get better, but that's partially for my own selfish reasons, too. I don't want to be tied down to being your caretaker for the rest of my life. I want to be able to base my decisions off something more than your ability to care for yourself each day. If you really think I've stayed here for me, I'm done."

Unwilling to give her another second of my time, I rush from the room, my mother's voice trailing behind me.

"Go ahead and leave. Walk away just like your father did."

I ZIP up my jacket and shove my hands deeper into my pockets. The early morning air is crisp and cold and the hour I've spent standing in it has left a chill in my bones that will take a while to thaw. My stiff fingers find a wrapper in my left pocket and squish it into a little ball, giving me a small task to distract myself with for a few seconds. I'm exhausted and shivering. I check my watch again. It's 5:30 am. This would have been easier if I knew what time they were planning to leave.

A horse trailer is already hooked up to Austin's pickup, parked down the side of the barn where their horses are kept. A floodlight shines down from the corner of the barn, giving me some light even though the sun has yet to show its face today. Eventually, hushed voices come around the barn, and I push off the side of Austin's truck as they approach.

"What are you doing here, Kate? Wanted to have another go at beating me up?" Austin asks, stepping past me to throw his duffel bag in the bed of the pickup where mine is already waiting. Caleb trails behind him, following suit, and opens the back of the horse trailer to load up their horses. Caleb guides his palomino, BoJack, onto the trailer first, his hooves thudding on the trailer floor. Next, he loads Austin's grullo, Trigger, while Austin and I talk.

"I guess after all these years I should know better than to try." I follow him to the cab of the truck where he starts the ignition to let the truck warm up while they load.

"Probably. But I'm sure I'll give you plenty more reasons to try again."

"Undoubtedly."

Austin leans against the side of his truck and cocks an eyebrow at me. "Seriously, though. Why aren't you at home?"

"I'm going on the road with you," I say, briefly distracted by Caleb and the horses.

"No, you're not." Austin folds his arms over his chest.

"Why not?" I mimic his stance, not about to back down that easily.

"Where would you stay? In the motel room with me and Caleb? Yeah, that would be cozy. And what about your job?

And Mom? The animals?" Austin motions for Caleb to go ahead and get in the passenger side of the truck.

"Mom said she doesn't need me anymore. My job isn't going anywhere, and the neighbor agreed to make sure the animals are tended to."

"Kate—" Austin takes me lightly by the shoulders, his own expression softening.

"We had a fight, okay? I finally got an appointment with that doctor who could really help her, and she refuses to go. She's given up and I can't help her anymore. She accused me of being like Dad."

I stare up at my big brother—hopefully my eyes look pleading. He can't deny me when he knows what I've given up for our mom.

"Wait, she said what?" Austin's expression instantly turns to ice.

"She's taking advantage of me," I say with a shrug, my arms falling limply to my sides as I shake my head in defeat. "Please don't make me stay here."

Austin takes a step back, hanging a hand across the nape of his neck, contemplating what to do. He studies me a moment longer then taps on the window of Caleb's door. Caleb rolls the window down, looking back and forth between us expectantly.

"What do you think about Kate coming on the road with us?" Austin asks.

Caleb's expression is frozen, almost as if his brain has short-circuited. Finally, as things start to get uncomfortable and I'm afraid Austin is going to take Caleb's lack of reply as his answer, an affectionate grin stretches across his face.

"Sounds like a blast if you ask me," Caleb says. He hops out of the truck and holds the door open for me to climb in. "Shortest gets the middle."

I roll my eyes at the declared seating rule of our youth and climb into the truck. It's going to be a snug ride, but there's no way they're leaving without me.

CHAPTER THIRTEEN

caleb

Really though, how am I supposed to explain to Austin what a bad idea it is to bring Kate on the road with us? We've always let her tag along. The difference this time is the length of time we'll be gone and my intensified struggle to keep it in my pants when she's close. *Hey, remember that time a couple days ago that I nearly boned your sister in broad daylight against the side of a barn? No? Huh. I do. Boy, do I ever. I've about given myself carpal tunnel ever since.* If Kate goes with us we won't have to worry about running out of warm water to shower. I'll be strictly bathing in cold.

It almost feels like old times, the three of us riding down the road together, rodeo songs on the radio. Kate's leg rubs against mine, sending sparks through me, but she doesn't lean into me like she usually does. A heavy tension hangs over us, and I hoped that as the hours on our trip passed the heaviness would, too. But it doesn't. Austin seems to have won her forgiveness by agreeing to let her come with us, but I must not be forgiven yet. There's a rigidity to her that I don't think will fade until I find a way to make amends.

At lunchtime, Austin finds a diner to stop at with a sizable open lot in the back. The lot will give us a place to let the horses stretch their legs and have some water and rest. I'm more than ready to jump out of this cab and get some space.

Once the horses are tended to and resting, Kate heads straight to the bathroom while Austin and I grab us a booth. The server comes around for our drink order, and I make the executive decision to go ahead and order for Kate since they have her favorite drink on the menu. By the time Kate sits down our drinks are already on the table.

"I saw they have gooseberry lemonade so I ordered you one," I say.

No reply. She scoots her drink aside and opens her menu instead. Austin looks up from his cell phone, his eyes sliding from Kate to me. I shake my head and go back to reading the list of lunch specials. Before long, our server returns to collect our orders.

"Oh, and could I get a water, please?" Kate asks sweetly.

"Sure," the server says and leaves to put in our orders.

Kate successfully makes it through lunch without speaking a word to me or touching the gooseberry lemonade. The silent treatment is new. She's never been one to be silent, and it puts my nerves on edge. Earning her forgiveness is all I can think about. Believe it or not, when we return to the truck, the tension has only grown. The turmoil she's causing me is ridiculous. Her silence eats at me from the inside out until suddenly her head is resting on my shoulder. I peer down at her. Her eyes are closed and her breathing steady. She's asleep.

"You want to know the messed-up part?" Austin asks, breaking the silence.

"What's that?"

"If she wakes up and realizes she was lying on you, you're going to be the one that pays for it." He's not wrong. I knew this already. "What did you do, anyway, to piss my sister off so bad?"

My blood runs cold. I don't truly know, but I have a hunch.

"I'm sure I'll figure it out." I turn to the window, not interested in exploring this particular dilemma with Austin.

"Must be something pretty bad. I've only gotten the silent treatment from her once. It was the first time she got dumped for being my sister. Even then, she only held out for a couple hours."

Music fills the cab when I don't respond, and we listen to the radio for the rest of the trip. When Austin pulls up to the rodeo grounds an hour later, I send up a silent prayer that Kate doesn't bite my head off when she wakes up to find herself snuggled into my side. I don't have it in me to push her aside, despite the punishment that may find me.

Austin shuts off the engine, and Kate starts to come to. My prayers have been answered because she seems to have forgotten in her sleepy haze that I'm the enemy.

"You two get the horses unloaded while I handle the paperwork for the stalls we're renting," Austin says, sliding out of the truck.

We make quick work of unloading BoJack and Trigger. All the while Kate refuses to make eye contact with me. It's not long before Austin's done, and after feeding and watering the horses and parking the trailer, we head to the motel.

At the motel, I hold the door open for Kate as she slides out of the truck. Grabbing her duffel bag along with mine from the truck bed, I motion for her to lead the way. She doesn't protest, so I carry her bag and admire the view on our way to our room. Her jeans complement her curves, and I'd like nothing better than to wrap her ponytail around my fist. Even with the attitude she's giving me.

The room is small and hasn't been updated in the last couple decades, but everything appears clean. I set our bags on one of the beds and head to the bathroom. Leaning against the counter, I study myself in the mirror. This only has to be as awkward as I make it. I can get through this.

"So, what's the plan with the bed situation?" I ask, coming back into the room.

I'm only slightly concerned how I'm going to conceal the inevitable morning wood I'll have knowing Kate spent the night in the same room. Austin shoots me a look like I'm stupid.

"Kate and I will share a bed and you can have the other to yourself," Austin says. "Unless you want to sleep on the floor . . ."

"No, that arrangement sounds fine to me."

"I'm going to take a shower." Kate makes a point of looking directly at Austin as she says it.

"You guys good with pizza for dinner?" Austin asks after giving her a nod. "I'll run out and grab some."

"Good with me," Kate says and closes the bathroom door behind her.

"Yeah, sounds good," I add.

Austin takes off, and I make myself comfortable on one of the beds before flipping through the channels on the TV. I need something to occupy my mind. Fifteen minutes pass by before the pipes in the wall creak as the water kicks on in the shower. The image of water running over Kate's tight, bare skin in the steamy shower fills my head. What I would give to be able to climb in the shower with her and run my soapy hands over her body, washing every inch of her. With a frustrated groan, I try to push the thoughts away, but nothing on TV is interesting enough to take her place.

Exasperated and fighting a hard-on, I swing my legs off the side of the bed and look around the room for something to distract myself. Coming up short, I rummage through the nightstand drawers. All I find is a Bible. Desperate, I deem it worth a shot. I pull the Bible out, my fingers sliding over the smooth leather cover, flip to a random page, and read. How do people make any sense of this stuff? I'm about a page in when the door swings open and Austin, pizzas in hand, freezes in the doorway, his startled expression fixed on me.

"Are you reading the *Bible*?" Austin asks incredulously.

"Don't ask." I slam the book shut and toss it in the drawer.

"Kate still in the shower?" Austin closes the door behind him and sets the pizza on the desk. The smell of pepperoni, garlic, and bread instantly fills the room.

"Hell yeah," I say, failing to hide my frustration.

Following Austin's lead, I dig into the pizza. By the time Kate emerges from the bathroom wearing an oversized T-shirt and yoga shorts I'm already four pieces of pizza in. Her wet hair hangs over one shoulder, and evidently, she's not wearing a bra because her nipples are threatening to cut through the fabric of her shirt—a shirt that looks so much like one I used to wear all the time.

Kate grabs a slice of pizza from the box and sits across from me on her bed. My mouth goes dry as I watch her, instantly transfixed. Austin's phone buzzes on the nightstand, and he wipes the grease from his fingers before picking it up.

"Hey, Emily, hold on," he says into the phone. "I'm going to step out for a minute," he tells us and leaves the room.

A sensual moan brings my whole body to attention. Kate. She swallows and takes another bite of her pizza, moaning again.

"This may be the most delicious thing I've ever put in my mouth," Kate says, licking the sauce from the corner of her mouth.

Kate leans back, propping herself up on a hand positioned behind her, and takes another bite, moaning again. The blood drains from my face and rushes to a particular appendage very uncomfortably positioned at the moment. This arrangement is not going to work.

"Fucking hell," I mutter.

Grabbing a pillow from the bed, I hold it over my lap and make my way to the bathroom. I toss the pillow to the bed once I'm out of her line of sight and lock the door behind me. Kate's soft giggle follows me, barely loud enough for me to catch. I groan and peer down at the tent in my pants. Let the cold showers commence.

BoJack might be the only way I make it through the season. Competing like this was never my thing. It's already a stretch being out here on the rodeo circuit with Austin. Adding in the complication of Kate being on the road with us—and a mad Kate at that—I'm completely out of my depth.

"You've got my back, don't you, BoJack?" I offer him the other half of my apple. He scoops the apple from my hand, and I accept it as his commitment to helping me survive this summer.

After I finish feeding and watering BoJack and Trigger, I return to the motel. Kate is awake when I walk in.

"I bet the horses were lonely last night. Maybe you should consider staying with them tonight. You know, so they are well rested and ready to compete and all that," Kate says.

I guess the silent treatment has worn off, but with that comment she clearly hasn't forgiven me. I'm standing in the bathroom shaving when she comes up next to me, squeezes a dab of toothpaste onto her toothbrush, and scrubs her teeth clean. The spearmint from her toothpaste nearly clears my sinuses. While she brushes, she watches each meticulous sweep of my razor. She may have something on her mind she's considering sharing with me, but it feels more like she's hoping I cut myself. That may be my guilt talking though.

Finished with the razor, I rinse off my face in the sink and pat it dry on the hand towel. Kate gently hip checks me and takes my place in front of the sink, spitting and rinsing her mouth before dabbing it on the corner of the towel in my hands. She arches an eyebrow at me, turns, and leaves.

"You about done in here? I need a quick shower," Austin says, filling the doorway now.

"Yeah. I'll get out of your way."

I find Kate sitting on the bed. She's braiding her hair, pulling the ends over her shoulder to finish the job. When the bathroom door clicks closed, I take a seat across from her.

"We need to talk," I say quietly.

"Then talk."

"I don't know what I did to upset you, Kate—"

"Stop right there. You don't know? Let me help you get started. You show up at my house, drunk off your ass, and you tell me how badly you want me." Kate stands from the bed, takes a couple steps toward me, and crouches down till we are eye level and practically nose to nose. "You nearly ravage me against the side of a barn and instead of talking it out with me like the grown-ass man you're supposed to be you make plans to cut town without so much as a goodbye. Does any of that sound familiar?"

"It sounds pretty accurate. But you're wrong about one thing. I wasn't trying to leave without saying goodbye. The whole rodeo plan happened quickly. We were still working out the details earlier this week. I want to do what I can to help Austin out."

"Help him out with what?" Kate's fists land on her waist, one hip popped out to the side and the same angry glower fixed on me.

"Earning enough money to save your mom's house and land." Kate's eyes widen slightly, and her shoulders drop a couple inches. She steps back and sits on the bed, seemingly taken aback. Did Austin not tell her? "He thinks we can earn enough prize money to make the necessary payment to the bank. It was all very last minute, but I thought you knew what the plan was."

"And what about the kissing part?" Kate asks with less force this time.

"I'm sorry for what I did." My apology earns an exaggerated

eye roll from her. Shit. "I do care about you, Kate. A lot. But what I did was a mistake."

"I'm a mistake. Got it. Forgive me for tripping you up." Kate's voice drips with sarcasm.

"No, Kate. Fuck. That's not what I mean. None of that was supposed to happen. I can't be anything more than a friend to you, don't you see that?"

"Oh, you've made that perfectly clear." Kate stands, signaling she's done with our conversation, and my redemption remains elusive.

"Kate—"

"You guys about ready to go?" Austin asks, interrupting our conversation as he joins us from the bathroom.

"Beyond ready," Kate says and walks out the door without so much as a glance in my direction.

CHAPTER FOURTEEN

The days pass slowly, stuck in close company with each other. Close in reality, but still separated by the jumble of my inadequacies. Caleb and I can never be anything more than friends. I know what the words mean, but I don't understand. I don't understand why he would say the things he did—even if he was drunk—if he only wants to be friends. I've never had a friend kiss me the way he did. And it didn't feel very *friendly* when he did it. It felt raw and vulnerable. It felt real. But it did *not* feel friendly.

Ever since he said he wants me, I've wondered if it's true. He says he cares, but if a friendship is all he's interested in I'd rather he keep his feelings to himself. What good does it do for him to say those things if he's going to keep me in the friend zone? I'd rather not know how he feels than for him to dangle the carrot in front of my nose with no intention of sharing it.

It's hard being at odds with Caleb, especially in such close quarters. We *are* friends, and it's a friendship I've relied on over the years. The mixed signals he's throwing at me are really complicating things. He's supposed to be a safe place for me, but it's feeling more like a war zone. I don't understand him. One minute, he's pressing his erection against me, the next he's trying to leave. And they say women are complicated and hormonal.

Caleb comes out of the bathroom, still shirtless, brushing his teeth. His skin is dewy, and his jeans hang low on his hips making him look like he should be modeling for a calendar of sexy oral hygiene-conscious cowboys somewhere. My eyes trail like magnets to his sculpted abs before drifting along the V cutting into the waistband of his Wranglers, but as soon as I catch my anger mutating into lust, I sever the link and pretend to check my phone.

When Caleb heads into the bathroom, I allow myself to take another glimpse, greedily memorizing the muscles in his back and the way his ass fills out his Wranglers. I have to bite my lip to fight the smile toying at the corners of my mouth. Do I believe it's wrong to objectify people? Absolutely. But good golly that man makes some delicious eye candy.

"What was that?" Austin glares at me suspiciously from across the room.

"Hmmm?" My cheeks burn with embarrassment over being caught shamelessly ogling Caleb's body.

"I saw the way you were looking at him, Kate."

"I wasn't really looking at him. I was lost in thought, and he happened to step into my line of sight."

"Yeah, okay." Austin stalks over, his eyes narrowing at me. "I'm only going to have this conversation with you once, so listen up. You and Caleb are not a thing. You'll never be a thing. And if I get even the slightest hint that you and he are messing around, I'll send your ass back home so quick you won't know what happened. Do you hear me?"

"Stop being an ass, Austin. I told you it was nothing."

"Yeah, you keep reminding yourself of that. It's nothing. Because if it were to become something, he'd end up making a fool of you"—my eyes shoot up to Austin's—"just like Dad made a fool of Mom."

"Really? You think that little of your best friend?"

"No. Caleb is a good guy. He wouldn't do it on purpose. It would just happen, because that's what happens with relationships. They all turn to shit."

"I'm not Mom, and Caleb isn't Dad. But that doesn't matter anyway because like I said, there's nothing there, and there never will be."

"Exactly."

I stand, keeping eye contact with Austin. "No, this isn't going to work for me anymore. I've been more than patient with this whole overprotective, bossy big brother thing you've got going on, but I'm done with it. You may have had to step up and play dad for a bit after ours left, but you're not my dad. You're my brother, and it's time you figure out what that role is supposed to look like because this isn't it."

"You fall for guys way too quickly, Kate."

"I don't have to share your opinions on relationships, and you don't have the right to force them down my throat."

"Maybe so, but I don't want to watch you get hurt."

"Then close your eyes."

Austin scoffs. "Fine. I'll back off. On one condition, though. Caleb is off-limits—at least for now. Nothing good will come from you trying to hook up with him while we're all on the road together."

"Fine."

"Fine."

I focus on keeping my breathing slow and steady, trying to conceal my real feelings and avoid exposing myself any further. After a few more seconds of our staring match, Austin finally breaks and walks away.

The tension is steady all the way to the fairgrounds. When we get there, I hang around with the boys, helping them with the horses and preparing for their competition. When Caleb answers his ringing phone, Austin glares at him.

"I miss you too, Monty. The summer will go by quickly.

And maybe if we compete in a rodeo closer to home you can come watch." Caleb gives Austin an apologetic shrug.

Austin is a stickler about being zoned in and focused on the competition even before making it into the arena, so Caleb taking a phone call right now is undeniably all over Austin's nerves. If it was anyone other than Monty on the other end of the line Austin would have already made him hang up.

"We'll hang out in a couple weeks. I'm trying to stop by and see you as often as I can. And after we finish the season, we will be back on our normal schedule of hanging out every weekend. I promise."

Monty looks up to Caleb like a father figure. He's the only one Monty has been able to count on these past couple years, and Caleb being less accessible has rocked the boat for him already. I know this isn't easy for either of them.

"Here." Caleb hands the phone to me. "He wants to talk to you."

"Hey, Monty, what are you up to?" I ask.

"Nothing. Why did you go, too? We could have hung out while Caleb was gone."

"I know, and I would have loved having you all to myself, but this is just the way it worked out."

Once Monty is done talking, I end the call and hand the phone back to Caleb who's preparing for the competition ahead of them. I wish Austin good luck, purposefully ignoring Caleb, and make my way to the stands to find a seat. By the time I claim a spot, Caleb and Austin are already on their horses, waiting for the turn they drew and sizing up their competition.

The fairgrounds are covered in a crowd of wranglers, boots, and concession stand foods. There's no escaping the smell of popcorn. Spectators fill the metal stands, with a constant stream of people coming and going, laughter and chatter all around me. Cowboys waiting to compete surround the arena. They're getting ready to transition into the team roping event now, and although this event doesn't have the biggest purse, it will help them build up points on their way to more money. I watch each team nervously, not wishing a bad run on any of them but hoping my boys will stand a fighting chance.

Taking in Caleb's form, I admire what I see. Even from here, his muscles are evident, despite being hidden under his dark-blue button-up shirt and brown vest. Maybe I've been too hard on him. I mean, it's Caleb. The man couldn't do anything hateful or selfish if his life depended on it. Even if I don't understand his reasons, I know they are valid to him. I don't doubt he thinks he's doing what he needs to do, but it would be easier to accept if he hadn't wounded my pride in the process.

But he did hurt me. And his attempt to fix things was lame. I don't know what I want from him, but I need more than a rushed "I'm sorry." That being said, my resistance to forgiving him is likely to follow him into the arena. If they don't ride well it will be my fault. None of us will get what we want, and our purpose here is bigger than me. When Caleb searches the stands, I wave at him, catching his eye. Even from up here I can see a smile fill his face. Just like that, I feel my heart begin to thaw. Sweet Caleb. He gives me a nod, but Austin, as serious as ever, pulls Caleb's attention away, and they ride up to take their spots.

A new steer is pushed into the chute, and Caleb and Austin get their ropes ready to swing. I scoot forward in my seat and nibble on my thumbnail. The steer sprints out of the shoot into the arena and the game is on. Caleb's rope goes up in the air and in a smooth motion he launches it forward, catching the horns of the steer. Austin follows, slipping the rope around the steer's back hooves. They pull their ropes tight, wrapping the slack around the saddle horn. Good enough to put them in second place. Austin will be pissed they didn't get first, but assuming none of the remaining teams slide into their spot at second, he should be bearable.

I rush down from the stands to find them when they ride out. Pushing through the crowd, I circle the arena till I get to the area where they should be waiting. Sure enough, I find them. Caleb sees me first. He's a little hesitant, probably afraid I'm still mad at him—I am a little bit—but I give him a fist bump in passing before wrapping Austin up in a hug.

"You did great," I say, doing my best to avoid eye contact with Caleb. I might be coming around, but I'm not ready to grant him my full forgiveness yet.

"We can do better," Austin says, all business. "Come on, Caleb, let's find somewhere we can work through some kinks."

Always a dutiful partner, Caleb follows with nothing more than a quick sideways glance in my direction, leaving me alone in the crowd of people. I watch a few more rides from the side before making my way back to the stands. Emily would probably appreciate an update, so I pull my phone out of my pocket and start typing out a text to her. More distracted by my phone than I realized, I walk right into someone's back.

"I'm so sorry."

The stranger turns to observe at me. To my relief, I'm greeted with a smile.

"Not a problem, ma'am," he says with a nod.

He's attractive, but only about my height with a slender, muscular build. A bull rider I'm guessing. I return his smile and sidestep to go around him but stop myself. Maybe this is the opportunity I've been waiting for. The cowboy in front of me seems like a great option to cleanse Caleb from my system.

"You a bull rider?" I offer my hand, noticing how soft his is in comparison to Caleb's when he takes mine in his.

"People call me Tuff. You're a bull riding fan, huh? What's your name?"

"My name's Kate. I'm here watching my brother. He's a team roper."

"I have some time before my event. Could I interest you in a hot cocoa or something?" Tuff asks, his tone hopeful.

"Sure. That'd be nice."

Tuff offers his arm to me. Linking my arm in his, I let him

lead me to the concession stand. The conversation flows easily enough, and soon, we are sitting together in the stands watching the rest of the roping events. Caleb must have satisfied Austin because they're standing by the arena watching, too. Caleb seems more interested in the action happening in the stands, though, as his gaze burns into me, distracting me from the moment. My body heats under his inspection, and a shiver runs through me at the same time. I turn my attention to the handsome cowboy next to me.

"Do you make it to a lot of your brother's events?" Tuff's eyes roam over me as he waits for my reply.

"Yes, actually. I'm traveling with him right now." I shrug and take a timid sip of my hot chocolate. The warm, watered-down chocolate flows across my tongue, which barely escapes a scalding.

"Where are you headed next?"

"Bigfork. You?"

Disappointment sweeps across his face.

"I'm not riding in that one. Are you going to be in Hardin next weekend?"

"Yeah, we'll be there," I say, looking up at him through my lashes.

"Maybe we could get dinner one night while we're there?" His hopeful gaze stays on me.

"I would like that." Tuff's warm hand covers mine on my knee, and his thumb strokes the fabric of my jeans. Although it's not the hand I've been hoping for, I soak up the feeling of being wanted. I'm not sure Austin is going to take too kindly to me going on a date, and with a bull rider of all people, but he's not going to have a choice in the matter. And neither will Caleb.

"As much as I hate to do it, I'm going to have to head down," Tuff says as the team roping comes to an end. "I don't have much longer till my ride."

"I'll walk down with you. I should probably find my brother anyway and see if he's ready to head out."

Tuff takes my hand in his as we slowly walk around the arena, neither of us in a rush to leave. We stop walking and turn to face each other. The natural ease of conversation suddenly dissipates as we wait for the other to initiate our goodbyes.

"I'm really glad I met you today," Tuff says, finally breaking the silence.

"Me, too. Thanks for the hot chocolate, by the way."

"Maybe I could get your phone number? That way we can make plans for when I see you again." Tuff offers me his phone.

I take it and put my number in before handing it back to him. He slides the phone into his pocket and softly tugs me closer. My insides flutter with nervousness and anticipation. After a moment of hesitation, he pulls me to him and gives me a hug. His warm breath tickles my ear. He takes his time, holding me close, before he steps away.

"I should go," he says.

"Yeah. Good luck."

"Are you going to stay and watch?" He flashes me a smile.

"I'm not sure. I'd like to. But I think my brother is probably about ready to get out of here. But text me and let me know how your ride goes."

Tuff nods. "I will. Take care, Kate. I'll talk to you soon." Tuff turns and walks away.

I continue pushing through the crowd to get to Austin and Caleb. They're standing at the fence talking to a couple guys I vaguely recognize. Caleb notices me first, but he doesn't say anything. Instead, he continues listening to the conversation. They're talking about rodeoing—big surprise there. I climb up and take a seat on the fence so I can see over the other heads and into the arena where the bull riding is starting. I don't know when Tuff will ride, but if I'm lucky, maybe I'll get to see him before we go.

A warmth is radiating next to me, and I know without

looking that it's Caleb. He stands on the fence at my side. Ignoring him, I focus on the arena. He doesn't deserve my attention as far as I'm concerned. If he thinks he's going to play games with me he's got another thing coming.

Tuff spots me on the fence. He gives me a crooked grin and dips the front of his cowboy hat to me. Hoping he can't see the blush burning my cheeks, I give him a little wave.

"Who's that? I saw you talking to him up in the stands earlier," Caleb asks.

"Just a friend," I say, not looking at him.

"Seemed awfully cozy up there to be a friend."

"Whatever." I jump down from the fence and leave Caleb there. "I'll be in the truck," I say as I walk by Austin and leave the rodeo behind.

caleb

We arrive in Bigfork without incident. Kate has warmed up to me a little bit, but I'm clearly not out of the woods with her yet. I get why she's upset. It was shitty for her to find out from Emily that Austin and I were leaving town. We should have told her sooner, but Austin thought it would be best for the three of us to talk about it in person. Kate doesn't do well with people leaving. It's understandable after what she's been through.

Then, add in my dick move of pinning her against the side of a barn and drunkenly professing my love to her before splitting town. But there's no changing any of that now. All I can do at this point is work to regain the trust I broke with her.

It's another dusty day of rodeo grounds, vibrant sun, belt buckles, and shit kickers. Austin and I are saddled up and waiting our turn. We have a few more teams ahead of us. If Austin is nervous, he doesn't show it. I guess he's competed enough times not to be bothered by it. The nerves get to me every time. BoJack is antsy, too. He is undoubtedly picking up on my edginess. Reaching down, I rub on his neck and try to soothe both of us.

Maybe if it was only the best friend's little sister thing it would be easier to overlook it and be with Kate. It still wouldn't be ideal. If I focus on it for too long, I start feeling guilty. Kate and I essentially grew up together. Three years' difference in age isn't all that much, but when we were younger it was. Kate was like a little sister to me in those days. She was just a kid. Now there aren't as many lines drawn between us by our age. Instead, it's obligation separating us: my obligation to Austin, and my need to safeguard Kate from the consequences of a relationship with someone like me. Someone that wreaks havoc on those who are closest to me—my parents, my aunt and uncle, my cousin.

I can't date my best friend's little sister. That's not a boundary that should be treated lightly, especially considering what I owe him. I can't bite off the hand that saved me. It's not right, regardless of how I feel about her. And even if I hadn't promised to help protect her, I couldn't live with myself for putting Kate in the line of fire. It's best if I keep my space.

Austin and I ride into the box, ready for our run. BoJack shuffles on his feet, apparently feeling my anticipation. I rub my gloved thumb over the grooves of my stiff nylon rope, ready to swing—my personal ritual for good luck at the start of each run. The combination of leather, livestock, and earth fills my nose, and almost instantly the nerves give way to the comfort of familiarity.

The steer is released, and we get at it, slinging dirt into the air behind us. Within a few rotations of my rope, I'm launching it forward. My rope sails through the air and lands nicely across the horns of the steer. With a quick yank, the loop slips taut around the horns and I wrap the slack a couple times around my saddle horn to secure it. Austin releases his rope in time with the steer's gait, looping the hind legs before pulling his rope tight and ending our run. They clock us at 5.2 seconds, giving us the lead.

When we make it out of the arena, Kate is waiting for us. She's cheering excitedly. She reaches up and high fives Austin, but after that ride, I want more than a fist bump or a high five. I slide off BoJack and wrap her in a hug, picking her up off the ground. She stiffens slightly, probably remembering I'm in hot water, but she doesn't throat punch me. Sometimes the risk is worth the reward. I set her down on her feet, and Austin dismounts, joining us on the ground.

"How many more teams are left to compete?" Kate asks.

"Four, I think. But I doubt any of them will beat us," Austin says.

Sure enough, the event finishes with us in first place. We claim our winnings, get the horses fed, watered, and settled in their stalls, and head to the motel.

"I'm getting in the shower," Austin says once we're inside our room.

Kate grabs the remote and starts flipping through channels while Austin gets clothes together. I sit on my bed, propping the pillows up against the headboard. Kate finally settles on a show, but she doesn't seem to be paying much attention to it. Her phone keeps buzzing. She replies to whoever is texting her, and moments later it buzzes again. She doesn't seem too happy with the conversation, and secretly, I hope things are already going sour between her and the cowboy from the last rodeo.

"Are you still mad at me?" I ask finally.

Kate sets her phone down with a huff.

"I'm not so mad anymore as I am disappointed,"

"Disappointed in me or the situation?" I'm watching her, but she stares at the TV.

"Both." She turns to face me now, swinging her legs off the side of the bed. "I get it, okay? I get that Austin can be a jerk, and I get that you don't want to make him feel like you're using him to get to me. That feeling sucks. I wish things could be different. I wish Austin wasn't so overprotective, and I wish we could follow our feelings and be together."

"Is someone making you feel used?" I ask, picking up on her comment.

Kate grabs her phone and switches over to my bed, curling up next to me.

"Emily." Kate rests her head on my shoulder, looking deflated.

"But you and Emily became friends while Austin and I were gone to college. You think she's using you to get to Austin?"

"I don't know. We weren't that great of friends at first. Just work friends, you know? We didn't hang out outside of work. Not until you two came home for the weekend and stopped by the diner to see me." Kate peers up at me now, making me wish I could kiss her sadness away.

"Oh. Well, that doesn't necessarily mean she's using you."

"No, it doesn't. But I've been noticing lately that she really is a shitty friend. For example, she's been making jokes about how I can't even get your attention when I'm sharing a motel room with you," Kate says, twirling the ring she's wearing on her thumb.

Emily really pisses me off.

"She's a bitch, and she doesn't deserve your friendship." My blood is ready to boil over from the way Kate's friend leaves her feeling inadequate. "She doesn't know her ass from a hole in the ground. And for the record, you have my attention. You have more of my attention than I care to admit, if I'm being honest." I give her hand a squeeze and rest my chin on the top of her head.

"Even so, I'm getting tired of the backhanded remarks from her."

"Hand me your phone."

"What?"

"Your phone. Let me see it. I'll take care of Emily for you, but I don't have her phone number. Let me call her." I reach across her for her cellphone, but she stretches her arm out away from me.

"No way." Kate giggles as I continue reaching across her,

practically lying on top of her as I try to capture her flailing hand.

When the giggles subside, I look down at her, making sure I'm not crushing her in my pursuit to get the phone. I'm not, but I am completely dominating her personal space. Although her expression has sobered, it doesn't reveal sadness. Instead, longing filters through. Kate watches me silently, her arms resting on the pillows now above her head and her lips barely parted.

Suddenly, I'm acutely aware of every inch of her body pressing against mine. My pulse quickens, and the hand that was reaching for her phone has found its way to her hip. As though it has a mind of its own, my hand slides up her side, pausing over her silky skin exposed by her T-shirt riding up. Her breath hitches under my touch as I linger over her, and I know I should pull away. It would be so easy to let myself have another taste of her. But that wouldn't be fair to either of us. I suck in a deep breath as I roll off her, returning to my spot on the bed. Kate clears her throat and scoots up on the mattress till she's sitting upright again.

"Maybe it's wearing on me extra today, I don't know," Kate says, like nothing just passed between us. "And it seems like every time we talk, she is asking about Austin. Why doesn't she talk to him directly instead of asking me about him?"

"I thought that's who he's been talking to every time he leaves the room." I look over at her.

"I think it is. But I think she's afraid he's going to be messing around with other girls because he won't label himself as her boyfriend."

"Oh." I nod.

"Yeah."

"I can't speak for Emily, but I can tell you this"—I lock eyes with her, making sure to keep my expression stern—"I'm abso-lutely not using you to get to Austin." Kate giggles and rolls her eyes at me.

"Are you sure? Because you seem a lot more worried about his feelings than mine."

"Ouch. That was a low blow." I reach over and take her hand in mine again. "And I do care about your feelings. I might be doing a shit job at handling them, but I do care about them. And seriously, if you want me to talk to Emily, I'll happily put her in her place."

"No need. I can handle Emily. But thanks."

The water cuts off in the bathroom and Kate raises her head off my shoulder to look at me, pausing briefly before rising from the bed and heading over to her duffel bag. She rummages around inside it for a minute and turns to me with a deck of cards in her hand.

"How about a little poker?" she asks and sits on my bed, this time at the foot of the bed, facing me. She pulls the cards out of the box and shuffles them.

"Strip poker?" I ask before Austin walks out of the bathroom, a cloud of steam following behind him.

"Hey, Austin, we're playing strip poker. Should I deal you in?" Kate asks.

Austin swings around and glares at us, his brow furrowed.

"The fucking hell you are," he says, and Kate busts into a fit of giggles. I hold my hands up, silently pleading innocence.

"I'm kidding. No need to get your panties in a wad." Kate winks at me and deals out the cards.

CHAPTER SIXTEEN

caleb

With a day to spare, we head to Hardin for the next rodeo. Kate has been in better spirits, and I'm grateful for that. Her phone buzzes again in her pocket, and she pulls it out and reads the text message that just came through with a big grin on her face. Her thumbs get to work, typing out a reply. I try to turn my focus to the road in front of us, but at this point, the scenery all looks the same. It's all open fields and mountains until we make it to the next town.

We've fallen into a routine, and we all play the game by going through the motions. Austin drives ninety-five percent of the time, and I try to ignore the magnetic pull that keeps scooting me closer to Kate in the already tight cab of the truck. The motel rooms change, but let's face it, they're all the same: two queen beds wearing paper-thin dark, ugly blankets, the carpet worn from countless feet treading on them over the years, and a shower with squeaky pipes. The names change, but everything else is constant, like the longing I deny day after day. It wears away at my resolve, and I constantly find myself questioning my reasons for staying away. Maybe I'm making things more complicated than they are. Maybe the obstacles between us are all in my head. At least, that's what I want to believe.

Kate's texting conversation that seems to have gone nonstop since our last rodeo is absolutely none of my business. That's what I keep reminding myself of anyway. Just the same, her phone's vibration gives me a similar sensation as nails on a chalkboard.

This time I sneak a look to see the name Tuff with a heart emoji after it. It must be the "friend" she made at the rodeo. If it was someone from town I'd have at least heard of them. I don't know anyone named Tuff.

We did decent the other day at the rodeo. I took what I needed out of my winnings for expenses and gave the rest to Austin to go toward helping his mom out. That is, after all, the whole reason we are here. And while I do have fun rodeoing, I'm past the days of living on the road. I'm ready to put down roots.

Kate's phone vibrates, and this time when she reads the message she giggles. I blow out a long breath and try reminding myself not to care. Her fingers are typing away and I'm tempted to snoop and see what this Tuff guy said that's so damn funny. I don't, though, because it's none of my business. At least she's been in a better mood since he's been texting her. She's not holding a grudge against me anymore, but I'd rather grovel for her forgiveness than watch her flirt with another man.

I clear my throat and shift in the seat again. It's been a couple hours since our break, and the cab keeps closing in on me a little more with each text exchange Kate makes with that joker. When I'm ready to combust, I roll down my window and lean out into the wind, hoping my frustrations blow away.

With the horses settled in their rented stalls, Austin pulls into our new motel and claims a parking spot. I climb out and hold the door for Kate, who is currently typing out another message on her phone. She goes to grab her duffle bag, but I reach over and grab it instead.

"I've got it." I wink at her.

"Thanks, bud," Kate says, barely glancing up from her phone.

She continues typing out her message while somehow following behind Austin to our room. Bud? She's never called me bud before. What is that about? Whatever it is, I don't like it.

My brain is working overtime trying to decipher the change in Kate's demeanor since this guy came along. Austin slides the key card unlocking our motel room door. He holds it open for me and Kate. After I set our bags down, I announce that I'm going for a walk to stretch my legs.

"You want to go with me, Kate?" I ask.

She typically enjoys going on walks. This time, however, she waves me off absentmindedly.

I march down the sidewalk, releasing some of the pent-up frustration from the ride here. After a couple turns, I find myself on the main drag through town. Quaint shops line the street, and when I happen upon an old-timey country store, I can't resist going inside. I browse the aisles, taking in the merchandise that hasn't been regularly produced in decades. On an end cap, I find a massive display of duct tape, printed in multiple designs. It makes me think of Kate and all the hell she gives me for my obsession with the product. Picking a roll printed with pinks and purples, I head to the counter to make my purchase.

The walk doesn't do much to clear my mind, but at least it helps work out some of the soreness of riding in the truck for most of the day. When I make it to the motel, Austin is stretched out on one of the beds watching *Cops* on TV and Kate is lying across the other bed, phone in hand.

"I got you something, Kate," I say and toss the roll of duct tape onto the bed next to her.

With eyebrows scrunched together she picks up the roll and studies it before looking up at me.

"What the hell is this for?"

"As much as you've been texting today, I thought you might need to heal your sore thumbs."

Kate acts like she's going to chuck it at my head. Instead, she stands and sets it on the desk before disappearing wordlessly into the bathroom. I take a seat on the bed she vacated and try to let the show numb my brain.

"I'll be back after a while," Kate says, coming out of the bathroom and heading straight for the door. A faint floral fragrance trails through the room as she passes. Is she wearing perfume? Austin and I both sit up on our beds at attention.

"Hold up. Where are you going?" Austin asks, bewilderment on his face.

"Out with a friend. Don't wait up. I've got a key." Kate flashes the key card at us. She's wearing a pair of tight dark-wash jeans and a lacy white top with a scoop neck that shows a hint of cleavage. Her hair is down loose around her shoulders rather than being pulled up in her typical ponytail, and she's wearing makeup. She's gorgeous.

"What friend do you have out here?" Austin asks. "And where are you and this friend going?"

"I met him the other day at the rodeo. He's a bull rider. His name is Tuff. And it just so happens he's never heard of Austin Farley, so I think I've found the one guy in the state of Montana who isn't afraid to date me."

"Yet," I murmur under my breath. Kate shoots me an angry "fuck off" look, but I don't mind. Austin isn't going to let her leave. I hope he hunts down this Tuff guy and gives him the what for. He has me for backup if he needs it, but I know he won't.

"I don't like it," Austin says, his eyes narrowing. "How well do you even know this guy?"

"Well enough. And I don't need your permission." Kate folds her arms across her torso, and it's evident she has no intention of letting Austin hijack her plans. His hesitation has my eyes darting back and forth between the two of them. He can't seriously be considering letting her go.

"Drop me your location when you get where you're going," Austin finally says. I about fall off the damn bed. What's wrong with him?

"Okay," Kate says, a smile spreading across her face.

"What time are you going to be back?" Austin asks.

"Not sure. But I'll text you, if you want."

Austin gives her a nod. "Be safe."

Flabbergasted, I sit on my bed, my jaw practically resting on the floor. My eyes bounce from the door to Austin who is settling down on the bed to watch his show.

"What?" he asks in response to my frozen stare.

"You're seriously going to let her go out with this joker?" I ask, waving an arm toward the door.

"He's a bull rider." Austin shrugs.

"Exactly. She's likely to catch something from him. And then get her heart broke when she finds out he's got girlfriends all up and down the rodeo circuit."

"It won't last long enough for her to get hurt. Who knows if we'll even cross paths with him again."

"Chances are pretty good, actually."

Austin's glare narrows at me. "What's your deal? Why do you care what Kate does?"

"I don't. You're acting weird, that's all." I shrug and lean back against the headboard of the bed, but he doesn't ease up.

"Is there something going on between you and my little sister?"

I huff. "No."

"You'd better not be hiding anything from me. Are you sure there's nothing between you two?"

"Positive, man. I wouldn't go there. You know that."

Austin lets it drop, thankfully. I try to focus on the show, but my mind is on Kate. Austin's phone buzzes on the night-stand between us. He picks it up and swipes to answer the call, getting up and leaving the room. It must be Emily. He only takes his phone calls outside when she calls.

When my phone vibrates next to me, I grab for it, ready to take off and rescue Kate. It's not Kate, though. It's Monty. Clearing my throat, I swipe my finger across the screen to answer.

"Hey, little man, what's happening?"

"Caleb? Where are you?" Monty's hesitant voice floats through the line.

"I'm in Hardin. Are you okay?"

"I'm hungry," Monty says, drawing out the words in his soft tone.

"What did you have for dinner?" I ask, checking the time. It's late enough that he should be in bed by now.

"There isn't anything here to eat. I had the last piece of bread at lunch."

"What about the snacks I sent you?"

"They're all gone."

"All of it?" There's no way he already ate it all.

"Yeah. Mom's friend has been over a lot. He doesn't listen when I tell him they're mine."

My head pounds, probably from my blood pressure rocketing to new heights.

"Where's your mom, Monty?" Sitting up, I drop my legs over the side of the bed. I wanted something to distract me from Kate—this will definitely do it.

"She's asleep on the couch."

"Go over to her and wake her up. I want to talk to her." I drop my face into my free hand and massage my temple. In the background, Monty's little voice pleads with his mom, begging her to wake up. "Monty? Did she wake up?"

"She said to go away and went back to sleep," Monty says.

What am I supposed to do with this? I'm two and a half hours from him. He's as good as unsupervised, though I'm sure his mom would disagree if she was coherent enough to have even a brief conversation.

"Monty, I need to get off the phone. I want you to wait for me to call you before you do anything, okay? Just sit tight."

"Okay. I'll wait right here."

Letting out a deep exhale, I search my contacts for Monty's neighbor. She gave me her number once upon a time. Scrolling through the contacts saved to my phone, I finally find her, give her a call, and explain the situation. Moments later, I'm calling Monty, telling him to answer the door for his neighbor who he gets to spend the night with tonight. It's a short-term solution, but he'll be safe tonight. Tomorrow I can reach out to the CPS worker.

After a while, Austin comes in and goes to bed. I have no idea how he can sleep at a time like this. I stay up watching TV, flipping aimlessly through the channels, and unsuccessfully ignoring the clock while waiting for Kate to return from her date. In between that fun, I'm stressing over Monty's situation. Living on the road isn't working out too well for me. I always give Austin crap about acting like an old man, but maybe I'm the one aged beyond my years.

Eventually, unable to sit still any longer, I decide to get ready for bed. Changing into shorts, I don't worry about putting a T-shirt on. With nothing else to do, I climb into bed and try to fall asleep. It's pointless. I can't sleep. I lie in bed watching the window for Kate's silhouette to appear, unable to clear my mind.

Close to 1 am voices outside our motel room pull my attention to the window. Sure enough, two silhouettes appear outside. Kate and Tuff stand at our door, clearly neither wanting the evening to end. A gentleman would turn over and give them their privacy, but I'm not feeling very gentlemanly.

Dread sits in my belly like a giant boulder as I watch Tuff close the space between them, until their separate silhouettes join into one. My fist clenches at my side, my jaw grinding together so tight my teeth hurt. The jealousy coursing through my veins sends me into a silent frenzy. Sitting up in bed, I search the dark room for something I can plow my fists into. Not finding any reasonable solutions, I head into the bathroom and splash cold water over my face. My breathing is unsteady, and I can't get it out of my head that every second Kate stands outside that door is another second someone else's hands are touching her body. I can't do it.

Quickly, I dab my face on a towel but don't worry about catching all the drops that run down my bare chest. Marching silently to the motel room door, I swing it open. My abrupt manner startles Tuff and Kate and successfully ends their make-out session. Kate stares at me with rage exuding from her countenance.

"Hey, I thought maybe you forgot your key," I say casually, grinning at them. "Hey, man, you must be Tuff. I'm Caleb. Nice to meet you." Extending my hand to him, he shakes it and mumbles something I don't care enough to listen to. "You ready for bed, Kate?"

If looks could kill.

"I'll see you at the rodeo," Tuff says, turning again to Kate.

He's trying to play it cool, but I can tell my little stunt rattled him. I stand there waiting for their goodbye while the streetlamps buzz overhead. Tuff shifts on his feet, his eyes darting back to me a few times, probably trying to figure out the unexpected situation he's found himself in.

"Yeah, I can't wait." Kate gives him a faint smile and shoves past me through the door.

Closing the door in Tuff's face, I turn back into the room. Kate is already in the bathroom, changing I assume. After a few minutes, she appears. Even in the dark I can see the anger flashing over her expression. She slowly stalks toward me, but I hold my ground, ready to take whatever she is about to dish out to me.

"That was a real dick move, Caleb," she says in a loud whisper, pointing her finger into my bare chest. "You had no right to interrupt us like that. For once in my life my brother isn't cock-blocking me, so you decide it's your turn?"

"Are you seriously interested in that guy, Kate?" I ask, motioning toward the door.

"I could be, yes. But frankly, it's none of your business."

"You are my business, Kate. You know that. You've always been my business." What will it take to make her understand?

"You are not my brother, Caleb. And you sure as hell aren't my lover. So, no. I'm not your business. I'm nothing more to you than your buddy's little sister who you rescued once upon a time. But I don't need you to rescue me anymore. I don't need anything from you."

Kate turns away, crossing the room to the bed she's sharing with Austin. The room is silent aside from our breathing as she climbs under the covers and turns to face the wall. After a moment of quiet, I return to my bed, her words on repeat in my brain while I toss and turn through the night.

CHAPTER SEVENTEEN

The morning passes slowly, and it's probably Caleb's fault somehow. Okay, I don't actually think it's Caleb's fault, but I'm so mad at him I want to claw away the smile that's always on his face.

"How'd your date go last night, Kate?" Austin asks, breaking the silence as we drive to the fairgrounds.

"It went great. I had a fantastic time."

"Yeah?"

"Yeah." I make a point to look at Caleb as I add, "Tuff's an awesome kisser."

"Okay, we don't need to go there." Austin shivers dramatically.

"Seriously, though. Probably the best I've ever been kissed."

Caleb blows a heavy breath out his nose and turns to the window. I steal another glance at my phone. I haven't heard from Tuff since Caleb's little showdown last night, and I hope it's not because Caleb scared him off. On top of that, I haven't heard anything from Mom since I left, and I'm anxious to know how she's doing. But I won't be the first to reach out. If she needs my help, she's going to have to ask for it this time.

This rodeo will last a few days for us. Hopefully that means a few days with Tuff, if luck goes my way. When we make it to the fairgrounds, I break down and send him a text since I haven't heard from him yet, and I don't want to come off as desperate. For all I know, Caleb gave him the wrong impression last night.

> Me: Hey. Just made it to the fairgrounds. Maybe we can meet up when you aren't busy.

Several minutes tick by before my phone buzzes. I pull it out of my pocket, hoping it's Tuff. It is.

> Tuff: Be there soon.

I smile and tuck my phone away. Maybe I've been worried for nothing. I busy myself helping Austin get his stuff ready and actively ignoring Caleb. Once Tuff texts me that he's free, I go meet up with him and leave the boys to fend for themselves.

"Hey." I give Tuff a peck on the cheek.

"Uh-oh," Tuff says. "Don't tell me we're moving backward."

"What do you mean?"

"Last night you were kissing me on the lips and this morning it's the cheek?" Tuff teases. I relax and smile, instantly dropping my guard.

"Last night was so long ago," I quip. "Maybe you could remind me how it went?"

Tuff gives me a crooked grin and pulls me to him. Tipping his cowboy hat out of the way, he presses a kiss to my lips. It's nothing like it was with Caleb, but it makes me giddy just the same. When he starts to back away, I catch sight of Caleb glowering at us and lean into Tuff, prolonging our connection. He's happy to oblige and pulls me tight against him again, letting his hands drift over my body.

"That was much better," he says once we break apart.

I glare back at Caleb, not realizing Tuff is watching. He follows my line of sight, and a frown forms across his face when he sees Caleb.

Without a word, Tuff takes my hand, and we walk aimlessly around the grounds, chatting. We weave through the trailers and around the arena, taking our time as we stroll along the gravel paths.

"People are always surprised to hear that I grew up in the city," Tuff says.

"You grew up in the city? But how did you get into bull riding?"

"I was at a party at some kid's house out in the country. His family had a ranch. I was dared to jump on their bull's back."

"Oh. How long did you make it?"

"What do you mean?"

"On the bull you were dared to jump on."

"Oh, well, he wasn't strapped up or anything."

"Right, but was that it? You had to jump on him and get out again?"

"Pretty much. And I almost did it, too, but their ranch foreman caught us and kicked us out."

"So, you didn't do it?"

"No. Not that time. But that's where it all started."

"Oh."

Realizing how different his childhood was from mine, I find myself silently comparing him to Caleb. I don't mean to do it, but Caleb was a part of most of my childhood. There are very few memories that don't involve me, Austin, and Caleb finding trouble together.

"What about you? Do you have any crazy stories from when you were a kid?" Tuff asks. I watch the ground as we walk. If sneaking into his mean neighbor's backyard to retrieve a ball, or getting dared to jump on a bull is his idea of crazy childhood experiences, I'm not sure I want to share our mischief with him.

"Um . . . " I think back, trying to come up with one of our

milder shenanigans. "Our yard has a slight drop to it but not enough of a hill to get going good on a sled. So in the winter, Austin and Caleb would put a ladder up to the porch roof. We'd climb up with our sled and launch off the roof. It gave us enough of a start to get some good speed."

"Off the roof? Your parents allowed that?" Tuff asks, leading us around the arena now.

"They usually didn't know what we were up to." I shrug.

"Ah. This Caleb guy . . . he's the one that came to the door last night, right?" Tuff stops walking and turns to face me.

"Yeah. That was him," I say, kicking at a dried-out pile of dung at our feet.

"He seems . . . protective." Lifting a gentle finger to my chin, Tuff guides my face up to his, making me look at him. "You sure there's not something more than friendship there?"

"Caleb and I never dated," I answer honestly.

"But that's not what I asked." I was hoping he wouldn't pick up on my avoidance.

"Listen, even if there was something between us, nothing could come of it. Caleb's loyalty lies with Austin, and Austin would obliterate him. I'm essentially Caleb's little sister by extension. That's all." I slowly start us walking again, pulling Tuff along at first till his feet catch back into motion with mine.

"So, I don't need to worry that the woman I like is currently sharing a motel room with an attractive man that she shares zero DNA with?"

I stop in my tracks and face him.

"I share a bed with my brother. Caleb happens to be in the room."

"Hmmm," Tuff says, walking again. "Not going to lie. I don't like the guy. Personally, I think he'd be in your pants in an instant if you gave him the chance."

"That's not happening."

"If I were a betting man, I'd bet it already has."

His comment stops me, and my hand slips from his. Heat rises to my face as my hands ball into fists at my sides.

"And I'd bet that your chances just plummeted." I fold my arms over my chest.

Tuff adjusts his cowboy hat on his head and steps closer to me.

"I didn't mean it like that. I'm sorry."

I understand where Tuff is coming from, but I also can't deny the instinctual protectiveness his comments spike in me for Caleb.

"Whatever you meant, you're going to have to get over it. And you better get used to Caleb. He's not going anywhere."

"What's that supposed to mean?"

I shrug. "Caleb is nonnegotiable. He's always going to be around."

Tuff doesn't reply, but his posture stiffens, and if I'm not mistaken, I catch a slight flinch in his jaw. After a few beats of silence, he changes the subject completely, and we continue our walk around the grounds as though nothing happened.

Once the events start, we head up to the stands to watch among the busy chatter of the other spectators. The announcer's voice booms over the speaker, announcing scores and encouraging people to spend their money at the vendors set up around the arena. Caleb doesn't come back up in our conversation, but the tension from earlier hangs heavy around us, leaving me questioning my interest in Tuff. Caleb and Austin take first place in their event. It's going to be a good evening. When it's time for Tuff to get ready for the bull riding, I walk him down, my hand in his. We find a spot to pull off from the foot traffic so we can say our goodbyes.

"What are the chances I could take you to breakfast in the morning?" Tuff asks.

I hesitate momentarily, unprepared for his question. Maybe he isn't as hung up on Caleb as I thought he was. I do have a history of misreading things where Caleb is involved. All the same, his comment—however he meant it—stung, and even if Tuff is ready to move past our little tiff, I don't know that I am.

"Maybe." I give him a weak smile and peer at our surroundings, distracted.

"I'll text you later and we'll set up the details," Tuff says, pulling my attention back to him. As I turn toward him again, his lips brush against mine in an awkward half peck.

"Sounds good."

I pull back from him and see Caleb watching us from where he and Austin are talking to some other ropers. Did he see our botched kiss? I'm not sure why the thought makes my cheeks burn. I drop my head between us, giving me a moment to gather myself before trying to salvage the situation. Looking back up at him now, I pull him into a quick hug.

"Ride hard, cowboy," I say, tapping the brim of his hat when we break apart, but Tuff catches a glimpse of Caleb, too, and tightens his arm around my waist, pulling me back to him and solidly landing a kiss this time. I push him away, ending the kiss.

"What's the deal?" Tuff asks, leaning toward me for more.

I twist out of his arms. "No sense in making a scene."

"Yeah." He looks across the crowd at Caleb again. "I bet that's all it is."

Tuff struts off into the multitude of people, not bothering to look back. My head is spinning, and guilt is creeping up on me. How does he do that? How does Caleb interfere without even doing anything? And then it dawns on me. It's not Caleb this time. It's me. My subconscious takes over, searching for Caleb again. A weary sigh slips from my lips as my eyes land on him, roaming down his body. Is there any man out there that will compete with the hold Caleb has over me? If so, I haven't found him yet. I want more than looks or money from the man I settle down with. I want warmth. Someone who carries themselves with a steadiness through whatever challenges they meet. Peace.

I finally meet someone that Austin doesn't give me a hard time about dating just to discover that I don't even want him. As far-fetched as it is, I want Caleb. Anger rushes my veins as I let myself mull over those recent slips from Caleb—telling me he cares and then ignoring me the next day. Losing himself with me, but not allowing us to become anything—telling me we can never be more than friends. And yet my heart is so wrapped up in him that I can't let go. I don't want to let go, to quit hoping. And I hate him in this moment for telling me I need to.

Caleb looks up, meeting my gaze. As quickly as he does, I avert my eyes. I don't want his scrutiny right now. Turning from the arena, I wander through the crowd, seeking a retreat where I can take the time I need to get my head on straight. My hands are shaking, and the burn of oncoming tears assaults my eyes. I don't want to want him anymore.

The announcer's voice booms over the speakers, mingling with the chatter of the throngs of onlookers. I cut around the corner of the concession stand where there are no crowds of people, only extra bales of hay in a little alleyway between structures, and smack into a tall, unexpected figure, finding myself tangled in his arms.

It's Caleb, but I'm not supposed to relish the feel of his arms around me. His touch is warm and strong, but it stings me with emotions I no longer have the energy to deal with.

"I was wrong, Kate."

His words fall on deaf ears, and I erupt.

"Let me go, you fucking barbarian!" I shove against him, letting the anger win despite knowing he only had hold on me to steady me from our collision.

He's always there. Always reminding me of what I'm not allowed to have. Austin is right. Caleb would make a fool out of me. In some ways, he already has. He drops his hands and takes a step back, eyeing me up and down, but doesn't speak a word for several seconds. I shake my head, ready to run from him.

"Listen to me. I'm trying to tell you I'm sorry. I was wrong,

Kate. We both were. You mean too much to me to risk losing. I'd never leave you. We can do this—do us. I want to be with you."

"What about Austin?"

"Fuck Austin, baby, this is me and you." Caleb shifts toward me, bringing our bodies together again.

And now the next move is mine. I hesitate briefly, wanting to give my head a chance to be heard over my heart. I want to believe that dreams do come true, even for me. Desperation grows in Caleb's stance, and I know that despite his past reservations, he's sincere in his declaration. The choice is mine. I can walk away and never look back, or I can take the moment I'm being offered.

I pound on his chest with my fists. "Fuck you for playing with me like this. You can't keep going back and forth, wanting me one minute and not the next. I might not be anything special, but I'm better than that."

He catches my wrists and stops me. "I know you are, and I'll prove it if you'll let me. I don't want to go another minute without you."

"Fuck you, Caleb."

I break free from his hold on me, twisting around to make a break for it and find somewhere else to be—anywhere he's not.

"Just as long as you're the one doing it, darlin'."

I freeze mid-step and peek over my shoulder at him. What did he say? Meeting his gaze was a mistake. His steel-blue eyes smolder with an intensity that locks me in, and I find myself gravitating toward him until I'm close enough to touch him again.

Caleb's mouth crashes against mine. He wraps his arms around me, pressing me tightly against him. My anger vanishes, and I'm practically purring for him. His lips desert mine, trailing up my jaw to my ear and shooting heat straight to my core.

"Does he make you feel like this when he kisses you?" Caleb

whispers in my ear, his voice raspy. His teeth lightly nip and suck my earlobe. "Does the world disappear when his lips are on you? Does it?"

"No," I whimper. My hands fist his shirt, pulling him closer until my brain catches up, and I shove him away, shaking my head. "We've already played this game, Caleb. I was the one who lost. I'm not interested in round two." I start to spin away from him, but he catches my wrist, stopping me. I can't look at him. I can't carry his feelings on top of my own.

"Please, wait," Caleb says softly, and he drops my wrist before cupping my face with both hands, and despite knowing better, I allow it. "I don't want to hold back anymore. I want to be with you. If you've truly moved on and are no longer interested, I understand. But if there's any chance you still have feelings for me, Kate, please give me this chance."

Without wasting any more time, I press into Caleb, forcing him back till he lands on the hay bales behind him. Straddling his lap, I crush my lips to his. His fingers climb up to my braid, wrapping it around his hand and tugging my head back. His heated breath trails down my neck till his mouth picks the perfect spot to tease. My breath hitches, his touch intoxicating me. My hips rock against him on instinct, but there are too many barriers between us. As he loosens his grip on my braid, I claim his mouth again, needier than before, and let his tongue explore.

"Caleb"—I pull free and force myself to breathe—"there are too many people here. Where can we go?"

With a heavy exhale, Caleb deflates. His forehead falls gingerly to my shoulder for a moment before he raises his eyes back to mine. He wants this as bad as I do. It's written all over his face.

"I don't know. I don't think there is a place here. Fuck," Caleb says. "We could go to the truck."

I shake my head. "No, there's too many people coming and

going, and there's no tint to the windows. We'd be better off right here."

"It's going to have to be later, I guess." Caleb's voice drips with dismay. "Let's go out tonight. We can get dressed up and make a real date of it."

Austin's words from the day he caught me checking out Caleb and threatened to send me home come back to me: *"If I get even the slightest hint that you and he are messing around, I'll send your ass back home so quick you won't know what happened. Do you hear me?"* I cock an eyebrow at Caleb and slide off his lap. "There's no way. Austin can't know about us."

"What do you mean, Austin can't know? We're supposed to hide this from him? Kate, we're all living in the same motel room."

"You know as well as I do he'll lose his shit if he finds out there's something going on between us."

Caleb stands and adjusts himself. "Which is why we should tell him."

"He can't know. Not yet. Maybe once we aren't all sleeping in the same room we can tell him, but not right now. We need to keep it between us."

Caleb takes my hands in his, and I watch him expectantly, waiting for his reply. When none comes, I turn away from him and straighten my disheveled clothing, making sure there's no evidence left of our encounter. He turns me to him again and softly kisses my lips before hugging me.

"We'll find opportunities to be together. I know sneaking around isn't ideal, but we'll make it work until we can be public about it. I promise," I say.

Soon, we're weaving through the crowd in search of Austin. He's standing close to where Caleb left him, only now he's wearing a scowl. I do my best to act like nothing has changed between me and Caleb, despite exactly all that has changed being the only thing I can think about.

"Where have you two been? I've been looking all over for you," Austin says.

"That's weird," Caleb says. "You ready to leave?"

Austin narrows his eyes at us and takes a step toward Caleb, studying him. "You're not up to any funny business, are you?"

"Nope"—Caleb shakes his head—"serious business only."

I stifle a giggle. There's no way we're going to make it very long without Austin catching on. Austin turns his scrutiny on me now. I clear my throat and straighten under his gaze, sobering to the challenge of keeping our secret. Although I'd rather tell Austin what is going on, sneaking around could be fun. Plus, there's no way Austin will let me stay on the road with them if he finds out Caleb and I are together.

"Let's go," he finally says.

CHAPTER EIGHTEEN

Caleb discretely nudges me with his elbow and winks at me when our eyes meet. Austin is rattling off a list of things we need to do during our free evening, and he puts me and Caleb on laundry duty together while he tends to the horses and takes the truck for an oil change. Who knew laundry would be something to look forward to? My phone buzzes in my pocket, demanding attention.

> Tuff: What time should I pick you up for breakfast?

Right. Tuff. He asked me out to breakfast tomorrow, and I avoided committing. That obviously can't happen now. It wouldn't be fair to him or to Caleb, and besides that, I'm not interested anymore. My intrigue was already starting to wane before Caleb made his move. I chew on my thumbnail while considering the kindest way to word what I need to say.

> Me: Turns out breakfast isn't going to work.

> Tuff: Drinks later?

Me: I can't see you anymore. I'm sorry. I hope you understand.

Tuff: No, actually, I don't understand. What changed between this afternoon and now?

Fair enough question. Just earlier today he asked me if there was anything going on between me and Caleb, and I assured him there wasn't. If I tell him the truth, I'll seem like a liar and probably hurt his feelings. Surely, there's a way around it—an honest answer that will appease him? I give it a try.

Me: Look, there isn't any hope of a future with us. I don't want to continue down this road only to wind up hurting us both. Who knows if we'll even have the chance to see each other again after this rodeo. And I'm not looking for anything long distance. It's best we end it now.

I set my phone aside, hoping that does the trick.

Tuff: It's that other guy, isn't it? Caleb? He's always hanging around you.

Me: It's not about him, Tuff. I'm not looking for a hookup. And given our situation, a relationship isn't in the works for us, either. Why prolong the inevitable?

Caleb and I unload our bags of dirty laundry from the back of the pickup, and Austin drives off as we shuffle our way into the laundromat. The door hinges squeal as they're put to work opening the door. The air inside is hot and stuffy, heavily fragranced by the various detergents used throughout the day in the washing machines. Luckily, it's not too crowded now. Two dryers are currently in use along the wall; a lone woman sits in a chair reading a book with a scantily clad couple wrapped in each other's arms decorating the cover. She pays us no mind as we walk by her and the long row of empty machines. At the end of the row of machines, a laundry cart sits with clothes already hung across the top bar. After we pass the cart, a table on the back wall of the laundromat becomes visible.

We plop our bags and tub of detergent down on the table and sort the garments into piles. Between the three of us, we have two loads to wash. Caleb and I claim a couple washers side by side. I pour the detergent in, and Caleb follows behind me with a handful of quarters, starting each machine.

I push our bags aside and perch myself on the table. Caleb saunters over, his eyes running over my body as he approaches me. I kick my feet and give him a smirk.

"You've got your mind in the gutter again," I say. "I can see it in your eyes."

"You do, too." Caleb scans the room behind him, leaning to see around the curtain of clothes hanging on the cart before brushing his lips over mine. My arms slide over his shoulders, relaxing around his neck and keeping him close. We're cheek to cheek now, his breath tickling my ear. "Tell me I'm wrong."

"You're wrong," I whisper, soaking up the feeling of having him close like this.

"Liar." Caleb tenderly kisses the lobe of my ear and pulls away, leaving me flushed and feeling empty.

A rapid succession of buzzing from the dryers in use draws the woman's attention from her book. She empties the contents of the dryers into a couple laundry hampers, stacking them and carrying them out the squeaking door to her car. It's not until she drives away that Caleb notices her book sitting in the chair she vacated.

"Should we see what was so intriguing?" Caleb scoops up the book and holds it up for me to see.

"Do you think those were her clothes as well?" I ask, motioning to the cart of abandoned clothes that blocks our view of the door. Caleb shrugs and flips through the pages as he walks back to me, still seated on the table. He rests against the table next to me, and I prop my chin on his shoulder, reading along with him.

"Wait, what?" I reach for Caleb's hand, stopping him from turning the page before I'm ready. "What did she say she did with his brother?"

"I'm pretty sure you read that right." Caleb flips the page.

"She's letting it all out, isn't she?"

"Did you make it to the part about his dad?"

"I'd love to be a fly on the wall at their Thanksgiving dinner," I say, shaking my head in disbelief. Caleb chuckles.

"No, you wouldn't. Read this part." Caleb points to a group of paragraphs on the next page, waiting quietly for my reaction.

"No . . . There's no way!"

Before long, our tutelage on the art of romancing your way through a single family tree is interrupted by the buzzing of the washing machines finishing their cycles. Caleb and I move the wet clothing from the washers over to the dryers, add some quarters, and start the machines.

I slide up on the table again, this time pinching my shirt right below the neckline and flapping it to cool off from the heated room. Caleb stands in front of me now, his warm hands heating my thighs.

"You warm?" Caleb asks. I lean back and continue fanning myself with my shirt, not answering him. "The easy solution would be taking off your shirt."

I let my head fall back as I laugh at his unsurprising suggestion. When I lift my head back up, Caleb is leaning into me, a grin spread over his face and pure bliss floating over his countenance. The warm air intensifies his rich, woodsy scent, sending his pheromones swirling through my senses. I straighten upright and press a kiss to his lips. His arms wrap around me and tug me toward him. I relax into his kiss, melting into him.

When the hinges of the laundromat door screech again, I'm too enraptured by the urges climbing my body to consider the warning they call out to us. My hands slide up into Caleb's hair, raking through his wavy strands. A sudden splatter and pop of cardboard and liquid on the concrete floor startles us out of our reverie.

"Damn it to hell!" Austin's voice rolls over the humming of the dryers.

Caleb jolts back, wide-eyed, and peers around the cart of clothes as I slide off the table and smooth my hands over my clothes. Caleb walks down the row of machines, approaching Austin, and I follow close behind. A bag of fast food and two drinks sit on the washer next to the third cup, smashed open and spilled over the floor. Austin is unrolling some paper towels and Caleb bends to pick up the cup and accompanying lid.

"You're back quicker than I expected," I say.

"That's your drink on the floor, Kate," Austin says. "Sorry. You can have mine if you want it."

The dryers buzz, notifying us that our clothes are ready. While Austin soaks up the spilled beverage, Caleb helps me pull the laundry out of the dryers. He nudges me and peeks over his shoulder at Austin before holding up the lacy panties he found in the load he's collecting. He winks at me and silently slides the panties into his pocket with a smirk. I dramatically roll my eyes in response, hook my finger in the exposed loop hanging out from his pocket, and sling them into my basket of clothes. This guy.

The tension is palpable between us on the way to the motel room. It's the good kind of tension, though. The kind that swirls around in your body leaving you all hot and bothered and wanting more. Boy, do I want more. Spontaneous combustion may be in my near future. How we're going to keep Austin from figuring us out, I have no idea. Surely the energy trapped inside with us feels different to him, too. He's undoubtedly going to sense it.

No sooner than when we get to the room, Caleb heads for the shower. What I would give to join him right about now. Instead, my phone buzzes in my pocket, stealing my attention away from the naked man behind door number one.

Emily: "bumped into your mom" like you asked me to do. She seems good. Says she's feeling a lot better.

Me: Did you notice any of her symptoms? Anything stand out?

Emily: Nope. She seemed steady. She wasn't her old self but definitely seems better than she has in the last six months or so.

Me: Ok. Thanks for checking on her Em.

Emily: You know you could just call her.

Me: Except then I'd have to talk to her.

Emily: What's Austin up to? Has he said anything about me?

Me: You know you could just call him.

Emily: Bitch.

Me: He's sitting here next to me. He's watching TV, so he isn't talking much about anyone except John Wayne.

Emily: Ok. Well let me know if he says anything about me.

Me: I will.

Caleb comes out of the bathroom, freshly showered and dressed. Worries about my mom instantly melt away as I run my eyes over his dewy skin. I wet my suddenly dry lips, and Caleb smirks at me, clearly aware of what's currently running through my mind. If I could get him alone for even fifteen minutes . . .

I plug up my phone and gather clothes for showering. I'm glad Mom seems to be doing well. I've worried about her. I'm usually the one taking care of her from day-to-day, and despite how I left, it's hard suddenly not being around. But she made her choice clear.

By the time I get out of the shower, the lights are out except for the TV, and Austin is quietly snoring from our bed. Instead of climbing in beside him, I take a detour and slide into Caleb's bed, already warmed by his body heat. I tuck myself into his warm body and kiss him. His woodsy scent envelopes me, renewed by his recent shower.

"You're going to get us in trouble," Caleb says in barely a whisper, pulling away and glancing over his shoulder in the dark to Austin's motionless form.

"He's a sound sleeper," I whisper and kiss him again.

Caleb's calloused hands slide over my body, drawing me closer. Heat pools inside me, and despite our bodies being flush now, I want more. He shifts onto his side, pushing me on my back, and his lips find my neck, right below my ear. Slowly, he roams over my body, his warm mouth shooting shivers through me. When a soft moan accidentally escapes between ragged breaths, Caleb quietly chortles and captures my mouth with his again before resuming his tour of my body.

I squirm under his wandering touch, trying to urge him on silently. Just the same, he takes his time exploring, never rushing. Gradually, his hand finds its way, sliding underneath the waistband of my underwear. Thoughts of Austin and rodeos drift from my mind, leaving only me and Caleb in our happy little bubble. I clench my teeth, trying to swallow the moans vying to escape.

Austin snorts and rolls over in his bed, facing us now. We freeze, and I suck in my breath, hoping he didn't wake. His quiet breathing resumes, and Caleb twists to peer over his shoulder at Austin and make sure he's sound asleep before turning to me again.

Kissing my lips tenderly, Caleb winks at me. "You better go to bed before we wake Austin."

"But—"

"It's fine, Trouble." Caleb grins at me. "We've already pushed our luck."

He kisses me again, and I'm reluctant to let him go.

"Or—hear me out—I could sleep with you tonight and we can pretend like I was sleepwalking and ended up in the wrong bed."

"You're trying to get me killed, aren't you?" Caleb smirks at me. "Go on. Get out of here."

Grumbling quietly, I climb out of Caleb's bed and claim my spot next to Austin. Caleb goes to the bathroom, and I can't help but wonder if he's taking care of the problem I created for him—in which case I definitely should be in there, too—or if he's going to put himself to bed with blue balls. I'll make it up to him later.

THE NEXT DAY at the rodeo, I choose to stick with Austin and Caleb until it's time for their run. Austin doesn't seem to notice. He's too zoned in to the rodeo to pay attention to anything around him. That's how he gets when he is competing. Caleb and I are perched on the rough, splintered fence, above the sea of cowboy hats and pretending to watch the events currently happening in the arena. Caleb's thumb nonchalantly brushes over my fingers next to his on the fence. It sends sparks through me that heat my cheeks. The fans cheer from the stands as the announcer calls out scores in his deep, booming voice.

"Someone is giving you some awfully dirty looks." Caleb's

warm breath brushes against my ear and neck and sends shivers down my spine.

"Who?" I scan the crowd in search of the sender.

Caleb nods over to our left, and I see him. Tuff is glowering at us.

"Poor kid. Want me to go tell him to move along?"

"No, it's fine. Let's ignore him." There's no sense in making a bigger production of it.

Finally, it's Caleb and Austin's turn to rope. I give Caleb's hand a quick squeeze, wishing him luck and then reclaiming my spot on the fence for a better view as they ride off to the box. It's another successful run, earning them first place again.

This time, instead of collecting the winnings and leaving, we hang around to enjoy the festivities. We walk through the vendors, checking out the merchandise for sale, Caleb and I always within each other's gravitational pull but careful not to touch or give Austin anything to be suspicious of.

"Slut."

The word is barely uttered above a whisper as we walk by, but it's heard by all three of us. Chills trickle down my spine, and Caleb and Austin's heads whip around to locate the offender. Not even trying to hide himself, Tuff stands squared off and facing us in the walkway.

"You care to repeat yourself?" Austin is already on him, personal bubbles be damned.

"Your sister is a whore—"

"Stop!" I grab Austin's coiled fist before it explodes, wedging myself between them.

"Caleb, get her out of here while I take care of this twerp."

Caleb breaks his readied stance to do as he's instructed but halts at my protest.

"No, stop. He's not worth it."

"He's not going to talk like that about you, Kate."

"What are you going to do? Challenge him to a duel? My honor does not need to be defended. I don't care what he says.

But if you punch him, he's not going to take it on the chin like a man. He's going to call the police. And you two will go to jail. Come on. Ignore him." When Austin fails to move I try again, this time sterner. "Now, Austin. He's not worth it. Let's go."

By the grace of God, Austin and Caleb listen and turn away, their nostrils flaring and their jaws clenched. We settle on hot dogs from the concession stand and find seats to watch the rest of the rodeo. The final event of the night is bull riding. Caleb nudges my side when Tuff drops down on the bull, readying himself for his ride. The bull flies out of the chute, bucking and twisting. Tuff only makes it about four seconds before getting tossed. He stands, collects his cowboy hat, and chucks it into the dirt again before stomping out of the arena while the boys whistle and cheer. Caleb snickers quietly at my side.

"That's embarrassing. Did you know he couldn't ride?" Austin asks, reclaiming his seat.

"Stop." I elbow Austin in the ribs.

"That's the problem with those bull riders," Caleb says. "You can't get more than eight seconds out of them on a good night."

"Ha ha. You're hysterical," I deadpan.

"He's not getting away with talking about you like that." Austin wads up his trash, tucking it in the palm of his hand to throw away later.

"And you're not touching him. So, I'm not sure how you're going to do anything about it."

"I have an idea," Caleb says, wearing a pleased grin.

CHAPTER NINETEEN

caleb

I type out a text on my phone and hit send. Kate grabs her phone and reads the text message that buzzed through to her device. As she reads, a big smile spreads across her face.

> Me: Hey Trouble.

> Kate: We're in the same room, Caleb. You could just speak to me . . .

> Me: Not the way I want to. Austin would definitely catch on that there's something going on between us if he hears me say the things I want to say. Like how it's killing me that you're so close, yet I can't touch you.

> Me: Or how badly I want to take you out on a date.

> Me: Or how all I can think about is running my fingers across your skin.

The buzzing coming from Kate's phone draws Austin's attention. He glares over at her from the TV, irritation marking his face. When she catches him watching, she tries to wipe her smile away, unsuccessfully.

"Who's blowing you up?" Austin asks.

"It's nobody," Kate says, setting her phone aside.

> Me: Ouch! I'm nobody, huh?

> Kate: Stop. You know you're not a nobody.

> Me: Go on a date with me.

> Kate: When? How?

> Me: I'll figure out the details. I just need to know if you're in.

> Kate: Absolutely.

"Are you two texting each other?" Austin asks me now. His eyes bounce between me and Kate. "You two need me to leave the room?"

"Sure," I say, offering a smirk.

Kate freezes briefly in a silent panic, no doubt thinking I'm about to out us. I'm not, but it would be more suspicious of me to pass up an opportunity to give Austin hell. His expression turns to stone, and he straightens in his seat.

"The fuck I'm going anywhere. Who are you texting?"

"It's a girl," I say with a shit-eating grin. "I found me a buckle bunny."

Austin shakes his head, but it doesn't disguise the relief that's plastered all over his face as he relaxes again on the bed. "It's about time you get laid. Make sure you wear a condom and don't catch anything from her. You never know how many cowboys the buckle bunnies have been with, but you can be sure you are neither the first nor the last."

Kate stifles a giggle. I look over at her and give her a wink. I don't want to sneak around to be with her, and I hate lying to

Austin. But if Kate needs me to keep us under wraps for now, I'll do it for her. I adjust the way I'm sitting so I can continue texting without making it so obvious what I'm doing.

Kate: I'm a buckle bunny now, huh?

Me: I mean, if the shoe fits . . .

Me: But I'm not sharing you with the other cowboys so don't get any ideas.

Kate: I'm only after one cowboy. You might know him. He's tall, handsome, and he sweet-talks the girls.

Me: He sounds run-of-the-mill if you ask me.

Kate: Oh, he's not at all. He's quite talented too. So many talents.

Me: Jack-of-all-trades, master of none?

Kate: No.

Kate: He's a master of at least one. But I'm willing to bet more, too.

Me: I'm intrigued. What's he mastered?

Kate: He's a gold medalist in mouth to mouth.

Me: Mouth to mouth?

Kate: Yes! And the things that man can do with his tongue...

Me: Tell me more.

Kate: Well, he starts with his lips on mine, which is fabulous. He moves down to my neck and stirs up all of these feelings . . . But there's so much more I'd like him to try. So many more places I'd like his mouth to explore.

Me: Yeah? What else would you like him to try?

I wait anxiously for her reply. Our texts have taken a turn I didn't expect. When her text comes through, I make sure Austin is preoccupied by the TV before reading. As I read her words describing the ways she wants me to touch her, my dick twitches. I stare lustfully across the room and blush spreads across her cheeks. And me? I'm turned on and itching to make her suggestion a reality.

"I need some ice cream," I say, standing from the bed and stretching. Hopefully this plays out the way I want it to. "You interested, Austin?"

Austin checks the time. "No, man. It's too late to be eating ice cream. I'm about ready to go to sleep."

"Okay. Kate? You interested?" I ask, looking up at her.

Please say yes.

"Yeah, I wouldn't mind some ice cream," she says with a mischievous glint in her eyes.

"Keys are on the dresser." Austin nods at them.

Kate slips her boots on and grabs a jacket. Snatching up the keys, we make our way down to the truck. That was surprisingly effortless. I thank my lucky stars my best friend is an old man trapped in a twenty-eight-year-old's body. Unfortunately, we aren't going to be able to get away so easily every time we want to be alone. There is always the chance he'll choose to go with us, and even if he doesn't, if we start taking off together all the time, he's bound to get suspicious.

Kate scoots over next to me on the bench seat and I put the

truck into gear. I pull out onto the road with one hand resting on her thigh. Kate cuddles into me, and we ride in silence for a few minutes.

"Do you actually want ice cream?" I ask.

"Not really." Kate looks up at me through her lashes, her cheeks stained pink.

"Me either." I pull into an empty lot.

The lot is dark with no working lights, and I find us a secluded spot near the rear. The truck has barely stopped moving before Kate has her arms wrapped right where they belong around my neck. She presses her lips against mine. The radio plays softly, barely loud enough to be heard, and a faint taste of watermelon hangs on my lips from the chapstick Kate is wearing.

"Come over here." Kate leans back onto the seat.

One little phrase and my dick is rising to attention.

"Abso-fucking-lutely," I say, crushing my mouth down on hers and hoisting myself up, resting my knee in the seat to turn my body to hers.

When I sink down closer to her, her legs wrap around my waist like they were made to fit perfectly around me, and I want to spend eternity between them. Kate pulls my shirt up, and we break our kiss just long enough for her to pull it over my head. With my tongue exploring her mouth, her hands run down the bare skin of my chest, faintly dragging her nails across me, sending shivers across my skin.

"I like your shirt," I say, breathing heavy and nodding at the T-shirt she's wearing. It's another one of mine that somehow ended up on her.

"Yeah?" She peeks down at it before flashing me a wicked grin and biting her lip.

"Yeah. It's never looked sexier. But we can explore that more later. For now, it needs to come off." I pull the shirt off her and suck in a breath at the sight of her lace bralette she's wearing under it, her nipples peaked and ready for my attention. Kate pulls the bralette over her head, fully exposing her breasts to me. "Fuck, you're gorgeous."

Grabbing the waistband of her leggings and thong at the same time, I pull them off in one fell swoop. She sits up and impatiently helps me with the buckle of my pants. I shove them down before laying her back on the seat, my own greedy hands anxious to roam her body and make the fantasies she texted to me a reality.

I have months, no, years to make up for with Kate. I am absolutely going to take my time and treasure every single inch, every single moment with my girl.

KATE SNUGGLES into my bare chest, our clothes strewn all over the cab of the truck. The windows are fogged up now, blocking our view of the darkness around us. Crickets chirping compete with the quiet crooning of the radio. Truthfully, it's kind of fun sneaking around like I'm sixteen again, but Kate deserves more than this. She shouldn't be loved in the shadows and ignored in daylight. That's not what I want for her, and it's not what I want for us.

Her fingers smoothly trace over the tattoo on the left side of my chest, the soft glow from the streetlights at the other end of the parking lot providing barely enough light to make out the dark ink on my skin. I don't have many tattoos, but I have a few scattered about. Kate lifts onto her elbow to take a better view. The loss of her skin pressed against mine leaves my side chilled, and goose bumps spread across my skin. Inside the horseshoe border, a young girl with long hair and angel wings rides a bareback pinto. The artist that did this one was amazing, drawing every little detail in realistic strokes.

"What inspired this one?"

"I got it for me, to help me remember, but I also got it for her," I say, pointing to the girl on the horse.

"Who is she?"

A flood of emotions pour over me as I release the memories I've kept locked up so tight. After a beat of silence, I exhale and search for the words.

"My little cousin, Anna. When I was in college, I taught riding lessons."

"I remember that."

"Anna was one of my students. She was seven years old. I was running late one day for her lesson. I called my aunt to let her know, and I hauled balls to get there. Anna was impatient and went ahead and mounted Jasper, her horse. She was riding him around the front of the property, which of course I didn't know.

"When I came up the driveway, I wasn't expecting Anna to be out there." I spoke softly, my mind drifting through the memory, a familiar ache filling my chest. "She and Jasper were coming around the corner to the barn, probably to greet me if I had to guess. They came around the corner as I drove by, slinging gravel. It spooked Jasper. He reared back, and Anna fell off him. I slammed on the brakes, jumped out, and rushed over to her. My aunt saw the whole thing through the window and ran out from the house."

I pause, squeezing my eyes closed at the memory of Anna on the ground. After taking an extra breath, I continue. "There was so much blood. Anna's lifeless little body lay there, and I didn't know what to do. My aunt called 911, but when the paramedics made it, they couldn't find a pulse. She was already gone."

"I'm so sorry, Caleb. I remember hearing about her accident, but I had no idea," Kate says, hugging me tight.

"You wouldn't. It's not something that is talked about."

Kate rests against me, her fingers splayed over my chest. After a moment, she looks up at me again.

"That's why you volunteer with the Buddy Up program, isn't it?"

"I couldn't help Anna, but there are other kids I can help." I grab hold of her hand and kiss it.

"Like Monty."

The accident put me in a really bad place for a while. I was so upset with myself for being late that day. Maybe if I'd been on time, she would still be alive. Maybe if I hadn't been driving so fast to get there, I wouldn't have spooked the horse, and everything would have been okay. It got to the point I could hardly get out of bed every morning. The guilt was eating me alive, and I couldn't seem to pull myself out of it. I stopped going to class and stopped teaching my other riding students. I dropped everything.

Austin saw the toll it was taking on me. He kept showing up every day, despite the way I'd cuss him and push him away. He showed up just the same. When I was in my darkest moment, Austin was there. He did for me what I couldn't do for myself.

It took time, a lot of it, but slowly he was able to draw me out of the darkness. I don't even like to consider how differently things would have gone if Austin hadn't been there. I owe everything to him, and I don't think I'll ever be able to repay him. The memories turn our blissful evening to one of guilt, thinking about sneaking behind Austin's back after all he's done for me. It's been a long time since I've let my mind run over that period of my life. Austin is right. It was bad. Even the memory of it hangs heavy on my mood, and suddenly the cab of the truck is closing in on me.

"It's getting late," I say, sitting us both up. "We should probably get going before Austin gets suspicious." Together we gather our discarded clothing, sliding each piece on before buckling in our seats.

Austin was there for me when nobody else could be. I would do anything for him, because I owe him everything. Austin and I are thicker than blood, and Kate . . . Kate is everything.

CHAPTER TWENTY

caleb

On my drive to the motel after feeding the horses, I make another call to Monty's assigned CPS worker. It's been a few days, and she hasn't followed up with me. Legally, she's limited in what she can tell me, but I need to hear that Monty is okay from an adult. I'm not sure that boy is familiar enough with the conditions considered appropriate to know whether he's okay or not. I press the phone to my ear, drowning out the roar of the engine, and focus on the sealed gravel road ahead of me.

"Hi, Caleb. What can I do for you?" Amy's voice replaces the ringing.

"How did things work out with Monty's mom? Is she using again?"

"Cutting straight to the chase today, huh?" There's a tired edge to her voice. "You know I can't answer that. Not without a release from Monty's mom."

I don't even try to disguise my frustrated groan. "You've got to help me out here, Amy. I'm out of town. My time is not my own this summer, and I can't go see for myself what's happening."

"I know. I get it. Monty is lucky to have someone like you in his corner. He's a good kid, but honestly most of them are." Her voice is softer now.

"How is he doing? Can you tell me that?"

"He's okay. I've offered services—"

"That she's probably not taking advantage of if history bears any significance."

Amy ignores my comment and continues. "And I'm checking in on Monty more diligently knowing your visits with him are limited right now."

"And if nothing changes?"

"Theoretically, because I can't disclose this information to you, if I don't see any changes after offering services and working with the parent, I would petition the court to remove the child from the home."

"And Monty will go into foster care?" I shift my phone to my other ear.

"If the court sees sufficient effort on my part to help the parents make the necessary changes without any progress from the parents, yes. They will grant the removal and the child will be entered into the foster care system."

I pull into the spot in front of our motel room and shut off the car engine, silently debating whether Monty going into foster care would be a positive or negative thing for him. I don't want him to go through that, but things can't continue like they are at home. It's not a safe environment for him, and he shouldn't have to worry about when he's going to get another meal or be left unsupervised and unprotected by an inebriated adult.

"If he goes into the system will I still be able to see him?" I ask, barely able to get the words out through the constriction in my throat.

"It depends. I would be happy to pass your information on to the foster parents and the caseworker who would take over the case. If the foster parents aren't comfortable with it, the caseworker may be willing to set up visits." After a beat of silence, Amy continues. "Or you could consider applying as a kinship placement to take Monty."

"I don't know how to take care of a kid."

My mind tries to picture what being Monty's full-time caregiver would look like.

"You don't give yourself enough credit. It would make the transition into care easier on Monty, too."

"I can't raise a kid on the road." My head drops back against the headrest.

"Allowances could be made for the travel since it's summer, so he wouldn't be missing school. You would mostly have to ensure he made it to his arranged visits with his mom, were that to happen. Once school starts, he would have to attend daily, of course."

"Yeah, and live in a bunkhouse with a bunch of rowdy ranch hands?"

"Well, no. You would have to find a suitable residence."

Even the possibility of this whole situation is infuriating. Grunting at the thought of everything it would take to turn me into an acceptable placement for Monty, I drop my head into my hand.

"Keep me posted, will you?"

"Caleb, you know I—"

"Can't disclose information to me on the case without signed consent from Monty's mom. Yeah, I got it." I let out a defeated grunt.

"I know this is frustrating and scary, but the important thing is that Monty is in a safe and stable environment. Even if that means he ends up staying somewhere else while his mom works on being able to provide that for him."

"I know. You're right. I want what's best for Monty."

Hanging up the phone, I head inside the motel room and review the rodeo schedule Austin has put together for the next two weeks. There's no way I could keep up with this schedule with a seven-year-old tagalong, but I made a promise to Monty before I left. A promise I mean to keep. The question now is what does keeping that promise look like? Austin has kept us busy traveling from rodeo to rodeo around Montana, and we've done decent so far, placing in most of the rodeos we've competed in. I was on fire for the first several competitions after Kate and I started messing around. Our secret is starting to get to my head a bit now, and I feel like it's creating a strain on my communication with Austin. We aren't as smooth together in the arena as we usually are, and my betrayal is the only reason I can come up with.

AUSTIN IS COLLECTING our winnings when I see the short kid gearing up to ride—Tuff is here, too. That means it's time to give the guy some special attention. Catching Austin's attention, I throw a nod in Tuff's direction. Austin follows the movement with his eyes, then he looks at me with a shit-eating grin. Great minds think alike.

I've had plenty of time to dwell on possible attacks, and I think I have the perfect one for today. We head out to pick up some dinner, and I add in an extra stop before we choose a place to park and eat. None of us are too anxious to shut ourselves back in the motel room, staring at the same four walls for the night.

I slide off the tailgate and gather up the trash from my dinner. Austin and Kate haven't finished theirs, so I grab the grocery bag from the cab and lay out my tools. Austin watches me as I work, but he doesn't say a word. I lay out the latex gloves, the fishing hook and line, and my pocketknife then grab the small lunch-size cooler from the bed of the truck. By this time, Austin and Kate are done eating—perfect timing—and I crack open the cooler. Within seconds, the putrid odor makes its attack against our senses and we're all bent over, gagging.

"What the hell?" Austin coughs out, finally gaining control of his dry heaving.

I don my gloves, take a deep breath from over my shoulder, tie some clear fishing line to my hook, and reach into the cooler for my first victim. Pulling out a small dead fish, I thread the line through the corpse and tie it, leaving myself about a foot of extra line on it. One by one, I repeat the process while trying to hold down my dinner.

"Where the hell did you get these fish, man?" Austin asks.

"Don't worry about it. You feel like going for a drive?"

"Where to?"

"The Mountain Lodge."

"Caleb Huxley, what are you up to?" Kate narrows her eyes at me.

"You'll see."

We load up and ride over to the motel, cruising slowly through the parking lot till we spot Tuff's truck. Conveniently, he's parked in a shadowed area of the lot, so the dark night will work in our favor. Kate stays in the pickup while Austin stands watch and I use a clothes hanger to unlock Tuff's truck door. Another perk of old trucks. You don't have to worry about a car alarm.

I get his door open and slide into the seat. One by one, I pull out the vent covers on his dash, drop a dead fish down the vent, and tie the loose end of the string around one of the grates of the vent cover. See? I'm nice. I'm making it easy for him to remove them once he figures it out. Clipping the vent cover into place, I move on to the next one. It only takes me a few minutes to finish.

Now, step two. I pour a bottle of milk into the cheap spray bottle I grabbed at the store and spritz the milk over the upholstery, making sure to sufficiently saturate the bench seat of his truck. Once I'm satisfied with a job well done, I lock the truck door and toss the cooler and gloves into the motel dumpster. I have no interest in trying to scrub the smell from that cooler. It's best to sacrifice it for the cause.

"You think that's sufficient punishment?" Austin asks as we take off down the road.

"Nope. But it's a start. And a good one. Can you imagine how much worse that's going to get after sitting in the hot sun? When he figures out he's got rotting fish in his vents, he'll think the problem is solved once he removes them. But by then, the milk should be thoroughly spoiled and stinking."

"You are a bastard, man."

"He has a lesson to learn. And we're limited in our options, thanks to this one." I poke at Kate's ribs, making her squeal. "He's not going to get away with talking trash about Kate."

"I couldn't agree with you more."

Kate huffs and shakes her head at us.

We make our way back to our motel to rest up for our second day at the rodeo—don't want our extracurriculars interfering with our performance. We go to bed early, opting for the extra sleep and feeling the satisfaction of a job well done.

When morning comes, we ready ourselves for another day spent at the fairgrounds. It's another hot one: eighty-six degrees. I've nearly sweat through my shirt by the time we rope. We have a decent run but end up in second place. Austin curses under his breath as we ride out to watch the rest of the event.

The evening perks up when we head to the motel. As luck would have it, we spot a truck pulled off the shoulder of the road. Austin slows down a bit and hugs the left side of the road, trying to give the truck room. As we get closer, we see Tuff hop out of his truck and puke over the guardrail. I roll my window down and hang halfway out of it as we pass, Kate yanking on my shirt, trying to pull me inside. Austin and I whistle and holler at him. He spots us over his shoulder and shoots us the bird. It's a glorious sight.

CHAPTER TWENTY-ONE

The dust stirs around me as I fight my way through the crowd, trying to find somewhere quiet enough for the conversation on my phone. It's Dawn, my boss from the diner back home.

"How about now, Dawn?"

"Yeah, sweetie, I can hear you better. Listen, sorry to bother you. I know we agreed you could take the time you need, and you can. Here's the thing, though. I had a mild stroke and I'm going to be out for a while. I've got to find someone to run the place till the doctor releases me to come back to work."

"I'm so sorry. That's dreadful. Are you recovering okay?"

"I'm taking it day by day. It could have been a lot worse, so I'm counting my blessings. The doctor thinks with therapy and time I should make a full recovery. But in the meantime, Kate, I was really hoping you would be willing to run the diner for me. There's nobody that knows the place better than you do. What do you say?"

"Dawn, I'm honored. But I'm a bit at the mercy of my brother, being as he's my ride. Can I get back to you with an answer?" There's no way I'm going back home to face my mom, but maybe I can figure out a solution.

"Sure, sweetie. Let me know."

I end the call and huff out a heavy breath. Things are going so well with Caleb right now, and I'm not interested in putting miles between us. It may not be made to last, but we're having a good time, and who knows, maybe we could be a forever thing. Maybe.

I search over the expanse of cowboys to find the ones that belong to me. Finding them, I settle my gaze on Caleb, watching every confident movement he makes. It's unrealistic to think we can continue on the road together like this all summer. It's a recipe for disaster. Dawn needs my help, and if Caleb and I stand any chance at something long term, we need to give it a try outside of our road bubble. Emily's roommate moved out recently. Maybe she would be up for a new one.

It's time to go home.

I peek over my shoulder at the door, making sure the coast is clear for Caleb and I to continue our conversation while Austin is out of the room. Caleb holds my hands in his, waiting for my answer. We'll be leaving—heading for home—when Austin gets back. Previously, we'd decided to keep our relationship a secret while we were all on the road together, but now that I'm going home, we have a decision to make. Austin's words resound in my head, telling me Caleb is sure to make a fool of me. Is he right? I can see it happening—Caleb growing tired of being with me and breaking my heart. Our little town would have a field day gossiping about what happened between Caleb Huxley and that poor little Farley girl.

"We could tell him now," I say, unable to hold Caleb's gaze. "But maybe we should wait a little longer."

"How long?" Caleb watches me intently.

"I'm not sure. Till the season is over for you two? I mean, he's not going to take the news well regardless of when we tell him. One way you'll be stuck in a motel room with him for the rest of the summer, and the other way you'll only have to deal with him at work."

Caleb doesn't respond right away.

Finally, he speaks up. "You have a valid point. But as soon as we finish rodeoing, I want to tell him. I don't want to have to continue sneaking around with you."

"We will. We'll tell him right away." I nod.

Austin returns and ushers us to the truck. The unplanned trip back home is going to add to their travel time and we need to get going if they're going to make it to their next destination in time. We pile into the truck and pull out of the motel parking lot.

As we drive down the highway, Austin breaks the silence. "You sure you're ready to face Mom again?" Without the usual music and conversation, the only sound is the hum of the engine. I keep my sight on the mountains ahead of us, my hands tucked between my thighs as the miles pass.

"I'm not going to stay at the house. Emily said I can stay with her. Her roommate moved out last month, and she's been debating getting a new one. I'm going to take the room for now."

"Not going to lie, I'm bummed you aren't going to be on the road with us anymore," Caleb whispers in my ear.

I peer up at him, hoping he can't sense the hesitation rushing through my veins. "Me, too."

Why did I think leaving him was a good idea? I was optimistic to think we could turn into something long term. I could be trading the last of our good days away without even realizing it. And if I'm not around, who's to say the girls on the circuit won't earn his attention?

After a long day on the road, Austin drives us through the center of town, making our way to Emily's. Nothing has changed in our quiet town, aside from the wild hyacinths now in bloom. There's a distinct comfort in being home, even amid the exhaustion from all the travel and turmoil of the last twenty-four hours I've spent weighing my choices.

The boys drop me off, and my self-control melts away as I watch them drive away, standing in the doorway of my new home. Emily, startled by my tears, hugs me tight.

"Hey, it's okay, girly. They'll be back. And I'm sure if you decide to go hang out with them for a few days on the road again, they'd be all about that."

"I know," I say with a tearful hiccup. "It's just all changing."

"Are you sure everything's okay?"

I turn to face my friend, debating whether to keep my secret or not. Emily certainly wouldn't win any bestie awards, but she has been there for me at times I didn't have anyone else. And I desperately need a friend right now.

"You remember me telling you I met someone?" Emily nods. "We might ought to sit down for this one."

We close the door and take a seat on the plush red couch in the living room. Pulling my knees up to my chest, I scrunch my toes over the suede fabric. I wipe the moisture from my cheeks and take a deep breath. The smell of coffee is steadily growing in the room as the automated coffee maker on the kitchen counter works through its brewing cycle. I start from the beginning, telling Emily about my encounter with Caleb at the ranch, about Tuff, and about Caleb and I finally getting together.

"You mean to tell me after all these years of daydreaming about Caleb, you finally got him?" Emily's eyes practically pop out of their sockets.

"Got a taste of him, at least. I don't think you could say I have claim of him."

"And how was it? Did he . . . *taste* good?" Emily wiggles her eyebrows at me.

"As a matter of fact, he is better than I could've imagined." I groan and drop my face into my hands. Wiping the tears away, I observe Emily as she dishes her next backhanded comment.

"Of course, you don't have much to compare him to."

"No, I don't. And I know the experience I did have was outrageously bad, but I can't imagine how it could be any better than it is with Caleb."

I lost my virginity the summer before my senior year of high school when I met a guy from Kansas finishing up his freshman year at Montana State in Bozeman. He didn't know my brother, and I thought maybe if I spread my legs for him, he'd stick around. I showed up at his dorm prepared to seduce him, and I succeeded, unfortunately. He had no clue what he was doing, and I obviously was no expert. It ended up being a painful experience with no happy ending—no happy ending for me, anyway. He got his quickly. Very quickly. And once we were cleaned up and dressed, he informed me he was dropping out of school and moving home. No strings attached.

"Austin is going to flip if he finds out."

"Yeah." My voice is barely more than a whisper. "He definitely will."

"I know I promised not to bring you into the middle of anything, but I have to ask. Was Austin seeing any other girls while you all were out on the road?"

"No, why?"

"I don't understand why he refuses to commit to a relationship. We're sleeping together, I talk to him every day, and it feels like a relationship. But it also feels like he's trying to keep me at arm's length. I thought maybe it was because he had another girl on the road."

"No, Em, I told you before you started seeing him,"—I shake my head—"he doesn't believe in relationships. You can thank our parents for that. He thinks labeling a relationship is meaningless. He says if marriage doesn't stop people from walking away, what's the point?"

"I guess that makes sense."

And just like that, the conversation shifts to Emily's efforts to snag my brother. Just another typical day of being Emily's friend.

THE WEEKEND PASSES QUIETLY with my focus on the diner. Dakota is waiting for me when I walk in, my eyes drawn to her mess of curly auburn hair. I am instantly jealous. She's new in town, and for her first shift, she'll be training with me.

I give her a smile as I tie my apron on, then I clock in, and Dakota and I get to work. She catches on quickly, and by the end of our shift, she's able to work independently on a few things.

"Did you grow up here?" she asks as we reset tables.

"Yeah, I've lived here my whole life."

"If you know anyone looking for a place to live, I'm hoping to take in a roommate. The house I'm renting isn't huge, but it's a two bedroom and it's a decent place. The rent is a bit higher than I was hoping for, though."

"I'll keep that in mind and let you know if I hear of anyone," I say.

I wipe down the last table and reset it. Lunch today was busy. It was the perfect rush to keep me focused on the moment and on serving my customers. I punch in the order of my newest table and prep their salads alongside Dakota.

We carry them out to the dining room and the plates of food clink against the table as we set them down. I check to make sure my customers have everything they need for their meal, and with the promise to return with refills for their drinks, I head to the main counter. Out of nowhere, my mother steps into my path, stopping me in my tracks. It's the first time I've seen her since I ran off with Caleb and Austin. She seems to be moving well today, but she's carrying a definite sadness.

"Kate, I heard you were back in town. I was hoping that might mean you'd come home."

"I moved in with Emily," I say, silently evaluating her visible symptoms. "I need to do me for a while."

Mom fidgets with the strap of her purse. "Kate, I'm sorry

for the things I said. You were right. I was giving up on myself and I was blind to the way if affects you and Austin." Silence hangs in the air between us. "I've started seeing that new doctor since you've been gone. I've only been to him once so far, but he seems to have a much better grasp on things. I think he might finally have some answers for me."

"I'm glad, Mom. You should have a doctor who cares about you getting better and not masking your symptoms."

"Looks like I haven't been giving my girl enough credit. It seems like you've been right about a lot of things."

"Have you been doing okay?" I finally allow myself to ask.

"I've been okay." She nods. "I don't want to get ahead of myself, but I feel like I've been having more good days lately."

"That's great. Well, I better get to work. Are you here to eat?"

"No, just wanted to stop by and see you. I won't hold you up any longer."

I reach out and wrap her in a hug. Good gracious, how I've missed her.

"I love you, Mom."

"Love you too, bug. Come by the house sometime. Don't be a stranger," she says with a wave, and I watch her walk away.

Grabbing the refills I'd promised, I drop them off before making the rounds to my other tables again, leaving the check for a couple of them. All the while I let the conversation with my mother soak in. The space we've had since I left with Austin and Caleb has possibly served us well. I don't know that Mom would have made the decision to fight for herself if I hadn't left. I think we both had become too complacent in our own ways. This time apart has been helpful.

CHAPTER TWENTY-TWO

caleb

Austin is in a mood. Per usual, he's put it behind him and is focusing on our competition. We are fifth in line. These guys have a lot of try and are running good times, but even so, I think we stand to place high. I slide my hands into my gloves and fidget with my rope, ready to go. For whatever reason, the crowd is lighter today than most days. It could be because of the dark clouds hanging overhead. Regardless, I shouldn't be experiencing this level of nerves. The announcer's resounding tone isn't helping.

When it's finally our turn, we run our best time all season, taking first place again. If we keep up this winning streak for the rest of the season, we should be close to reaching Austin's goal. We collect our winnings and return to the arena to watch for a while. We have one night left here and hit the road in the morning.

"Hey, isn't that Tuff over there?" Austin asks, nodding toward a cowboy eyeing us from across the arena.

"Yeah, looks like him," I say, taking a sip of my soda.

"I wonder what his deal is."

"Who knows. Probably looking for Kate or something."

I turn to the bronc riding in the arena and try to ignore

Tuff's stare down. It's not hard to do until he's standing right in front of us, a scowl on his face. His stance is wide, his hands clenched at his sides.

"Can I help you?" I ask.

"I should kick your ass," Tuff says, stepping into my personal space. Austin looks back and forth between the two of us and snickers.

"Uh-huh." I glower down at his maybe-a-hundred-and-seventy-pounds-sopping-wet physique. "And what gives you that idea?"

"I know it was you who screwed with my truck. And I also know you're the reason Kate broke up with me."

"Wait a minute." Austin straightens up from leaning on the fence, suddenly vexed. He stares me down. "What would you have to do with Kate breaking up with this joker?"

I shake my head. "Kate stopped seeing you because you're a twat. It wasn't because of me," I tell Tuff before glancing back to Austin. He's glowering at me suspiciously but leans back on the fence again, his arms crossed over his chest.

"I had something special with her," Tuff says, stepping up and shoving me. It causes me to sway, but I regain my balance without uprooting my feet.

"Something special, huh?" I ask.

"Yeah. She could have been my forever."

"That wasn't very nice of you, Caleb," Austin scolds me, though he's clearly amused by Tuff's demonstration. I roll my eyes and turn back to Tuff.

"Don't flatter yourself. You couldn't have handled her." I turn from him now. "Come on, Austin, let's get out of here."

"Actually, I think we should see how this plays out," Austin says.

"I'm not afraid to fight you for her." Tuff tries to get in my face and act all . . . well . . . tough.

Austin stifles a chuckle.

"And how exactly do you think that's going to work out for

you, little man?" I ask, crouching down to his level. "Do you seriously think you can take me on?" The size difference alone gives me an unfair advantage. Even if Tuff is a better fighter—which I doubt—he would be lucky to win this match.

"I'll sure as hell try."

"Fortunately for you, my mother taught me not to whoop up on kids littler than me. Come on, Austin. It's time to go."

This time Austin follows, laughing as we leave Tuff standing there by himself. That kid has a few things to learn, and I'd rather not waste my energy teaching him a lesson—like the fact that it's usually not a good idea to pick a fight with someone twice your size.

"I was really hoping for a showdown between you two," Austin says when we get to the truck.

"You're a jerk," I say, but I'm laughing.

"Why don't you get off that damn phone before you piss me off and get your head into the competition?" Austin is fuming next to me.

I could argue, but what's the point? I let Kate know I'm putting my phone away for a while, and I do my duty as Austin's partner. Truth is, being away from Kate has been harder than I expected. Having Austin around all the time makes video chats and even phone calls nearly impossible. Add in Kate's busy schedule running the diner, and we get very few moments to talk.

Tomorrow is our last day here, then we head to Stanford, Montana, for the weekend. We have a decent run but get beat out by two tenths of a second for first place. Austin isn't very happy about taking second place, but we're still in good standing. I hand Austin the drink I bought him from the concession stand and take a sip of my own.

"Hey, cowboy," a sultry voice says.

"Hey." I give the woman and her friend a polite nod but turn back instantly to the arena.

"My name's Lena. What's your name?"

"Look, I'm not trying to be rude, but I'm not interested," I say.

"I guess I have a confession to make," the woman continues, linking her arm in mine. "I already know your name. I know your buddy's name, too. And if you boys are open to having a good time tonight, we know just the spot." I glance over at Austin who stifles a snicker.

"Ma'am"—I turn to face her this time—"as I've already told you, I'm not interested. And I'm pretty sure my friend here isn't interested, either. Now I'd appreciate it if you'd kindly go about your business elsewhere." She pouts at me for a minute but eventually turns and struts away, and I go back to watching the rodeo.

"Why do the buckle bunnies always approach you, but none of them ever approach me? What's that about?" Austin asks.

"Probably because of your resting bitch face."

He chuckles at the jab. "I was thinking they're too intimidated by my rugged good looks."

"Should we start a poll? I don't mind going around and asking the ladies for you, but my money is on the big 'fuck you' that's always plastered to your forehead."

We've seen Tuff around a couple times since he threatened to beat me down. Austin continues to get a kick out of it and constantly gives me crap. Tuff must have come to his senses because he hasn't approached us again. He glares at me and boos us when we make it into the arena to rope. I'm not sure what Kate saw in the guy.

We cut out of the rodeo to find ourselves something besides concession stand food and pizza for dinner. Despite our slip from first place, Austin is in a decent mood, and we opt for a steakhouse dinner. Probably the hardest thing about being on the road so much is the food situation. We're constantly eating out for meals, and it often leaves us feeling like garbage. Evidently, I also forgot how to eat with a fork because I drop a piece of steak covered in steak sauce down the front of my shirt like a toddler.

"We're still good to swing through town Monday, right?" I ask as we leave the restaurant.

"Planning on it. Did you decide to go to the meeting about Monty?"

"Yeah. I need to officially get the ball rolling on it. You excited to see Emily?"

Austin cocks a brow at me. "I'm pretty sure I'm going to drop her. Truthfully I already have, kind of. Except she can't seem to get the message."

"What do you mean?" This is news to me.

"I told her a week ago I was done. She has called me ten times and I've lost count of the number of texts she's sent at this point."

"No kidding."

"She's a clingy one, man. I should have stayed away from the start."

When we get to the motel, I check my phone for missed messages from Kate but don't have any, so I kick my boots off, setting them aside, and pull off my sauce-covered T-shirt. Austin already has the TV turned on and I take a seat on the bed where I pretend to focus on the show instead of obsessing over the lack of messages coming to my phone.

I take my watch off and set it on the counter and check my phone again. No messages.

> Me: Hey, Trouble. Been thinking about you. Call me when you have a chance. I'd love to hear your voice right about now.

I drop my phone onto the counter and finish undressing for my shower. Checking the water temperature, I climb in and soap myself up while my mind runs free. Living out of motel rooms is starting to wear me down. I'm ready to be home with my people. I try to remember what our schedule looks like. Once we finish out this week, we should be able to make it home for a visit. We have a couple more weeks of back-to-back rodeos, followed by a week off, and then the final. After that, I'm free.

I rinse the soap away and stand under the spray of the water, letting its warmth sooth the soreness in my muscles. If I've learned anything this summer it's that I'm not interested in another season of rodeo life. I'm ready to settle down. And Kate might just be the one to settle down with.

CHAPTER TWENTY-THREE

Clicking through the time cards for each employee, I submit the final approval for paychecks for the week and send Dawn an email letting her know it's done. I slump back in the chair and groan. It hasn't been a horrendous experience with Dawn being out, but it's not too far from it. Most of the employees have handled the temporary transition. Of course, the one choosing to take issue with it is my best friend. What else could I expect?

> Me: You were supposed to be here 20 min ago. Where are you?

> Emily: Running late. You can MANAGE a few more minutes without me, right? Be there soon. 😉

Damn it, Em. This is the third time this week she's been late. When Dawn asked me to run things, I thought we were talking operational. I didn't even consider disciplinary issues. Leave it to my bestie to make sure I get to cover all my bases.

I print off the new schedule for the upcoming week and post it to the board outside the office. I was supposed to be out of here an hour ago. At this point, it feels like I'm always at work. Normally, it wouldn't be a big deal since Austin and Caleb are out of town and Emily has been acting up. Today, however, I actually have plans—plans that Emily's tardiness is getting in the way of.

When Emily finally makes her grand entrance, I request a word with her in the office.

"I gave you a warning that the next time you were late I'd be writing you up, Em." I slide the prepared form across the desktop to Emily.

Emily laughs. "You can't be serious."

"I couldn't be more serious, actually. You've always shown up to work on time. This pattern of tardiness has developed since Dawn left me in charge. We're best friends, Em. I know you haven't had any major life changes or struggles that you're dealing with all of a sudden. That means it's one of two things. Either you're taking advantage of our friendship by showing up late for your shifts, or you're blatantly disrespecting me because you have an issue with me. Either way, it can't happen. Not here at the diner. If you have a problem that you need to take up with me, it needs to be handled at home."

"Everything is always about Kate, isn't it?" Emily scoffs. "I knew you'd get a big head from filling in for Dawn. But the funny part is, you're nothing special. You're just Dawn's little puppet for a few weeks till she gets back, so get off your high horse, Kate. I'm not signing that write-up. You do what you want with it. As soon as Dawn is back, you'll be nobody all over again."

Emily storms out of the office and into the dining room. That went well. I drop my face into my hands. I need a break. I need out of this diner. I need something else to think about for a while. With a steadying breath, I lock the office door behind me and make my escape.

But I barely make it out the door before my attention is captured by the poster hanging on the diner window. There's going to be a small local rodeo competition this year at the county fair hosted by our town. Each night will be a different rodeo event, including barrel racing. I haven't competed since I dropped out of the rodeo in high school to take care of Mom.

Getting back into barrel racing isn't something I've considered before, so I'm not sure why the idea hits me today. Maybe it's because for the first time in a long time, I've started thinking about things in terms of what I want versus what I should do. This could be a good chance for me to see if I'm ready to give up barrel racing on my own terms. I jot down the information for registration and head out to my truck, knowing I'll have to think on it some more before I'm ready to make a decision.

In my truck, I check my phone for any missed calls or messages. I was supposed to call Caleb forty-five minutes ago. It's been almost impossible to find a chance to talk since they brought me home. Austin is always around Caleb, making conversations difficult. This was supposed to be the first time all week that our schedules lined up. I press the call button, praying he's available to talk. Ringing fills the silence on the line until eventually his voicemail picks up. Damn it.

I try one more time on my way to Mom's house, only to get his voicemail again. She called this morning asking for my assistance with cleaning out the big front closet. We never used it for the things it was meant for, like coats and such. We couldn't. Mom shoved box after box of things she didn't want to deal with into that closet. Now, it's one giant mess that we've avoided for years. There's no telling what we're going to find in there. Mom says a lot of the stuff is mine and Austin's, so she wants me to go through it with her and make sure she doesn't get rid of anything important.

I stand on the porch and knock on the door, something I'm not used to doing. Mom must have been close because she almost instantly opens the door.

"Good afternoon, bug. I'm glad you were able to come," Mom says, stepping to the side so I can enter.

"Yeah, no problem. You ready to get started?"

"I think so. I can't remember the last time we got into this stuff."

She opens the rickety closet doors, making them moan a bit from old age, and we get to work, sitting on the wood floors of the entryway, slowly figuring out a system. We sort through one box between us at a time. Mom and I dig through random contents and sort them into one of four piles: trash, mine, Austin's, and Mom's. It's slow and somewhat tedious, but we both find enjoyment in it.

"Remember this dog leash?" Mom asks, pulling the blue leash from the box. I smile at the memory.

"We worked so hard to talk you into getting a dog. We couldn't believe it when you finally agreed and took us to the pound to pick one out. Good ole Roscoe. We didn't keep him long."

"He kept peeing on Austin's pillow. We could never figure out why he did that."

"Remember how every time someone opened the door, he somehow escaped? We spent hours running after that damn dog."

"He lasted a month before you and Austin were sick of him, and we gave him to the Clarks down the road. They had him for about five years before he died." Mom sighs. "Do we trash the leash or hold on to it for the memories?"

"Trash it." I laugh. "We might be able to laugh about him now, but we hated that dog."

Item after item, we sort through the boxes together. It would go quicker if we didn't pause for the stories along the way, but it wouldn't be nearly as therapeutic.

"Do you remember this?" Mom passes a folded slip of paper over to me. I open it to discover my middle school suspension slip. Before I can respond, Mom is retelling the story. "You were wearing a new dress, like every year on your birthday. It was some sort of special field day, so Austin was outside, too. He said you were playing on the monkey bars. You were about halfway across when some little boy—well, he wasn't too little—came over and lifted your dress for everyone to see. You dropped down off those monkey bars and punched him right in the eye. He was twice your size at least, but he dropped to the ground, holding his eye and crying like a little baby. When Austin told me what happened, I don't think I could have been any prouder."

"I got suspended for a week from that incident. He got off scot-free. Well, kind of. He didn't get in trouble with the school, but Austin had words with him."

"That's the last birthday you wore a new dress. You said you were never wearing a dress again."

"I was so humiliated."

"You started wearing Austin's hand-me-downs instead. And Austin and Caleb started teaching you how to fight." Mom reaches over and squeezes my hand. "I'm sorry you had to go through that. I'm glad Austin stepped up for you over the years and tried to fill the hole your dad left. I'm just sorry there was a need for him to do it."

"You didn't have control over Dad's choices. That wasn't on you."

"Maybe not. But I do have control over my choices. I never should have allowed you kids to take on so much." She runs a hand up and down my arm resting on the box between us.

"It's okay. We've made a decent team over the years, and if anyone is to blame, it's him."

"Things weren't always so bad with your father. I've always been the damsel in distress and him the knight in shining armor who rides in and saves the day. That's how we met after all. I was stranded on the side of the road with a flat tire, and he happened to stop and help. After the tire was changed, he asked me for my phone number. We fell in love, married, and then Austin was born. A few years later, you joined us. We had the perfect family. Somewhere along the way, life placed its wedge between us, and we grew apart."

"You didn't notice his armor had rusted," I continue for her. She nods. "We said some hard and hurtful things to each other before you left. Maybe there's a better way we could have had that conversation, but it was a conversation that needed to happen. After all, you finally found a new doctor and I don't think I ever could have separated myself from helping you like I was without the extra shove. It was ugly, but it initiated the change that needed to happen. And we're better now for it."

"I like that spin on it, Kate."

I grab another item from the box, holding it up for Mom to see. It's a slow process, but eventually, we make it through the last box of memories. Scanning over the piles we made, it hits me. I've been so stuck in the routine of caring for her that I'd pushed aside the experiences and relationship we had before she got sick. And I hate the abrupt end to the junk she saved. So many years of missed opportunities.

Mom reaches over and gives my hand a squeeze. Her eyes have their sparkle back, and she has color in her cheeks again. We still have a ways to go and repairs to make, but we have our foundation again.

CHAPTER TWENTY-FOUR

caleb

The hardest thing I've ever done? Being face-to-face with my girl for the first time in weeks without devouring her instantly. That's it. Thankfully, it doesn't take Emily long to lock Austin away in her bedroom, leaving me and Kate the chance at a more appropriate reunion.

Deciding to avoid any possible complications, we take to the back roads in search of privacy. I know the perfect spot, on the property of a friend. The little grove of trees used to conceal a camper, but these days, all that's left is the weathered wooden deck and the old firepit.

We sit, wrapped up in each other, in the back of my pickup after making up for lost time. Kate snuggles into me, as though there's any space left between us. I breathe in the coconut scent of her, stirred up by my fingers twirling through the loose strands of her hair.

"Coming home was a shit decision," Kate says, breaking the peaceful quiet and making me laugh.

"Yeah, it wasn't your best idea, was it?" I rest my chin on the top of her hair.

"I needed to, but I didn't know how hard it was going to be."

"What do you mean?" My free hand captures hers on my chest, pressing it to me.

"It's not what I expected it to be. Any of it. Work is driving me nuts. Emily's being an ultra bitch. I feel like I never get to talk to you anymore, as if never seeing you isn't hard enough. And finding the new boundaries with Mom is weird."

"It's been hard for me, too. And I don't have all the extra crap you've been dealing with."

"I'm sorry. I'm not trying to play all 'woe is me.'" Kate sits up, one arm hooked around a raised knee. "And the last thing I want to do is waste the time you're home with griping about the time you're not home."

I straighten, following her example. "I know. But I want you to know you're not alone. It sucks being gone, and I miss you, too."

Kate's eyes drop. "You sure? You're not having too much fun to notice?"

"Having fun dealing with Austin in competition mode all of the time? You're kidding . . . No. I'm not having fun. I'm constantly thinking about getting home to you."

A smile slowly blooms across Kate's face again.

"I've got an idea. What do you say we knock off one of your bucket list items?" I ask.

"Which one?"

"Tattoo. We can both get something. To remind us we aren't so far away from each other even when it feels that way."

"I love that idea."

Within the hour we're at a tattoo parlor. Kate and I sit in neighboring seats while our artists prep their areas. Kate is bubbling with nervous energy.

"Are you sure we aren't going to regret it?" I ask.

"Yes, I'm sure. It looks good, right? And you trust this guy?" Her artist throws back his head and laughs. Kate holds the mirror up, eyeing my scrawl stenciled along her collarbone, ready to be tattooed.

Forever in my heart

I'm standing next to her now, hooking my finger around her chin so our eyes meet.

"It's perfect."

"Let me see yours again."

I turn my arm to display her stenciled script.

Always on my mind

"I can't believe you let me talk you into it. We shouldn't do it. This is permanent. Once it's done, there's no going back, no washing it away in the morning. It's a done deal." I take Kate's hands in mine, ready to combat the panic radiating from her.

"Hey, Trouble, listen to me. You are absolutely right. This is permanent. But so am I. I'm here, and I'm never leaving. If I have to take a beating from Austin every damn day, I'll still be here showing up for you. It's up to you whether you get a tattoo. You can do something totally different and mark off your bucket list item. But I can promise you one thing—if you get the tattoo today and one day find yourself regretting it, it won't be because I'm gone. Not even a tattoo can outlast me where you are concerned."

"Okay. Okay. We've got this. Are you sure we have this?" Kate asks, taking a deep breath.

"No doubt in my mind."

Kate leans forward and kisses me. "Okay. I'm good. Let's do it."

She lies back and gives the tattoo artist a nod, and as the tattoo gun buzzes to life, I reclaim my seat. I hate that my girl has had such a hard time lately. I know it's not just because of me, but I hate that I can't fix it. Hopefully these tattoos will make the hard days a little easier on both of us.

Kate makes it through her first tattoo like a champ. I

couldn't be any prouder. By the time we're done, Austin's been blowing up my phone, telling me to get to the ranch. Making sure the evidence of our day is covered, we go to the ranch to meet up with everyone.

Thankfully, Austin doesn't hold me hostage at practice for long. After a handful of rounds, the other guys start rotating in, and before long, our practice has turned into a social gathering.

"Let's go out tonight," Kate whispers in my ear. She's propped up on the fence next to me, watching the ranch hands make fools of themselves. Emily is standing on the fence several panels away, leaning into Austin. Trevor's horse whinnies and throws its head back, dancing to the side, agitated by something, and Ducky helps him calm it with a soothing tone.

"How are we going to manage that?" I want to spend every possible second with Kate, but Austin is going to get suspicious if we are sneaking off together the entire time we're home.

"I'll tell him I'm going out with Trevor. You tell him you're checking up on Monty or something."

Her solution catches me off guard, pouring a mixture of panic and jealousy over me. We never talked about exclusivity, but I assumed we were on the same page. We just got tattoos together for crying out loud. My pulse quickens, as my stomach churns.

"Are you still talking to Trevor? I thought that was over as quick as it started."

"No, of course not. But Austin doesn't know that. I've been here, and you two have been on the road."

Relief whooshes from my lungs. "Okay. Let's do it."

At the end of the day, Austin and I feed and settle BoJack and Trigger in their stalls, then we load up and drive to Emily and Kate's. Austin looks beat. When Emily turns on a chick flick, he doesn't even grumble. He must be tired. So much for him dropping her, I guess. I sit with them while Kate is getting ready. She wanted a few minutes to clean up before we left.

I've noticed Kate's been wearing makeup more and dressing

a bit frillier, but I'm not sure why. She looks good dressed up, but I personally think she looks just as gorgeous in her typical jeans and T-shirt. But if it makes her feel good about herself, it's worth the wait. She texts to let me know she's only a few more minutes away from being ready. I stand and stretch out my stiff muscles.

"I'm going to go check on Monty," I tell Austin. He doesn't even look up, just nods.

Soon, I'm leaning against the truck, waiting for Kate, when I see her appear from around the corner. Damn, she's gorgeous. I've got her door open by the time she makes it to the truck. She presses a kiss to my lips before climbing in.

"Where do you want to go?" I ask, getting in the driver's side.

"Let's find a bar or a pool hall somewhere outside of town. Somewhere we can get some drinks and have a good time but not have to worry about running into anyone."

"Works for me."

We end up in Bozeman and find a dive bar on the far side of the city. The place is packed when we get inside. We push through the crowd, my hand resting on the small of Kate's back, searching for an open seat. Just as we approach, a couple gets up from the bar and leaves, freeing up two seats. Kate and I claim them before anyone else can, and we wait for the bartender to make his way down the bar to us. When he does, we order a couple beers.

"What's on your mind?" Kate nudges my side from her stool next to me.

"What do you mean?"

"You look like you're miles away, and you have been nursing that beer like it could be your last." She smiles at me, but there is concern behind it.

"I'm sorry. We're supposed to be having fun." I finish off my beer and signal for the bartender to send another couple beers our way.

"It's okay. You can talk to me about whatever it is if you want." Kate's soft hand takes hold of mine and gives it a squeeze.

"I'm worried about Monty. I talked to the CPS worker and it sounds like things are moving toward Monty ending up in foster care."

"Things aren't going well with his mom?"

"Evidently not. Amy suggested I apply to be his foster parent if that happens."

Kate leans back in her chair and blows a raspberry. "Are you going to do it?"

I swap my empty glass out for the full one the bartender placed in front of me. "Nah. That would be crazy." I drag my finger down the condensation on the outside of the glass before glancing up at Kate. "Right? I couldn't do it. There's no way."

"Caleb, I think you might be the most capable person I know. I think you're thinking about it all wrong. If you want to do it, I think you should. You have the biggest heart of anyone I've ever met. You will find a way to make it work if you decide to do it."

A table of big biker-looking guys at a booth near us start getting rowdy, interrupting our conversation, and I let it fall by the wayside. It's too heavy for a night out with my girl. I need to snap out of it.

Pushing aside my worries, I wrap an arm around Kate. I have one more night with her after tonight, and I want to make the most of it. After our third round of beers, I switch to water and order pretzels and beer cheese to get some food in my belly. Hopefully I'll be ready to drive by the time we're ready to go. If not, we'll have to kill some time parked in the shadows. That would be a shame. How would we ever entertain ourselves?

Kate sets her empty glass on the bar, orders another beer and slides from her barstool with some change in her hand to pick a song on the jukebox. I watch from the bar, defending our seats. On her way by the table of noisy bikers, she catches a wolf whistle.

"Hey, baby, why don't you come settle down over here on my lap. I promise I'll show your fine ass a real good time," the one who appears to be the leader of the pack says.

Kate turns on her heels, fury radiating from her, her fists clenched tightly at her sides. She's one fiery-ass drunk. I hop up from my seat and put myself between Kate and the biker before she can start something that I'm not likely to be successful at finishing.

"Nope. We're not doing this tonight," I say, pushing her toward our seats. "Ignore them and come sit back down."

Thankfully, Kate complies easily enough. That could have turned into a nasty situation. Somehow Kate manages to get another beer down, along with a couple shots. I offer her some pretzels, but she's not interested. She's not going to enjoy herself in the morning.

"I've got to piss," Kate says loudly in my ear.

"Okay, do you need help getting there?" With as much alcohol as she has sloshing around in her belly, she's not likely to be very steady on her feet.

"No, I'm good." Her words slur together. "I'll be right back."

I watch her walk away, ready to go after her if she seems too off-balance. Surprisingly, she isn't doing too bad. Relaxing a little when I see her make it through the bathroom door, I turn to my water again.

"Let me buy you a drink, sexy," an attractive redhead now hanging on my arm says.

"No, thanks. I'm done for the night." I hold up my water and turn to face the bar again. She doesn't get the point.

"Well, that's no fun," she pouts. "I know a spot where we can find a little privacy."

Her hand slides up my thigh in the direction of my package. I stand abruptly, grabbing her hand and turning her down again, this time with less civility. She has horrible timing because Kate sees the whole thing. Kate shoves the redhead off me, making her totter back. I try to step between them and get Kate to her seat, but I'm not quick enough to stop Kate from landing a punch square on the girl's face. I grab Kate around the waist, pulling her off the redhead, but she's still swinging, determined to land at least one more hit.

"Damn, you sure caught that tiger by the tail, didn't you? I bet you've trained her real nice," the biker dude yells at me. "You sure you don't want to loan her out? Because I'd love to see her juicy lips wrapped around my cock."

And that, folks, was the magic phrase to make all common sense and self-preservation instincts go right out the window. By the time my fist collides with his face, his three buddies are already out of their seats. I'm a big guy, and I've been in my fair share of fights, but I'm not arrogant enough to think that I stand a chance against these guys. One of his cronies steps up to the plate now with a swing and a miss till someone grabs me from behind and the guy lands a few good ones on my face.

Kate, not interested in missing out, swings her foot up between my captor's legs from behind, hooking her foot on his junk. He drops to his knees, letting me go, and I grab Kate's hand, making a run for the door with our new friends charging behind us.

Traffic is on our side, and I'm able to pull straight onto the road, putting distance between us and the local watering hole. In the seat next to me, laughter bubbles out of Kate, and I let out a sigh of relief.

"Holy shit, can you believe that just happened?" Kate yells into my ear, making me flinch.

"No. No, I can't. That was a clusterfuck, Kate. We're lucky as shit we made it out of there."

Finally, we make it back to Kate's, but I don't get out. Instead, I look her over. She's too drunk and high on adrenaline to recognize the reality of the situation we were in.

"Are you okay?" I ask, examining her.

"I'm good, Caleb. That was so awesome. Did you see—" She sobers quickly, getting a good look at me. "Shit, babe! Look at your face."

I wince as she not so gently turns my face toward the mirror. My left eye is nearly swollen shut, which I already knew by my steadily decreasing vision. My jaw is already bruising, but my split lip has stopped bleeding.

"That guy really did a number on my moneymaker, didn't he?" I say, making light of the situation for Kate's sake. Tears are streaming down her face, her emotions magnified by the alcohol.

"I'm so sorry, Caleb. I'm so sorry," Kate says between sobs. I pull her to me, trying to soothe her.

"It looks bad, but it's nothing, Trouble, trust me. With a little bit of ice, I'll be as good as new in no time."

"This is all my fault."

"It's not your fault. I'm the one who started it. It's on me. But it's all good. We're both fine. Now what do you say we get inside and try to sleep it off?"

"Okay," Kate says, calming a bit.

Inside, Austin and Emily are already in bed, and Kate silently pulls me into the bathroom with her. She pushes me down on the toilet and turns to the sink to wet a washcloth. Holding onto the backs of her thighs, she stands between my legs, cleaning the blood from my face. When she's done, she kisses each spot with a tenderness I don't often see from my rough-around-the-edge's tomboy-turned-woman.

We both take some ibuprofen and get changed for bed. Kate climbs into her bed, and I curl up on the couch with a bag of ice, hoping to take some of the swelling down. I send up a silent prayer that I won't be stepping up for round two in the morning when Austin wakes.

CHAPTER TWENTY-FIVE

My mouth might as well be stuffed full of cotton when I wake, and my head feels like someone took a jackhammer to it. I roll over in bed, a groan escaping my lips as the light of the new day seeps through the curtains. And that smell . . . What is that smell? My nose crinkles at the mixture of sweat and alcohol.

Oh. That's me.

I sit up slowly, holding myself up with one hand and rubbing my temple with the other. Austin walks out of the bathroom looking refreshed and ready for the day. He stops briefly in my doorway to take me in. Yeah, I'm sure I'm a sight to behold this morning. He comes into my bedroom and takes hold of my hand, inspecting my knuckles.

"Your knuckles are bruised." Austin studies me for an explanation.

"Oh." I pull my hand away and slide it under the covers. "It's nothing. Got in a little squabble last night is all. You should see the other guy."

"Trevor?" Austin asks, his jaw clenching.

"No. He didn't do anything. I'm fine."

"You need to get in the shower. You smell awful. And take some medicine for your head. I know it's got to be pounding."

"Yes, sir." I salute him and yawn before collapsing back on my pillow.

"I'm going to leave in a second to grab some breakfast. You want anything?"

"Sure. That would be nice. Surprise me."

I force myself up from the bed and gather a clean change of clothes before locking myself in the bathroom for a shower. Turning the water on to warm it up, I pop a couple more ibuprofen in my mouth, hoping it will ease my headache. Using a generous dollop of toothpaste, I brush my teeth, doing my best to scrub away the taste of stale beer.

The shower gives me new life as it washes away the sweat and the grime. Once I convince myself I've scrubbed every speck of last night away, I shut the water off and wrap up in my towel. My headache has begun to ease a bit, and I think I might make it through the day. If I'm lucky.

Dressed now, I walk into the living room to check on Caleb. Austin isn't here. He must have left to pick up breakfast like he said he was going to. Hopefully he gets pancakes or biscuits—something to help soak up the alcohol that's still sloshing around in my system. Caleb groans and sits up, earning a gasp from me. His face only looks worse in the daylight.

"How are you feeling?" I ask, rushing to the couch.

"Like I was outnumbered in a bar fight," Caleb says. "Oh, wait. I was." I hand him a bottle of water and drop some pills into his hand. "Thanks."

I'm inspecting Caleb's face when the door swings open. Austin stops, the door hanging ajar, his gaze narrowing in on Caleb. I drop my hand from Caleb's cheek and take a step away, clasping my hands behind me.

"Would somebody like to explain to me what exactly happened last night?" Austin's voice booms through the silence.

When neither of us speak, he slowly stalks into the room, his glare flashing from Caleb to me and back again. "Kate's knuckles are bruised like she's punched somebody, and your face looks like it was used as a doorstop on a revolving door."

"I know how this looks, but I swear to you, Kate did not beat me up," Caleb says, rubbing his purple jaw.

Austin starts toward him like he's ready to add his own brushstrokes to the colorful masterpiece on Caleb's face. "Caleb, I swear to you—"

"I started a fight," I say quickly. "I punched some chick, and he broke it up." As soon as the words leave my mouth, regret pours through my veins. I single-handedly exposed us by giving away the fact that we were together last night. Caleb lets out an audible breath of dread, and Austin surveys us suspiciously, trying to match the bits and pieces of what little he knows together. "I was on my way here when I saw Caleb's truck at the bar," I explain, hoping my impromptu story doesn't land us in a bigger mess than what I've already got us in. "I told Trevor I wanted to stop in and see what Caleb was up to. We got in a scuffle with some other people at the bar, and we came home. End of story."

Austin continues to study us, letting the dust settle from my tale. I'm not sure if Caleb appears so miserable because his face hurts or from the stress of Austin discovering our secret. I'm pretty sure the latter is at least a significant factor.

"Is that what happened, Caleb?" Austin asks.

"That sums it up well enough."

"You sure about that?"

"I'm sure," Caleb says, accompanying his words with a gentle but pained nod.

"Get up and get showered. We're burning daylight," Austin says, shoving a bag of food into my arms and stalking out of the room.

"I'm so sorry." I sit on the edge of the couch next to Caleb, hoping he's not mad at me. "I was trying to save us from trouble and nearly blew it all out of the water."

"Maybe we should come clean and tell him we're together."

"No, not yet." My answer comes too quickly, and the resulting sting is visible in Caleb's expression. "It's not that I don't want to, but I just don't think it's the right time. I think we need to give it a little more—"

"It's okay," Caleb whispers back. "I better get up and get ready. We're supposed to be on the road soon. Last thing I need is to make us leave late, too."

I stand, offering a hand to help him to his feet. He accepts it, but when I press a kiss to his lips, he barely kisses me back. Dropping my hand, Caleb disappears down the hallway and the bathroom door clicks closed behind him. I sink onto the couch, flustered. What just happened? That clearly wasn't the answer Caleb was hoping for, but I can't shake the feeling that outing ourselves would be a death sentence to our relationship, and I would be the one left looking like the fool. I don't have long to speculate before my trainwreck of worries is interrupted.

"Kate. We need to talk."

My eyes shoot up to the opening of the hallway, but it's Austin, not Caleb. He's leaning against the wall, his arms folded across his chest. The pit in my stomach opens wider.

He knows.

I rise, facing him. Unsure of what to do with my hands, I tuck them into the back pockets of my jeans. I don't speak. If he has something to say, he can start. The silence is almost as uncomfortable as the turmoil Caleb left me with when he made his escape to the bathroom.

"Is what Emily said true?"

"That would depend on what Emily said."

"Are you hazing her at work?"

"What? She claims I'm hazing her?" I fold my arms in front of me. This has to be a joke.

"She says you've been giving her a hard time—"

"Your little girlfriend has been a complete bitch lately."

"First off, she's not my girlfriend. Second, you need to take it easy on her."

"Please tell me you're kidding." I turn away, running my hands over my face.

I don't have the patience for this right now. Frustration tries to escape my body through my jittery hands, and I suck in a sharp breath.

"She says you've been running around town with people you shouldn't be, Kate. Bringing different men home. She's worried about you, and honestly, I am, too. I don't want you to end up like Mom with a couple kids and no spouse to help you provide for them."

I spin around and take a step toward Austin.

"Are you being serious right now? Yeah, I know. I'd make a shitty mom. That's why I'm never going to be one." I shouldn't yell, but I'm beyond caring about composure. I step up toe-to-toe with Austin. "Even if any of that bullshit was true, you have no business caring about what men I bring home. Surely whatever habits are good enough for my big brother should be suitable for me as well."

"Grow up, Kate."

"I have grown up. You're the one who's struggling to see that. I'm not a little kid. My sex life is none of your business, but no, I'm not bringing men home. I'm not hazing Emily or doing any of the other crap she's said. I can't believe you would question me like this. Why are you so ready to believe anything that you hear about me?"

Austin's fiery eyes drop from mine to my neck. "Tell me, Kate, are those bruises from your bar fight? Or are those love bites?" His finger grazes my neck and I smack his hand away. "Is that what the fight was about? You got caught up with a taken man?"

"Fuck. You." The staccato of each word falls in time with each shove against Austin's chest.

Austin's brows furrow and his finger hooks the wide neckline of my T-shirt, tugging it down my shoulder. "Is that a fucking tattoo, Kate?"

"What the hell does it matter?" I yank away, covering myself before he can read the words. "Is that another one of your double standards? You can have all the tattoos you want, but I have to keep my skin unblemished? You're such an asshole, Austin."

"I don't know what's gotten into you, Kate, but you need to take a hard look at who you're becoming and decide whether you like it before it's too late."

"I hate you. I fucking hate you." I choke out the words and shove past him to my room.

caleb

K ate climbs off me and collapses on her stomach then props herself up on her elbows, resting her chin in her hand with a lazy grin on her face. I roll onto my side so I can better appreciate her naked body stretched out next to me on the bed and smoothly run my fingers up and down the knobs of her silky spine.

"I like you like this," Kate says.

"Like what?" Unable to resist any longer, I lean forward and kiss the dimple peeking through on her left cheek.

"In my bed, wearing nothing but a shit-eating grin." Her fingers trace the muscles in my arm.

"I like you like this, too." My grin stretches further across my face. "Naked, satiated, and . . . ready for round two?"

Kate laughs and stretches her torso up to reach a kiss to my lips. When she pulls away, though, her smile is gone. She tucks her arms against her chest, cuddling into me, her head resting on my bicep.

"I'm sorry about how things went with Austin this morning." I swipe away the hair that has fallen into Kate's face. Although she pretends to be unaffected by the memory, her features harden at the reminder. I can't help but wonder if we should be putting our relationship on hold until we can be upfront with Austin about it.

"Why? You're not the one that made him a colossal asshole."

"Maybe not. But I gave him the ammunition."

"Not you, Emily. And I don't want to spend our last few minutes together in who knows how long talking about my brother."

She has a point. Kate and I won't be seeing much of each other until we finish the season. It naturally puts us on ice for now. I check the time. Austin went to load up while I was showering, but he should be back before long. The last thing either of us needs is to have Austin find us like this.

"Do you have to go?" she asks, freeing an arm to skim her fingers across my bare chest.

"You know I do, Trouble. I wouldn't leave if it wasn't necessary. We've got your mom's house to save."

"Maybe I can come back out on the road with you two." Kate peeks up at me.

"As much as I'd love that, I don't think it's a good idea. But maybe you can come watch us at some of the closer rodeos. And I'll swing through town every chance I get."

"It's not the same." She groans and lays her head on my shoulder.

"I know. But it's not for very long." I kiss the top of her head and hug her to me then groan as I rise from the bed and start gathering my clothes. Kate remains stretched out on the bed watching me as I dress. Her eyes roam down my body, and her lip disappears between her teeth. "See something you like?" I wink at her.

"Absolutely, I do." She flashes me a naughty smirk. I step over to the bed and give her a kiss. She fists my shirt and tries to pull me onto the bed with her.

"Can't," I rasp. "Austin will be back any minute to pick me

up." That earns me a pout that resonates with my soul, but Kate gets up and throws her clothes on as well.

The faint rumble of a diesel engine outside, followed by a couple long honks announces Austin's arrival. Kate rolls her eyes at me. She holds tightly to my hand, leaning against my progression toward the front door. Austin blows the horn again. I open the door and give him a wave, so he knows I'm coming, and pull Kate in for a goodbye kiss. With her back against the inside wall where he can't see us, I lean down to her, pressing a long, sweet kiss to her lips. Kate's hand skims across the back of my neck, roaming up into my hair. Her other hand slides under my shirt, and I'm ready to toss her over my shoulder and carry her to the bedroom like a caveman.

"I don't have all fucking day, dipshit. Let's go!" Austin yells out his window.

"He's his usual jolly self." I chuckle. "I better go before he kicks my ass."

Kate steals one more kiss before she releases me. What I would give to have her riding in the middle again. I'm supposed to be a big tough guy, but I'll be the first to admit I left a chunk of my heart in Kate's hands. She has the power to determine my fate.

We've barely made it outside of town limits and all I can think about is getting back to her. But maybe it shouldn't be. I couldn't make out the details of their argument, but I caught the part about the hickeys and the tattoo. Austin doesn't know about us yet, and I'm already driving a wedge between them, slowly chipping away at the relationship they have with each other. I don't want Kate to become the next victim—the next person I inadvertently hurt.

There's always the option of cooling things off, but maybe telling him would change everything. He would undoubtedly be livid at first, but I'd rather he takes it out on me than to let this misunderstanding continue to break apart his relationship with Kate. I wish I could get Kate on board.

I glimpse at Austin, finally escaping my head. The roar of the engine is the only sound in the cab. Austin stares ahead, his eyes fixed on the road with an unusual determination.

"Sounded like things got pretty heated between you and Kate earlier."

A few silent seconds pass, making me think he isn't going to answer. "What of it?" He doesn't look away from the road.

"Nothing more than wondering if you were able to settle your argument before we left or if it's going to be weighing over you while we're competing."

It's just as well he doesn't look at me, because I'm not confident of how convincing I am right now.

"It's not my head anyone needs to be worrying themselves with. I'll be fine. Kate, on the other hand, needs to get a hold of herself and stop making stupid choices before she goes and does something she can't undo."

"So, you didn't make up."

Austin regards me, his eyebrows furrowed. "What the hell do you want?"

"Nothing. Nothing at all." I turn back to the window, slouching in my seat.

If it comes down to it, Kate could find herself having to choose between me and her brother. I wouldn't put that choice on her, but he might. And if he does and she chooses me, I don't know if I can live with the consequences for her.

Time is already dragging without Kate around, so I scroll through my messages with her, calculating the days until I can swing back through town. With a grunt, my head falls back against the headrest, defeat washing over me.

CHAPTER TWENTY-SEVEN

Either Emily moved out and forgot to tell me, or she is doing her best to avoid me. She had the last two days off work, and I haven't laid eyes on her since Austin and Caleb left a few days ago, which is why the tap on my door catches me off guard.

"Yes?" I look up from painting my nails.

The door creaks open and Emily peeks her head inside. "Hey, girl. Can we talk?

"Oh, you bet we're gonna talk." I twist the top back on the bottle of polish. "I've been waiting for a chance to have words with you."

"I know. The thing is, I owe you an apology." Emily wrings her hands, moving into my room.

Her unexpected start to the conversation throws me off.

"Damn right, you do. I'm really curious to hear your excuse for the lies you told Austin."

"I screwed up. I know that. But things haven't been going very good with Austin. Kate, he told me he didn't want to see me anymore. Over a text message, while he was on the road."

I scoff. "You two seemed pretty cozy while he was here."

"That's only because I convinced him to have one last hurrah when he came to town. He says we're done now. I've tried everything I can think of, and I can't make him care about me."

"I told you from the start that nothing would come of it with him. And you promised that you wouldn't take it out on me when things didn't work out." I cross my arms over my chest.

"I know, but Trevor told me a couple weeks ago that Brock heard I was seeing Austin, and that douchebag laughed at me. He said it had to be a joke, because guys like Austin Farley would never be interested in a girl like me."

"This is about your ex?" I ask incredulously.

"Not just any ex. It's Brock, the one that got away. And he thinks I'm pathetic now. I wanted to prove him wrong."

"Good hell." I shake my head. "Please explain how this involves me."

"When nothing I said changed Austin's mind about ending what we have together, I thought maybe if he needed me for something more, like to give him updates on you, that he'd continue seeing me."

"So, you made up a bunch of shit about me? Emily, have you lost your ever-loving mind?" I ask, aghast.

"I'm so sorry, Kate. I'm prepared to call Austin and tell him the truth. I never should have involved you. It was dumb, and I've been a total bitch."

"You realize that's only a portion of what you should be apologizing for, right?"

Emily stares back at me, her expression blank.

"If any hazing has been happening"—I stand from the bed—"it's been you hazing me."

"You're not wrong. I haven't made things very easy on you."

"You're supposed to be my friend—"

"I know. I've been a shit friend." Emily bites her lip and

shifts her weight from one foot to the other. "Can we please go back in time and start this summer over?"

I huff and drop on my bed again, Emily watching me silently. Part of me wants to accept her apology and hopefully move past all the recent drama with her. That's what the old me would do. If I'm being honest with myself, however, I'm not interested in stepping back into our one-sided friendship. Plus, she's never apologized to me before, so why now?

"Em, I'm willing to let go of all the things you have said and done, but I'm not okay with being used. I won't hold a grudge over past mishaps, but if you're interested in my friendship, you'll have to earn it."

"Totally, girl." Emily fluffs her hair and pulls the ends over her shoulder. "We should go out this weekend and hang out like old times."

"Yeah, maybe. I'll think about it."

"Okay, well, let me know."

Emily slides out the door, and I check the time on my phone. Dakota should be here soon to pick me up. We haven't decided what trouble we want to get into tonight, so we decided to ride together. I slip into my boots and clip my hair up off my neck. Gravel crunches outside, alerting me to her arrival, and I head out to her car.

"I grabbed us some snacks on the way over," Dakota says when I open the car door.

"Hey, this is random, but how would you feel about Emily tagging along with us tonight?"

"Emily? I didn't see that one coming. Yeah, sure. I don't have a problem with it if you don't."

"Hold on." I go back inside and extend the invitation to Emily, who drops what she's doing without hesitation and follows me out the door.

As I settle into the passenger seat, Dakota hands me a bottle of Diet Dr. Pepper—my beverage of choice—and gives Emily the option between the extra drinks she brought.

Dakota turns the car onto the road, and the tension immediately blows out the open window with the warm, summer air caressing my skin. I sink into my seat and inhale deeply, filling my lungs with the fresh scent.

"This is exactly what I needed," I say, stretching my hand out the window now, letting it glide through the breeze.

"Rough day?"

"Not bad, just not great, either. And this whole long-distance relationship thing sucks."

"Tell me about it." Dakota nods in agreement. Her boyfriend Derrick lives a couple hours away. "But it's worth it, right?"

Is Caleb worth it? I can't repress the grin that spreads across my face.

"Yeah. It's worth it." I take a sip of my drink. "We were planning to keep our relationship a secret until the summer is over, but I'm beginning to think we should tell people."

"Are you only keeping it a secret because of Austin?" Emily asks from the back seat.

"Mostly. And because I was worried whether Caleb would stick around or if I'd be a fling to him. It's nearly impossible to talk to him as much as I'd like while he's sharing a motel room with my brother, but I think he might be as crazy about me as I am about him."

"If he's as good looking in person as he is in the pictures you've shown me, I don't know how you're not telling the whole world. Clearly, you have way more restraint than I do." Dakota turns us down a road that leads into the canyon.

"He is," Emily says with a sigh.

It's not about restraint. It's fear that has kept my secret. The dread of following too closely in my mother's footsteps, of proving Austin and his doubts right, and of having to pretend I'm okay if Caleb gets bored with me.

My reservations are shrinking every day, chased away by

Caleb's promises and reassured by his touch. I don't want to bring it back up to him until I'm sure, but every day I'm a little closer to the benefits of making our relationship public outweighing the drawbacks.

caleb

As luck would have it, Tuff is riding at the same rodeo as us again this weekend. He's cooled off a couple degrees from what he's been, but he's clearly pissed at us and wants us to know about it. He hasn't said as much, but he doesn't have to—his scowls are sufficient. That's okay. I'm enjoying this silent war.

Austin and I wait across the street from Tuff's motel, watching the bubble on my phone's GPS move across the map toward the motel. We have one more errand to handle before we leave for our next rodeo. This one involves a special delivery being made to our friend this morning.

"He's here," I say, slipping my phone into my pocket.

I anxiously scan the walkways till I spot the delivery man walking up the stairs to the second-level balcony. He walks down the row of doors until he makes it to the right motel room and waits for someone to answer his knock. Tuff opens the door and accepts the package from the delivery man who doesn't waste time hanging around. Confusion creases Tuff's brow as he reads the shipping label.

I moan in frustration when he turns into the room and closes the door.

"Man, I was looking forward to seeing the look on his face when he opens that package."

"How did you even find a place to deliver a thousand live crickets?"

"The internet. Where else?"

Shrieks ring out from the motel across the street, catching our attention again. The shrill screams continue, and Tuff barges out of the motel room, sprinting down the balcony to the stairs, swatting the air around his head. His screams bring other motel guests hesitantly to their doors to see what the fuss is about. One brave guest tiptoes over to Tuff's door, still ajar, to inspect. After a moment, he walks over to the rail and yells down at Tuff.

"It's just crickets, dude!"

Austin and I double over in laughter. Tears are streaming down my face, and I'm laughing so hard I can't catch my breath. Tuff jumps into his truck and squeals his tires as he speeds down the road. Austin and I wipe away our tears and try to regain our composures.

"That was worth every penny," I chortle.

Austin pulls away from the curb and drives to the fairgrounds to grab the horses. It's time to head to the next town with yet another motel and another couple days of rodeo. Kate and I have continued playing phone tag, seldom finding moments we can both talk. Since Austin confronted Kate about the alleged hazing, Emily has been a little bit nicer to her. I think she feels bad about causing the fight between them and is trying to make up for it. Regardless, it means she's also demanding more of Kate's time and our lack of communication is taking its toll, but maybe it's a good thing. The space has given me extra time to think about what the right move is. I don't want to wreck Kate's life, and I'm not sure if that's more likely to happen by me staying or me walking away. Either way, I'm pretty sure the only ending to this story involves Kate getting hurt.

If we are going to make this work and come out in the open about our relationship, I should figure out the best way to tell Austin about us that will win me the fewest broken bones and bruises. There's no chance Austin will let me off easy.

I could try coming right out and telling him I fell in love with his little sister. I could ask him for his blessing to date the younger sibling he vowed as a teenage boy to protect. Ultimately, broken bones will heal. The main thing I need to worry about is keeping him away from sharp objects and my dick.

Dusk is settling over the landscape by the time we make it to the new motel. We're getting settled inside when my phone screen lights up with a notification. It's a message from Kate. I open our texts to see what she said. I'm excited when I see it's an audio message because I'll get to hear her voice again. I slip into the bathroom where I can listen to her message in private. My thumb hits the play button, and I turn the volume up.

"Seriously, Kate." It's Emily's voice. "I know you want to stay shut up in your bedroom all night with *Charlie*. But you've got to leave your room at some point. You're going to waste away."

"Do I, though?" Kate's voice rings out from my speaker. "Oh, shit. I'm recording an audio message somehow."

Who. The. Fuck. Is. Charlie?

Just like that, in the span of thirteen seconds I go from lovesick fool to jealous, raging caveman. I storm out of the motel room, needing space to deal with this new development. Austin is sitting in his usual fashion, boxers and a T-shirt, watching crime shows on TV. That's probably where his ideas of retribution will come from when I tell him about me and Kate. If I tell him.

My hands shake as I dial Kate's number, waiting for her voice on the other end of the line. The rough concrete of the sidewalk scratches at the soles of my feet as I pace back and forth. If she doesn't pick up, I may go insane. Eventually her voice drifts through the speaker, but it's a recording. I got her voicemail.

Immediately, I hang up and dial again, walking back in the other direction, away from the putrid odor seeping from the dumpster. Maybe she didn't answer because she's already with him. I'm already obsessing over this Charlie fucker and all the places his hands and mouth and . . . other bits will have the time to touch Kate before I can get back to town to stake a claim on my girl.

I stop. Maybe I've misinterpreted things. I run a hand through my hair. Maybe she's been so out of touch lately because she's seeing someone else. My mind races to replay each conversation over again and pinpoint a time when we discussed exclusivity. We did, didn't we? Shit, I don't think it ever came up. She's been talking to this Charlie dipshit while I've been on the road trying to save her mother's house? No, I won't accept that lying down. If she doesn't want me, that's fine. It's her choice to make. But I'll be damned if I'm going to stand to the side while she bangs some other dude.

"Hey, Caleb," Kate's voice finally answers, relieving a smidge of the pressure building up in my chest.

"Who the fuck is Charlie?" I ask as calmly as I can muster, given the situation.

I know it sounds like an accusation. A woman walking by with her child pulls the kid in closer and hustles by me, giving me a dirty look as she passes.

"Excuse me? What are you talking about?" Kate asks, the pitch of her voice rising.

"Please, just tell me. Who is Charlie? Is he there now?"

In the background, Emily bursts into a hyena-like fit of laughter.

"Oh, Charlie hasn't shown up yet," Emily yells loud enough for me to hear. "He doesn't usually come around until Kate's all curled up in bed."

Emily explodes into another fit of laughter. I lean against the rail for support and massage the growing bubble of pain in my chest.

"Em! Stop," Kate scolds.

I'm ready to kill this guy, whoever he is. The thought of another man's hands on her body rips my soul to shreds.

"Where is he? I want to talk to him." I force my voice to sound calmer than I am.

"I . . . He . . . It's not what you think."

"Come on, Kate. Are you going to tell him, or do I have to?" Emily asks, her voice muffled. "Fine. I'll say it." Emily raises her voice again. "Charlie is the nickname for Kate's vibrator. You want to get your hands on Charlie? He's in her nightstand drawer. Better take some extra batteries though. Even the Energizer Bunny can't keep up with Kate for long."

"Emily!"

I am such a fucking moron. I run my hand through my hair again and let out my breath in a rush, the tension slowly fading from my muscles.

"Kate, is that true?"

"Well, the bit about the Energizer Bunny was a little exaggerated."

I can imagine the glare Emily is receiving from her right now.

"But I got all fired up and ready to beat up a vibrator?"

"Yes. I haven't been with anyone but you, Caleb."

A sigh of relief the size of Mount Everest escapes my lungs. A door closes on her end of the line, and I'm guessing she's sought privacy after Emily's hijacking of our conversation.

"I got that audio message—"

"I'm sorry. That was a mistake. The phone was in my hand, and I guess I somehow started the message without realizing it. When I tried to delete it, I sent it instead. I didn't even think about the conversation it recorded or how it might be received."

"Obviously, I freaked out a little bit. I'm sorry, Kate. I don't want to lose you."

"Me neither, Caleb," Kate says, and I know she's speaking the truth.

I don't want to jinx it, but I think we've finally made it to the best part.

CHAPTER TWENTY-NINE

I'm counting down the days till I get to see Caleb again. The weeks creep by, and despite the days dropping off one by one, it feels like I have an eternity to go before this rodeo season is over for Caleb and Austin. It's ironic that Caleb and I finally get together after all these years just for us to have to do the whole long-distance thing.

I. Hate. It.

Caleb has made it home for one quick overnight—which included a short visit with Monty. Other than that, we've had to settle for FaceTime, phone calls, and texting.

A car door slams outside. Great. Emily must be home. After her apology, I thought maybe she'd gotten whatever issue she had out of her system and things were going to go back to normal between us. We've hung out a couple times, but it's hard to pretend like nothing happened. Plus, she gets jealous about the time I spend with Dakota and has reverted back to her evil self. It's been sneers and attitude with her ever since.

Emily walks in while I'm in the kitchen making myself lunch, music playing quietly on my phone. She glares at me before taking claim of the couch in our living room.

"Bitch." I hear her say, barely audible and accompanied by a snicker. I'm pretty sure it's Emily trying to taunt me, but I ignore it and go on cooking my dinner. A few seconds pass. "You heard me, bitch," Emily says a little bit louder this time.

"Excuse me?" I ask, poking my head around the wall separating the kitchen from the living room. "Were you saying something?"

"I don't want to hear your shitty music. Why don't you take it somewhere else? Like maybe back to your mommy's."

My blood instantly boils. The urge to come across the living room and throat punch her smart ass is almost too strong to resist, but I've turned over a new leaf. I've decided I'm not fighting anymore. I'm going to be a fucking lady. So, instead, I take my earbuds out of my pocket and smile delightfully at Emily as I pop one in my ear.

Once my lunch is done, I take it to go. I have plans to meet up with Mom for milkshakes at the diner before my shift anyway. Milkshakes at the diner was a weekly trip we did as a family when it was only the three of us. It slowly drifted to an end after Austin moved off to college and Mom's symptoms started getting less manageable.

Mom is already waiting at the diner when I arrive. I join her in the booth she's sitting in, and we place our orders. We make small talk while we wait for the milkshakes. She looks good. Possibly the best I've seen her in a couple years. Our milkshakes arrive and we both take a couple long draws off them.

"How's things with the new doctor, Mom?"

I take the cherry from the top of my milkshake and pluck it off the stem. She dabs her mouth with her napkin before answering.

"So good. You would really like him. He has a mindset much more like yours, and I've started making progress since working with him."

"I'm glad. You look like you're doing well."

"When I told him about filing for disability, he told me to throw the papers away. He thinks I could start looking for a part-time job. You know Austin's friend Jacob from high school? He is looking for part-time administrative help doing filing and answering phones. I've got a meeting set up with him this afternoon to interview for the position."

Actually, I'm acutely aware of who Jacob is. Yes, it's a small town, and yes, Austin went to high school with him. It's more than that though. Jacob is the man Caleb's ex-girlfriend broke up with him for. I wish I could hate her—you know, dated my man before me and all of that—but she's really nice.

"I'm proud of you, Mom."

"Thanks, bug. What have you been up to?"

"Not a whole lot. Just been working." I focus on my milkshake, twirling the straw between my fingers. There's so much I want to say, but I don't know if I should, yet. Not without talking to Caleb first. Then again, I already know where he stands. He's waiting for me, and I think I might be ready. "I did start seeing someone though."

"Oh? Who? Do I know him?"

"Yes." I focus on the straw rolling between my fingers. "It's Caleb." I watch her, expecting her to be surprised, but she's not. Her smile is soft and knowing.

"Well, it's about time. Does Austin know?"

"No. Not yet." I shake my head. "I'm afraid he won't be too happy about it." Mom reaches across the table and takes my hand in hers, giving it a squeeze.

"So what? He'll come around. I've been waiting for you and Caleb to get together for years." Mom must see the shock on my face. "What? You didn't think I saw the way you two look at each other? He's been your person for years now, Kate. And I could be mistaken that you've been his person as well, but I don't think I am."

"I had no idea I was that obvious." I press my hands to my cheeks, trying to ease the burn of embarrassment.

"There's been a lot of things wrong with me, but there's nothing wrong with my vision. Plus, I'm your mother," Mom says, tapping her finger on the table. After a few beats of silence, she continues. "There is something else we need to fill Austin in on."

"What do you mean?"

"I received another notice from the bank." Mom pulls an envelope from her purse, slides the letter out, and straightens it on the table.

"Are we out of time?" I push my milkshake aside, giving her my full attention.

"Not quite. The payments Austin has been making have helped, but it's a slow process." She slides the paper across the table to me. It's a formal letter from the bank. "The bank has decided to expedite the process of foreclosing on the home."

"Why would they do that?" I scan the documents.

"We've barely made the installments we agreed to in order to catch up. The bank doesn't think we're going to pull through, so they've moved up the deadline. Can you tell Austin for me? Our schedules seem to be completely opposite, and I don't want to leave it in a voicemail."

"Sure, Mom. I'll call him tonight." I push the papers over to her, and she folds them up and slides them into the envelope.

Conversation continues to flow while we finish drinking our milkshakes, but before long, it's time for me to clock in and start my shift. We stand from the table, and I wrap Mom in a hug. I'm so happy with the way things are going for her health. Hopefully soon, we will have the mortgage figured out, too.

My shift drags on, the news about the bank rushing the foreclosure occupying my mind the entire time. At last, I'm free and able to clock out and head home. But I don't make it far. Sitting in my truck in the diner parking lot, dreading the conversation I'm about to have with Austin and knowing there's no point in delaying it, I pull out my phone and dial his number. No sense in putting it off. The conversation goes about as well as I expected, with Austin pissed off and ready to burn down the world. After our phone call, I grudgingly make my way home. I have plans with Dakota tonight and desperately need a shower before I go. Thankfully, Emily isn't home when I pull into the driveway.

I'm stepping out of the shower when my phone rings. It's a FaceTime call from Caleb. Securing the towel wrapped around my body, I swipe to answer his call.

"Hey, beautiful," Caleb says, his typical smile filling his face. "Looks like I'm late."

"Late?"

"For the shower," Caleb says with a wink.

"Come home and you can join me next time."

"I'll hold you to it."

Carrying my discarded clothes and the phone, I cross the hall to my bedroom and perch myself on the bed.

"How was your day?" I ask.

"Nothing special. We got third place today, so Austin's a little bitchy tonight, but other than that, just the typical. Are you going to give me a show or what?"

"A show?" I shoot him a raised eyebrow.

"Yeah, or am I supposed to be able to focus on a conversation with you while you're sitting on your bed wearing nothing but a towel?" His sly grin makes me smile.

"No show for you until I get to see those pretty blue eyes in person." I set the phone down on the bed and quickly throw on some clothes.

"Soon. I'll be there as soon as I can be. You know that."

There's a peck on the door and Dakota sticks her head inside my bedroom.

"Hey, girly, don't mean to interrupt. Just wanted to let you know I'm here whenever you're ready to go. I'll wait out here," she says quickly and pops back out.

"What was that?" Caleb asks.

"Dakota and I are going out this evening."

"What are you ladies getting into? Do I need to worry?"

"No, she's my moral support. I'm crossing another item off

my bucket list. I'm getting a piercing tonight." I slide my feet into a pair of flip-flops.

"What are you getting pierced?" Caleb asks, a wicked glint in his eyes.

I can't hold back my grin. "You'll have to wait and see."

"Kate . . ."

"I should go. Don't want to keep her waiting." I grab my purse off the dresser and flip off my bedroom light.

"Kate!"

"Bye! Talk to you soon." I swipe the screen to end the call. I'm getting a daith piercing, but I'll let him ponder on all the possibilities for a while longer.

I'M PLEASANTLY surprised to see Dakota working lunch with me today. She's already turning into someone I would consider a friend. Plus, not only has she not met Austin yet, but she has a boyfriend. I can confidently say my friendship with her is not based on her level of attraction to my brother.

"How's the piercing feeling?" Dakota asks, prepping a salad.

"It's still a bit swollen and sore, but I'm managing. No regrets," I say, clocking in.

"That's to be expected. You're only a few days out, after all. It's going to be sore for a while. It's been a busy day, but it's been good for tips. I'm surprised it's been so busy, being a Tuesday and all."

"Tuesdays are the day the old timers like to meet up for breakfast here. On Friday mornings, they go to the bakery for coffee and pastries. They like to come and go first thing, so they don't have to wait for service."

"That would explain it," Dakota says. "When's that boyfriend of yours supposed to be back in town?"

"Not till at least next week. A lot of the rodeos are sched-uled too close together to warrant the drive home in between."

"That's got to be hard."

"It is. I miss him. I'm not really used to going so long without seeing him. Even while he was in college, I saw him most weekends," I say.

"What's your schedule look like this weekend then? Maybe since both of our boyfriends are MIA, we should hang out instead."

"That actually sounds like a great idea," I say. "Hey, are you still looking for a roommate?"

"Yeah, you know someone?" Dakota looks up from the ketchup bottles she's marrying.

"Would you consider me? Emily's so hostile. I think it's time I leave."

"Oh my gosh! I would love that! I hate living by myself. I'm chickenshit and get freaked out at night. Plus, it would be nice to have someone to split rent with. You can move in as soon as you want. I'm not worried about prorating the rent or anything. You can start paying with me on the first. The rest of this month is on me."

"Can I move in this weekend?"

"Absolutely!"

Maybe it's Dakota's good luck, but the lunch shift does seem heavy for a Tuesday. My tables keep me busy during my shift, and I have to hang around a few minutes later to finish wrapping silverware.

When I get home, Emily is standing in the kitchen eating one of my yogurts. She stares at me as she finishes the yogurt, licks her spoon clean, and drops the empty container into the trash can containing the other six yogurts I had in the fridge when I left for work today.

"Oh, I forgot to throw those out, didn't I? Hopefully you don't get sick. They expired last week," I say with a shrug. Her eyes bulge briefly before she composes herself.

"Whatever, bitch."

"By the way, as much as I've cherished my time living with

you, it's time I move on to bigger and better things. I'll leave my key on the kitchen table when I move out this weekend."

"We're already halfway through the month. I'm not giving you a refund."

"I don't expect one. First, it's short notice. Second, you would have to have at least a minuscule amount of maturity and class to do that, and you clearly lack both."

Emily shoulder checks me as she passes by me on her way to the door. At least I'll be able to pack in peace tonight.

caleb

I'm ready for a break from the heat, but we aren't getting it. We'll be leaving Glasgow, Montana, tonight after we compete and head to our next rodeo in Helena. It's in the eighties there, and I'll spend three days roping, riding, missing my girl, and looking for opportunities to play pranks on jerks. The fairgrounds are filled with excited energy—the stands stay full, and spectators bustle about the grounds. We're only a month out from the finals, and the reality of that has given everyone's dopamine levels a boost.

Austin and I get ourselves checked in, and we settle in for the day, making sure our horses are ready to go. I pick up a different rope than what I've been using and start messing around with it.

"You're joking, right?" Austin glares at me.

"I'm feeling like mixing things up today." I bite my cheek, trying to avoid the smile that is fighting to be freed.

Austin grinds his teeth, watching me for a few more seconds before going back to prepping his own gear. He takes choosing ropes and gloves for each competition seriously. You don't mess with a combination that's working well. Not if you want to continue to win. If I go with a different rope and we don't make first place, I'll be carrying the blame.

We're second to last in line to rope today. After us is the team that nudged us out of first place at the last rodeo. To say Austin is on edge is an understatement.

"Where the hell is my glove?" Austin is tossing our truck cab, looking everywhere for the damn thing and cursing himself the whole time.

"I've got another pair of gloves if you want to borrow mine," I say, knowing I'm setting myself in the line of fire.

"Are you as stupid as you look?" Austin glowers across the cab at me. "No, I don't want to use your damn glove. Do I look like I want to lose today?"

"Just offering." Austin turns his back to me, looking in the compartments of the door for his glove. "Hey, what's that in your back pocket?" His glove is hanging halfway out. Austin's hands fly to his pockets.

"Good hell, I was about to lose it." Austin pulls out his glove and puts it on.

"About to?" I chortle, and Austin glares at me as if daring me to continue speaking.

Several of the ropers ahead of us clock some good times tonight but nothing crazy enough to get us too worked up. Once it's our turn, we do our thing. I get the horns, Austin gets the heels, and we make it look easy. The hands reset while we exit the arena, and we watch from horseback as the last team gears up. They have a clean start, quicker than ours. I'm sure they are going to push us down to second place again, when the heeler only ropes one hoof. That's an automatic five-second penalty on their time, solidifying our place for the night.

We stop for dinner on our way back to the motel. With half of my burger eaten, my phone vibrates on the table next to my plate. Flipping it over, I see Monty's name on the screen and exchange looks with Austin who's sitting across from me in the '50s-style diner we stopped at. With a swipe of my thumb, I answer the call. Monty's sobs meet my ears before I can get any words out.

"What's wrong, Monty? Are you okay? Are you hurt?"

Austin drops a fry to his plate, his full attention on my conversation. My heart isn't the only one Monty has won over.

"Mi-Miss Amy ca-came and sh-she took me away."

"Take a deep breath and try to calm down, little man. What do you mean she took you away?"

"Sh-She took me fr-from Mommy. She says I ca-can't go home."

"Where are you right now?" My fingers tap anxiously on the table.

"At h-her o-office. Sh-she says she's f-finding m-me a new home. I don't wa-want a new home."

"I know, buddy. Take another deep breath for me. It's going to be okay. Miss Amy is trying to help. Is she there with you now? Can I talk to her?" Austin shifts across from me, listening intently.

"N-no. Sh-she went to g-get me a sn-snack."

"Okay. I'm going to call her on her cell phone and talk to her about what's going on, okay?"

"Okay." His little voice steadies.

"And Monty? You're not alone. I know this is scary, but you're going to be okay. Miss Amy is going to find you somewhere safe, and you always have me, too."

"Caleb?"

"Yeah, little man?"

"Why can't I live with you?" The sobs have been replaced with hope. "Miss Amy doesn't know my daddy, either. I could tell her you're my daddy."

Just like that, all the air is sucked out of my lungs. "Monty, it would be an honor to be your daddy. But above all else, we need to be honest and tell the truth. That wouldn't be honest of us, would it?"

"No." Although I can't see him, I know his little chin is tucked down to his chest like he does when he's disappointed.

"Don't you worry. I'm going to talk to Miss Amy and see what we can figure out for you."

Monty is sounding in slightly better spirits by the time we get off the phone. His situation shouldn't be such a surprise to me. Amy all but told me it was about to happen. But my heart breaks for him, and I hate that I'm so far away and helpless when he needs me, even though it wouldn't make any difference if I was there tonight. There's red tape to go through in a situation like this, and we have to play by the state's rules. Amy's contact information comes up on my screen and I push the phone icon to call her. It's time to make some serious decisions.

AMY CLOSES the folder in front of her which holds a stack of papers filled with my personal information and notes from the team meeting we just completed. We were able to swing through town on our way to Glasgow to get the process started with DCS. Monty is grinning up at me like I hung the moon. I hope this works out. I was hesitant to fill in Monty on my decision to try to get custody of him. If things didn't work out, I didn't want to disappoint him. When Amy talked to his foster parents about it, we discovered Monty was determined that things would happen this way anyway, so we decided if things don't work out, it would be better for Monty to know that I tried than for him to think I didn't care.

"Am I going to live in the bunkhouse with all of the cowboys?" Monty asks, his expression lit with excitement.

I chuckle and observe the amused grins around the room. "That would be pretty cool, but it would get boring after a while. I think we better find our own place. What do you think?"

"Yeah! We should get a house with a pool."

"I don't know about all that. I'm getting ready to go look at a house with my realtor. It's supposed to be a pretty good one. Do you want to go with me to check it out? You can give me your vote on the place."

"Can I really?"

"Let's ask and see if you have time today."

Monty jumps from his chair and runs to the other end of the table where his foster parents sit. His hyper voice pleads for permission, and when they nod in agreement a resounding "Yes!" echoes through the room.

Monty jabbers the entire way to the house about how great it will be to live in a house together and get to see each other every single day. He doesn't slow down enough for me to reply to any of his questions but just keeps rattling on. My realtor, Greg, is waiting for us on the front porch when we arrive. Monty is out of the truck and halfway up the porch steps by the time I make it from the driveway to the sidewalk.

"I think this is going to be a good option for you, Caleb," Greg says, reaching out a hand to shake mine.

"How much of the land comes with the house?"

"It's only two acres with the house, but you're surrounded by the neighbor's farmland, so you get the feel of a huge piece of property without the upkeep."

"Except I want the option of using the acreage. You know that. We already discussed acreage is a nonnegotiable, Greg."

"Humor me. Let's look inside and try to keep an open mind until you see what all this property has to offer."

We walk into the house, and Monty takes off running through each room, exploring every closet and nook. The house is newly remodeled, and I can see why Greg wanted me to see this one, but I've been clear about what I want. And this house isn't it.

"I don't really like this house," Monty says as he comes into the kitchen where Greg is pointing out the quality of the cabinets and the updated appliances.

"Why not?" Greg asks, crouching down to Monty's level.

"It doesn't have any furniture. And there's no barn. Where will we keep the horses?"

I don't bother trying to hide my amused grin.

"You bring your own furniture to put in the house." Greg stands again, and the look of annoyance on his face pisses me off.

"I agree, Monty. We've got to have a barn for the horse."

Monty runs for the door, done with our tour, and I follow.

"I haven't even shown you the upstairs yet," Greg says in protest.

I stop and turn to face him. "What did I tell you about acreage, Greg?"

"It's a nonnegotiable, I know, but—"

I walk out the door, not waiting for him to finish. "Non-negotiable, Greg," I call over my shoulder.

CHAPTER THIRTY-ONE

It takes several trips, but eventually, all my belongings are loaded into the back of my pickup. I take one final walkthrough of my room, making sure I haven't left anything behind, and I place my key on the center of the kitchen table with a note for Emily letting her know I'm officially moved out. Who knows, maybe having some space will allow us to get on better terms again.

Locking the door behind me, I pull it closed and climb into the driver's seat of my truck. Relief floods over me almost instantly. No more worrying about Emily messing with my stuff or being on the receiving end of her glares and misplaced judgment. I mean, she's still working at the diner, but that's now the only place I have to face her.

The drive over to Dakota's is a short one. In the driveway I give myself a moment before climbing out and getting to work. The curtain in the window flutters, and soon, Dakota is bounding down the front steps of the little rental cabin. It only has two tiny bedrooms and a bathroom that's closer to the size of a closet, but it's quaint and cute and free from Emily's neverending attacks.

"Hey, welcome home," Dakota says following me to the back of the truck.

"Thanks, again. I can't tell you how much I appreciate you letting me move in. I don't know how much longer I could have survived under the same roof as Emily. She's brutal."

"Don't mention it. You're doing me a favor, too. I hate living alone almost as much as I hate depending on a man." Dakota is smiling but with a wicked glint.

I pause and inspect her carefully. "What did he do?"

She doesn't need any clarification. She knows I'm asking about her boyfriend. Rolling her eyes dramatically, she reaches for a couple bags from the bed of my truck.

"Oh, just the usual. Overpromising and underdelivering. Again. He was supposed to be coming to visit me this weekend. He was going to be here in time for dinner, leaving work early and everything. But wouldn't you know, something came up. Again. Now he's not coming at all. Not worth the trouble to see me, I guess."

"Dakota, that's horrible. I'm sorry." I grab a couple bags as well and follow her into the house.

We step into the living room and peace instantly crashes over me. I've been to Dakota's house countless times, but knowing it's my place too has drastically changed the energy here. A leather couch lines the back wall facing the entertainment center positioned between two front windows. A potbellied stove sits off to the side, a tidy stack of logs accompanying it.

"Has he been here to visit yet?"

"No. Always claims to be too busy. The only time I get to see him is when I go to him. And even then the attention isn't what I want it to be. He says it's because they are so much busier during the summer, and come fall, he'll be able to make more time for me."

Dakota pushes open the door to the spare bedroom—my bedroom—and sets the bags she's carrying on the floor. The room fits a full-size bed and a nightstand on the wall across from the built-in drawers and closet.

"Maybe you should be too busy for him, too." I'm only half joking.

"Maybe you're right."

Dakota and I continue unloading the truck. "You're off this afternoon, right?" I ask.

"Yep, off till closing shift tomorrow. You?"

"Same. How do you feel about a road trip?"

Dakota pauses, turning to face me. Curiosity flits over her expression and I know I've caught her attention with my suggestion.

"Where to?"

"Caleb and Austin are competing tonight in a rodeo only two hours from here. I was considering surprising them."

"I think that sounds like a blast. What time do we need to leave?"

"Not for a few more hours. Maybe we can get permission to take Monty with us, too. Caleb would freak out. And Monty has been dying to see Caleb compete."

"Let's do it."

It doesn't take long to finish unpacking with Dakota's help. She sticks with me the entire time, helping me find homes for all my belongings and gossiping about our men. It's such a nice change not having to listen to details about my brother's sex life for a change. If no other good has come from my broken friendship with Emily, that alone is a pleasant perk.

After reaching out to Amy, Monty's caseworker, and getting clearance to take him with us, Dakota and I get ready to go to the rodeo. I take my time, trying to apply my makeup perfectly and choosing the most optimal outfit for the occasion.

"You look gorgeous. Caleb is such a lucky guy," Dakota says earnestly. "You sure know how to rock a pair of jeans. I never see you wear a dress though."

"Yeah, I haven't worn a dress in years."

"Why not?" Dakota cocks her head to the side and a frown overtakes her face. I tell her the whole humiliating story, and she responds with sympathy. "What a punk. I'm glad Austin didn't let him totally get away with that."

"Yeah, Austin is always ready to come to my defense."

"Well, if you ever have interest in trying a dress again, I've got several I'm happy to share. I bet your legs would look a mile long in a sundress."

She's right. I do have nice legs, but I never show them off. Her offer plants the idea firmly in my head, and suddenly, I'm wondering what Caleb's reaction would be to seeing me in a sundress.

"You sure you wouldn't mind if I borrowed a dress?"

"One hundred percent." A smile spreads across her face. "Are you interested?"

"Maybe."

"Come on. I'll show you what I have to choose from."

Dakota leads us into her bedroom, a flipped carbon copy of my own, and lays out dresses on her bed. When she said several, she wasn't kidding. My fingers graze over each dress until one captures my interest. I lift it from the bed, letting the silky fabric glide through my fingers.

"Can I try this one on?"

"Try on any of them you want."

Before long, I'm standing in front of a full-length mirror, fisting the skirt at my sides. The hem of the dress falls right above my knees, a soft-white floral print covering the navy fabric. Releasing the fabric trapped in my hands, I twist back and forth, letting the skirt dance around my legs. The bodice hugs my body; its puffy cap sleeves claim my shoulders.

"What do you think?" Dakota asks.

"Honestly, I love it."

"Keep it."

My head whips over to Dakota. "What?"

"Keep it. That dress fits you like a glove. From now on

anytime I put that dress on, I'll remember how much better it looks on you than me, and I'll probably never wear it again. And that would be a shame. It's an amazing dress. So, you keep it." Dakota shrugs.

I look over myself again, twisting and turning to get a glimpse from every possible angle.

"Thanks."

On our journey to the rodeo, we pick up Monty from his foster home. He excitedly climbs into the middle of the bench, sitting between me and Dakota. Smiling up at Dakota, he watches her closely.

"Is your hair real?" Monty asks, his eyes roaming over Dakota's head.

"It sure it." Dakota looks at me and we both laugh.

"Are you sure?" Monty turns to me now. "What do you think, Kate? Have you ever seen hair that color?"

Dakota and I burst into a fit of laughter. "That's called auburn," I tell him. "It's beautiful, isn't it?"

Monty looks back at Dakota now, tentatively reaching up to touch a strand. "Auburn?"

"Yep." Dakota smiles down at him. He seems to be lost in thought. Finally, his eyes rise to meet hers again.

"You're beautiful. I've never seen a girl as pretty as you." He rubs the ends of her hair between his fingers.

"Thank you. That's quite the compliment."

"You want to be my girlfriend? I don't have one right now. I asked a girl at the park yesterday to be my girlfriend, and she said yes, but my foster mom said that doesn't count."

"As tempting as that is, I already have a boyfriend."

"Figures. All the good ones are taken." Monty turns forward in his seat now, his shoulders slumped.

"You'll find the right one someday," I say, trying to hold back my smile now.

The remainder of the trip is uneventful aside from Monty chatting our ears off in excitement for the entire two-hour drive.

By the time we arrive, he's stolen Dakota's heart, and I'm pretty sure she's stolen his as well. Her boyfriend better watch out.

Monty walks between us now, holding both our hands as we search the grounds for the two cowboys we came to see. Somehow, Monty spots Caleb first. He's perched by himself on the fence near the barn, where their horses are probably staying in rented stalls, waiting for the rodeo to start. It takes all the restraint I can muster not to take off running to him.

"Caleb!" Monty screams as soon as we are in earshot. Caleb's gaze shoots straight to him, and a brief flash of confusion is replaced by the sweetest grin. Caleb hops down from his seat and his eyes trail up to me, holding Monty's hand. Just like that, I lose all restraint.

caleb

Nearly tackling me in excitement, Kate climbs me like a damn tree. I fall backward into the fence as she plants kisses all over my face. Setting her down, I try to silently calm her. Truth be told, I'm as excited as she is.

"What are you guys doing here?" I ask once she's firmly on the ground. My eyes roam over her, taking in every inch. She's wearing a dress, and I can't get enough of it. I haven't seen her in a dress in years.

"We had the day off and wanted to surprise you," Kate says. "Where's Austin?"

"He went to the bathroom. He should be back—"

"Kate? What the heck are you doing here?" Austin cuts me off.

Kate doesn't immediately go in for a hug like usual, clearly not completely over the tiff they had. Austin tugs her to him anyway, and once they collide, Kate's arms wrap loosely around him.

"I owe you an apology," Austin says.

Kate's eyebrows shoot up. That's not a phrase that Austin spouts often.

He continues. "I was out of line the other day. I should've

never believed Emily over you. I don't know what I was thinking."

"You're right. You shouldn't have, but thanks for the apology."

"I'm not going to see her anymore. A little birdie has been telling me about some of the shit she's pulled on you. When I found out, I ended things with her."

"Thanks." Kate shifts, ever so slightly wringing her hands. "Oh, this is Dakota. Dakota, this is Austin," she says, pointing to her brother before turning to me. "And this is Caleb."

"Nice to meet you," Austin says, taking her hand and holding it a moment too long.

I lift Monty up overhead and spin him around. "And what are you doing here, little man? Have you been making moves on these ladies to get them to bring you to the rodeo?"

"No!" Monty giggles, pleased with the attention. When I lower him, he catches his arms around my neck and hugs me. "I missed you, Caleb."

"I missed you, too." I squeeze him tight before setting him on the ground.

"Austin, they need you in the press office," a lanky cowboy hollers over.

Austin nods in reply. "Guess I better see what's going on."

Before long, Monty pulls Dakota away in conversation, holding tight to her hand as he leads her along the side of the arena. I motion for Kate to see the way Monty hangs on Dakota's every word. I think my little friend has a crush. Taking advantage of the distraction, I grab Kate's hand and we disappear into the barn behind us.

"I've missed you so damn much." I wrap her in my arms and hold her tight, pressing my body against hers and breathing in her scent.

"I've missed you, too," she says as her hands slide up my chest to my face. She pulls me down to her level, pressing her lips to mine.

"This is the best surprise ever."

I wrap a hand around the back of her neck and lean into her, bringing her mouth to mine and dipping her slightly backward. She hooks her arms around my neck, and in one fell swoop, I lift her, wrap her legs around me, and carry her into a nearby empty stall. She giggles as I press her against the wall and kiss every inch of her exposed skin. As my lips wander over her, her giggles transform into soft moans.

"Stop." She giggles again when I hit a ticklish spot. "Austin could come back any time. He's likely to come in here and beat you up."

"If I had to take a beating every time, it'd still be worth it," I say, my voice gravelly, then I kiss her dimple.

"I'll take that as a compliment." Kate strokes my cheek.

"You should. You're thoroughly perfect."

"You're only saying that because you want to get laid." Kate kisses me again.

"Hell yeah, I want to get laid. There's no question about that."

I press my hips into her, letting her feel the effect she has on me. She gasps and grinds against me, her legs around my waist.

"What's stopping you?" Kate asks in a breathy whisper.

My mouth crashes against hers again, and I slide her down my body till her feet meet the ground. Breaking our kiss, I kneel in front her. Her curious, hooded gaze watches me. "You're sure about this?" I ask, looking around us. The stall we've claimed isn't rented, but we could easily be found.

"Please, Caleb."

Her simple plea is all it takes for me to completely lose myself in her, no longer thinking, only doing and feeling. Our bodies tangle together, making up for lost time. Once the summer is over, I never want to be away from her again. As I bury myself in her, I know we aren't meant to be apart.

Eventually, we come up for air, satisfied for the moment.

With my face pressed into her mess of hair, I breathe her in and kiss down her neck as I wait for my legs to steady.

"You okay?" I ask.

The side of her face is pressed against the wall, mouth agape.

"Oh yeah. Guess I can cross 'quickie in a barn' off my bucket list now."

I chuckle and release her hands I'm holding captive over her head. Taking a step back now, I retrieve her underwear and pass them to her.

Then I pull up my pants, buckle them, and place one last kiss on Kate's lips before we amble down the breezeway, hand in hand.

We buy food from the concession stand and claim a spot in the bleachers to watch the starting events of the rodeo. Austin is distracted by Dakota. He's not competing with Monty for her attention, but my buddy might be as enraptured by her as his competition.

Monty bounces excitedly in front of me in the stands. It's not his first time at the rodeo, but it's his first time this season. He slaps at my arm for my attention and points out the rodeo clown hiding in one of the barrels. Eventually, he jumps up from his seat and his half-eaten hot dog capsizes against his shirt. He turns to me, wide-eyed and unsure of what to do next.

"Oh no. That's no good. You can't go around wearing ketchup for the rest of the night." I use the napkins we have left in an attempt at cleaning him up.

Taking his hand in mine, we make our way out to the vendors, where we find a booth with button-up western shirts for sale. There's one close to Monty's size and I purchase it for him. We swap out his soiled shirt for the new one, and he runs his hands down the front of it, clearly proud to be dressed like the other cowboys.

"Now I need a hat," Monty says. He drags us along to another vendor where I fit him for a cowboy hat and make the purchase.

When the roping events draw near, Austin and I pull ourselves away from the girls and get ready to compete. I want a good run now more than ever. The two most important people in my world are sitting in the bleachers watching me tonight. When it's our turn, we ride out to our boxes. I wave up into the stands at our fan club, now on their feet to watch us. Monty stands on the bench, Kate's arm wrapped around his waist, holding him steady. It's a sight I hope to be able to admire for years to come. Focusing back on the arena again, I wait for our steer to be released. We make it through our run like a well-oiled machine, taking first place again.

At the end of the evening, it's time to part ways. I wouldn't have thought it was possible, but saying goodbye this time around is even harder than it was the last time. Maybe it's because I already know how bad my chest aches when Kate's not with me. Maybe it's the worry that she's going to need something, and I won't be there to help make sure that she gets it. I know she's a grown-ass woman and she can take care of herself. She's more than capable. But just because she can doesn't mean she should have to. If it was up to me, she wouldn't lift a single damn finger unless it's something she wanted to do. The woman is my queen, and I'm already committed to a lifetime of servitude to her.

Kate is wrapped up in my arms, her head tucked beneath my jaw. Her tears drip from her cheeks and soak into my shirt, eroding my soul with each little drop. If it lightens her load even in the slightest, I'll take it till it washes me away.

"We won't be apart as long this time, Trouble," I say in a hushed voice and kiss the top of her head.

"I don't want you to be gone at all."

"I know. And I don't either. But we've almost made it through. We only have about another six weeks until the final rodeo. And the week before that is wide open." Kate shifts in my arms to look up at me through her wet lashes.

"Will you promise me something?" Kate asks.

"Anything."

"Once this circuit is finished, never do it again."

"Deal." That is one promise I know I can keep.

"Dakota seems nice," I say. It's been a few days since the girls surprised us, and Austin and I are on our way to get checked in at our next rodeo.

"Yeah, seems a hell of a lot more stable than Emily ever was," Austin says without looking at me. He probably doesn't think I noticed how much attention he was giving Dakota the whole night.

"She's pretty, too. And has that curly-hair look going on. Looks a lot like your type." Austin catches on and glowers at me.

"She's got a boyfriend, dickhead."

It's hot as hell tonight, the August air stale and thick. We're last to rope, giving me plenty of time to get caught up in my head and let the nerves take over. Austin watches each run quietly, and I try to follow suit. Finally, after I've nearly sweat through my shirt, it's time to glove up and go.

We ride into our boxes and wait for the steer to break loose before charging after it, ropes swinging. We rope it clean and pull a solid time, squeezing us into first place by a tenth of a second. Another night for the win. We have two more nights here before we head to Wolf Point for a few days.

"Whatever rope or glove or underwear you're using," Austin says as we ride out of the arena, "don't change them. We keep this up and we are going to be looking pretty for the final in September."

I try to quash the smile fighting to be freed. I know exactly what my lucky charm is, but I bite back the comment on the tip of my tongue, opting not to start any trouble by telling him where my luck is coming from—his sister.

kate

Nothing could ruin the mood I'm in today. It's another busy day at the diner, and Dawn is slowly taking over again. Caleb and Austin should make it to town sometime late tomorrow. Caleb seemed sure of what he wanted when I talked to him on the phone last night, and I think I'm ready to believe him when he says he's not going anywhere. It sounds like we're on the same page with telling Austin about our relationship. All the pieces are finally coming together.

I grab the two plates of pancakes off the warming rack and carry them out of the bustling kitchen to the table, sliding them in front of my customers. I do a quick visual check to ensure they have everything they need. The sweet maple scent of the syrup rises from the table as they dress their pancakes.

"Is there anything else I can get you?"

"Nope, I think we're good for now," the woman says.

Glancing over my tables, I head toward the kitchen to check on another order, following up at the drink station to grab refills and deliver them to the appropriate tables. As I head into the kitchen, my phone vibrates in my pocket. My orders aren't up yet, so I take the moment to pull out my phone, hoping it's Caleb.

Tuff: I can't believe you dumped me for him.

I roll my eyes. Tuff has been texting me the last couple weeks. At first, I responded, but after a few different episodes of his whining, I decided to ignore him.

Tuff: He's not being faithful to you. I've seen him with buckle bunnies at every rodeo since you left.

Tuff: You chose the wrong guy to bet on.

"Kate, is everything okay?" Dakota asks, coming over to me.

"Yeah, this guy can't seem to get the hint." I slide my phone back in my pocket.

"Is it that cowboy from the rodeo again?"

My phone buzzes several more times, convincing me to check it again.

Tuff: You're a whore.

Tuff: You deserve whatever you catch from that loser.

Tuff: I've already told all the other guys on the circuit what a slut you are. Even gave your phone number out to a few.

Tuff: Better have your price list ready because when they call you asking for favors, they'll be ready to pay up.

"What the hell is wrong with this guy?" I hand my phone over to Dakota so she can read the messages.

Alarm washes over her face, and her mouth falls open.

"Kate, are you sure he's stable? What type of person would go off like this after one date?"

"Do you think I should text him back?"

"I don't know. He might be harmless, but who knows. Maybe you should tell your brother."

"I'd rather not have to bail Austin out of jail." I laugh, but it's forced.

"Maybe Caleb then? I feel like they should be aware that this guy is harassing you. Especially if their paths are going to be crossing at the rodeos."

"You might be right." I put the phone away and grab the entrées for one of my tables.

We finish up breakfast and the lunch crowd teeters in. My phone has continued to go off all morning with texts from Tuff. Reaching my breaking point, I switch the phone off, hoping to forget about the harassing messages.

As things start to slow down a bit and I'm only running refills to tables, I start rolling silverware on my downtime. I wouldn't usually say this, but I'm ready for the summer to end.

Dakota grabs a spot next to me to work on her silverware. She's become someone I can trust and confide in. She's so different from Emily. Her boyfriend lives in Missoula, about three hours away, so she understands the struggle. When we aren't working, we hang out together, but she's not breathing down my back constantly, trying to get me to go out drinking with her or asking me about my brother. It's been refreshing to say the least.

I make it home from my shift excited to be only a day away from seeing Caleb. And my brother. But mostly Caleb—except the messages from Tuff come back to mind. Caleb never gave the buckle bunnies the time of day while I was on the road with them, but what if my absence changed that?

There's a loud knock at the door. Confused, I make my way to the front of the house and look through the peephole. All I can see is a mess of blue. I sling the door open, and I'm greeted by a bouquet of blue wild hyacinths and the most handsome grin I've ever seen.

"Caleb." I leap into his arms, not waiting for an invitation. "What are you doing here? I wasn't expecting you till tomorrow."

"I wanted to surprise you." He squeezes me tight, lifting me and carrying me back inside. "These are for you," he says, offering me the bouquet.

"They're my favorite. I can't believe you remembered." I grab a vase from the cupboard, stuff the stems in, and fill it with water. "They remind me of you."

"Me?" Caleb chuckles. "Because I'm dainty?"

"Your eyes, actually."

"My eyes are dainty?"

Laughing, I say, "Nothing about you is dainty." I give him a pointed look and a smirk spreads across his face. "It's the color. They match your eyes."

Caleb steps into my space, his sudden nearness sending electricity through my body.

"Do you have plans tonight?" Caleb finally asks, skimming my arm with the backs of his fingers.

"No."

"Will you go out with me?"

"On a date?" I can barely focus on his words, my senses basking in Caleb's presence: his scent; the deep, velvety tone of his voice; the feel of his calloused fingers; the warmth of his breath on my skin.

"Yes. I want to be with you, Kate, and I want us to do it right." His voice dances softly to my ear as he inches closer. "No more sneaking around or caring what other people think."

He nuzzles my hair, shooting warm currents straight to my core. I stand silently, soaking in every bit of him. Finally, my tongue breaks free from the trance.

"Yes. I'd like that."

Caleb presses a kiss to my forehead. "Whenever you're ready."

"I need to change."

It's dark by the time we leave. We get in the truck and Caleb drives us out of town, down a familiar road. I scoot in closer to him. His hand drops from the gear shifter to my thigh and gives it a gentle squeeze.

"Caleb."

"Trouble."

"Are you taking me to Lover's Lake?"

A mischievous smirk spreads across his face. "What if I am?"

"Are you trying to give me a reputation?" Leaning away from him, I fold my arms and feign offense.

Caleb winks at me. "The only reputation I'm interested in giving you is the reputation of being my girl."

"Yours, huh?" I lean back to him and hug onto his arm.

"Mine."

"I like the sound of that."

It's not surprising that we are the only ones at the lake. Actually, I don't think people are supposed to stay up here past dusk, but they don't have a gate blocking it off, so nothing is stopping us. Caleb lifts me down from his side of the truck and grabs a basket, blanket, and lantern from the back seat. We stroll down the path that wraps around the lake, my hand tucked securely in his. Finding a clear spot along the trail, Caleb spreads out the blanket while I hold the lantern, and we claim our spots.

"I brought some snacks and drinks." Caleb pulls containers from the basket.

"What are you up to?" I eye him suspiciously. "Most people don't picnic in the dark."

"You caught me. We aren't really here for a picnic, but I didn't know if you'd had a chance to eat after work, so I brought a few things."

"What are we doing here?"

Caleb moves the basket and food aside, lying back on the blanket, and pats his shoulder, inviting me to use him as a pillow. I comply, curious to see what his plan is, and once I settle, he switches off the lantern.

"What do you think?" Caleb asks in a soft voice, holding me close.

There's no light pollution up here. The only thing I can see in the blackness of the night is what's illuminated by the crescent moon, which isn't much. Lying here, the sky wraps around us, presenting us with the most magnificent display of stars—stars so bright they feel close enough to reach up and pluck from the sky. The quiet water of the lake reflects the scene, only engulfing us more.

"It's beautiful, Caleb."

"We're supposed to have a meteor shower tonight. In about an hour, actually. I thought this would be the perfect place to witness it." He kisses the top of my head.

The perfect tranquility nearly convinces me we're the only two people on earth. The chill in the air kisses my skin, threatening to break me out in goose bumps, but the heat radiating from Caleb protects me from the effects of the crisp night.

Sure enough, the night sky puts on a performance for us. At first, it's one or two stars streaking across our view. Gradually, they become more frequent, their fiery tails blazing through the expansive sky.

This right here, lying under the stars with this magnificent man, is what life is supposed to be like. It's what I've been waiting for. Maybe I can have it all, too. For some reason, I can't escape the whisper in the back of my mind telling me it's all too good to be true.

As the show comes to an end, I yawn, fighting the exhaustion from the stresses and excitement of the day.

"You ready to go home, Trouble?" Caleb shifts, angling

himself toward me, and gently swipes a stray strand of hair from my face.

"Are you coming with me?"

"Do you want me to?"

"I'll be offended if you stay anywhere else tonight."

Smiling, I rest my palm on the side of Caleb's face. He leans into me, kissing the dimple I've learned he's obsessed with before trailing kisses to my lips. My hand slides into his hair, and I deepen our kiss, savoring the taste of him.

Caleb breaks our kiss, his breathing ragged. "Let's get you home before you get us in trouble."

Caleb's phone lights up on the blanket next to us. He quickly slides it into his pocket without checking the message first. That's weird, right? The accusations in Tuff's texts from earlier today drift into my mind and the words escape before I have time to think. "Tuff said you've had buckle bunnies all over you at the rodeos since I've been gone."

It's not an accusation, but I want him to confirm what I already know to be true. Caleb sits up, his smile vanishing. He rests his forearms on his knees, staring out into the lake.

"You've been talking to Tuff?" Grabbing a twig from beside the blanket, he tosses it into the water.

"No." I sit up and when I grab his bicep, he looks over his shoulder at me. "I don't talk to him. He's been blowing up my phone."

"I don't have any interest in anyone but you. Seriously, I hope you know you can trust me. I would never cheat on you, Kate. I might do a lot of dumb things, but that's not one of them." Caleb twists toward me.

"I know that," I say, and I mean it. "I guess I didn't realize he got in my head until you ignored the message you just got on your phone."

Caleb pulls his phone back out and offers it to me. "Here. Check it."

I shake my head. "I don't have to. I know better."

"I don't care if you do. I want you to see for yourself, because I've got nothing to hide from you, Kate." He unlocks the phone and shows me the notification. "It's a reminder for myself to talk to you about telling Austin. I think it's time."

"You had to set a reminder?"

"What can I say? I get a little distracted around you."

"I think it's time, too. Plus, I really want to keep you around because Charlie gets a bit temperamental sometimes and I have to knock him on the nightstand to get him going again."

When Caleb smirks, I can't hold back my grin.

"What are you saying, Kate?" With a handful of his shirt, I pull him into me. His hand slides around the back of my neck. "I do a better job than Charlie?" We are nose to nose, and I instinctively wet my lips in anticipation of his kiss.

"I never said *that*."

"Maybe we can settle it once and for all right now."

Suddenly, his lips are on mine, and I'm pulling him closer. His fingers release the tired ponytail holding my hair up and wind through the strands, sending goose bumps across my skin. I brace myself on his muscular shoulders now and hoist myself onto his lap, wrapping my legs around his waist. It's been too long since we've been together, and every touch from him ignites my body with desire.

Craving the heat of his bare skin pressed firmly against mine, we are both stripped naked in a matter of seconds. I gasp as he flips me onto the blanket, and when he climbs over me, his warm tongue on my cool flesh making me instinctively arch into him, I know without a doubt that I will be forever safe in his arms.

CHAPTER THIRTY-FOUR

Strong, warm arms hold me as I drift in and out of sleep, and I remember it's Caleb in bed next to me. My heart is full, and I don't think I've ever experienced a bliss like this before. One of his hands rests on my breast, the other hand on my waist, pulling me against him, the little spoon to his big spoon. We made love last night before coming back to my place and fell asleep together. We woke up a couple times in the night and made love all over again. I could happily spend my whole life like this. It's as though I've walked into a dream, and for once, I'm sure enough about the outcome to want to tell everyone I know.

I reach between us, surprised to find him wearing his boxer briefs. Undeterred, I slide my hand inside them, earning a tired moan from Caleb. He's already hard, and I'm ready for another round.

"Why do you have these on?" I ask after trying to clear the sleep from my throat.

"I had to pee. Didn't want to risk surprising Dakota," Caleb says.

I roll in his arms onto my back so I can reach his lips and

kiss him. He shifts, lifting his body over me and sliding his legs between mine.

"Damn, you're gorgeous. I'm one lucky man," he says, sweeping my hair off my face.

He's kissing me again and ever so slowly descends my body like it's his personal mission to kiss every inch. Reaching down to where he has settled between my legs, my fingers rake through his hair, grasping a handful as a moan escapes my lips. I sleepily arch into him. His hand snakes up my body to my breast, the warmth of his calloused hand on my cool skin making me shiver.

My bedroom door swings open, slamming against the wall. I scream and try to cover myself with my arms. Caleb's head pops up and he shifts himself off me, covering me with the blankets.

Austin stalks into my bedroom, fury emanating from every pore. For the first time in my life, I understand why people find my brother so terrifying. Caleb climbs out of the bed, ready to face my brother's wrath.

"Austin, we need to talk—"

Austin's fist connects with Caleb's face and my scream pierces the room. Emily gasps, standing in my doorway next to Dakota. What is happening? Why is Austin here? How did he find out about us? My mind is spasming, shock holding me in place.

"Okay," Caleb says, "that's fair. Now let's put the fists away for a minute and talk about—"

Smack.

This time Austin's fist lands on Caleb's bare side, hunching him over in pain. Before he straightens, Austin is already rearing back and punching Caleb in the face again. This time blood streams from his nose. My brain finally catches up, and I'm able to move from screaming hysterically to lifting myself off the bed, my blanket wrapped around my naked body, and rushing to Caleb.

"Austin, stop this!" I scream through tears. "Why are you doing this?" Austin doesn't acknowledge me. Instead, he swings again. "You're going to fucking kill him, Austin, stop!"

"Damn right, I'm going to kill him."

He sets himself up to strike again, only this time Caleb steps back and straightens.

"Okay, Austin. I let you get a few good swings in, but I've paid my dues. No more," Caleb says, wiping blood from his face with the back of his hand.

Austin doesn't hesitate to lunge at Caleb, initiating a sparring match between them. After a couple exchanges with no sign of resolution, I take matters into my own hands. Austin isn't expecting it when I throw my fist into his jaw. He hobbles back, more stunned by the unexpected blow than the force behind it. He rubs his hand over the spot where my fist connected with him, and it finally looks like I have his attention.

"If you don't leave my room this instant I will never speak to you again," I say, low but firm.

If he cares enough about me to do this to Caleb, surely he cares enough not to risk losing me. And he does. A grumble reverberates from his chest, and he stalks out of my room, Emily following close on his heels. I drop down next to Caleb who is sitting on my bed holding his T-shirt to his gushing nose.

"Let me see," I say, despite not knowing what to do. "I don't think it's broken. So that's good."

Caleb lets out what could almost be a chuckle. "Do I have all of my teeth?" He pulls back his lips for me to see.

"It appears so." I delicately hold his battered face in my hands.

"Damn. Least he could've done is make me look like a tough guy."

"By knocking your teeth out?" I ask incredulously.

Caleb shrugs. "Would you date me if I was missing my front tooth?"

"Well, yeah, but—" The throbbing in my hand demands my attention, and I wince in pain.

"Did you hurt yourself?" Caleb gingerly takes my hand in his and inspects it. "We should get ice on it."

"It's okay. Really." I pull my hand from his. "Anyway, you're injured enough for the both of us."

Caleb flashes me a swollen grin. "Get your clothes on, Trouble. I need to go talk to a man about dating his sister." Caleb pats my naked thigh.

"You're not going to talk to Austin. Are you crazy? Did he give you a concussion?" I turn his face toward mine so I can inspect his pupils.

"Who said I was talking to *your* brother?" Caleb teases, earning a smack on the shoulder from me. He captures my hand and kisses it.

"Okay, smart-ass." I stand and pull away from him. "Let's see how you do against him without anyone intervening this time."

I drop the blanket draped around me as Caleb watches with a greedy smirk. This will never get old. Grabbing clean clothes from my dresser, I put them on under Caleb's watchful gaze before I help him into his pants while he continues to hold the shirt to his nose. I pull open one of my dresser drawers and remove a shirt that once belonged to Caleb.

"Here, this should do," I say, helping him get it on. He looks down at the shirt and smirks.

"I've missed this shirt. I was wondering where I lost it."

"I couldn't say," I lie, shrugging at him. "Let me see your nose again." The bleeding has stopped, and I look over my battered man and press a gentle kiss to each mark he took for me. "I'm so sorry. I had no idea he'd lose his shit like that on you of all people. And you didn't even do anything."

"I mean, I thought I was doing something, but if you disagree, we need to have that conversation." I give Caleb a puzzled look, not following. "He walked in on his best friend's face buried between his little sister's legs. That's enough to shake anybody up. And I know I barely started, but if you couldn't tell I was doing anything—"

"Stop!" I laugh, shaking my head. "That's not what I meant. Pervert."

Caleb kisses me and leads me by my uninjured hand into the living room where Austin is pacing across the floor, and Emily has nearly chewed all her fingernails off. Austin stops when Caleb and I walk into the room, his gaze dropping to our clasped hands and up to Caleb's face.

"Who the hell do you think you are?" Austin asks brusquely, coming nose to nose with Caleb. I push Austin back and stand between them.

"It's okay, Kate," Caleb says in a low voice. "I don't want to risk you getting caught in the crosshairs."

"Of all the people in the world, I never actually expected you to fuck my sister. I. Trusted. You." Austin shoves Caleb's chest with each word.

"I know, but I'm not using her for sex, Austin. I care about her. I want to be with her. We weren't trying to hide anything from you. We were going to tell you today."

"That's convenient. As soon as you get caught, you have plans to tell. Yeah, I smell bullshit, Caleb. How long have you been fucking her?"

"I told you," Caleb says, shoving Austin. "It's not about the sex, and you're going to piss *me* off if you keep talking out of your ass like that." Austin staggers back a couple steps, his jaw clenched tight. "I've been crazy about Kate for years now, but I didn't make my feelings known to her until recently."

"Bullshit."

"I swear. You can ask her."

"Kate?" Austin asks, waiting for my input.

"It's true, Austin. Caleb didn't want to sneak around

behind your back. He wanted to be upfront with you. I didn't want to tell anyone right off but planned to tell you today."

"Fuck you both," Austin says. "You deserve each other." Austin shoves past Caleb to the door.

"Wait, how did you find out about us?" I ask him.

He pauses and turns to me. "Emily called me early this morning. Told me Caleb was in your bed. Evidently, your *bestie* is just as self-serving as mine is and doesn't think it's fair for you to get to be with Caleb. I tried calling you—both of you. But neither one of you answered."

"I must have left my phone in the truck." Caleb pats his pockets.

"And I turned my phone off yesterday when Tuff was texting me," I say.

"Wait, Austin, I need a ride home." Emily stands from her seat.

"You can fuck off, too, Emily." Austin slams the door behind him.

After a beat of silence, Austin's explanation sinks in, and it's my turn to be enraged. Emily called Austin and told him Caleb was here? She's the reason things played out the way they did?

"Emily," I say, turning to her now, "you told Austin? Why would you do that?" Emily pushes off the armrest of the couch where she is perched.

"I didn't think he would freak like he did," Emily says, wringing her hands. "I just thought . . . I hoped . . . "

"You hoped what? What did you honestly think was going to come from ratting us out?"

"I don't understand why he won't date me." Emily finally breaks down with a stomp of her foot. Her eyes well up with tears. "Trevor said his brother is coming to town at the end of the summer for a visit, and I was really hoping to introduce Austin as my boyfriend. I thought maybe if I was useful to him somehow he'd finally commit."

"So, you broke the news to him that his sister and best

friend were hiding a relationship from him? Emily, that doesn't even make sense." My mind spins as I try to comprehend her line of thought.

"It's not fair, okay? You've had a crush on Caleb for years and nothing was ever going to come of it. Suddenly you two are screwing around and professing your love for each other, and I can't get a damn thing more than an orgasm from Austin."

"So, your answer was to betray me?"

"Kate, I'm sorry."

"No, you're not. You're sorry your little scheme didn't work out the way you wanted it to. That's what you're sorry about," I say. "You're a really shitty friend, you know that? Honestly, this shouldn't even surprise me. Everything always has to be about you."

"I see how it is. You finally start sleeping with Caleb, and suddenly you're superior? Well, I have news for you . . . You aren't that special. Caleb is like every other pussy-chasing pig. He'll get bored with you before long, and you'll just be another notch on his belt—"

"That's enough!" Caleb says, stepping up to my defense as my open palm collides with Emily's cheek, the force slinging her head to the side. She gasps and covers her splotchy cheek with both hands.

"You will keep his name out of your slimy mouth." My index finger pokes at Emily's chest. "You do *not* have the privilege of talking about our relationship. I'm done with your blatant insults and your shitty friendship. You and me? We're done. Get out of my house."

Emily shuffles out the door, sobbing.

"Kate, I'm so sorry," Dakota steps up now. "I had no idea. Someone was banging on the door, and I saw it was Austin. I answered it without even considering. He barged right in, and I couldn't stop him. By the time I recognized what was happening it was too late."

"It's okay. It's not your fault." I shake my head.

"I know, but still. I knew Caleb was here with you and I knew you hadn't told Austin. I should have immediately put it together."

"It wouldn't have made a difference. I'm sure of it. It's okay." I give her a reassuring smile. "Come on, Caleb, let's get you cleaned up."

THERE ARE several things about Caleb that I find attractive. In fact, everything from his Viking-like physique to his sweet, playful personality does it for me. But there's something else I find wildly attractive about him, too. Watching the way he has taken Monty under his wing and dotes on that kid has my heart spazzing out.

We pick Monty up from his foster home after the blowout with Emily and bring him to the ranch. Last summer, Monty talked Caleb into teaching him to ride horses. Ever since, he looks forward to his trips to the ranch. Monty looks up to Caleb and wants to be just like him. Honestly, when Caleb mentioned he's considering applying for custody of Monty, I wasn't surprised. Caleb loves with his whole heart, and he doesn't hold anything back. He's always been that way.

As we pull onto the road leading to the ranch, I dig my phone out of my purse. In the surprise of Caleb showing up and the drama this morning, I completely forgot about turning it on. Pressing the button, I wait for it to power on before releasing it. In rapid-fire succession multiple text messages buzz through.

"What's all that?" Caleb asks, glancing over from the driver's seat.

"Remember last night I told you Tuff has been harassing me? Well, I turned my phone off yesterday because it was distracting me at work."

"Let me see." Caleb reaches for my phone, but I dodge him in protest.

"You're driving, mister. And it's no big deal. I'm going to go through and delete them."

Caleb stops the truck in the middle of the road and holds out his hand, silently asking for my phone. I huff through gritted teeth and roll my eyes, but I hand it over. It's not that I care about him reading them per se, but I'm concerned about what will come from him after seeing the horrible things Tuff has been saying.

We sit in silence as Caleb scrolls through the messages. His jaw twitches, and a scowl grows deeper on his face as his thumb slides up the screen. When he looks up at me, handing me back my phone, pure rage dances in his eyes.

"Please don't do anything stupid, Caleb. He's not worth it."

"He may not be. But you are." His voice is gruff, no doubt straining to hide the depth of his anger from Monty who's watching us closely from the back seat with a solemn expression.

"Promise me." I squeeze Caleb's hand and hope he'll comply.

He doesn't respond, doesn't move. Just stares back at me, his breathing heavy. Finally, when I think I'm going to lose, he answers.

"I won't hurt him. Physically."

"Or do anything illegal," I add, nodding my head.

"Kate . . ."

"Promise me, Caleb."

"I won't get in trouble, okay? I'm not letting him get away with talking to you this way. It's not okay for him to talk to anyone like this, and my girl is the last person on earth he'll disrespect."

"Who's getting in trouble?" Monty asks from the back seat, looking back and forth between us.

"Nobody's getting in trouble, little man. It's okay." Caleb

starts driving again, and within a few minutes, we're at the barn, saddling up a horse for Monty to ride.

"I think I'm ready to start roping," Monty says from atop the gentle mare Caleb put him on.

"You do, huh? And what do you plan on roping?" Caleb asks.

"Bulls, obviously." Monty makes a show of rolling his eyes at Caleb, who is trying to suppress a chuckle. "I'm going to grow up to be a roper just like you, Caleb!"

Yeah, Caleb's a goner. Honestly, though, who wouldn't be? You'd have to have a heart of stone to resist that sweet kid.

"You'll have to jump down from that horse if you want to learn to rope."

"Why? You rope from your horse all the time."

"Yes, I do. But that's not where I started. First, you learn how while standing on your own two feet. Once you've mastered that, you can try roping from the saddle."

Monty sulks, but he dismounts the horse, stirring the loose dirt under his feet as he lands. Caleb picks one of his old ropes and hands it over to Monty. Almost like father and son, he and Monty stand side by side, each with a rope in their hands. He helps Monty find the right grip on the rope and, in slow motion, demonstrates the swing. Monty watches closely, absorbing each detail, and mimics Caleb's motions. Speeding up now, Monty tries again, releasing the rope this time. Caleb gives him a high five, and Monty grins across the corral at me.

"Did you see that, Kate? I'm going to be as good as Caleb in no time!"

"You're doing great. Already way better than Caleb was at your age."

Caleb smirks at me and goes back to coaching Monty.

While the two of them practice roping, I make my way toward the barn, hoping to find Austin. I don't think there has ever been a riff like this between Austin and Caleb, and I hate that I'm the cause of it. Hopefully Austin has cooled off enough to talk to me. Not finding any trace of him in the barn, I'm about to try the bunkhouse when the clink of a metal cap bouncing across the floor above me snags my attention. Why didn't I think of that before? I climb the rungs to the hayloft, finding Austin in what was our favorite spot to hide away in our barn at home. All of life's troubles were solved from the hayloft when we were kids.

"Hey, you." I pause briefly at the top of the ladder.

The light streaming into the barn through the open hay door highlights the little particles of dust and dirt floating in the loft air. It's a familiar and comforting scene. Austin barely shoots a glimpse my way. I step into the hayloft anyway.

"What do you want, Kate?" Austin takes a sip from the glass bottle in his hand.

"A little early for a drink, don't you think?" I make my way over the dusty boards and sit on the haybale next to him. My comment earns me a scowl. "Look, I know finding out about me and Caleb must have been a shock for you—"

"You think that's the problem? I'm pouting because I was last to find out about your boyfriend? I don't care near so much about the way I found out as I do the fact that you two are together in the first place."

"Why is that a problem?"

"You're going to wind up getting hurt, Kate. Why can't you see that? He may think he has the best of intentions now, but everyone breaks up eventually. And when you do, I'll be left to pick up the broken pieces and try to glue you back together all by myself. I don't know if I can do it alone. Caleb has always been there to help. But when you break up, he won't be anymore. For either of us. And he's supposed to care about you more than that."

"He's not going to break my heart, Austin." I link my arm through his and rest my cheek on his shoulder.

"You don't know that," Austin grumbles, taking another

swig. "And I meant it when I promised you that I wouldn't let another man hurt you."

"You are by far the best big brother a girl could ask for. I'll be the first to say so. But you made me that promise when you were a kid yourself. You know as well as I do that you don't have control over that. Nobody really does. Getting hurt is a risk of living, Austin, and I'd rather take that risk than lock myself away." An indistinguishable grunt sounds from Austin's chest. "Caleb's your best friend. You know him well enough to know he wouldn't get with me just because he can. He's a great guy and you know it. I never intended to stay single like you choose to be. Eventually, I was going to start dating someone. Wouldn't you prefer it be someone like Caleb that you already know and trust?"

"He's our friend, Kate. He took advantage."

"No, he didn't. I've had a crush on him for years, Austin. I was as surprised as you when I found out he has feelings for me, too. He's *had* feelings for me. Feelings that he's fought out of respect for you. But it shouldn't be one or the other. He shouldn't have to choose between a relationship with me or a friendship with you. Don't ruin this for me because of your own insecurities. You know Caleb is a good guy, and deep down, I don't think you could ever deny that. You should be happy for us."

"You're delusional." Austin rolls the empty glass bottle between his hands.

"Whether I'm delusional or not, you need to make amends with Caleb."

"Why?" His voice is sharp.

"Because he's your best friend, dork. And because I think I might be in love with him."

Austin's head whips over to me, his gaze burning into me. He wasn't expecting that, I'm sure, but it's true. We passed the point of ending this without a broken heart a long time ago.

His expression turns stony. "You're not in love. You're in

love with the idea of love, and you're too smitten to see this for what it is. Caleb is the asshole, and you are the fool. When he breaks your heart—and it's only a matter of time—don't bother running to me."

I watch in disbelief as he stands and heads for the ladder. He turns into a teary blur before he can disappear beneath the floor of the loft. I swallow the lump in my throat and attempt to dab the moisture from my cheeks. Austin finding out about us was a mistake we'll never be able to take back.

caleb

"Where do you want to go?" I ask Kate after another painful goodbye with Monty at his foster home.

It's been a crazy twenty-four hours for her, and she has a lot to process. We agreed to make our relationship public, she was betrayed by Emily, her brother beat the shit out of yours truly, and her boyfriend is fighting for custody of a seven-year-old kid. That's a lot for anyone to unpack.

"I don't know. Somewhere just the two of us?"

"Okay. I think I can figure out a place for us to go."

I turn the truck around and we follow the road away from town. Kate sits quietly, holding my hand and staring at the mountains in the distance. My heart aches for her. I hoped things with Austin would go better than they did. When she reappeared from inside the barn, I could tell by the look on her face that she tried to talk with him again, and it was plain to see that it didn't go well.

After driving about three miles outside of town, I slow the truck and pull onto a dirt road leading into an open field. It's a bumpy ride, but we take it slow. After a few minutes, we make it to the top of a hill, and I slow the truck to a stop. I hop out and hold the door open for Kate. She slides out of the truck, and we drop the tailgate for a place to sit. The empty valley stretches out below us with a mountain backdrop, no signs of civilization within sight. I wrap my arm around Kate, pulling her tight against my side, and she rests her head on my shoulder.

"What's on your mind?" I ask.

"Everything. Everything is on my mind and it's all one big jumbled-up mess. I can't seem to work through any of it."

"Want to talk about it?" I ask, looking down at her.

"I think so."

"You start, and I'll listen." I kiss the top of her head.

"I'm worried about Austin. I don't think the two of you have ever had a fight like this before, have you?"

"No, nothing this bad, but I'm certain he'll come around. I need to try to talk to him again."

"I don't want him to be without a friend. I never dreamed he would react the way he did. I thought he would be mad, and I didn't expect him to like us being together, but I didn't expect this. I can't believe the things he said." Kate sniffles, and I give her a reassuring squeeze.

"We'll make amends, Kate. It might take a little time, but it will all work out in the end."

"I hope so. And can you believe Emily's nerve? I don't get that girl's thought process. How did she really expect that to end for her?"

"I'm kind of happy about that part. I never liked the way she talked to you. She never comes straight out and says anything, but she was always condescending toward you."

"She's a bitch. And it felt good to put her in her place."

We sit quietly for a spell and watch as the sun starts to sink behind the mountains, the sky full of reds and pinks and oranges. It's a peaceful reprieve from an uncertain reality, and despite the circumstances, there's nobody I'd rather share it with. Gradually, the night creeps in and darkness invades. Kate sighs and looks up at me.

"Take me home, Caleb?"

"Sure thing, Trouble."

Kate snuggles into my side on the drive to her place. I walk Kate to the front door, waiting with her as she unlocks it. She steps inside without saying a word, pauses, and turn back to me.

"Are you not staying?" she asks, disappointment coating her voice.

"Do you want me to?"

"Please. I don't want to be alone."

I lock the door behind us and follow her to her room. We both undress for bed. Kate grabs my discarded T-shirt and slides it on over her head then climbs into bed. I can't help but smile. My girl loves to wear my shirts, and I love the way she looks in them. I climb into bed with her and pull her tight against me, stroking her hair until her breathing slows to a steady pace and she falls asleep.

But sleep doesn't find me as easily. I'm basking in my own guilt. My girl is hurting right now, and while I may not be the one that lit the match, I'm the string leading to the stick of dynamite. Eventually, exhaustion takes over, but the dream I find myself in isn't any better than reality. It's a jumbled mess of angry words and Austin cutting ties with me and his family, Kate falling into a deep depression, and me calling out for Monty with no response.

I slide out of Kate's bed at daybreak, hoping some fresh air will clear the nightmare from my mind. I can't shake the feeling that I'm being selfish and screwing up.

I return to Kate's with a box of her favorite doughnuts from the bakery in town. She's sitting on her bed, writing in what appears to be a journal. I quietly slide into the room and carefully sit on the bed next to her, trying not to jostle her while she writes. She peeks at me, her pen continuing to move against the paper for a moment. I prop open the doughnut box.

"Got your favorite."

Kate smiles and kisses my cheek before taking one. "Thanks. You only got Boston cream. What's your favorite?"

"You're my favorite." I bite into the doughnut that's left.

My phone rings, my realtor's name lighting up the screen. I answer.

"Caleb. I have a house for you. We need to move fast though. Do you have time to go see it?"

"Yeah, send me the address, and I'll meet you there."

There aren't too many houses for sale in a town this small, especially with the specifics that are a must for me. If I'm going to buy a house, there are a few things I'm not willing to go without. Like land. I'm not a subdivision type of guy. I don't have any plans of starting up a full-fledged ranch, but I want a place for BoJack and any other horses or animals. The option of homesteading is a must. And I want a tree in the yard. One big enough to tie up a tire swing. I loved tire swings when I was a kid, and Monty loves them, too.

Within thirty minutes, Kate is riding shotgun as I pull into the driveway of what could possibly be my new home. We walk hand in hand up the stone sidewalk to the front door.

"Caleb, it's beautiful."

Greg is waiting for us inside, excitement written across his face as he shows us through the house.

"It needs some updating, but nothing major. The property belonged to an older couple. The husband passed away and the wife, too old to handle the upkeep on her own, moved out of state to live with her daughter. They did a surprisingly good job with upkeep, considering their age. I'm guessing they had hired help," Greg says.

"I like the older style of the house." Kate smiles broadly.

She slowly spins around, taking in the details of the living room. The dark hardwood floors look original but well kept. A stone fireplace stands as the focal point of the room.

The living room leads into a dining room, followed by a galley kitchen. It's not big, but it's sufficient. Next to the laundry room and rear exit is a set of stairs leading up to the garret, now divided into two bedrooms.

"Is it only the two bedrooms?" I ask.

"The master bedroom is downstairs off the hallway by the living room and half bath. Come on, I'll show you."

We head down the stairs and Greg shows us around the master bedroom and bathroom. There aren't any fancy walk-in closets or ornate showers, but the old clawfoot tub has Kate nearly drooling. The image of Kate naked and soaking in that tub has *me* drooling.

"How much of the land goes with it?" I ask.

"Only about a hundred acres. But this hundred is surrounded by larger ranches. You probably noticed on the way in that there aren't any neighbors for a while."

"What do you think?" I ask Kate.

"Show me the barn."

I chuckle and nod at Greg. "You heard the woman. Let's see the barn."

After a tour of the barn and outbuildings, Greg prompts me for a decision. "Not to rush you, but if you want this place, we need to get your offer in as soon as possible."

"Would you choose a house like this to raise your kids in?" I ask Kate.

She shrugs. "I don't want kids. But I think this house would do nicely for someone who did. Someone like you."

Her comment knocks the breath out of me. "You don't want kids?" How did I not know this?

"No. I'm not mom material. Are you kidding?"

"Hmmm. I disagree with that part." I brush my thumb over her cheek and call over my shoulder to Greg. "I want it."

We discuss numbers, and Greg steps aside to make the call.

Kate hugs onto my side. "Does this mean—"

"I hope so. Still a few more hoops to jump through first."

"Like finishing your training."

"Yes. And hopefully since I already have my documentation

handled, we will be able to expedite the closing on the house if they accept my offer."

After brief deliberation, an agreement is made and the house is officially under contract. Yet another box checked off in the grueling process of getting custody of Monty.

We ride down the road in silence, both lost in thought. I should know better than to think there's nothing left for me to learn about Kate, but her revelation today surprised me. A faint ringing beside me snags my attention. Kate has her phone pressed to her ear. After a few more rings, Austin's muffled voice sounds through the speaker. It's barely there, but the volume on her phone is loud enough I can make out most of what he says.

"Do you need something, Kate?"

"No, I haven't heard from you since our talk, so I thought I'd check in."

"Yeah, well, I thought about what you said, and it doesn't matter. I'm not okay with it. He's another bad choice, and he's one I'm not going to stand by and watch you make. As long as you're seeing him, don't bother calling."

"Austin—" Kate looks at her phone screen, verifying the silence is from an ended line.

Her phone drops into her lap, and tears stream down her face. I adjust in my seat, wrapping an arm around her shoulders, and clutch her against my side. A quiet sob escapes through her hands that are now covering her beautiful face. I press a quick kiss to the top of her head.

"I'm sorry, Kate."

"I don't get it. He's my brother. He's the one person who I'm supposed to be able to rely on unconditionally, and suddenly, he's pissed and not talking to me."

"He probably needs some time to let it all soak in. He'll be back to bossing you around in no time."

"I don't know, Caleb. He's never shut me out like this before. It hurts." Kate swipes at the loose tears, determined to clear them away as quickly as they formed. "But that's fine. If he wants to be an ass, I can, too. I know how all his games work."

This is what I didn't want. I didn't want to obliterate Kate and Austin's relationship. I didn't want to cause her suffering. But it's what happens to the people who hang close to me. My parents missed out on having the family they'd always dreamed of. My aunt and uncle. Austin. They've all endured different degrees of torture thanks to me. And now Kate is going to be next. She's already losing her brother over me. And it's devastating her. If Austin doesn't let me finish the rodeo season with him, the loss of the homestead will be one more casualty I've caused. Who knows how much more she will face? It's selfish of me to make her go through that.

Plus, I already have things in the works with Monty. I assumed she wanted kids eventually, but it's not something we've discussed yet. She's known about Monty. She encouraged me to go for custody of him. Why would she do that if she didn't want to have kids . . . unless she never expected us to last. I won't force Kate into a role she doesn't want to play, but I also won't break my promise to Monty.

I slow to a stop in front of Kate's house, switch off the ignition, and sit back in my seat. Instead of getting out, I stare quietly ahead. The pit in my stomach has grown over the course of the drive here and is gaping large enough that it's summoning physical pain. Kate stirs beside me, gathering her things.

"You're coming in, right?"

"For a minute. But I can't stay."

My somber tone douses her with worry. I can see it in the way she stiffens. Knowing there's no sense in drawing out the pain, I step out from the cab of my truck and follow Kate inside. Getting involved with Kate was a mistake. This wasn't a good idea for either of us—I see that now. Dakota is curled up in a blanket on the couch in the living room as we pass, watching a movie. She gives us a happy wave as we walk by to

Kate's bedroom. I drag my feet down the hallway, and when Kate disappears through her bedroom door, I get lightheaded. A couple deep breaths and a long, tight blink steadies me, and I follow Kate into her room.

"What's going on?" Kate asks, spinning around to face me after the door clicks closed behind us. "You know something. Is it Austin? Did he say something to you?"

With my head hung forward, I rub the back of my neck, dreading the words that I know I need to speak. I need to say it. Get it over with. Quick. Like a Band-Aid. Maybe it won't hurt so bad. Slowly, I scan up her body, taking in each detail that I know will haunt my dreams over the nights to come. One last touch. I can give myself that much. I hold out a hand to her and she takes it without hesitation, stepping into me. Cupping her face, I stare into her troubled eyes, a reflection of the vast mistake I've made by pursuing her.

"Caleb, you're scaring me."

I lightly press my lips to hers. Just barely at first, soaking in the warmth of her mouth, memorizing the way her lips fit to mine. My fingers graze the silky skin of her neck and thread through her hair, fisting it delicately, eliciting a moan from her. She tries to pull me into her, deepening the kiss, but I can't. If I fall in, I'll never be able to wade my way to shore again. And she needs this from me.

I break our kiss and swallow the lump in my throat.

"I've been thinking," I say as I step away, my voice gravelly. "This thing between us has turned into something way more than I ever meant for it to. I think it's best if we call it."

"What are you talking about? You're not making any sense." Kate stares up at me with furrowed brows.

"Look, Kate, it was fun while it lasted. I had a good time, and I think you did, too. We were tempting fate by trying to be more than friends, and it stirred up a bunch of drama." The words are like sand filling my mouth. "That's not a good thing for either of us. I think it's best we call it now before any more damage is done. It's over . . . We're over."

Kate's chin trembles as realization blooms. "I hate you." Her words come out in a whisper at first but grow louder each time she repeats the phrase. "I hate you. I hate you. I hate you." Her fists pound against my chest as the tears burst free.

My breath catches, the aching inside me growing too strong to ignore.

"Get out. Get. Out." Her demand roars through the room.

I don't hang around any longer to watch the destruction I've caused. Instead, I comply and flee like the scoundrel I am, knocking into Dakota as I rush down the hall. The world molds into a blur around me as I escape out the door and never look back.

kate

"Kate?" Dakota pokes her head into my room. "Is everything okay?"

I shake my head, still standing in the center of the room, right where Caleb left me moments ago. His words echo in my head as tears pour down my cheeks.

"It's over. We're over." The words escape in a whisper.

Dakota is standing in front of me now, her eyes wide, gliding over my face, looking for clues. "What do you mean? What's over?"

"Caleb." My body feels weak, like I might topple over.

"Did you have a fight? This doesn't make sense. I thought everything was good between you."

I shake my head. "He left. He wasn't supposed to leave." Frantically, I pat my pockets for my phone. I need my phone. I need to call him. He wasn't supposed to leave. I scroll to his name and press the green phone icon. It rings three times and goes directly to voicemail. He ignored my call. I hang up and call again. Voicemail. I'm about to press the call button again when Dakota swipes the phone from my hands and tucks it in her pocket.

"Look at me." Dakota grabs my shoulders, demanding my attention. "What happened?"

I force myself to focus on her. "Caleb broke up with me." The words tumble out of me, stealing the breath from my lungs as they go. I crumble in Dakota's arms, the dust finally settling. "He left. He was supposed to stay, but he left. He broke up with me."

The sobs rack my empty body—the gaping hole in my chest swallowing all my strength and making my limbs go numb and weak. I cling to Dakota for support, finally accepting the truth: He's gone. Dakota and I drop to the floor, tangled together as she holds me tight.

"It's going to be okay." Dakota's hand rubs firmly against my back in soothing circles.

"He was supposed to stay."

STABBING pain in my shoulder chases away the troubled sleep that finally found me. I squint, trying to get my bearings. My eyes ache, and my nose is stuffy. After I ran out of tears yesterday, Dakota and I camped out on the couch in the living room together, watching mindless shows. Rolling onto my back, I find Dakota lying on the floor next to the couch where I must have fallen asleep at some point. She stayed by my side all night.

Muffling my groan, I rise from the couch and hobble my way into the bathroom. Staring into the mirror, I poke at the soft tissue around my swollen, bloodshot eyes and wince. My whole face is puffy. Grabbing my hairbrush from the counter, I work through the rat's nest that's formed on the back of my head.

Everything aches, and yet I feel numb at the same time. Hollow. Am I supposed to lose everything this summer? Emily's friendship may not be one I should mourn, but the loss hurts just the same. Austin has turned his back on me. Technically, he said as long as Caleb and I are together, but I won't give him the satisfaction of me crawling back to him now and begging his forgiveness. And now, Caleb. I sweep my hair over my shoulder for a better angle with the brush and my shirt shifts along with my movements, exposing the black ink on my collarbone.

Forever in my heart

Trembling fingers trace Caleb's script across my skin as his words from that day flood my mind.

"This is permanent. But so am I."

My swollen face crumples in the mirror, and I grab up the washcloth and scrub at the tattoo as his velvety voice comes back to me.

"I'm here, and I'm never leaving."

I scrub harder, wanting it gone, wanting to be freed from his words.

"Not even this tattoo can outlast me where you are concerned."

My skin is red and raw and burning, but his words still brand me, lying to me. Over and over again he lied. But the words don't fade. I scrub harder until a hand lands on top of mine and arms wrap around me.

"Hey, not like that. That won't help," Dakota says softly at my side. She drops the washcloth back into the sink. "We can fix it, but not like that. Come on. Let me fix you some breakfast."

Holding tightly to my hand, she drags me from the bathroom and down the hall to the kitchen. I lean against the wall, my body feeling weak and exhausted. Goose bumps break out across my skin, but Dakota doesn't miss a thing.

"Hold on."

She disappears around the corner, only to return lugging the plush chair from the living room and a blanket draped around her neck. She drops the chair in the middle of the kitchen floor, waves for me to take a seat, and tucks me in with the blanket.

"Coffee?"

"Please." My voice is scratchy and raw.

She pours me a mug and gathers supplies from the cupboards and fridge.

"I'm thinking French toast. What do you think?" She looks over her shoulder at me while she works.

"I'm not very hungry."

"Sweetie, you just got your heart broken. You might not be ready yet, but here, soon, it will be time to rage. And a girl can't properly rage without a healthy supply of carbs. Trust me on this. French toast is exactly what you need right now."

"What do you mean?"

Dakota freezes. Slowly she turns to face me and leans back against the counter, studying me closely.

"Don't tell me you've never raged before."

I shake my head.

"Oh, boy. This is the first time a guy has truly broken your heart, isn't it?"

This time I don't respond, choosing to sip on my coffee instead.

"Double order of French toast it is." Dakota nods to herself, turning back to the stove. "You're gonna have to trust me on this one."

After several minutes, Dakota hands me a plate with four slices of French toast buried under whipped cream and fresh berries. The smell of the cinnamon instantly makes my mouth water in anticipation.

"I can't eat all of this."

"Give it your best shot. You might surprise yourself."

Dakota lifts her own plate off the counter before sliding down the cabinet and sitting on the kitchen floor in front of me. Immediately, she digs in.

"We can move to the table," I offer, secretly wanting to stay in my cushioned cocoon she so carefully tucked me into.

"Not a chance. This is perfect right here. Plus, I'm starving. Go ahead—dig in. Tell me what you think."

The metal fork is cold between my fingers, but as soon as the first bite touches my tongue, my mouth explodes with flavor.

"Dakota, this is delicious," I mumble through a mouthful of food.

"Thanks. It's my mom's secret recipe. She would make them for me any time I was having a bad day. They were her cure-all. Until they went up against the one thing they couldn't cure, anyway."

"What was that?"

"Cancer. She passed away last year."

"I'm sorry. I didn't know."

"Nothing to be sorry about. You didn't give her cancer, and I never mentioned it before. But enough about sad stuff. That's the number one rule with the cure-all French toast—you can't talk about depressing things while you eat it. What are we going to do with you today?"

"Do with me?"

"Uh, yeah. You are the only thing on the agenda today. What are we doing?"

"I have to work tonight." I shove another bite into my mouth, savoring the taste.

"I already told Dawn you won't be in. Come on, you must have something you'd like to do."

I think for a moment. "How do you feel about motorcycles?"

Dakota pauses mid-bite and looks up at me with a smirk. "They're sexy as shit. Why?"

"Austin has one."

"Of course he does." Dakota rolls her eyes and stuffs an oversized bite of French toast in her mouth.

"He's never let me on it before, but he's leaving town today. And I know where he keeps it."

Dakota just about chokes on her food. She raises an eyebrow at me. "A broken heart leads you to grand theft auto? I like it. Do you even know how to start the thing?"

"Eh. How hard could it be?"

caleb

Sleep evades me most of the night, giving me an excess of time to wallow in guilt and obsess over all the ways I'm failing at life right now. By and by I drift to sleep, only to be startled awake again by Ducky's snore. Popping upright in bed, I bang my head on the bunk above me, disoriented. I cuss, dropping my feet over the edge of the bed, and run my fingers across the knot forming on my head. With a tap on the screen, my phone lights up, displaying the time. It's nearly six. I'm not sure how much sleep I finally got, but it couldn't have been more than a few hours. My eyelids are like sandpaper, scratching my eyeballs with each blink, and a soft pounding keeps rhythm in my head. There's no way I'm getting any more sleep. Instead of lying back down, I head to the barn to take BoJack on a ride.

It's a quiet morning, and although the ride doesn't cure the aching in my chest, I return with a little more hope than I left with. When BoJack and I ride up to the barn, Austin is busy loading up his truck. I can tell by the scowl on his face that his mood hasn't improved much over the last forty-eight hours, and I dismount and approach him slowly, a little nervous about poking the bear. Austin peers in my direction briefly but doesn't acknowledge me. I walk around to the other side of the truck bed and rest my arms on the side.

"What's the plan for the rodeo?"

"You can make your own plans. I'm headed out today," Austin says without looking at me.

"But you need a partner."

"I'll find someone." Austin stops now and looks across the truck bed at me.

"Come on, man. I can still rope with you. Nothing needs to change."

"Of all the women you could have, why did you choose my fucking sister?" Austin scowls across the truck at me. His hands grip the bed till his knuckles turn white.

"Because she's the only one worth taking a beating to be in a relationship with. Look at me, man. You worked me over good yesterday."

"You're lucky we taught her how to fight. My jaw is still sore where she punched me," Austin says, rubbing his jaw, but I can see the pride he has in her.

"She's one of a kind. That's for damn sure." I can't keep from smiling when I talk about her.

Austin sobers again.

"So are you still sleeping with my sister?"

"No. We broke up. I made a commitment to help you save your mom's homestead, and I want to follow through on that."

I don't know what's going on in Austin's head, but I can see the wheels turning. Austin walks slowly around the truck to where I'm standing, his penetrating glare fixed firmly on me. He stops in front of me, toe-to-toe, his hands flexing at his sides. The seconds tick by without either of us speaking.

"You can come on the road with me," Austin says, breaking the silence. I exhale a sigh of relief. I didn't think he was going to come around so easily. "But to make myself clear, I am not okay with what you did." Austin shoves my chest, making me stumble backward. He follows, keeping himself in my personal space. We stand nose to nose like two angry bulls. Austin exerts his dominance, and I let him. "This does not mean we are okay. I need to save my mom's house. That's all this is. And once our season is over, I want nothing to do with you."

"Understood."

Within the hour, we are on the road, headed out of town. The wild hyacinths wave goodbye, mocking me. I make it an hour outside of town before I can't stand it anymore, and I scroll through the messages on my phone. Possibly the hardest thing I've ever done was ignore Kate's phone calls yesterday after I left. I hope she's okay. Surely, she is. I shoot a text to Dakota, feeling weak.

> Me: Please let me know how she is.

> Dakota: How. Dare. You.

> Me: Please. I missed her calls. I need to know she's fine.

> Dakota: Of course she's not fine. She trusted you and you blew it. I really liked you for her, Caleb. I thought the two of you could be the real thing. Shame on you for using her. I thought you were better than that.

> Dakota: Lose my number.

I throw my head back against the headrest and groan in frustration. Dakota's right.

"Nope. You don't get to act like a lovesick fool. I will kick you out of this truck and make you walk."

"Man, we might have broken up but that doesn't mean I don't care—"

The roaring of the rumble strip drowns me out as Austin pulls the truck off the side of the road. Coming to a complete stop, Austin glares at me and points to the door.

"Get out of my truck."

"Austin—"

"Now." His voice is clear and determined, the authoritative tone that he uses on employees who screwed up.

Without arguing, I unbuckle and step out of the truck. Austin says nothing. He checks the road behind him in his side mirror and pulls back onto the road. The passenger door swings shut, waving goodbye.

"Fucking asshole."

I search the road in the direction we came from. Nothing. Looking forward, Austin's truck has nearly disappeared. It's only me on this two-lane road in the middle of nowhere running through the middle of a golden field surrounded by mountains. Lifting my hat off my head, I run a hand through my hair before replacing the hat and start my hike in the direction Austin drove, grumbling to myself.

Evidently, I have a lot of ass-kissing to do.

Sliding my phone from my pocket, I debate calling someone to pick me up. My finger lands on Ducky, and I press the green call button, but it only beeps without completing the call. I have no service out here. That's fucking great. Accepting my fate, I stuff the phone into my pocket and focus on the road ahead.

I have no interest in losing my best friend. Our friendship is one I thought would last our entire lives. I never thought there would come a day that I felt like I couldn't rely on Austin. But as hard as that is on me, it's got to be harder on Kate.

The sun beats down on me as I continue ahead, focusing on the horizon. What the hell is Austin thinking anyway? I get that he's pissed at me, but seriously? Hopefully he turns around at some point and picks me up. Surely he won't make me walk for too long. The longer I walk, the further behind schedule we'll fall. This rodeo is too important for him to leave me stranded for long.

A quiet hum behind me gradually grows louder, and I peek over my shoulder, catching sight of a small car headed my way.

Stepping off to the side of the road again, I hold out my thumb. I've never actually hitchhiked. Never had a reason to. The car swerves into the other lane, only slightly slowing as they drive by. Yeah, I'd probably be leery about stopping to pick me up, too. What sane person would find themselves stranded on this empty road in the first place?

Eventually, a building comes into view ahead. As I slowly draw closer, I can make out Austin's pickup and the horse trailer parked to the side of the building—a convenience store maybe? Relief washes over me as the hole in my belly fills again. I was right. Even if he doesn't give a damn about me, he cares about his schedule. And punishing me for too long will only turn back on him and ruin his day, too.

When I finally make it to the truck, Austin is leaning against the front fender, a drink in his hand. I stop about six feet in front of him, waiting for him to break the silence.

"Are we clear?"

"Yes, you've made your point."

"Get in the truck. We've got time to make up."

kate

"Hey, Jazzy girl. Are you ready to come out of retirement?" I rub my horse's nose and lead my buckskin friend to the large corral Austin's boss is letting me use on his ranch. I've set it up with my old barrels. It's been a while, but hopefully it will come back to us. It's been two weeks since Caleb broke up with me, and Dakota has done her best to keep me occupied.

"She's gorgeous," Dakota croons, stopwatch in hand. "Okay, so how are we doing this exactly?"

I mount Jazzy and head toward where Dakota is standing at the gate.

"I'm going to take a few slow practice runs first. Make sure we've got the motions. When I tell you, you'll start the stopwatch when I come through the gate and stop it when I finish. Sound good?"

"Sounds great. I can't wait to see you in action."

I take my practice runs, muscle memory leading the way. It goes smoother than I expect, boosting my confidence. Reaching down, I rub down Jazzy's neck and we line up to go again. This time Dakota times me. It's clean, but it's not pretty.

"Austin's calling. You want to take a break and answer it?" Dakota asks, waving my phone at me.

"Ignore him. Let's run it again."

Austin has called relentlessly since he left town. Obviously, Caleb told him we broke up. But I have nothing to say to him.

Dakota salutes me and I line up, taking the right barrel first; we stick close. Jazzy switches her gait as we head to the left barrel and take the turn. Pushing forward, we make it around the final barrel and shoot straight to the gate. It's better, but it's going to take some work to get where I need to be. And if I'm being honest with myself, it's not giving me the same satisfaction that it used to.

"You getting back into the rodeo, too?" Ducky yells across the corral to me.

"Just dusting off some old memories I think." I ride over to where he's standing, one foot up on the bottom rung of the panel.

"Have you ever thought about coaching? I know a guy looking for a coach for his little girl."

"I never really thought of it. You think I could?"

"Why not? Especially someone new to it that needs to learn the basics."

"Yeah, I suppose you have a point. That could be fun. Pass them my number if they're interested."

"Okay, will do." Ducky gives me a nod, and I ride over to Dakota.

"What's next?" Dakota asks.

"I think I'm done for the day. After I get Jazzy squared away, you want to get some takeout and veg out at home to a movie?"

"I think that sounds like a fabulous idea."

"Thanks, Dakota. I don't know what I'd have done without you these last couple weeks."

I don't give her a chance to reply. Instead, I ride off toward the barn. My breakup with Caleb crushed me. The ache still fills my chest every single day. But every day, Dakota has been there. She doesn't hover, but she makes herself available to make sure I'm not left alone to rot in my bed.

I miss him. Somewhere over the years we built a solid friendship between us, and I hadn't considered how much I'd miss it if I couldn't talk to him. If someone asked me who my best friend was over the years, Emily was probably the name I would give. In reality, she was my backup plan. She was there for the things I couldn't talk to Caleb about. Like how I about lost my shit every time I watched him and the other guys doing something reckless that could get him hurt or how my heart skipped a beat when he touched me. I don't have either of them anymore, but I do have Dakota.

We make it home with takeout in hand. My phone buzzes again for what seems like the millionth time in a row. Austin has called on repeat nearly the entire way home.

"What do you want?" I ask, finally giving in and answering the phone.

"To talk to my sister, obviously." Austin's gruff voice booms through the speaker. "How are you, Kate?" he asks, softer now.

"Terrible. What do you care?" I climb out of the car and follow Dakota inside.

"I do care. I've always cared, Kate."

"You're a jerk, and I'm not sure what difference you caring makes."

"I know. I've been worried about you. I've been worried, and there's been nothing I can do, because I screwed up and you wouldn't even take my calls. I even tried checking in on you through Dakota, but she's like Fort Knox. She wouldn't tell me a damn thing."

"That's because she knows you're an asshole, too. You owe her an apology, by the way, for barging in like you did when she answered the door. That was incredibly rude and inconsiderate of you."

"You're right. I'll do that."

Silence fills the line.

"Kate, I'm sorry. I was out of line. I've been out of line. I thought I could keep you safe, but I think I ended up making things worse. I'm not going to interfere anymore."

"It's a little late for that, don't you think?" I try to laugh, but it comes out more like sobs.

"I've made a real mess of things, haven't I? I'm sorry, Kate."

I sniff back the tears that threaten to fall.

"You really cared about him, didn't you?" Austin's voice is tender, filled with regret.

"I already told you, Austin. I loved him."

"Loved? Or love?"

"What does it matter now? It's over. We're over, and I need to move on." I plop onto the couch and hug my knees to my chest.

"For what it's worth, I don't think he's having any easier of a time with it than you."

"I don't care what kind of time he's having. You were right. He made a fool of me."

"Did he? Or did I?"

"It doesn't matter anymore."

"I want you to be happy, Kate."

"I will be. Dawn is back at work. I'm helping her out, but she's officially running the diner again. That makes me happy. Emily was driving me nuts."

"Things are looking up then."

"Things are looking up."

A COUPLE TIMES A WEEK, I meet Mom at the local walking trail. Today is one of those days. The walking has benefited her immensely after spending so much time in her recliner. Truth be told, I've begun to treasure these snippets of time with her.

It's helped us repair and strengthen our bond after so many years spent with me acting as her caregiver.

"Are you nervous about competing again?" Mom asks as we walk at a comfortable pace down the trail.

"A little bit. Not the riding itself, I guess, but how it might change things."

"What do you mean?"

"I think I'm ready to give it up, officially. But what if I ride and I'm not? What if it suddenly becomes a necessity for me like it used to be? After spending time on the road with Austin, I don't think that's something I'm interested in. I prefer being home."

"Regardless, I'm glad you're getting the chance to give it another try. How's things with Caleb? I haven't heard you mention him lately." She gives me a sideways glance as we continue walking.

"That would be because we broke up."

"Oh, Kate. Austin got in the way again, didn't he?"

"I don't know. Maybe." I shake my head. "But truthfully, if Caleb wanted to be with me badly enough, he wouldn't have let Austin stop him. I don't think our relationship meant the same to him that it did to me. That's my fault. I should have known I wasn't special enough to keep a guy like Caleb interested for long." I try to make my tone sound light but fail miserably.

"Do you love him?"

"Gosh, why do people keep asking me that? What does it matter? He's not here." I kick at a rock on the path.

"You never know, he may realize his mistake and try to win you back."

"It would be pointless for him to try. I already let him fool me once. It won't happen a second time."

"I hope one day—" She checks her cell phone and trails off as she reads the name. Her fingers find the charms of her necklace. "It's the bank."

I freeze. What if we're out of time? She answers the call and I mouth for her to put the phone on speaker so I can hear.

"We aren't going to be able to wait much longer," a gruff voice leaks from the speaker of the phone.

"I told you we're taking care of it," Mom says. "We just need a little more time."

Without thinking, I grab the phone from Mom's hand and continue walking down the trail, away from her. "Sir, I don't know who you are, but we made an agreement on this account. We will have it paid up by the end of the rodeo season, and you calling to harass my mother isn't going to get you your money any sooner."

"I'm sorry?" The man's confusion is evident. "You're saying the repayment on the account is dependent on winning rodeo money? It's a very small chance that you can pull that off."

"No, it's a small chance that *you* could pull that off. You don't know us." His silence echoes through the line. "Don't you ever call my mother again."

I end the call, swiveling on the ball of my foot to return the phone to my mother, but she's already there, right behind me. She reaches out and takes the offered phone, sliding it into her pocket.

"Do you really think Austin is going to come up with the money?" Mom asks, the question weighing heavily on both of us.

"I don't know. But I hope so."

caleb

After exiting the arena, I jump off BoJack and fling my gloves to the dusty ground. Austin rides up behind me and dismounts his horse. We had our worst run yet, and it's all on me. Instead of stealing the first-place spot that we should be in, I disqualified us by missing my mark entirely.

"What was that?" Austin asks with a scowl.

"It was this damn rope," I lie, unable to look him in the eye. "I must have grabbed the wrong one."

"Was it your rope's fault yesterday, too? Or how about the ride before that?"

"Alright. You've made your point." I turn to him now. "I don't know what the problem is. I told you from the start I wasn't a good choice for a partner."

"Bullshit." Austin steps into my space. "You're every bit as good of a roper as I am, Caleb. You need to get your head out of your ass and focus on what's important."

Catching myself before running off at the mouth, I let out a heated breath. "You're right. I'll be focused tomorrow."

"You better be, man. If you don't figure it out, we're going to run out of time and chances. Whatever you need to do to, make it happen tonight."

"I'll get it handled."

Austin nods and turns to the arena to watch the rest of the competition. Truth is, I don't know how to fix it. I don't know what to do with this Kate-sized void. I can't focus on anything. I can't eat, can't sleep. Even getting out of bed feels like an accomplishment most days—one I wouldn't be making if Austin wasn't sharing the room, giving me a reason to do it.

Unable to wait any longer, I check my phone for any missed calls or texts. Notifications for both light up my screen, but none of them are from Kate. My resolve has weakened over time, and I've justified trying to rekindle the friendship I had with Kate before we got together. I've tried reaching out to her, but she ignores my texts and calls. I was slow to reach out at first, hoping that a little bit of time would give her a chance to cool off. Or maybe miss me a little. It didn't seem to have the desired effect.

Positioning myself next to Austin, I watch the other ropers with him. Austin is justified in calling me out. I've got to start doing better. We came out here to make money, but all I've been doing since the breakup is costing us money. We have another week on the road before we get a break and head home for a week before the final. At this point, we can't place lower than second in the finals if we are going to reach our goal.

But I can't concentrate on what's going on in the arena. It's like staring my failure in the face. Today's run really hurt us. I haven't had my head in it since getting back on the road. All I can think about is Kate, and it feels like I'm spiraling all over again. I don't know how to do life without her in it. I've never tried before. If these last couple weeks are any indication, I don't think I can.

The crowd fills the stands, cheering the cowboys on. As the roping wraps up, barrels are brought in and the arena is prepared for barrel racing. I groan and turn my back on it, leaning on the fence now. As if Kate wasn't already all I can think about, she's the first thing that comes to my mind when I see barrel racing.

"Okay, man. This is your free pass. Get it off your chest now, or never speak of it again," Austin says, interrupting me from my thoughts.

"I don't know what you mean."

"We both know what your problem is. This is your chance to say what you need to say."

I study Austin. He's carrying his typical bad attitude, but he's been softer since I overheard his call with Kate the other day. He doesn't look at me, just stares out into the arena as though we're talking about the rodeo schedule or something. I debate whether to open my mouth or stay silent. But Austin wouldn't offer if he didn't mean it, and I'm desperate to be able to talk to my friend.

"I miss her. I knew it would be hard—I'm not stupid—but I didn't think it would be this hard." The words rush out without effort.

"You *are* stupid. If you were smart, you never would've broken up with her."

"I was trying to protect her." I straighten and turn to face Austin. "I didn't want her to get hurt. I thought this was the best way."

Austin rears back, his face scrunched up like he's tasted something sour.

"You didn't want to hurt her so you decided to break her heart? Honestly, man, I should beat your ass for that alone. But I did tell you two to break up, so I'll spare you this time. What were you thinking? She's crazy about you. I knew something was up well before I knew what it was. I haven't seen Kate that happy and lighthearted since she was a kid. You did that. You lightened the burden she's been carrying in a way I've never been able to. Tell me, what did you think you were saving her from by breaking up with her?"

"You know as well as I do that I end up hurting everyone

that's close to me. Kate was already getting a taste of it. She was losing you over being with me."

"Man, what are you talking about? Kate and I would've made up eventually. We always do. She's my sister. And what's this nonsense about you hurting people? You are probably the most harmless person I know. You're the freaking BFG." I raise a questioning brow at him. "Big Friendly Giant? You've seriously never seen that movie?"

I shake my head. "It's been my whole life, Austin. Literally since the day I was born. I wasn't supposed to be an only child. My parents wanted a big family. There were complications with my birth, though, and my mom couldn't have any more kids. She carried that burden every single day. Then there's my aunt and uncle. They've never been the same since Anna's accident—"

"For the last time, Anna's accident wasn't your fault. It was an unfortunate mishap."

"You don't know that." I shift my weight from one foot to the other.

"Actually, I do. Her horse didn't start bucking after it came around the corner, Caleb. That's just when you saw it. Your aunt was already running out to help Anna before the horse threw her. Anna hung on for a good while according to your aunt. And that's because of the lessons you gave her. But she wasn't strong enough, and the horse threw her before your aunt could get to her. You showed up at an unfortunate time to see the end of a horrible catastrophe. It wasn't your fault."

Austin's hands are on my shoulders now. I shake my head.

"No. I would've known. All this time, that's not how the story went."

"It is, Caleb. They tried telling you, but you couldn't hear through the grief, and then you shut down completely. You cannot continue carrying the blame for everyone else's misfortunes. It will ruin you. It's already ruining you. You broke up with a girl who's in love with you because you're still paying for other people's problems that you didn't have a hand in."

"I want what's best for Kate. I didn't want to hurt her. I thought it would be better to let her go than drag her down with me."

"I get what you're saying, but it's faulty reasoning. By trying to save her, you made her biggest fear a reality. You left."

Austin's words nearly take me down on the spot. They weigh heavily in the pit of my stomach, making it hard to catch my breath. My mind is reeling, trying to process the information Austin laid out for me—Anna's accident, Kate . . . How did I not think about that? I'm such an idiot. Grabbing the fence, my head dips forward and I try to breathe through the nausea of my realized mistakes. Kate's script on my forearm catches my eye.

Always on my mind

I made so many promises to her. So many promises that never even crossed my mind as I ripped each one to shreds. I've ruined everything. Sucking in a breath, I meet Austin's gaze.

"What do I do now? How do I fix it?"

"You go get your girl, man."

CHAPTER FORTY

I put the cleaner and rag away after wiping the empty tables down, clock out, and put in an order for myself. Missing Caleb has nothing to do with why I'm ordering the burger I created for him. It's a delicious burger. I sip on my Diet Dr. Pepper and scroll social media while I wait. Neither Caleb nor Austin are active on their social media accounts, unfortunately. If I want to know how things are going for them, I'll have to suck it up and ask them directly. Which isn't happening.

"Here's your food, Kate," Dakota says, bringing it out to me.

"You're working dinner, too, right?" I ask, taking the bag of food from her.

"Yeah. I'm closing tonight."

"Okay, well, I'll see you later I guess." I slide off the stool.

"Hey, are you not taking the flowers home?" Dakota motions to the ridiculous display of flowers Lacey brought over from the flower shop earlier today with an apology from Caleb. It's filled with blue wild hyacinths and a few other flowers I don't know the names of. It's a beautiful arrangement, but it doesn't change anything. He may be looking for my forgiveness, but he's not getting it.

"Trash them." I shake my head. "I don't want them."

The bag swings at my side as I walk out to my truck then drive home, going straight to my bedroom when I get there. Once I'm settled and comfortably sitting on my bed, I open the takeout box and eat my hamburger and fries.

My phone vibrates next to me. It's a text message.

Caleb: Hey beautiful.

Scoffing, I promptly toss it to the bed. No, thanks. It took him so long to reach out to me that I don't know if I'm relieved or pissed off. Instead of answering him, I cram another bite of my burger in my mouth.

Ten minutes pass. I'm full and unable to finish the rest of my food, so I scoot it aside. My fingers slide across the embossed cover of my notebook now sitting in front of me, and I journal about my day. It's something new I started since I've been home. Journaling doesn't fill the void Caleb left, but it's a start. Surprisingly, it seems to be good for me even though I don't have much going on to write about. Since the breakup, if I haven't been working, I've been at home trying to find something to do to occupy my mind.

My phone vibrates on the bed again, distracting me from the mostly empty page in front of me. This time it's a phone call. It's Caleb, so I hit the fuck-you button and continue writing without giving him a second thought. Until my phone lights up again.

"What?" I finally answer his call.

"Hey. I wanted to check in. See if you got the flowers." Caleb's velvet voice carries through the speaker. Good heavens, how I've missed hearing him . . . talking to him.

"I got them, and then I threw them away. Now if that's all—"

"Kate, please. I don't know how else to tell you I'm sorry."

"That's just it, Caleb. Sometimes sorry doesn't cut it." My discarded pen lands on my blanket, next to the open notebook.

"For what it's worth, I miss you." I know he's telling the truth because I can hear it in his voice. I massage my temple with two of the fingers of my free hand.

"What do you want me to say?" My tone is softer now. Of course I miss him, too, but I'm not ready to confess. I'm still so angry, the wounds he left too raw.

"Anything, honestly. I needed to hear your voice. How are you doing? Things going okay for you?"

"Oh, I get it." The anger takes over. "You're feeling guilty. That's why you're checking up on poor little Kate. You're probably afraid I'll run and cry to Austin with my broken little heart. Well, rest easy, Caleb, because I'm not fourteen anymore, and you would've had to have my heart in order to break it." I sit up a little straighter on my bed.

"Kate, that's not—"

"I'm doing fine without you. Honestly, I've been so busy I haven't had time to dwell on it. I've worked every day. I finally got all my stuff moved from Mom's to Dakota's, and when I haven't been working, I've been going out with friends. And, believe it or not, with Austin out of town, the boys aren't cowering as much as usual. So, that's been nice."

"You've been dating?" There's a noticeable hardening to Caleb's voice.

"I wouldn't call it dating, exactly," I say, thankful our conversation is happening over the phone and he can't see my tells exposing my lie. "More like . . . scratching an itch."

"A particular itch that I'm no longer scratching?" Caleb mutters his question.

"Really, it's not a big deal. They've been quite capable."

"They?" His jealousy seeps through the phone.

"Well, a ménage à trois does require more than one partner."

"Okay." Caleb draws out the word. "See, I don't think you're being serious right now, but frankly, I can't really tell."

"Speaking of which"—I ignore his comment—"I have somewhere to be tonight. I really need to start getting ready."

"Oh. What are you doing tonight?"

"I would tell you, but I don't want to make you jealous. Have a good night though and tell Austin I said hello."

I hang up on him before he can say anything else or ask me any more questions. As a matter of fact, I do have plans. I have a hot date with Charlie Hunnam in his movie *King Arthur: Legend of the Sword* and a pint of mint chocolate chip ice cream. And if things get crazy, my vibrator just might get lucky tonight. Yes, I did name my vibrator after my celebrity crush. Charlie is better than a man.

Charlie doesn't make false promises and break my heart, because let's face it, Caleb *did* have my heart, and he didn't just break it—he shattered it. Thanks to Dakota, I'm slowly learning how to glue it back together, reclaiming each little shard one piece at a time. The rage helps, giving me something else to focus on besides the pain. But from time to time, the fury fades, and I catch myself missing him again and missing what we were together. And that is a dangerous place to stay.

A COUPLE DAYS have passed since I talked to Caleb. I stare at the most recent text message from Caleb this morning, debating my next move. This time, it's not about us. It's about Monty. I reread the message.

> Caleb: Monty is having a hard time at his foster home. His mom has missed her last few visits with him. He's hysterical, and there's nothing I can do from out here. Please, Kate. Go see him for me? I'm trying to get to him, but it's going to take time.

Monty means the world to Caleb. We all care about the kid, but Caleb is in it deeper. I can only imagine the turmoil he must be feeling right now, unable to come immediately to the rescue for Monty. There is, of course, no question about what I'll do. I send a text to Monty's caseworker and get ready to go.

Luckily, the foster family agrees to meet me at the park. Time drags during the drive over, giving me too much time to dwell on all things Caleb, but I can't allow myself to fall back into that headspace—I'll be useless for my visit with Monty. I try to focus on him instead. I'm not sure what my plan is or what to expect. Does Monty feel the same way I did when my dad left? It's different circumstances, but it's no doubt just as hard. Only Monty doesn't have anyone else to rely on. Except Caleb. Poor kid. Hopefully it works out better for him than it did for me.

I don't have any trouble locating him when I get to the park. He's sitting on the railroad tie at the edge of the play area, his face drawn into a frown, and he picks at the ground with a stick. He doesn't notice me approach, and I stop first to talk to his foster mom.

"How is he doing?" I ask.

"He's struggling with the transition, but he's a good kid." I don't miss the depth of sympathy floating in her voice. It tells me what her words don't.

"I'm going to talk to him for a bit, if that's okay." I gesture toward him, and she nods in reply before seating herself on the bench nearby to wait.

Monty continues digging at the ground with his stick. He finally looks up after I sit next to him on the railroad tie, and I watch the myriad of emotions that wash over his face as his mind processes my sudden appearance.

"Kate!" Monty slings himself against me, hugging me with all his might. He stands now, looking around the playground excitedly. "Where's Caleb?"

"He's at the rodeo, bud. But he asked me to come by and see you because he misses you so much."

"Oh." Monty slouches down in his seat.

"Come on." I nudge his side. "Let's go for a walk."

Monty groans but stands and takes my hand. We stroll around the park, kicking the dandelion puffballs as we go. Eventually, I work a giggle out of him, and his playful side starts to emerge.

"Bet you can't catch me!" Monty yells, and he takes off across the field at full speed. We play a few rounds of tag until we're both out of breath and collapse onto our backs in the grass.

"I miss him, too, you know." I lace his fingers through mine.

"You do?"

"Yep." The weight of my confession holds me against the ground.

"Do you think Caleb misses us?" Monty rolls onto his side to face me and props his head up on his hand.

"I know he does. Caleb never forgets about people who are important to him. And *you're* the most important to him."

"Yeah? How do you know?" Monty wipes his runny nose on the sleeve of his shirt.

"Does he call you?"

"Yeah."

"That's one way you know. He also talks about you all the time. And even when he has important things going on, he tries his best to make sure you're okay."

"That *does* sound like Caleb."

Caleb's endless calls and texts to me over the last couple weeks flood my mind. Even when he has important things going on, like trying to save my mother's house and making sure this sweet boy is taken care of, he tries his best to make sure I'm okay. A lump fills my throat, and I try desperately to swallow it down. Good hell, I want things to be right with us again. Despite my best efforts, a tear escapes and trails down toward my ear. It's quickly caught by the hand of a little boy smelling of earth and sweat.

"It's okay to miss him, Kate. He'll come home soon. Right?"

I sniffle and blink several times, trying to clear any remaining tears.

"That's right, Monty. He'll come home soon."

caleb

The mountains slowly slide by my window, and the miles gradually pass. I catch myself scrolling through messages with Kate again, unable to think about anything other than being back with my girl. I've got some major begging in my future, but I think I'm ready for it. Checking the time, only ten minutes have passed since the last time I looked. The scenery all looks the same. It's gorgeous, but that's not what I'm interested in right now.

Not much irritates me more than Austin barely driving the speed limit like a retired old man when I have places to be. Namely, at home making up with Kate. We're headed home for a week. After our week off, we head to Billings for the final rodeo of the season. Hopefully, we'll bring home the money we need to save the homestead, and I'm able to win Kate's forgiveness. Assuming we ever make it home at the rate Austin is driving.

"Gas pedal is on the right, man," I say, urging him to drive faster.

"Would you like to drive?" Austin asks, clearly tired of my whining.

"Yes!"

"Too bad. You scare the shit out of me when you drive us home. You're like a damn barn sour horse," Austin says.

I groan and check the time again. We're never going to make it home.

Despite it all, we do *eventually* make it to town. Austin pulls into Kate's driveway, and suddenly, I'm not in such a rush. I stay in my seat, staring at the door. Austin clears his throat.

"What's the problem?"

"I think I need a pep talk."

Austin chuckles. I'm glad he finds this funny because I'm sure as hell not laughing. It's too hot in this damn truck. Beads of sweat break out across my forehead, and I swipe them away.

"Get out of the truck. Go on. I'll wait right here."

I groan but do as I'm told, and before I know it, I'm standing in front of her door. Balling my hand into a fist, I tap on the door several times. Soft footsteps from inside draw closer until finally the door swings open. The very sight of Kate melts my heart. I've clearly surprised her. Her mouth hangs open, and tears fill her eyes. I can't wait to feel her warmth as I wrap her in my arms and beg for her forgiveness. But there's no chance.

"Kate—"

The door slams shut in my face, narrowly missing my nose. Austin's laugh taunts me from behind. I knock again, softer this time, knowing she's on the other side of the door. Bracing myself with a hand on either side of the doorframe, I lean into the door.

"Kate, please talk to me."

"Go away."

"I'm sorry. I need to talk to you. Please, can we talk?"

The door swings open, but instead of Kate, it's Dakota.

"She asked you to leave," Dakota says firmly

"I'm trying to make things right. I need to talk to her."

"And I can already pinpoint part of the problem: You're not listening." Dakota steps out onto the porch, grabbing hold of my ear and dragging me back toward Austin's truck. "Kate doesn't want to talk to you. She doesn't even want to see you. That means you need to use those big ole ears of yours to listen, and you need to leave."

With a final shove, I stagger against the hood of Austin's truck, and Dakota releases her hold on me.

"Ouch." I rub my tingling ear.

"Hey, Dakota." Austin leans out the window and waves, a broad smile filling his face.

"Hmmm." Dakota stares back at him through narrow slits before turning and marching back inside the house.

I reclaim my seat in the truck. That didn't go as planned.

"I think I need a plan B."

"I think you need a miracle."

I CATCH a flash of Dakota's curly auburn mane from around the tower of toilet paper and hustle into her aisle of the grocery store. My boots skid across the polished tile floor, and I'm unable to stop myself before sliding into the side of her grocery cart, nearly toppling the whole thing over.

"What the hell? Are you following me?" Dakota's angry question attracts curious looks from passersby.

"Happy coincidence. I promise." I try to right the contents of her buggy that spilled over from our collision.

Dakota snorts. "What do you want, Caleb?" She folds her arms over her torso.

"Breaking up with Kate was a mistake."

"Yeah, it was. Sucks, doesn't it?" Her eyebrows shoot up on her forehead.

"I want to make things right with her. I want to win her back."

"You don't deserve her." Dakota grasps the handle of the cart and starts to walk away.

I dart out in front of her, blocking her path. "I know. You're right. But I love her, and I never should have broken up with her in the first place. If she'll give me another chance, I know I can prove myself to her."

"Shouldn't you be talking to her, not me?" Dakota's hand finds her hip, popped out to the side.

"Yes. But recent events made it evident that I'm not going to be able to get to Kate without either earning your cooperation or hog-tying you. So here I am, begging you to let me try to win my girl back."

"I don't see much begging going on."

I come around the cart and drop to my knees in front of her, clasping my hands together at my chin. "Let me have a chance to talk to her. That's all I'm asking of you. Don't block me from Kate. If she doesn't want to take me back, that's her choice to make, but she needs to be the one to make it. I love her—"

"Good hell, get up off the floor." Dakota nervously surveys the store. "Are you *trying* to cause a scene? Can you imagine the gossip this would start?"

Obeying, I stand and wait patiently for her response. When the coast is clear, her gaze steadies on me.

"Okay. I won't get in the way. But Caleb, I'm telling you, if you hurt her again, I will personally hunt you down. You already had your chance, and you blew it. Personally, I don't think you deserve another one, but I'll keep that opinion to myself. For now."

"Thank you. One other thing."

"Yes?"

"Would you slip me her work schedule?"

Dakota huffs and turns away, pushing her cart down the aisle. "I never said I would help you. I said I wouldn't get in the way. Take what you can get." Dakota tosses a package of paper towels into her cart and continues down the aisle, not bothering to look back.

That was easier than I expected. Forgetting my shopping

list, I head out the automatic doors. They flutter closed behind me. I've got to figure out how to show my girl I'm here to stay. My truck roars to life and I take off toward Kate's. I'm not sure what my plan is, but I've got to try something.

Kate's truck is missing from the driveway, but I pull in anyway. She isn't responding to any of my texts or phone calls. She wasn't at work this morning when I went to the diner for breakfast. I'm betting my best chance at getting in front of her is to stake out at her house and wait.

I knock on the front door a few times for good measure, to make sure she's not here. If she is, she's not coming to the door. I take a seat on the steps and wait. The sun is setting by the time Kate's truck appears. It pauses on the road, and for a moment, I think she's going to drive past. She doesn't. She pulls into her spot and gets out, a determined expression claiming her face. I stand, waiting for her to approach.

"What are you doing here, Caleb?"

"I need to talk to you."

"I have nothing to say to you and no interest in hearing whatever it is you think you need to say to me. We're over. Remember? You're the one who called it."

Kate shoves past me and stomps up the steps of the porch, working her key in the door as quickly as she can. I trail behind her, propping an elbow on the doorframe next to her. If she'll give me a chance to talk, I might be able to fix this.

"Kate, please. Hear me out. I never should have left, but you were hurting, and I was the cause of it. Plus, there's the whole Monty thing—"

Kate's expression twists and she finally pauses to look at me. "What does Monty have to do with this?"

"You said you didn't want kids. I'd never even thought to ask before, and you were always so encouraging when I talked about fighting for custody of him that I just assumed . . ."

"I would never get in the way of that little boy having a safe home—"

"I know that. And I didn't want you to sacrifice your happiness for my choices."

The door opens and Kate steps inside, removing the key from the lock as she goes in. The scent of her shampoo intensifies the torturous ache I've become accustomed to.

"That's when a conversation should have happened, Caleb. I can't be in a relationship with you if you're going to bail every time I say something you don't agree with."

"I'm here to prove to you that I won't leave you again—"

The door slams shut in my face. Not another word from Kate. I'm not a fan of this new dynamic between us. I heave a sigh and drop onto the step again. I'm not leaving till she talks to me. If she needs me to show her that I'm serious, I will. I'll stay here as long as it takes to prove to her that my intentions are sincere. I have all the time in the world and nothing I want more than to fix things with her.

When Dakota comes home, she watches me suspiciously while grabbing bags from the back of her car.

"Want help?" I ask, ready to take advantage of any opportunity.

"Nice try. If Kate isn't letting you in the house, I'm not either."

Dusk slowly turns to night. Eventually the lights turn off and the house goes quiet. I adjust, stretching my legs across the stairs and leaning my back against the rail. I feel helpless sitting here, but what else can I do to prove to Kate that I'm here to stay? I can't screw this up like I've done everything else.

Austin's explanation of my cousin's accident comes to mind. Whether her accident was my fault or not, I still would have felt the loss. I loved my cousin, and the role I had teaching her to ride allowed us the opportunity to form a bond I don't have with some of my other family. But if her accident wasn't my fault, that changes so much. I've carried that heaviness for years.

I pull up my uncle's contact information on my phone and

press the call button. Within a few rings, he's on the other end offering me a greeting.

"Hey, Uncle Wesley. Do you have a minute to talk?" Emotion already weighs on my tone.

"Yeah, Caleb, what's wrong?"

Aunt Loreen's muffled voice is in the background. "Is that Caleb? Put him on speaker, Wesley."

"Your aunt's on the line now, too, Caleb. What do you want to talk about?"

"Anna has been on my mind a lot lately." I clear the lump from my throat. "And her accident."

A heavy silence fills the line before Aunt Loreen speaks up. "We have those days, too. But then I think about my girl on the back of that horse and how much joy filled her little soul every single time she rode. I try to focus on those moments instead."

"She really looked up to you, Caleb," Uncle Wesley says. "The days you came over for her lessons were her favorite days."

"I just . . . I wish I could go back. Maybe if I'd been on time—"

"Stop." Uncle Wesley's tone turns stern. "There are a million different things all of us wish we'd done differently that day. There isn't any question whether someone would have prevented her accident if they could have. Blaming yourself isn't going to fix anything."

I drop my face into the palm of my hand. "I was talking to Austin the other day and he said it wasn't me that spooked the horse. I don't know if he knows what he's talking about or not, but I'm so sorry I wasn't there when I should have been. It was my job to teach her, and I failed."

"Caleb, honey, none of it's your fault," Aunt Loreen says. "If there is any blame to lay it's on me. I'm her mother, and I'm the one that was responsible for watching her when it happened. I should have made her wait in the house till you arrived. I knew how excited she got for her lessons, but I never thought she'd go against everything all of us had taught her about not getting on the horse without an adult. She was wild and free, and you know that."

"Did the horse really start bucking before I came up the driveway?"

"How do you think I got there so quick when it happened? I'd gone upstairs and happened to look out the window and see her on that horse. And then Jasper started bucking, and I ran down to help her. You'd just pulled up when I came out the front door."

"I didn't know. All this time I thought I was the one that spooked Jasper."

"We thought you knew. If we'd known you thought you were responsible . . . "

"You all were grieving the loss of your child. You shouldn't have had to look out for me, too."

"I'm sorry you've carried that burden all this time," Aunt Loreen says, and the line goes silent for several seconds.

"You'll be coming to the family reunion this fall, won't you?" I ask, ready to move on from the pain.

"Yeah, we'll be there."

We spend a few minutes catching up before ending the call. It's a call I should have made years ago, but I didn't know. What a mess I've made from acting on my perception of things without stopping to question if I'm seeing things right. Maybe now I'll be able to find some peace in Anna's memory.

I prop my head against the rungs of the porch steps and drift in and out of sleep, waiting for morning to come.

A shrill scream startles me awake around sunrise. I totter down the stairs, forgetting where I am. Splayed out on my back on the brick sidewalk, two heads pop into view above me.

"What the hell, Caleb?" Kate asks. "Did you stay here all night?"

"I told you I needed to talk to you and that I'm here to stay this time."

"You're absurd. Go home. We have nothing to talk about."

They step over me now, dressed for a run, and I rub my hands over my face before sitting up. That was really smooth. I stretch and reclaim my spot on the steps while I wait for their return. This might be a dumb idea, but Kate's bound to cave before too much longer. Even if it's only to get me to go away. And I've got to talk to her if I have any chance of winning her back. My stomach grumbles, reminding me I haven't eaten since breakfast yesterday.

They're gone about thirty minutes when they come jogging back to the house. A thin sheen of sweat covers Kate's forehead. She stops in front of me, her hands on her hips, her breathing heavy. Without speaking, she slides her eyes over me from head to toe. Finally, I break the silence.

"I see you've taken up running."

"I see you've taken up stalking."

"I'm not stalking you, Kate. I want to talk to you. I want to explain myself and apologize."

"You already have. And I don't have to accept it unless I want to. You seem to be missing that fact. Go home. I don't want to see you."

Kate shoves by me. Dakota shrugs as she follows Kate into the house. I'm not making much progress. Grumbling, I plop onto the steps again, determined to outlast my stubborn girl. The swish of the curtains inside catches my eye. Moments later, the door creaks open, and Dakota appears.

"You hungry?" She offers me a plate of eggs, bacon, and toast.

"Helping the enemy?" I raise an eyebrow at her.

"Kate's in the shower. Eat quick. If I'm questioned, I'll deny everything."

"You didn't fill it with laxatives or something, did you?"

"No." Dakota shoves the plate at me. "Eat. Before I retract my offer."

I take it and shovel the contents into my mouth. "I appreciate this," I say through a mouthful of eggs. A small clump falls out of my mouth and rolls down the front of my shirt.

"That's wildly attractive. It's a wonder why Kate hasn't already taken you back. *Love* a man with food all over his face."

I chuckle. "Depends on the meal. She never complained when it was her—"

"Okay! Let's keep it PG, why don't we. Are you finished yet?"

I smirk.

"Men." Dakota rolls her eyes. "Give me your plate. I've got to get rid of the evidence."

"Thanks for breakfast."

"Don't mention it. Literally," Dakota says and disappears inside the house.

kate

Dark clouds are rolling in overhead. Caleb is crazy. He hasn't moved from our steps. He needs to go home. I slowly step away from the window, trying to avoid being seen.

"Is he still out there?" Dakota calls from the other side of the room.

"Hell yeah. Maybe I dodged a bullet. Maybe he's crazy." I plop on the couch and aimlessly flip through channels.

Dakota looks up at me and cocks an eyebrow at me. "Really? You think he's crazy now?"

"No." I exhale, nearly blowing a raspberry, and drop my chin to my raised knee. "There's nothing good on TV." I switch it off and toss the remote.

"Maybe not. But there's a super juicy drama currently happening in our front yard." Dakota wiggles her eyebrows, making me laugh.

"Shut up. There's nothing juicy happening out there. Only a crazy guy who can't take a hint." I'm not about to admit that I secretly find it sweet of him to hang around, if not a touch insane. But it's best this way. I need to keep my distance.

"I don't know. It's kind of romantic in a way." Dakota claims the other end of the couch.

Now it's my turn to roll my eyes.

"Don't tell me you're falling for his tactics."

Before she can respond, the house shakes with the rumble of thunder outside. I straighten, my feet dropping to the floor. Neither of us says anything. Within seconds the roar of raindrops on our metal roof fills the room. I jump from my seat and rush to the window. Finally, Caleb will leave, and I can forget about him once and for all. But he doesn't. He's sitting there, getting soaked to the bone.

Shaking my head, I grab my phone from the couch. This is so stupid. He's been out there a ridiculous amount of time already. He's going to get sick if he stays out in this weather. I press the phone to my ear and wait. After several rings, Austin answers.

"Come get your dumbass friend off my steps." I peek out the window at Caleb sitting in the rain, his head tucked into his hands.

"You haven't succumbed to the charm yet, huh?"

"Austin. It's pouring rain. There's lightning. He's been out there since yesterday with nothing to eat or drink. I don't even want to think about what he's been doing about using the bathroom. Our potted plants may never be the same."

"Eh. The rain will wash them out for you." Another boom of thunder shakes the house again.

"Seriously, this is a problem. He needs to go home before he gets sick or struck by lightning. Come make him leave."

"I have a better idea. Why don't you invite him in? You could give him a towel to dry off and give him back one of his many shirts you've kidnapped over the years. Let the guy say what he has to say. Would it be that bad to hear him out?"

"Austin—"

"Come on, Kate. It's the least you can do. He's trying."

"Since when are you on *his* side? What alternate universe have I found myself in?"

"Go talk to him, Kate. You're both adults. Act like it."

The fucking nerve this man has. Without saying goodbye, I hang up the phone and throw it against the couch with a growl. It bounces off and lands on the floor. Dakota watches me quietly.

"I can't believe this." I storm across the room. "I have to do everything myself. Where is everyone's common sense? I mean, seriously, what is going on?" I swing the front door open and march out into the rain.

Caleb stands, backing into the yard as I charge down the steps, straight for him. Lightning strikes in the background, way too close for us to be standing outside like this, and the thunder shakes the ground.

"Have you lost your mind?" I scream at Caleb, pointing at my head.

"Yes. I lost everything when I gave you up."

"You can't be out here, Caleb. It's not safe. You've gone mad. At the very least you should go sit in your damn truck and wait till the rain stops."

"I'm not going anywhere till I get a chance to talk to you, Kate."

Rain pelts down on his face and shoulders, soaking through his shirt and plastering it against his skin. Droplets fall from his hair, streaming down his skin alongside the rain.

"Then talk. Say what you have to say and leave. I don't want you here, Caleb."

I shiver, my own clothes soaked through already from the rain, as the massive, cold beads of water batter against my skin. Caleb steps closer, taking my hands in his. Somehow his hands are warm, and mine are like ice cubes. The warmth sends goose bumps shooting up my arms.

"I didn't mean what I said when I broke things off with

you, Kate. We were always something, always an us, to me. I only said those things because I thought I was protecting you."

"Protecting me from what? Damn it, Caleb, I'm so tired of you and Austin justifying your actions by claiming you were trying to protect me. What the hell are you protecting me from? Where are all these imaginary monsters that I'm somehow blind to?"

"It was me, Kate. I thought I was the monster. I was trying to protect you from the hurt that I knew would come along with being with me."

"That's funny because the only hurt you caused was when you looked me in the eyes and told me that I wasn't worth the trouble and walked away."

The tears are welling up again, merging with the streams of rain as they race down my cheeks. Lightning strikes, followed by boisterous thunder that makes me jump. Caleb pulls me to him, wrapping his arms around me. I've missed this: the feel of his body pressed against mine; the warmth that radiates from him, making me feel safe and cherished. But it's a lie. It's all one big facade he made me believe. I know better now.

"I can see that. And I'm going to make it right—to prove to you that I'm here to stay."

I step away from him, despite the comfort I find in his arms. His words aren't enough to fix us. The pieces can't be magically glued back together. It's not enough. I shake my head, and his hands slowly trail down my arms as I step further away from him. His eyes widen with the distance between us, and when my fingertips drop from his, pain and loss play like a slideshow on his face, giving me a front row seat.

"Kate, please—"

"I can't." I shake my head, backing away slowly. I can't watch him fall apart like this. My heart splinters alongside him.

Caleb collapses onto his knees, his voice breaking as he speaks. "I'm begging you, Kate."

My throat is too tight to let out any more words. I can't

look at him. I can't watch him fall apart like this—to see the desperation win. It's too much. I spin around and rush back inside, slamming the door closed behind me and sinking to the floor as sobs rack my body all over again. Dakota wraps a towel around me, rubbing up and down my arms, trying to warm my body.

"Why don't you go put on dry clothes? I'll have hot cocoa waiting on you when you get back."

I nod through the tears and let Dakota pull me to my feet.

"What about Caleb? He can't stay out there in the cold rain."

"I called Austin again before you came inside. He's on his way over to take care of him."

I hug the towel around me without saying anything more and head to my bedroom to change. As promised, Dakota has a mug of hot cocoa waiting for me when I come back out. I carry it to the window, watching for Austin. Within minutes, Austin's headlights dance through the window. He crouches next to Caleb, still kneeling in the soaked grass, his head tucked into his hands. Austin rests a hand on his shoulder. After speaking a few soundless words with him, he pats Caleb on the back and rises, holding out a hand to him. Caleb takes it, allowing Austin to pull him up from the ground. I watch from the window as Caleb climbs into Austin's truck, and they drive away.

"I did the right thing, didn't I?" I ask, sinking into the chair and draping a blanket over my lap.

"Do you not know?" Dakota's eyebrows shoot up her forehead.

"After all the promises Caleb made, all the times he swore he'd always be here for me, he walked away. How can I ever believe him now? Even if he says all the right things now, he said the right things before, and that didn't stop him from leaving."

"True. You're probably better off playing it safe." Dakota shrugs.

"Do you really think so?" I shift, tucking my feet under me.

"Oh, for sure. I mean, men, right? You can't trust any of them. They say all the sweet things that they think you want to hear so they can get in your pants and poof, they're gone. It was all a lie. They're all a bunch of lying scoundrels. Honestly, your brother has the right idea. Have your fun, but never get close enough to anyone to get hurt."

My pulse quickens and I search Dakota's face. This is not the response I expected.

"Do you really think so?"

"Totally. See, your problem is you were playing defense. Caleb had all the control. You wanna play offense. You want to be the one with the ball, calling the shots. Otherwise, you'll get used just like Caleb used you."

Heat simmers in my veins, and my skin grows hot. "Excuse me? You barely even know Caleb. You've been around him, what, two times? Maybe? Caleb is one of the most empathetic and compassionate people I know. He would never intentionally use anyone, and the fact that you're accusing him of that tells me you don't know him at all. I mean, honestly Dakota, the man wouldn't . . . "

The words die on my tongue.

"Yes?" Dakota leans back in her seat with a Cheshire-cat grin. "Go on. The man wouldn't what?"

It was a trick. I see that now. And it worked. My chin quivers, and I set down what's left of my cocoa.

"Yeah, okay, I'm in love with him. But it's not that simple."

"Kate, it's as simple as you want it to be. If you want to love him, do it. Let that beautiful man ravish you. Let him spoil you for years to come and treat you like his queen. Have his beautiful big babies and thank your lucky stars that he chose you."

"That's not how it works in real life."

"Except it is, Kate."

I shake my head. "Not for me. Kids aren't part of the picture for me."

"Why not?"

"Clearly, you haven't met my mom. I don't have what it takes to be a mom. And kids are important to Caleb. Hell, he practically already has one. He was right to break up with me."

"Are you talking about Monty? Because that boy loves you, and you are great with him. Plus, you wouldn't be doing it alone. You'd be doing it with Caleb.

"You're not your mom, Kate. In fact, she's had you filling in her role for years. You've already earned the mommy merit badge, and you can't even see it because it wasn't a child you've been mothering all these years. It's a forty-eight-year-old woman. And shame on her for putting that on you."

"He broke me, Dakota. And instead of saying, hey, we should talk about this, because I'm in the middle of getting custody of Monty, he told me I was a mistake, and he left."

"Okay, well, that's obviously an issue you two need to work out."

"But if I wasn't important enough for him to have a difficult conversation with, why would I be now?"

"It's fine to not want kids. But if the only reason you don't want them is because you don't think you're enough, I'm here to tell you, you'd make a great mom. Especially to Monty. And I'd hate for you to lose Caleb over a false assumption like that."

"You may be right, but that doesn't change the fact that I wasn't enough to make him stay."

I rise from the chair, sniffling back the remnants of emotions that keep bubbling up, and lock myself in my bedroom. Life's not that simple. And neither is love.

I FORGOT about the nerves that come with competing. Jazzy shuffles underneath me, feeding off my energy no doubt. Austin and Dakota stand nearby offering moral support. They've decided to watch from the side of the arena rather than from the stands. I don't understand why I'm getting so worked up. It's not like this is a significant competition. It's nothing more than a bunch of locals from around the county.

I take in a few deep breaths of the dusty arena air and try to center myself. It doesn't even matter how I do today. If I place, great. If not, it's no big deal. Except I hate losing. But winning isn't what today is about. Today is about me quitting barrel racing on my own terms. I think I'm ready to kiss that chapter of my life goodbye, but my first time around the choice to quit or keep going was stolen from me. Stolen from me by my dad's absence, my mom's declining health, my own obligation to put family first.

This summer took a turn I never saw coming. It's been a summer of discovery—discovering what I want, what I'm capable of, and finding closure for old seeping wounds I never thought would heal. Me competing today is one more step down that path of closure.

"You're on deck, Kate," Austin says, tapping my leg. It's no surprise he's the one focused on me being in position when it's time.

Jazzy and I get in place, ready to make our run. Jazzy shuffles underneath me as I scan the crowd, surprised by the number of spectators that showed up, but it's the solo figure standing off to the side that sends a rush of emotion through me. For the briefest moment, our eyes lock.

The crazy part is I can picture it—me and Caleb and Monty being a family. Ever since my conversation with Dakota, it's all I've been able to think about. Maybe I've been wrong not to give Caleb a second chance.

He gives a subtle nod, and the whistle blows, giving me the go. As we ride through the gate, my nervousness dissipates, and adrenaline takes its place. We take the first barrel a bit sharp, knocking into it and causing it to wobble. I'm focused on the next barrel, though, before I see if the first one went down. Making our turn at the second barrel, we head to the third and final turn. Jazzy does her thing on the straightaway and we dash toward the gate.

Our cheering squad is waiting on us at the end of our run. The run was clean with no penalty, and I made an overall decent time for the arena. I search for Caleb, but he's gone. Did he watch me? Is he on his way over to try to talk to me? Not wasting any more time, I get Jazzy settled so we can enjoy the rest of our night at the fair.

"How did it feel being in the arena again?" Dakota asks later as we walk with our group around the fairgrounds.

"It felt good. I'm glad I did it, but I think I'm satisfied with calling that my last run."

"You sure?" Austin asks incredulously. "You looked pretty good out there."

"I'm sure. I don't think I could focus through a whole season. It was fun, but even while I was practicing in preparation for tonight, it never felt like my priority. It was another line on my to-do list for the day that I only wanted to finish so I could cross it off my list. I used to want to spend the whole evening riding."

"You took on that student, didn't you?"

"I did. I've already had a couple lessons with her. She's good." I nod. "I didn't realize how much I'd enjoy the teaching side of it. It's got me considering taking on some more students. Possibly make a business of it."

"That sounds like a great idea. Guess what I got us for tonight to celebrate your run?" Austin slides a few tickets out of his pocket and hands them to me. I flip them upright to read the print.

"You got us tickets for the Josh Turner concert?" I squeal and spin around to hug him, nearly tripping him up in the process. "I didn't even know it was him performing tonight."

"I sure did. We have about an hour to kill. Maybe we should get some dinner?"

We all decide on a vendor for food and make our purchases.

Dakota is unusually quiet tonight. Derrick was supposed to be in this weekend, but he had work stuff come up that held him in the city. It's been happening more and more lately, and I can see it wearing on her. She decided to come out with us tonight anyway, Derrick be damned.

We claim our seats when they finally open the gates for the concertgoers. When Josh Turner takes the stage, the crowd loses it. Everyone instantly hits their feet when his deep voice permeates the grounds. I'm right there with them. No amount of shame over my singing voice could keep me quiet, and I belt out each word. When he slows it down to sing a love song, Austin and Dakota stand awkwardly nearby, Austin pretending to ignore Dakota and Dakota fixating on the concert.

Everything was near perfect till the band starts the intro for "Your Man." The imaginary Band-Aid I'd pasted over my heart last night bursts open at the words Caleb used to serenade me with. I squeeze my eyes tight, determined not to break down in the middle of this crowd of people. A warm hand grabs mine, urging me around the seating to an opening. I resist at first, till I'm face-to-face with Caleb.

I know I shouldn't allow this. It would be better for both of us if I turned him down and saved ourselves the pain this is bound to cause us. Instead, I soak in his touch while everyone around us fades into the background. I may regret it later, but I need him right now. Holding onto a hand at both of my shoulders, Caleb leans in close to my ear.

"Do you know how to country cha-cha?"

I know I should turn away, not allow him to be so close, touching me. Instead, I arch an eyebrow at him. "You should know the answer to that. Of course, I don't."

"Let me show you. Start off with your left foot."

Together, we cha-cha forward, then back again, Caleb's strong arms guiding me through the steps I'm unfamiliar with. For a moment it's like we've been transported back in time, before things between us became so complicated. This man beside me is someone I never thought I'd have to learn how to do without. He's always been there for me, each and every step I take, protecting me, supporting me, and wanting me.

I'll allow myself this last moment with him, with the possibility of what we could have been. When this song ends, I'll force myself to face the facts and accept that it's time to move on. I'll put an end to Caleb's attempts to repair the relationship that has proved irreparable.

Caleb's familiar warmth engulfs me under the starry Montana night. When I look up to his handsome face, he's gazing down on me with that same unfaltering smile that lightens any burden. He winks at me and spins me around, somehow avoiding us becoming a tangle of arms. Our feet continue moving to the beat of the music, and I trust his steady hands as he drops me into a dip. With a sharp tug, I'm on my feet, Caleb's arms around me this time and his lips on mine.

I break away, the old familiar ache filling my chest—a reminder of the torment I've been through these last few weeks.

"Caleb, we can't . . ."

"I never should have assumed the things that I did. I never should have made the decision to walk away on my own—I see that now. Leaving like that broke me. It wasn't for me, Kate. I was doing it for you, despite how much it hurt me. But it wasn't a decision I should have made on my own. I should have talked to you and given you the chance to decide for yourself. It's a mistake I can promise you I'll never make again. I love you. With every part of me, I need you."

Caleb reaches across the empty space between us and brushes away the tear that breaks loose, trailing down my cheek. He's saying all the right things, but how can I trust his words?

"Take this." Caleb places a letter in my hand. "Read it tonight. It's time sensitive, and you have a decision to make. Promise you'll read it?"

"I'll read it."

Caleb kisses my forehead and disappears into the crowd.

caleb

"You did *what*?" Austin's hands shoot to his head as he spins around to face me.

Ducky and Josh snicker, both taking a few steps back in case Austin blows a gasket no doubt. Trevor walks unassumingly into the barn office, swinging a rope.

"Get the hell out of here," Austin says, grabbing the rope from him and tossing it back out the door.

"Geez." Trevor scowls and follows his rope.

Austin turns back to me, crossing his arms over his chest. "Start over and repeat what you just said. With more detail this time."

"I gave Kate a letter."

"Last night at the concert?" Ducky asks.

"Yes. Last night at the concert."

"After you made yet another move on her and she shut you down for what . . . the hundredth time?" Josh asks.

"Yeah. Something like that." I huff and rub my temple with the tips of my fingers. These guys don't believe in taking it easy on me.

"What was in the letter, Caleb?" Austin asks, glowering at me.

"I basically told her all the same things I've already told her—"

"That she said wasn't good enough . . ." Ducky chimes in.

"Right. I told her how I feel about her."

"Which apparently also wasn't enough . . ." Josh says.

"Are you guys going to let me spit it all out or what?" They hold their hands up in surrender, chuckling. I'm glad they're finding this so funny. "I asked her for another chance, and if her answer is yes, I asked her to wear one of my T-shirts to the rodeo tonight."

Ducky and Josh about fall over each other laughing. Austin squeezes his eyes shut and repeatedly knocks the back of his head against the office wall. He lets out a long exhale before daring to return his stare to me.

"That's what I was afraid you said."

"Why? What does it matter?"

"Are you kidding? Your head isn't going to be in competing tonight. It's going to be in finding Kate in the stands, assuming she even comes—last I heard she didn't even want to be in the same arena as you. If she doesn't come, or shows up not wearing the right outfit, you're going to be a blubbering mess and we're going to be an embarrassment. If she does show up in your damn shirt, your ass will likely be climbing the damn stands to get to her, and yet again, I'll be showing up in the arena without a header. There is no way this ends well for saving the homestead."

"I'll hold it together. I swear."

The peanut gallery breaks out in laughter again, and Austin shakes his head.

"It is what it is, I guess. For what it's worth, I hope she shows. Come on. We need to get loaded up."

The day creeps by, full of anticipation over what decision Kate will finally make. The smell of earth, hay, and manure fill the indoor arena. I scan the stands, swarming with spectators gathered to watch the rodeo, but so far there's no sign of Kate.

This is the competition that determines it all for us. This is where we save or lose the homestead.

Austin might be right. I shouldn't have involved the rodeo. That was such a dumb idea. There's no way I'm going to be able to focus on roping. I move further around the panels, trying to get a better look of the stands. There are so many people here. I don't know how I'll ever be able to spot her. This was a terrible plan. Austin rides up next to me.

"Have you heard from Kate? Is she coming? Have you seen her?"

"Good to know you're holding it together like you promised." Austin scowls at me, but then he searches the crowd with me. "Have you tried texting her?"

"No way, man. I told her I'd give her space to make her decision and wouldn't bother her. You text her."

Austin grumbles under his breath, but he sends a text to Kate. The announcer's voice booms over the noise, announcing the transition into our event. Austin's phone buzzes, and he checks it for Kate's reply.

He pauses briefly to read and looks up at me. "She's not here."

"Fuck." I pull my hat off, setting it over the horn of my saddle. "Damn it. What did she say?"

"She said, 'No, I'm not.'"

"Well, what did you ask her?"

"I asked her if she was here," Austin says, exasperated.

Hope blooms fresh in my chest. I place my hat back on.

"So she said she's not here, not that she's not coming."

"Hell, I don't know. You didn't tell me to ask if she was coming, you told me to ask if she was here."

I scan the crowd again, focusing on the entrance this time. Within minutes, Kate and Dakota appear. They're looking over the mess of cowboys waiting to compete, no doubt trying to find us. At last, we make eye contact across the arena. Kate lifts onto her toes and waves. She's wearing my shirt. I wave back and blow her a kiss.

"Isn't that sweet," Austin says, catching my eye.

"Don't be jealous," I say, giving Austin a wink. "Holy shit, I can breathe. I didn't realize how tight my lungs were before."

"Remember, you're holding it together. And it's going to be our turn soon."

"I need to ask you something," I say.

"About?"

"Kate." I reach down and rub my horse's neck, trying to release some of the nerves I know I'm transferring to him.

"And now's the time?" Austin asks, shooting me a look like I've lost my mind.

"Yes, now. I can't focus on anything else." Austin grunts and motions for me to let it out. "I want to marry your sister." Austin's head jerks toward me.

"Marry her? Don't you think you should get out of the doghouse before you try jumping to marriage? Are you even on speaking terms with her right now?"

"Eh. Details. She showed up in my shirt. That's the important part. That means I can fix the rest later. She does have a thing for barns—"

"Stop." Austin turns away from me again.

"I'm not asking her tonight. Maybe not even in the next month. I don't know. I haven't figured that part out yet, but I know I want to officially make her mine. And I want to know if you'd be okay with that." Austin removes his hat and wipes away the beads of sweat gathering on his brow. He's taking his time to answer, making my confidence waiver. He's come a long way, but maybe I'm pushing it.

"Caleb," Austin starts, his voice sharp, "as far as I'm concerned, you've been part of our family since the day we met in kindergarten. But if you ever do anything to fuck it up, I will fuck up your face. That being said, I'm glad she chose you. And

I take back what I said about wanting nothing to do with you once we wrap up our season."

"Wait, are you saying what I think you're saying?" I ask, sitting up a little straighter in my saddle. "Did I hear you right? Are you finally giving me your stamp of approval?" Austin scowls again, turning toward the arena.

"Don't turn it into a fucking ordeal, okay? I said what I said."

"That's probably the most agreeable thing I've ever heard you say, Austin. Thanks, man."

"Now get your head in the game, would you? I need second place tonight to stand any chance of saving my mom's house. I need you to focus, Caleb. I can't do it without you."

Austin's scowl is replaced by the sober expression he wore the night he asked me to come on the circuit with him. He's nervous. I've been so wrapped up in my own head that I hadn't noticed Austin's tells until now—the way he keeps adjusting his rope and shifting in his saddle. Austin never gets nervous.

"Alright, man. Let's show these folks how it's done."

I give Austin a nod, and we ride into the arena. Austin heads straight to the box. Unable to contain myself, I ride out to the center, stand in my stirrups, and do my best to yell over the crowd.

"I love you, Kate!"

The romantics in the stands cheer. Dakota nudges Kate who is currently beet red from the attention. She drops her face into her hands. Austin rolls his eyes and whistles at me, signaling for me to get into position, so I ride over to my box and get ready. Excited nerves flutter through my extremities. I look up in the stands, making eye contact with my girl. We clearly still have some making up to do, but the fact that she's on the edge of her seat and chewing her thumbnail tells me everything I need to know. She loves me, and I'm the luckiest man alive. Focusing on the task before me, I ready my rope and it's go time.

The steer rushes from the chute, and as the barrier rope flies free, my horse barrels out into the arena to put me in position. I'm not looking at Kate, and all I can hear is the sound of our horses' hooves beating against the ground, but I know my girl is cheering me on. I can feel it. Swinging my rope, waiting for the right moment to launch it at the steer, we close the space between us. My rope flies through the air, wrapping around the horns of the steer, and I quickly wrap the slack around my saddle horn, ready for Austin to get the heels.

Suddenly, the steer redirects, crossing in front of me and back toward my horse, cutting BoJack's legs out from under him. He tumbles downward, and I have no time to react. My body slams against the dirt, sliding and contorting as my 1,000-pound horse rolls on top of me.

CHAPTER FORTY-FOUR

Gasps followed by silence falls over the crowd as Caleb is crushed under the weight of his horse. BoJack kicks and squirms trying to right himself, but he's twisted up in the rope and can't stand. Instead, he mauls Caleb's lifeless form lying face down in the dirt. My heartbeat is all I can hear as the arena is rushed by cowboys running to Caleb's rescue. I try to run to him, but I'm glued to my seat until, somehow, I break free. It's like a nightmare where I'm stuck in slow motion while the murderer chases me on my heels. Only it's not the murderer who has my attention, and I am not the victim.

They say when you rodeo, it's not a matter of if you get hurt, but when and how bad. People typically think of the bull riders when they hear of another rodeo death, but when it comes down to it, death isn't so choosy. Death doesn't care if you're a man or a woman, an athlete or an artist. Death doesn't care if you're rich or you're poor, educated or uneducated, bull rider or team roper. It doesn't care.

At the base of the stands, I pause and wait a moment, expecting to see Caleb on his feet, waving to reassure the crowd that he's fine. It wasn't as bad as it looked. We all overreacted. Of all the standing cowboys, though, he is not one. They work at the rope, trying to avoid the flailing hooves of the horse. During the struggle to get free, one of BoJack's hooves clips the back of Caleb's head, and a strangled cry tries to escape my throat. Austin lunges for Caleb's head, sacrificing himself to shield Caleb from any further blows.

I leap over the rail, pain searing up through my feet as I land the six-foot drop to the arena floor. The tight pinch in my ankle suggests injury, but I don't care. I race toward the wreck, my feet sinking into the soft dirt like a sandy beach and my lungs fighting the iron clasps restricting their function. By the time I make it to him, BoJack has been freed and the paramedics are strapping Caleb to the stretcher, his body limp.

Austin holds me now, wrapping his arms around me, but I can't hear the words he says. He *is* speaking, isn't he? His brows are creased together and his lips are trying to tell me something.

I can't.

I need to get to Caleb.

I try to shove away from Austin, but he only pulls me back, trying in vain to get my attention.

Caleb is loaded into the ambulance, and the doors are closed. All too soon, and yet not quickly enough, the ambulance pulls away, lights and sirens blaring, racing to the hospital. It's Austin who gets me moving, pulling me along to where his truck is parked. My heart is aching, pounding in my ears. I can't catch my breath. Why is it so hard to breathe? I don't understand what is happening. This must be a dream, isn't it? It doesn't feel like real life. The pain is searing through me, but I can't find the source, and I don't understand the hurt.

Dark blurs swipe across the window and Austin speeds after the ambulance. It's raining now, and the raindrops further numb the world around me, turning it into a dark haze on the other side of the windshield.

The bold red block lettering of the emergency room sign is what catches my eye. Finally, something to focus on. Something I can understand. We're here to find Caleb. Austin tugs me inside, and we stop at a desk. The lady behind the desk types into her computer as he talks to her, but she only looks up at him and shakes her head.

Austin leads me over to a set of chairs in the nearly empty waiting room. We sit, and slowly, the tears burst free. He holds me tightly to his side, his strong hand holding my head to his chest as the tears pour out of me. The pounding in my ears fades, only to be replaced by my own sobs and Austin's voice trying to console me.

"They're working on him, Kate. The doctors have him. It's Caleb—he has to be okay. Everything will be fine. I know it will."

His hand rubs against my back, trying to ease the sobs.

Before long, Dakota joins us in the waiting room. When Austin has no news to share, she takes the seat on the other side of me and sits with us, holding tightly to my hand.

Time crawls by, and people come and go from the waiting room that has become my personal hell. Unable to sit any longer, I pace back and forth across the scuffed tiles. Austin leans back in his chair, his fingers dancing on his knees. Dakota sits quietly twirling a strand of curls around her finger, her eyes lost in another reality. Probably one much better than this one. After countless laps across the floor, I collapse in my chair again, exhausted in every possible way.

Footsteps moving down the quiet hall catch my attention. They move quickly, growing louder with each step. They're headed for us. The doctor in blue scrubs and a white lab coat searches the room.

"Family of Caleb Huxley?" she finally calls out.

I'm on my feet, charging toward the doctor with Austin and Dakota on my tail. The doctor's expression is heavy, throwing even more weight on my already drowning soul. She motions for us to follow and leads us into a small room with an oval table surrounded by chairs. Directing us to have a seat, we all file in and wait expectantly for her to tell us what's going on.

"First of all, I'm Dr. Anand. I'm the treating doctor on Mr. Huxley's case. Mr. Huxley was unconscious upon his arrival in our emergency department. It was ascertained that his accident caused a buildup of pressure on his brain, among other more minor injuries. We have been monitoring his intercranial pressure and treating him with medications to give him some relief and hopefully restore consciousness."

Air rushes from my lungs as I choke back more tears. Austin wraps an arm around my shoulders, squeezing me closer, his thumb rubbing across my shoulder.

Dr. Anand pauses, allowing me a moment before she continues. "He will hopefully wake up soon—"

"And if he doesn't?" My voice is scratchy, barely recognizable.

"We will have to monitor to determine the extent of his brain injury. During the accident, he also received other injuries due to being crushed underneath the horse. Thankfully, those are mostly mild in comparison. The most severe injury aside from his brain injury is a broken ankle we were able to stabilize. We will be consulting with ortho to determine the plan of action for his ankle."

"Can we see him?"

Dr. Anand nods at me. "Yes. I can take you to him now if you don't have any other questions."

I shake my head. "I want to be with him."

Dakota squeezes my hand. Dr. Anand stands and holds the door open for us to file out and follow her down the hall. She leads us down the winding corridor then comes to a stop, pushing open the door to Caleb's room. Not wasting any time, I rush inside, finding my spot at his bedside.

I brush my hand through Caleb's hair and press a kiss to his forehead, but it doesn't earn any response from him. He lies on the hospital bed, his eyes closed, his breathing steady, and the beeping of the monitor keeping time. I lace my fingers through his and give his hand a light squeeze before turning to the doctor.

"How long will he be unconscious?" I ask.

"We expect him to wake soon as the medications have more time to work. A nurse will be in after a while to check in and keep an eye on his progress," Dr. Anand says before leaving us.

Austin props his hands on the side rail of Caleb's bed, letting his head hang down between his arms as he exhales a shaky breath. Dakota stands off to the side, her arms wrapped around her middle.

Caleb looks peaceful, like he's simply napping. I lower the rail on my side of the bed and carefully climb up next to him, cuddling into his arm. This isn't the way things were supposed to work out. Our night wasn't supposed to end in a hospital, and mine and Caleb's story isn't supposed to end in tragedy. Maybe I should ask for another doctor to review Caleb's scans to make sure they didn't miss anything. Austin turns from the bed and paces back and forth across the room.

"Damn it, Caleb," Austin mutters under his breath. He pauses, his hands on his hips, and lets his eyes run over Caleb again. "I'm sorry, Kate. I've got to get out of here. I'm going to see if they have some coffee or something. Do you need anything?"

"No," I say faintly, wiping at the tears on my cheeks.

"Dakota?" Austin asks.

"No, thanks."

I PRESS the red end call button on my phone and toss it onto the chair next to Caleb's bed. His parents are on a cruise, and

I've been giving them regular updates as they work through finding a way home. Unfortunately, there have been very few updates to give. Caleb has remained stable throughout the night. The doctors seem positive, but they don't give me any of the answers I'm looking for.

Dakota finally left during the night. I think she felt like she was in the way or intruding on private moments. She promised to check in and make sure I didn't need anything later.

Austin walks in with a backpack, a paper bag, and two cups of coffee. He hands me a cup and the bag, but I have no appetite. Without even looking inside, I set the bag on the table and focus my red-rimmed eyes back on Caleb. If he won't wake up on his own, I'll will him to.

"No changes?" Austin's voice is barely above a whisper.

I shake my head.

"You need to eat something."

"I'm not hungry." And I'm not. I'm too numb to feel hunger, despite the growls coming from within my body.

"Damn it, Kate, don't make me beg." Austin stands at Caleb's bedside where I've been perched since last night.

"I'm fine, Austin. It's not me that needs help. It's Caleb." I link my fingers through his, hoping that maybe he'll give my hand a squeeze.

"We don't know when he's going to wake up, and it won't do him or anyone else any bit of good if you sit here wasting away while you wait on him." Austin grabs the bag from the table and pulls out a giant blueberry muffin. "The least you can do is keep yourself healthy for when he wakes up. He's going to need us to be strong for him, and if you're looking frail, he'll be too worried about you to worry about taking care of himself and healing."

Austin takes my hand and plops the muffin in it. Bits of the crumb topping crumble and fall to the floor. He's right. I know he's right. But that doesn't mean the gaping hole in my belly can be filled with food. I lift the muffin to my mouth anyway and take a couple bites to appease my brother before dropping it back down in the bag.

"I about forgot. Dakota sent this." Austin slides the backpack off and sets it in the chair. "Clothes and things for you. Stuff she thought you might need."

A nod is the best response I can muster.

A quick tap on the door announces the entrance of the nurse, bustling into the room to check Caleb's monitors and note his unchanged condition. She told me her name at shift change, but I can't remember. She gives me a warm smile, but it doesn't reach her eyes.

"Everything looks about the same," she says softly before settling her gaze on me. "Is there anything I can get you? I know hospitals aren't an easy place to sleep but we can bring a cot in for you if you want to try to rest some."

"No, thanks. How much longer do you think before he wakes up?" I ask.

She pats my knee, her expression somber. "It's hard to pinpoint things like that. It takes as much time as it takes."

The nurse leaves, and Austin takes her place at the bedside next to me. His hand rests on my shoulder, his head hung low. Austin's breathing hitches, catching my attention. I study his face, watching him closely. Slowly, his bloodshot eyes rise to mine.

"I'm sorry, Kate."

"Sorry for what?"

"I thought I was protecting you. I thought I was keeping you safe. I didn't want you to get hurt."

"Austin, what are you talking about?" I shift toward him in my seat.

"I never should have come between you and Caleb. I didn't see it at the time, but I do now."

"It's okay, Austin. This isn't your fault. Nobody could have foreseen this accident."

Austin observes Caleb now, refusing to hold eye contact with me. "But what if . . ."

I shake my head. "No."

"What if he doesn't wake up? Or what if he does and he's not the same? What if the time you two had is all the time you get?" Austin slowly turns to me but struggles to link his gaze with mine.

"We can't live for what-ifs. Nobody knows what's going to happen. We use our judgment and do the best we know how. That's all anyone can expect."

"Kate, I've seen the way you two have been looking at each other. I knew you two liked each other long before either of you spoke up and said anything. Probably before you admitted it to each other."

"And you still let me come with you guys?"

"I was dumb and thought neither of you would ever actually act on it. I thought my threats were enough, but I never should have tried to keep you apart. So much time was wasted because of me."

I shake my head. "If it wasn't you, it would have been something else. Or if we had gotten together earlier, who's to say we would have been ready? We could have broken up after a month and never spoken to each other again. You don't have anything to feel guilty about."

"I love you, Kate, and I want you to be happy."

"I know. I love you, too. Even if you are overbearing sometimes." I wink at him and reach over to squeeze his arm. "We're going to be okay, Austin."

"How do you know?"

"I can feel it."

"In that case, why don't you go take a shower and let me sit here with him." A muted smirk finds its way to Austin's face. "You stink. I'm tired of smelling you, and I'm sure Caleb is, too."

That almost makes me laugh. I release a heavy breath

instead, looking back at Caleb. "You're probably right. But if anything at all changes, you'll come get me?"

"Kate, the shower is about six feet from his bed. You aren't going to miss anything."

"Promise me."

"Okay. If anything changes, I'll get you."

caleb

A steady beeping fills my ears. I try opening my eyes, but my eyelids must be made of lead. Instead, I rest and listen to the beeping. When footsteps enter the room accompanied by a woman's voice sometime later, I try again, this time succeeding. I'm in a hospital room.

"Caleb, you're awake." The mattress shifts and Kate's there, sitting next to me. "Dakota, can you get the nurse and find Austin? How are you feeling?"

"I haven't decided yet. What happened?" My voice is dry and raspy. Dakota skirts around the end of the bed to the door.

"You had an accident. BoJack got tripped up. You don't remember?"

"It's fuzzy." I try to scoot up on the bed, but Kate shakes her head at me.

"Sit tight. We need to wait for the nurse or the doctor or something." She squeezes my hand and slides off the side of the bed.

I look over my body, at the IVs and the monitors. My body is aching, and I don't try beyond one lame attempt to climb out of bed. What happened?

"How long was I out?" I'm almost afraid of the answer.

"About a day. We've been worried sick."

A doctor walks in now, followed by Austin, Dakota, and a nurse. Kate stays glued to my side, one hand brushing through my hair while the other holds tightly to my hand. The doctor stands on the other side of the bed, my chart in her hand. She performs a quick exam and jots her findings in my chart.

"How are you feeling, Caleb?" the doctor asks.

"Like I've been hit by a truck."

The doctor shrugs. "Not far off. Do you remember what happened?"

I shake my head and instantly regret it. "Bits and pieces."

"You were crushed by your horse. We administered medication to relieve pressure from your brain. Aside from that, you do have extensive bruising, some damaged ligaments, and a broken ankle. From what I understand, your right foot was stuck in the stirrup, and the weight of the horse coming down on you must have broken the bone. We're waiting on the ortho consultation to determine whether surgery will be required. Overall, you're doing well, and we expect a full recovery, but we'll keep you here a bit longer for observation, to make sure we haven't missed anything. If everything goes well, you should be able to finish healing at home soon. Do you have any questions?"

"How long until I'm better?"

The doctor shrugs. "That's a loaded question. You may experience some headaches and fatigue for a while. Your ankle will probably take ten to twelve weeks. But again, ortho should be able to give a more accurate timeline when they come to speak with you later."

"Damn."

"If that's all, I'll leave you with your visitors." She snaps the chart shut, dropping it into its cubby, and leaves.

"Is BoJack okay?" I ask Austin.

"Yeah, he's going to be fine. I've got a buddy taking care of the horses. I'll go pick them up tomorrow."

"Your mom's house," I say, my mind slowly clearing. "I'm sorry, man. I ruined it. How are you going to get the rest of the money?"

"I have a week and a half to come up with something. Think we can pull off a bank heist in that time?" Austin asks.

"Seriously, what are we going to do? Fuck. If only I didn't screw us over."

"Don't worry about it. It was a freak accident. I was about to go after the heels when the steer cut back and under you. I never expected BoJack to get tripped up like that. And then you didn't bail off . . . "

"I didn't see it coming, either. I felt him going down, but my center of gravity shifted, and I didn't even get to drop my stirrup before I hit the ground," I say, bits and pieces of the accident coming back to me.

The nurse who introduced herself as Nurse Millie scurries about the room, checking my stats and making sure there haven't been any changes.

"As much as I hate to break up a good party," Nurse Millie says, "it's time for the rest of you to be heading home."

"Not Kate," I say.

"She hasn't left your side the whole time you've been here. I didn't expect her to start now," Nurse Millie says.

"Are you ready, Dakota?" Austin asks. I smirk at Austin, realizing they rode here together, and he flips me the bird when the girls aren't watching.

Goodbyes are said, and soon, it's just me and Kate. Kate lies on the edge of the bed with me, careful of where she touches. I hate hospitals, and I feel like absolute shit right now, but even a smile from her makes it so much better.

"You scared me." Kate curls up at my side.

"I'm sorry. I'm okay, though, Trouble." I kiss the top of her head and try to disguise the groan that slips out as I pull Kate tightly against me.

I mull over everything that's happened. Somehow, I seem to

have won my girl back, but yet again, I've caused her more heartache. Is she going to stay when her mom loses the homestead because of me? Because that's the reality of it: I ruined everything.

ANOTHER DAY of not-so-delicious hospital food and disrupted sleep later, the doctor finally signs off on my release. Kate drops the fresh clothes Austin brought for me on the hospital bed. Despite my excitement to get out of here, I can't shake this bad mood, knowing the consequences of my screwup.

"I can do it myself." I yank the shorts from Kate's hands and groan from the stabbing pain of moving my broken body.

"I just want to help," Kate says, stepping back. She's on edge, and it's because of me. I'm the asshole.

"Thank you." It comes out gruff, between gritted teeth.

I make a conscious effort to be nice as Kate helps me into the truck to drive me home. The ride is quiet aside from her occasional attempts to make conversation. Once we make it to my house, she nervously dances around me as I make my very slow trek from the truck to the house on my new crutches. Kate fluffs the pillows on my new couch, trying to make everything perfect, and hovers over me while I slide into my seat.

I don't deserve her. At all. Guilt eats away at me as she helps me get settled and all I can think about is how I've failed her and her family. I don't know if it's the lack of sleep or residue from my accident, but I can't shake this foul mood. Kate has done nothing but fuss over me since I woke up. I should be ecstatic. She showed up at the rodeo. She chose me. But it's overshadowed by my inability to follow through and help Austin win. I promised to help them save their mother's house, and instead, I single-handedly ruined all hope.

Kate has doted over me, always ready to help. The more

she's there for me, the more my anguish grows. More than once, I've taken my anger out on her, but she never left. She just takes it from me like she isn't worthy of more, and that only pisses me off, adding another stone to the weight I'm carrying.

There's a knock at the door, followed by Austin's voice calling from the entryway announcing his arrival. He's no doubt here to check up on me, too. Yet another person in my life that I don't deserve. Another person that I've managed to screw over.

Kate greets him, and he dumps himself into one of the recliners across from me, an unusual smile on his face. What does he have to be happy about anyway?

"Are you hungry?" Kate asks.

"No, I'm fine." I press my fingertips to my temple.

"How about a drink? Are you thirsty? How's your pain level? You can have some more medicine in . . . two hours."

"I said I'm fine, okay?"

It comes out harsher than I intend it to, and the whole room stiffens. I expel a heavy exhale, the already massive pressure on my chest growing almost unbearable. I was hoping to leave the outbursts at the hospital, but they've followed me home and are only becoming more frequent. Honestly, I don't know why she insists on sticking around after the way I've treated her since I woke up in the hospital.

"Oh. Okay. Well then. I think I'm going to go to the bathroom. I'll be back in a minute."

I can't lift my eyes from the floor. I can't witness the hurt I hear in her voice. As her soft footsteps tread away, Austin scoots forward in his chair, and I know he isn't going to let what happened pass without saying anything. When I find the courage to look up, Austin is staring straight into me.

"This is not going to happen," Austin says, his elbows resting on his knees and his fingertips pressed together.

"I don't know what you're talking about."

"Yes, you do, and I won't stand by and watch, Caleb. I don't know where your head is at, but you'd better find it and you'd better fix it. We've been down this road before, and we do not need a trip down memory lane. Especially if Kate is going to be one of your punching bags this time."

I know he's speaking metaphorically, but the statement disgusts me just the same. How could he say something like that? Does he really think so little of me?

"I don't deserve her. That accident should've never happened, but I can't do anything right."

"No, you don't deserve her, and you're right, the accident shouldn't have happened. But it did, due to no fault of your own. Falling into a depression won't fix it."

Fire spreads through my veins, and my breathing becomes heavy. I'm done with this conversation. I don't want to be here, and I don't want them here. I've already done enough. Can't they see that?

"I don't need your pity."

Austin scoffs. "Our pity? You think we pity you?"

"What else would you be doing here? I ruined everything. I single-handedly lost your family homestead. Me. I did it. If it wasn't for me, you'd have the money you need to take to the bank and save your mom's house. But I fucked it all up like I always do. I ruin everything I touch. Why did you have to choose me to be your partner? I tried to tell you to choose one of the other guys. You should have chosen someone else, Austin."

The bottled-up rage in my chest has nowhere to go. I probably can't even get off this damn couch without someone helping me. I can't leave. I can't move. I can't do anything.

"Is that what this is about? You think we care more about money than we care about you? That's pretty low, Caleb. I'm surprised to hear you think so little of us."

"That's just it, Austin. It's not you and Kate. It's me. And I don't understand why after all I've messed up you're giving me the time of day."

"Man, you're family. That's why. We love you, and no matter how you screw up, we're always going to be here. That being said, I'm not going to stand by and watch you disrespect Kate and hurt her because your head is stuck too far up your ass to see that the only thing we care about is you being okay."

"I failed her. I failed you." I lightly drop my head back against the cushions, trying desperately not to cry like a blubbering baby at the thought of letting down the woman I love.

"That wasn't failing. That was fighting. And you're still fighting. Failing Kate looks like you letting your insecurities dictate the way you treat her. Failing Kate looks like losing her. And you haven't lost her yet. Remember? She showed up for you. She came to the rodeo wearing the damn shirt. She stayed by your side in the hospital. You haven't failed anyone yet."

"Why don't you just kick my ass and get it over with, man?"

"I don't beat up on invalids." Austin stands from the chair. "Get your head on straight, or I'll change my mind. Now go fix it." Austin points toward the bathroom.

His footsteps disappear through the front door. He's right. He's right about all of it. I'm making up situations in my head, and I'm taking it out on the people that mean the most to me.

I take a deep breath, bracing myself for the pain and discomfort I know are about to follow. Slowly, I ease myself to the edge of my seat and lift myself to my feet. Well, my one good foot. Scooping up the crutches Kate propped against the couch, I head to the bathroom where Kate is hiding. Getting closer, I catch the sniffle not quite drowned out by the running faucet. Man, I'm an ass. I lean against the doorframe and peck lightly on the door. Silence overtakes the space between us, not even the hiss of running water filling the air. The door creaks open, and Kate stands on the other side. She smiles at me, but it's forced. Only her real smiles are blessed with the dimple that I love. Her skin is splotchy and her eyes red-rimmed.

"I'm sorry, Kate. I know those two little words are insignificant, and they aren't enough on their own, but really, truly, I'm sorry."

Kate visibly swallows. She shrugs like it's nothing, but she can't even look at me. "I don't know what you mean. Everything is fine. Do you need something? Can I get something for you?"

"Please, Kate, look at me." I shift off the doorframe, trying to balance, and reach for her. She doesn't pull away when my thumb strokes her cheek. Instead, she leans into my hand. "I've been an asshole. I've been in my feelings, and I haven't been treating you right. You've been there for me through all of this, and I couldn't be more grateful, but I haven't been showing it. Instead, I've been pushing you away."

Kate looks up at me now, fresh tears springing loose. "If I did something to upset you—"

"No, not at all. It's nothing you did. It's all me, Kate. I don't want to lose you, and I've been doing a crummy job at showing it."

"I don't want to lose you either, Caleb. I was so scared in the hospital that you might never wake up or you might have a complication or something. I couldn't bear the thought."

"Me either, Trouble." I hug her to me, holding her tightly against me, and kiss the top of her head. "You know what you need?"

She looks up at me, the sadness gone from her features now. "What's that?"

"A break. I'm going to fix you dinner tonight. What are you in the mood for? Maybe some lasagna alla Bolognese? Some tiramisu?"

Kate giggles. "You are not. You're going to sit your ass back down on the couch and we are going to order takeout."

"Wait and see . . . " I wink at her, as though there is any chance of me having the stamina to fix a fancy meal.

caleb

When Ducky and I pull into the driveway, Kate is waiting for us on the front porch. I barely slide out of the truck before she's there, ready to help. I'm one lucky guy. She kisses my cheek, and I pull my crutches out of the truck, resting them under my arms.

"Did you boys have fun?" Kate asks.

"A blast. Didn't we, Ducky?" I say, shooting him a wink.

"Sure did. Always a blast hanging out with this doofus," Ducky chimes in.

"Hmmm. Why do I feel like you boys are up to something?"

"We'd never." I give Kate a quick peck on the lips. "Thanks again, Ducky. See you later." I close the truck door, briefly losing my balance and hopping back a couple steps to catch myself.

"You good?" Kate asks me, resting a hand on my back as if she could stop me from falling.

"What would you do about it if I wasn't?" I ask, chuckling. "Get smooshed underneath me? Then we'd both be in a pickle." Kate rolls her eyes at me, but she's smiling. We make it up the front porch steps and into the house. "What time is the meeting with the bank? You did tell Austin I'm coming with you, right?"

"Yeah. He knows. We have about an hour before we need to leave." Suddenly, her whole demeanor shifts into one of sadness. "If they refuse the extension it's going to be hard watching them take the house from Mom."

"I know, beautiful. Maybe something will work out though. Don't lose hope." I kiss the top of her head and settle myself on the couch. This hobbling everywhere on one foot is for the birds, but I'll have to get used to it for now. Surgery is scheduled for next week, and the crutches will be sticking around for a while.

Kate fixes us some lunch, bringing our plates to the couch where I'm already settled. I don't know how I'd manage everything on my own right now. She's been a lifesaver. Thanks to Kate, Monty's bedroom is freshly painted and ready for him to move in. We had a family and team meeting for him yesterday and scheduled his move for two weeks from now. He can't wait, and neither can I.

Austin and Mrs. Farley are waiting with long faces in the lobby when Kate and I arrive at the bank. We join them and make small talk while we wait to be called back for the meeting. Eventually, a man in a business suit with slicked-back hair invites us to join him in the conference room. There are two other bank associates sitting at the long oval table when we walk in.

"Mrs. Farley, it's time to discuss the status of your mortgage account," the slicked-back gentleman begins once everyone is settled. "As you know, we're ready to move the process along."

"Which is bullshit," Austin says from his end of the table. The man simply acknowledges him with a nod before continuing.

"We received your request for an extension with your updated employment information. Unfortunately, we're unable to agree to your terms, and if you don't have the full remaining portion today that we previously agreed to, we will be filing the foreclosure this afternoon."

"Fucking hell." Austin's fist slams down on the tabletop, making everyone jump.

"I don't have the payment," Mrs. Farley says without looking up from her lap.

"I can come up with the balance, if you'll give us a little more time," Austin says, taking control of his anger.

"I'm sorry, Mr. Farley, but we are unable—"

"Yeah. Unable to agree to any of our terms but perfectly happy to auction my mother's home off and scrape in pennies of what the place is worth. That's obviously the better financial choice," Austin says.

I clear my throat before speaking. "Actually, I have a money order here written out to Mrs. Farley." I pull the money order out of my pocket and slide it across the table to the slicked-back man. "If you can deposit it into Mrs. Farley's account, I think you'll find it's adequate to cover the remaining balance."

The room is silent as all eyes turn on me, and I shift in my seat. The banker hands the money order over to one of his associates, giving her a nod before she rises from her chair and briskly leaves the room. I slump back in my seat, the room of unyielding gazes making me uncomfortable. I didn't want to do it this way. I'd have preferred to slip the money order to Kate or Austin and let them handle the whole thing. Despite their desire to save the house, though, I knew they'd never take it.

"Caleb, I can't accept that," Mrs. Farley says, her eyes wide.

"You can, and you will," I say. "Think of it as repayment for all the food I ate at your house over the years. It probably doesn't cover the way I ate you out of house and home or all the stuff Austin and I broke, but it's a start."

"Where did you come up with that type of money?" Austin asks, his expression unreadable.

"Took out a loan against my truck."

"That's what you and Ducky were up to this morning?" Kate asks.

I nod as the bank associate returns to the room, a receipt of payment in the hand that previously held the money order. She passes it across the table to Mrs. Farley.

"Well, that being handled," the slicked-back man says, "we have a few papers to sign, and you can be on your way."

Once we make it out the bank doors, Kate is on me, hugging me with her face buried in my chest. I wrap my arm around her, barely keeping hold of the crutch. Mrs. Farley joins in, hugging me over Kate.

"I'll pay you back every penny," Austin says. "You didn't have to do that, but I appreciate it. We all do."

"I know," I say. "It was my turn to return a favor."

WE RIDE to Bozeman with Dakota later that night and are the last ones to arrive at the bar. Austin, Ducky, and a few other ranch hands are there, some of them already a couple drinks in. Austin scoots a towering platter of nachos toward us as we sit down.

"Here. Help me eat these. I didn't know an order was enough for twenty people," Austin complains. Kate digs in without hesitation.

The place is crowded tonight, full of people ready to drink away their week. I get a waitress's attention and order a bucket of beers for the table. When I'm done, Austin is in the middle of telling everyone about the dead fish in Tuff's truck. I slide into the seat next to Kate and put my arm around her. She gives me a smile and leans into me.

"Tell them about the peanut butter," Austin says, turning everyone's attention to me.

"It's not that interesting—" I start, but the guys cheer me on, so I give in. "I can't admit to anything. You know, self-incrimination and all that. But this Tuff kid seems to think it was me who smeared a quarter-inch layer of peanut butter over all the windows of his pickup, his door handles, and his steering wheel."

"You didn't . . . " Kate's eyes bulge at me.

I guess I forgot to tell her about that one. "I never said it was me. He just claimed it was. Whoever it was, though, was kind enough to wrap the steering wheel in Saran Wrap first so the peanut butter didn't creep down into the crevices."

"That was mighty thoughtful of whoever did it," Ducky says.

The guys laugh, exchanging stories of past mischievous acts and plotting possible future ones. I tug Kate closer and lean into her, nuzzling her neck.

"What's the chances of me getting to dance with my girl?" I whisper in her ear.

Kate arches an eyebrow at me. "You think you can?"

"Absolutely."

She takes a swig of her drink and sets it on the table then leads us onto the dance floor. I pull her into me, my hands on her hips and my crutches tucked under my arms. Kate sways to the slow beat of the love song playing and I use it as an excuse to hold her close. She wraps her arms around my neck and tucks her head beneath my jaw. For years, Kate has been within arm's reach of me, but with her close like this, touching her, kissing her . . . I feel at home.

"I need to use the bathroom," Kate says a few dances in. "Meet you back at the table?"

"Want me to walk you?"

"Not necessary. I'll be back in a minute." She presses a kiss to my cheek, and I watch her walk toward the bathroom until she's lost in the crowd.

I slide into my chair at the table and tuck my crutches out of the way. Helping Austin with the remaining nachos, I join in the banter with the guys from the ranch. It's not long before a hand slides across my shoulders and a woman I've never seen before practically sits on my lap.

"Wanna dance?" the woman says so close that her breath tickles my ear.

"No, thanks."

"Come on, just one dance," the woman croons, tugging at my arm.

"I see you're keeping my spot warm for me," Kate says to the woman, rejoining us at the table. "You can be off now. I've got it from here."

The woman scowls at her. "Excuse me?"

This isn't likely to go over well. Austin and I exchange looks.

"That's my boyfriend you're hanging on. Kindly leave." Kate's voice is firm.

The woman releases me and disappears into the throng of people. Silence overtakes the table. Rather than sitting, Kate claims her spot standing between my legs, an arm wrapped around my neck. She grabs her beer, finishes off the bottle, and grabs a new one from the bucket.

"You tamed her, Caleb," Ducky finally speaks up. "Six months ago, that would have escalated into a full-fledged brawl."

The rest of the ranch hands, Austin included, laugh and agree.

"No, she's as wild as ever," I say. "I no more tamed her than someone could tame the wind."

"I'd rather conserve my energy for other things these days," Kate pipes up, winking at me.

"Ugh, Kate," Austin scowls. "No. Not okay."

"Come on, Kate," Dakota breaks in, taking her by the hand. "Let's go dance while the boys chat." Kate follows her to the dance floor, laughing and chatting as they go.

"Ducky's not entirely wrong, you know," Austin says. "She has changed this summer."

"We've all changed," I say.

"What I'm trying to say is you've been good for her." Austin finishes off his beer and I offer him another.

"I don't deserve her."

"No, probably not. I'm not sure any of us do." Austin leans back in his seat and takes a swig of his fresh beer.

"If you'll excuse me, I need to go join my girl out on the dance floor." I don't even try to hide my grin.

I find the girls on the dance floor and wrap Kate up in my arms. Balancing on my good foot, I lift her up, her feet dangling beneath her, and kiss her. My girl.

I've screwed up in a lot of different ways over the years, in both love and in life. I missed out on years with the girl I love, and some people may think our season on the rodeo was a waste. It wasn't the ending we had hoped for, but just the same, my temporary roping career ended better than I ever could have imagined. I roped the woman that made it all worth it. I roped Trouble.

CHAPTER FORTY-SEVEN

Dakota inspects my fingernails after we make it home, a broad grin spread across her face. "What do you think? Do you like them? I can't believe you've never had a professional manicure before."

"Believe it. I didn't even wear makeup before this summer. Why haven't you made me get a manicure before now? You've been holding out on me." I join her in admiring the classic French tips I chose to go with. It's been six weeks since Caleb's accident, and Dakota finally convinced me to leave his side.

"Wait till next time when we get pedicures. Those are to die for."

"I can't believe you caught Derrick cheating on you. It blows my mind that he would do that to you."

"Mine, too. I seriously don't know what he was thinking, but I'm better off without him. Thanks for coming out with me to cheer me up. If it wasn't for you, I'd probably be rotting away on the couch in front of a sappy movie."

"Oh, this is so much better than a sappy movie. What's next?"

"Let's get dolled up. We can do each other's hair and

makeup then go out somewhere and post some pictures so Derrick sees what he's missing."

I follow Dakota into her room, letting her call the shots. I was at Caleb's this morning when Dakota called me. I couldn't let her suffer alone. Austin came over to hang out with Caleb, and I hightailed it home.

"This dress is a must for you." Dakota holds up the emerald-green halter sundress to me. "Yes. Please wear this one."

I accept it from her, slipping it off the hanger and changing into it. It reaches right above my knees and fits like a glove.

"Which one are you wearing?"

Dakota flips through a few more dresses before landing on a black one. "How about this? Does this scream sexy and single?"

I laugh. "Absolutely it does."

"Good. I don't want him to think I'm wasting any time getting over him."

Within the hour, hair and makeup are done, and we're ready to hit the town. Dakota insists on driving, which is unusual, but I go along with it. She drives us across town toward the bar but misses the turn.

"Where are we going?" I ask when she makes no attempt to turn around.

"Oh, I thought we'd drive down this way. It's too early to show up at the bar. Don't want to look pathetic. Hey, isn't this your mom's house?" Dakota points to the house coming into view.

"Yeah. That's where I grew up." I tilt my head, studying her. "How'd you know where she lives?"

"Think she's home? I'd love to meet her." Dakota steers off the road, stopping in the driveway.

"Oh. Okay. Yeah."

When we walk inside, Mom is nowhere to be seen. I check throughout the house but come up empty. Right as worry creeps in, I hear her.

"Kate? Is that you? I'm out on the porch, bug."

My boots click on the hardwood floors with each step I take toward the door. The front door swings open, but instead of my mother, Caleb is sitting on the front porch steps, his back to me. Slowly, he stands and spins around to face me, balancing himself with his crutches. He's wearing a crisp, new button-up shirt, its grayness magnifying the depths of his irises. Vases of blue hyacinths line the steps. Those weren't there before, were they?

"Caleb, what are you doing here? How'd you get here? You aren't supposed to drive." I rush down the steps, inspecting every inch of him, trying to make sense of why he isn't at home with Austin right now.

"Kate." Caleb cups my face. "I didn't drive. I'm okay. Austin helped me. Dakota did, too."

"Dakota?" I twist back toward the house, but Dakota is nowhere to be seen. It's only me and Caleb.

"Caleb, what's going on?"

"I should probably wait, but I don't want to wait any longer. Life is short and you never know what's going to happen."

"What are you talking about? Wait for what? You're scaring me."

"Don't be scared, Trouble." Caleb takes my hand in his. "I hope this isn't a letdown, but when I thought about what I wanted this day to be like, all I could think about is how it started for me and you. And it started here, as kids."

Caleb slides a corsage on my wrist. I study the red rose before looking back at him. It's almost like déjà vu—like we're reliving the night he took me to homecoming.

"The first time I met you was in the backyard. You were on the swing. We were babies and had no inclination of what love was. We became friends running around on this farm, playing hide-and-seek in the barn, and making a fort in the hayloft. The first time I asked you out was right here on these front porch steps. And the moment I realized I'd fallen in love with you was over there in the side pasture, mending fences together.”

"Caleb, I don't understand. What's going on?”

"I want to marry you, Kate.”

"But—”

"I know we haven't been together long, and this is quick—”

"And kind of out of the blue.”

"Yes, that, too. But Kate, our history isn't like most people's. We weren't classmates who finally reconnected or a couple of random people who met three months ago in a bar. Our lives have been significantly intertwined for most of our lives. We've already seen each other at our best and at our worst, and we still chose to love each other. You are the first person I think of when I wake up and the person I hope to see in my dreams every night when I go to sleep. We've spent years fighting the attraction we have for each other. Years wasted that could have been time together. I don't want to waste any more time, and I know that another week or another month or even another year of dating you isn't going to change the way I feel about you. I want to marry you, Kate.”

Caleb reaches into the corsage on my wrist, exposing a diamond ring secured by a ribbon. With the slip of the ribbon, the ring is free. My mind is reeling, struggling to process his words.

"You want to marry me?” I ask, my eyes bouncing from the ring to Caleb's face.

"Absolutely.”

"Did Austin slip you some extra pain meds . . . ?”

"Kate, please. I've never been more certain of anything in my life. If you want me to get down on one knee right now, I will. It's a bit problematic and I don't know if I'll be able to get back up, but if it's what you need from me, consider it done.”

"No, are you crazy? What if you injure yourself?”

"Tell me you'll marry me, Kate. Please. I'll even beg if I have to.” Caleb's forehead drops to mine, his lips hovering close.

I remember the little girl who sat crying so many years ago on these steps, who had every single tear wiped away by this stunning man in front of me, and I remember the tenderness he's had for me year after year. This is the man who pieced me back together and made me whole again. And after years of waiting and hoping he'd notice me, I discovered he already had.

All the scrambled pieces of my day suddenly fall into place: the manicures, getting dressed up, the random stop at the homestead. It was all part of the plan. Warm, happy tears stream down my cheeks. I grab hold of Caleb's shirt and yank him into me, closing the distance between our lips. He about tips over, but I steady him.

"Say the words, Kate. Tell me you'll marry me." His voice is raspy, and I giggle against his lips.

"Yes. I'll marry you, Caleb Huxley."

epilogue

CALEB

Stepping down the front porch steps, I wince at the slight catch in my ankle. I've healed up from my accident last year, but my ankle still gets a little stiff sometimes, especially if I've spent a long day on my feet. It's been good being back at the ranch, though. And my current living situation is far superior to the bunkhouse.

I walk across the yard to the barn and corrals where Kate runs her business giving riding lessons and coaching barrel racers. I'm proud of my girl. She's growing a steady business, busy enough that she quit waitressing at the diner. One of her barrel racing students is showing real promise. Kate says the girl is going to be riding better than she was in high school by the time the new season rolls around.

"Hey, Trouble. You about ready to call it a day?" I ask her, walking into her makeshift office in the barn.

"Yeah, I just need to jot this one thing down on my schedule really quick." I scoot the vase full of blue wild hyacinths—like the ones Kate insisted on having in her wedding bouquet because she says they remind her of my eyes—and perch myself on the side of her desk. "Don't forget we have the rodeo next weekend to watch Austin and Josh rope in the finals." I nod and loop a finger in a belt loop of Kate's jeans, unable to keep my hands off her.

"Remember that time you and Dakota and Monty came to watch me and Austin rope last year?"

"Yes . . . ?"

"Remember the good luck charm you gave me in the barn?" I can't hold back my smirk any longer and it blooms across my face.

"I do," Kate says as I kiss the knuckle of the finger wearing a gold wedding band.

"I think I might need a good luck charm for today." I wiggle my eyebrows at her and pull her toward me. She laughs and pushes me away.

"We don't have time for good luck charms right now. Anyway, I don't think you'll need it this time around."

MONTY GIGGLES at the horrible joke I told him while tying his necktie and then straightening the suit he's wearing. For a little boy wearing a suit, he looks studly. Today is a big day for us. I check my watch. We need to be leaving soon if we are going to make it on time.

"Kate, are you about ready to go?" I yell across the house to the master bedroom where she's busy getting cleaned up.

"Yep. How about my handsome men? Are you all ready?" Her simple A-line dress hugs her body in all the right places. If we didn't have an eight-year-old chaperone right now we would be arriving late to our appointment today.

"We're ready. Let's get going."

Monty sits in the middle of the bench seat in my truck, choosing the music as we drive to town. I find a place to park on the street in front of the courthouse, and we all pile out. Kate gives us boys a last-minute check over, making sure our collars are folded down and our neckties are straight. Monty takes both of our hands, and we walk into the courthouse together to wait for our appointment time.

"Hey guys, it's good to see you," Amy, Monty's old caseworker, greets us. She leans down to Monty. "Are you excited?"

"Yeah!"

Before long, our attorney comes around the corner to collect us. We follow her into the courtroom where the judge is waiting and take our seats. The hearing begins with our attorney giving the judge the necessary information as he flips through the thick file containing our documentation. Finally, our attorney takes a seat, and the judge focuses on Monty.

"Do you know what you're doing here today, young man?"

"I'm getting adopted!" Monty bounces in his seat.

"That's right. Mr. and Mrs. Huxley here have petitioned the court to be your parents. How do you feel about that? Should I tell them yes?"

"Yeah! But you should also tell them I don't have to clean my room every day. That's the only part I don't like."

What a turd.

"It sounds like you and the Huxley's are adjusting well to life together if that's all you have to complain about." The judge turns to us now. "You understand that by choosing to adopt Monty you are taking sole responsibility for him, correct? Financially and otherwise. There is no return or exchange policy. Once these papers are signed, under the law you are seen as Monty's only legal parents."

"Yes, Your Honor."

"Okay. I don't see any reason why the state of Montana should be concerned about the finalization of this adoption. I'll sign these papers, then before you leave, my secretary will give you some official copies which you will need for getting a new birth certificate and such. Congratulations."

"That's it?" Monty asks, looking up at me.

"That's it."

Monty pounces from his seat, wrapping his arms around

our necks and hugging us as tight as his scrawny kid arms can squeeze.

We collect our paperwork and head to the park for our celebratory picnic dinner as requested by the newest member of the Huxley family. Kate and I sit stretched out on the blanket after our meal, watching Monty kick his soccer ball around the open field.

"What's on your mind?" I ask Kate who's watching Monty with a wistful expression.

"You're a good man, Caleb. You've changed this little boy's life."

"Our little boy." I wrap Kate up in my arms and kiss her. All too soon our rambunctious boy hops over to us, his ball tucked under his arm.

"Can we get a dog?" Monty asks, looking back and forth between us.

"We'll see," I say with a chuckle.

"We should stop at the animal shelter on the way home. That way we can be adopted on the same day," Monty says.

"Why not?" Kate grins up at me.

Without any warning, fifty pounds of little boy barrel into us, knocking us onto our sides, hugging us tight and cheering. If you asked me a few years ago where I'd be today, this would not be it. But only because I never thought I'd be this lucky.

And I am the luckiest man in the world.

Thank you!

If you enjoyed *Roping Trouble* please consider leaving a review. Reviews mean so much to authors and help other readers find our books.

ALSO BY AMORA BLAKE

Book 1 of Sweet Pea Ridge

Lacey and Jacob's Story

Get it here:

acknowledgments

When I wrote *Falling for Gypsy*, I didn't have any plans for writing another book. But then readers fell in love with the characters, and frankly, I did, too. I knew I had to write Caleb's story.

To my readers, thanks for taking a chance on a newbie author. There are so many books to read, and you took the time to read mine. Thank you! The only thing better than the accomplishment of writing a book is being able to share it with others.

Have I mentioned lately how wonderful my husband is? Because truly, he is. He encourages me to pursue my writing dreams whether it's a profitable business or an expensive hobby.

Jana, you've stuck with me through the long haul. Your critiques are priceless, and your friendship has kept me sane. Mostly.

And to Sarah, my editor, there is nobody I'd rather trust my book babies to than you. You are amazing!

Born in the summer of 1988, Amora was one of many generations of her family born and raised among the rich history of the Appalachian Mountains. Growing up on two hundred acres of farmland, shoes and propriety were optional, and exploration and imagination were plentiful.

After several years of unschooling on the family farm, Amora and her siblings graced the local public school system with their presence. It was during her stint at the local middle school that she found her first audience. Notebook after spiral-bound notebook, filled with her smudged graphite scrawl, was passed around her friend group.

In high school, Amora found herself obsessed with reading classics such as *Pride and Prejudice* by Jane Austin, *Rebecca* by Daphne du Maurier, *The Scarlet Pimpernel* by Baroness Orczy, and the *Anne of Green Gables* series by Lucy Maud Montgomery.

Amora's college years led her westward to the Rocky Mountains and beyond. She spent several years exploring the new landscapes of the West. She often found herself seeking inspiration from the deserts, mountains, and canyons for her writing. Amora's free time was spent scouting out caves, hiking through the local canyons, and rotating between genres of romance, mystery, and thrillers.

After many memories were made, Amora returned home to the Appalachians, where she met the man brave enough to take on her gypsy soul and who would months later become her husband. With over a decade of marriage and eight kids, they're still living their happily-ever-after.

Aside from creating bedtime stories, Amora's need to write was finally rekindled in the fall of 2019 when *Falling for Gypsy* poured from her fingertips, only to be tucked away and forgotten until four years later when it was rediscovered and rewritten beyond recognition to become her debut novel.

When Amora isn't writing, she's homeschooling her kids, hauling said kids to their extracurriculars, reading a good book, gardening, or coming up with yet another insane idea for her husband to roll his eyes at and lovingly support her in it anyway.

Connect with Amora through her website or on social media:

www.amorablake.com

Instagram

Facebook

TikTok